Sweetness in the Belly

—

Also by Camilla Gibb

—

*Mouthing the Words*
*The Petty Details of So-and-so's Life*

# CAMILLA GIBB

–

# sweetness

## IN THE

## Belly

–

William Heinemann : London

Published in the United Kingdom by William Heinemann, 2006

1 3 5 7 9 10 8 6 4 2

First published in 2005 by Doubleday Canada, a division of Random House
of Canada, Limited

William Heinemann
The Random House Group Limited
20 Vauxhall Bridge Road, London, sw1v 2sa

Random House Australia (Pty) Limited
20 Alfred Street, Milsons Point, Sydney
New South Wales 2061, Australia

Random House New Zealand Limited
18 Poland Road, Glenfield
Auckland 10, New Zealand

Random House (Pty) Limited
Isle of Houghton, Corner of Boundary Road and Carse O'Gowrie,
Houghton 2198, South Africa

The Random House Group Limited Reg. No. 954009

www.randomhouse.co.uk

A CIP catalogue record for this book
is available from the British Library

Papers used by Random House are natural, recyclable products made from
wood grown in sustainable forests. The manufacturing processes conform
to the environmental regulations of the country of origin

ISBN 0434 01453 2

Printed and bound in Great Britain by
Mackays of Chatham plc, Chatham, Kent

*For Abdi, Biscutti, Agitu and the ge waldach—*
*the children of Harar*

—

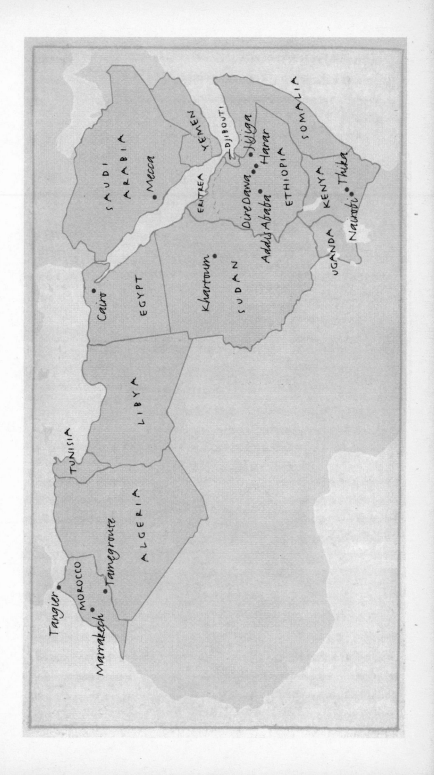

## Prologue.
### *Harar, Ethiopia*

The sun makes its orange way east from Arabia, over a Red Sea, across volcanic fields and desert and over the black hills to the qat- and coffee-shrubbed land of the fertile valley that surrounds our walled city. Night departs on the heels of the hyenas: they hear the sun's approach as a hostile ringing, perceptible only to their ears, and it drives them back, bloody lipped and panic stricken, to their caves.

In darkness they have feasted on the city's broken streets: devouring lame dogs in alleyways and licking eggshells and entrails off the ground. The people of the city cannot afford to waste their food, but nor can they neglect to feed the hyenas either. To let them go hungry is to forfeit their role as people on this wild earth, and strain the already tenuous ties that bind God's creatures.

A hundred years ago, when the city's gates were still closed at night—the key lodged firmly under the sleeping head of a neurotic emir—the hyenas were the only outsiders permitted access after dark. They would crawl through the drainage portals in the city's clay walls. But the gates are splayed open now, have been for decades, a symbol of history's turn against this Muslim outpost, a city of saints and scholars founded by Arabs who brought Islam to Abyssinia in the ninth century, the former capital of an emirate that once ruled for hundreds of miles.

For all the fear they inspire, though, if a hyena must die, one hopes it might do so on one's doorstep. Pluck its eyebrows, fashion a bracelet, and you are guaranteed protection from buda, the evil eye. Endure the inconvenience of having to step over a hideous corpse baking in the African sun all day, but be assured that by the following morning, thanks to hyenas' lack of inhibitions regarding cannibalism, the street will once again be licked clean.

As every day begins, the anguished cries of these feral children grow dim against a rising crescendo of birds quibbling in the pomegranate and lime trees of the city's courtyards. And then the muezzins call: beckoning the city's sleeping populace with a shower of praise for an almighty God. There are ninety-nine of them within the walls of this tiny city—ninety-nine muezzins for ninety-nine mosques. It takes the culmination of the staggered, near-simultaneous beginnings of a hundred less one to create the particular sound that is heard as godliness in Harar.

"But I don't want to go among mad people," Alice remarked.

"Oh, you ca'n't help that," said the Cat: "we're all mad here. I'm mad. You're mad."

"How do you know I'm mad?" said Alice.

"You must be," said the Cat, "or you wouldn't have come here."

—

*Alice's Adventures in Wonderland*, Lewis Carroll

**Part One.**

—

# London, England

1981–85

## Scar Tissue.

—

On a wet night in Thatcher's Britain, a miracle was delivered onto the pockmarked pavement behind a decrepit building once known as Lambeth Hospital. Four women standing flanked by battered rubbish bins looked up to a close English sky and thanked Allah for this sign of his generosity. Two women ululated, one little boy, shy and tired, buried his face in his mother's neck, and one baby stamped with a continent-shaped mole tried out her lungs. Her wail was mighty and unselfconscious, and with it, she announced that we had all arrived in England. None of us had hitherto had the confidence to be so brazen.

I was one of those four women. I trained in this God-forsaken building, a gothic nightmare of a place, a former workhouse where the poor were imprisoned and divided—men from women, aged and infirm from able bodied, able-bodied good from able-bodied bad—each forced to break a daily quota of stone in order to earn their keep. Adjacent is the old infirmary, which once had its own Register of Lunatics, among them a woman named Hannah Chaplin diagnosed with acute psychosis resulting from syphilis while in residence there with her seven-year-old son Charlie, some eighty years ago.

I don't share this history though I've moved within its walls. In the places I have lived, the aged and the infirm and the psychotic are not separated from the rest of us. They are part of us. I don't share this history, but as a child, I did see a Charlie Chaplin film in a cinema in Tangier through the smoke of a hundred cigarettes. I sat cross-legged between my parents on a wooden bench, a carpet of peanut shells at our feet, the audience roaring with laughter, united by the shared language of bodies without words.

Amazing that humour could ever be borne of this place. The building now stands condemned, slated for demolition, and I work at South Western, a hospital largely catering to the poor from the beleaguered housing estates in the surrounding areas: the mentally ill, the drug addicted, the unemployed white, the Asian and Afro-Caribbean immigrants and the refugees and asylum seekers, the latest wave of which has been rolling in from torn parts of East Africa, principally Eritrea and Sudan.

Many of these claimants avoid the hospital, overwhelmed or intimidated as they are by the agents and agencies of the state—the customs officers, police, civil servants, lawyers, social workers and doctors—with their unreadable expressions and their unreadable forms. I know this, because they are my neighbours. I encounter them in the elevator, in the laundrette, in the dimly lit concrete corridors of high-rises on the Cotton Gardens Estate. I've lived in a one-bedroom council flat on the fourteenth floor of one of these buildings since the autumn of 1974—compensation for the circumstances of my arrival.

My white face and white uniform give me the appearance of authority in this new world, though my experiences, as my neighbours quickly come to discover, are rooted in the old. I'm a white Muslim woman raised in Africa, now employed by the National Health Service. I exist somewhere between what they know and what they fear, somewhere between the past and the future, which is not quite the present. I can translate the forms for them before kneeling down and putting my forehead to the same ground. Linoleum, concrete, industrial carpet. Five times a day, wherever we might be, however much we might doubt ourselves and the world around us.

I was not always a Muslim, but once I was led into the absorption of prayer and the mysteries of the Qur'an, something troubled in me became still.

I was the daughter of two solitary renegades who'd met at Trinity College Dublin in the 1950s; freaks pulled by the magnet of shared disenchantment into an inseparable embrace. Alice and Philip, so convinced they had enough love, intelligence and language between them to make their way around the world that they took a leave of absence from university and obligation that would last the rest of their lives, setting off on foot, with me nothing more than an egg in my mother's belly.

Nomads, my father called us, though there was no seasonal pattern to our migration. I was born in Yugoslavia, breast-fed in the Ukraine, weaned in Corsica, freed from nappies in Sicily and walking by the time we got to the Algarve. Just when I was comfortable speaking French, we'd be off to Spain. Just when I had a new best friend, the world was full of strangers again. Until Africa, life was a series of aborted conversations, attachments severed in the very same moment they began.

There was a familiar pattern to the leaving speech. "You put roots down and they'll start growing. Do you know what I mean?" my father would say, poking me in the ribs.

"But why is that so bad?" I remember asking as we lurched and bobbed our way toward Yet Another Unfathomable Destination.

"It just makes the passage between places too painful. It's all about the journey. You don't want to spoil the journey by missing what you've left and worrying about where you're going" was his standard reply.

For them, the journey ended in Africa, while for me it had only just begun. After several months in Tangier, where I'd played in the streets of the medina while they lay about naked and high in the unbearable heat of our room in a crumbling hotel, we made our way south, to the Sufi shrine of Bilal al Habash on the Moroccan edge of the Sahara. Their friends in Tangier had suggested it: the saint was known as one who could bless pregnant women and their unborn children. My mother had suffered a miscarriage the year before, and she was willing to try anything this time, whatever lotions or potions or blessings might guarantee she carry this next baby to full term.

The saint's disciple, the Great Abdal, received us with some initial reservation, but softened once he'd placed his hand on my mother's stomach. It was too late: the baby lay still. She turned away, she turned inward, and I've always felt she blamed me somehow, as if I had robbed her of the capacity to bear more children. Some weeks later my parents told me they had business they needed to finish up in Tangier and they asked the Great Abdal if he wouldn't mind looking after me for the weekend. It would only be for three days.

I was not unused to being minded by relative strangers, and the Great Abdal seemed keen to use their absence as an opportunity to introduce me to the Qur'an. I'd already expressed some curiosity about his big green and gold book and the woollen-cloaked Sufis who mumbled and swayed in the courtyard surrounding the shrine. I had always envied children who went to school and so I welcomed the Great Abdal's lessons. My father had bought me a notebook in Tangier, and I'd already filled several pages with Arabic words I had learned in the streets of the medina. I began a fresh page for words from the Qur'an.

Three days became three weeks, my anxiety

eased somewhat by the repetition of new words, before the arrival of a friend of my parents' from Tangier. Muhammed Bruce Mahmoud was a large English convert with a white beard and algae-green eyes who had lived in North Africa for decades. We'd spent many nights in his company in over-lit sidewalk cafés and dimly lit bars.

He did not mince his words as one might with an eight-year-old, though he did feel responsible as the messenger. My parents had been killed in an alleyway in the city. He did not say how or why. He and the Great Abdal conferred and decided it would be best that I remain at the shrine rather than return to the city. I had no home to be sent back to—no relatives that I knew of, no England that I knew. The Great Abdal would be my teacher, my guide, my father in senses both spiritual and mundane. Muhammed Bruce would be my guardian, visiting me regularly and paying for my keep. And I would be absent and haunted for a long time while together they worked hard to fill the hollow and replace the horror with love and Islam. And so for me, the two have always been one.

Faith has accompanied me over time and geography and upheaval. From Morocco, to Ethiopia, to England. A faith that now binds me to my Muslim neighbours in this country my parents referred to—despite calling it a dark and oppressive place where the sun never shone and the English (Dad's people) hated the Irish (Mum's people)—as home.

In this country they called home, I became a nurse and began, fairly early on in my career, to bring my work back to the estate, to administer tetanus shots, treat head lice, sew stitches, mete out painkillers and counsel wives on the sofa in my sitting room in my off-hours. I hold my neighbours' children, listen to their stories, reflect in their silence and, in the most serious cases, insist on the hospital, accompany them there: men with fractures and hernias, women hemorrhaging from botched abortions, even one poor boy who'd lost the tip of his penis while his parents argued about whether or not he should be circumcised.

In all honesty, I'm not licensed to do half the things I do, but there is a need, both theirs and mine. Treating my neighbours restores my humanity after laundered and sterilized days of rounds spent injecting person after pain-riddled person with morphine, days when "nursing" feels more like a euphemism for euthanasia.

I'm certainly not licensed to deliver babies, but by the time I ran through the rain down the dark February streets after the two Eritrean women from my building who came to fetch me on that auspicious night in 1981, Amina's baby was well on its way.

They pointed at the Ethiopian woman squatting under the partial shelter of a gutter. It was too late to move her. I turned her chin toward the light. Her face was contorted with pain: a blood vessel in her eye had burst, her bottom lip, quivering with prayer, held the imprint of her teeth, and

sweat ran down her cheeks and plunged into the
tunnel between her breasts. For all the strain,
though, she made no more noise than the rain tapping gently against the gutter over our heads. A
young wide-eyed boy stood at the woman's side,
hand burrowed deep in his mother's hair.

One of the Eritrean women took off the veil she
was wearing, wiped the woman's twisted brow with
a corner and then suspended it like an umbrella
over this unlikely cluster squatting on the pavement. The other Eritrean moved to massage the
woman's stomach but I held her back by the hand.

"She needs no help," I whispered.

And she didn't. I held my hands under the
woman's voluminous skirt while she bit down on a
scarf to stifle a cry. She arched her back with a
blue surge of pain and out swam a puddle of black-
haired girl.

"Alhamdullilah!" the two Eritrean women
exclaimed.

Seven pounds, I guessed, as I lifted the girl up
before her mother's face. Ten fingers and ten toes
and one large, irregular mole on her cheek.

I cut the umbilical cord with the razor blade I'd
packed along with a towel and a bottle of rubbing
alcohol. I'd feared I might have to use that blade
for something else. If the woman had been infibulated the baby might have been in distress, might
have even suffocated by the time we'd moved her
into an operating theatre. In that case, I would
have had to cut through her scar tissue to open up
the birth canal, at the risk of injuring the baby, at

the risk of the woman hemorrhaging or going into shock. But we were lucky; it was just a minor circumcision: clitoris and labia minora.

Amina took the baby in her arms and touched the girl's cheek in wonder. "Masha'Allah," she wept, her tears now following in the tracks of her sweat. "Africa!" she exclaimed, outlining the mole with her finger.

The mole did indeed have the shape of a continent. We agreed to call it a miracle, even though, truth be told, it had a tail that made it look slightly more like South America. But that is the thing about miracles: it is perception that determines them as such, not facts.

## Alive and Kicking.

—

Sitta spent the first few weeks of her life in my bedroom. It is customary for mother and baby to rest for ulma—the period of seclusion after birth— baby feasting on milk, mother feasting on honey, both concealed out of range of heat and flies and the evil eye. We do not have heat or many flies here, but still, Amina sits ulma because the evil eye is everywhere. Even in England.

We draped sheets from the ceiling to enclose my bed, the bed in which mother and baby would lie for forty days. The Eritrean women had honoured Amina's request and buried the placenta at the base of a tree in the nearest park. I wonder how many placentas are buried in Kennington Park; how many drunken neo-Nazis fall asleep under those trees and whether they dream life-altering dreams when they do.

We lined the walls of my sitting room with pillows to accommodate the neighbouring women who came to visit Amina and her baby. For weeks, the flat was flooded with the smells of ripe bananas and garlic and incense smouldering on aluminium foil held over the flame of the gas ring in my kitchen. The rooms buzzed with spontaneous song, regular prayer and the constant chatter of women taking on the role of Amina's family and friends. There weren't many other Ethiopians in London yet—almost none living here on the estate, anyway—but with the help of the Eritrean and Sudanese women, and other Muslim friends like Mrs. Jahangir from down the hall, we managed to make it feel like a real ulma.

Amina had left a refugee camp in Kenya for a hostel room in Brixton so crowded the women had to sleep in shifts. Her husband, as far as she knew, was imprisoned somewhere in southern Ethiopia. I offered her a bridge, but her presence in my flat, her body and soul kneeling and praying beside me, gave me a way back to the life that I'd left behind. For the first time in years, I felt part of something. For the first time in years, I felt happy.

I'd had seven hard years here before Amina's arrival, years during which I could not even risk sending a letter. Whomever I might address could be indicted, if not specifically for their connection with me, then more generally for their association with the West. I carry the guilt of the specific and the mixed burden of the general. I ask questions in the hope of relief. Every time I introduce myself to a new neighbour or a patient I presume to be Ethiopian, I watch their faces soften, distrust yielding to uncertainty as they listen to the white woman with the Semitic tongue and peculiar accent reveal pieces of an Ethiopian history. I invite them to drink coffee, caffeinate before asking: Did you know a doctor there, by any chance? In the refugee camp? Dr. Aziz Abdulnasser from Harar?

On the eighth day of ulma, as I held Amina's baby while she dressed in the mismatched patterns of clothes donated by neighbouring women for the occasion, I could not help but wonder. Not a word for seven years, not a single sign, yet I'd managed to keep the fantasy of our future together alive. But the reality of this wide-eyed caramel-coloured wonder was arresting. *This* was the future, alive and kicking in my arms.

The day before the naming celebration, our Bangladeshi neighbour, Mr. Jahangir, went in search of goat meat. Tradition demands a trek to a shrine on the eighth day of ulma. In return, one is supposed to offer a goat. Here, we were, as we are with most things, forced to improvise. Mr. Jahangir wheeled his wife's carry-all to the Brixton Market and argued with the Jamaican women who refused to reveal their source. Then, so he reported, they demanded "a bloody greedy fortune" for the scraps they usually wrap into their take-away rotis.

"But I am no fool!" Mr. Jahangir said, standing on the threshold of my flat, shaking his head, hands gripping the handle of the tartan carry-all.

I waited for the end, where the good Bangladeshi man always wins. It's the way of all stories told by immigrant men: encounters end in victory because in the bigger scheme of things they feel (and justifiably so) powerless.

"Back and forth, back and forth, I'm playing with them," Mr. J said, drawing circles in the air with his hand, "and just when they think they have beaten me, I pull out what is called the trump card!" he shouted, his whole body an exclamation mark as he stood on his toes and paused for effect.

"What was that, Mr. Jahangir?" I asked.

He shrank then, adopting a demure posture. "Well, I said: 'Oh, dear ladies, perhaps I have misrepresented myself. This meat is not for my own personal consumption, no, it is for my dear Ethiopian friends, beautiful people who love the great Emperor Haile Selassie.'

"'Jah Rastafari!' the women shouted as if their lord had just entered the room. 'Blessed is he who comes in the name of Jah—take, take this meat to your friends, brother.'

"You see? From a bloody greedy fortune to take, take. It pays to know your history. Lucky thing I am an educated man!"

The next morning, Mrs. Jahangir helped me with the stew. We stood side by side, frying garlic and onions in ghee, and debated spices.

"But it's a wat, Mrs. J, not a curry," I insisted, replacing the mustard seeds in her hand with those of fenugreek. "Not better, or worse, just different. *Please.*"

"Yeah, yeah, okay," she finally gave in, waving a tea towel at me, "I'll make your smelly wat not."

I kissed her on the cheek.

I heard the pop of the mustard seeds as soon as I turned my back.

Amina sat on the bed behind the curtain, thanking each woman who filed into the room for coming. She engaged politely, remarked on her good fortune, exchanged pleasantries in Arabic and English, the languages of religion and exile shared among the women. But despite the smile, she was remote. I wondered how she must have been feeling: apart from her son, Ahmed, she had known none of us for more than eight days.

When everyone had arrived and crowded into my tiny bedroom, I asked Amina what she was going to name her baby. She turned to her son, who, although only four years old, was (so the Eritrean women teased him and only half-jokingly) now the man of the family.

"Obboleetii," he whispered shyly.

"Sister?" I asked, not sure if I'd heard correctly.

"Sitta?" he repeated, intonation and all, posing his first English word as a question. The women erupted with laughter and applause, and Ahmed buried his face in his mother's lap.

—

After the naming day, Amina's formality began to ease. When I returned home from work each day, I'd make us tea and sit down on the end of the bed while Amina breast-fed Sitta and Ahmed stared intently, eyes like wide-open windows, taking it all in—the sunshine, the inclement weather, the birds—as we talked.

Her English was good; she used to teach it, she

told me, to Red Cross workers in Ethiopia. She spoke matter-of-factly about the circumstances that had forced her to flee. Her husband had been linked to the Oromo Liberation Front, an underground movement the dictatorship deemed counter-revolutionary. All the Oromo at the agricultural college where he taught had been placed under house arrest. One by one they were taken in for interrogation; one by one they had disappeared.

"There are only two feelings left in Ethiopia now: fear and paranoia," Amina said, speaking of the horrors that had befallen the country since Haile Selassie had been deposed in 1974. The papers had reported the emperor dead of prostate cancer the following year, though no one believes he actually died of natural causes. There were rumours that he was suffocated with an ether-soaked pillow during an otherwise successful operation. We don't expect we'll ever know the truth.

Amina offered me a first-hand account of the violence I'd only gleaned since Mengistu had come to power. "People dragged from houses and gunned down in the streets in front of their families. Or they lined them up in city squares—yes, even in Harar—and in less time than you can say a prayer, the ground is covered with red." Qey Shibir, they call it, without subtlety or apology—the Red Terror.

And those who were merely sent to prison? I'd seen reports by Amnesty and Human Rights Watch: nearly one in fifteen Ethiopians was in prison by then, and prisons were notorious as houses of torture where men were hanged by their testicles and women were raped and sodomized with red-hot rods in order to elicit "confessions."

I don't look at his photograph any more. I can't bear to think of what might have happened.

—

On the fortieth day, we made a thick sorghum porridge and carried Sitta outside, where we showered her with rose petals under a brooding English sky. It was the end of ulma, and in two weeks time, Amina would have a two-bedroom flat of her own in the building. Ethiopians had suddenly jumped to the head of the housing queue. It was the beginning of the decade of the Ethiopian refugee.

The night before she moved, I rummaged through the drawers in my kitchen, trying to match an old set of cutlery for her. Amina sat at the kitchen table and poured us each a cup of tea. She spoke to my back, asking why I had been so kind to her these past few weeks.

I am drawn to Amina because of what we share. Not only is she from Harar but we are the same age—twenty-seven we were then, fifty-four years of life between us stretched across an African canvas, one lip of which is permanently stapled to the wall of the Ethiopian city that once circumscribed our lives, the other lip flapping loosely over the motley tapestry that is London. One side is permanently hinged, even if only in our imaginations.

I slowly pulled out the other chair and sat down across from her. I picked up the cup of tea in both hands, put my elbows on the table and sighed. "Because you remind me of people . . . people I love," I finally said. "And none of them are here."

She leaned forward and wiped a tear from my cheek with her thumb. Then she, who had not cried since the day her daughter was born, pulled an arsenal of toilet paper from between her breasts and handed it to me.

"Maybe they will come," she said with a gentle smile.

## Exile.

—

Sitta sits in my lap, busily twisting a paper clip in my ear while I stuff envelopes. For all her early unabashed bellowing, she is now, at four, terribly shy. She might grow out of it—Ahmed has—but perhaps we are at fault for overwhelming her. Every Saturday morning she sits here with us in the community association office, witness to the wildly shifting moods of the place. Opening a letter or answering a phone call is a lottery, as likely to inspire joy as to incite rage.

I've often wondered whether it is fair to expose her to all this, but Amina is adamant: her children will know their history, even where that history hurts. "She can have her dolls and her plasticine," Amina says, "just as long as she knows where she comes from."

Where she comes from is undergoing one of the darkest periods in its history, and that is written on the faces of everyone in the steady stream of people who come through the door of this office seeking news of loved ones and requests for help with housing, asylum applications, employment, English.

It's hard to know how much Sitta understands. What she cannot know is that Ethiopia has not always been this way, that there were happier times.

While Sitta sits in my lap, her brother is at the madrasa where he studies Qur'an alongside Iranian and Pakistani children in the Bible-scened back room of a church.

Amina stands behind me cheerfully bouncing coffee beans in a tin plate over a Bunsen burner perched on top of the filing cabinet. We had a call earlier this morning from someone Amina had known in the refugee camp in Kenya. He remembered her little boy and asked after him. Although his news was not entirely happy, it was news, and where there is a dearth of information, this alone can sometimes be cause for joy.

"Do you think Ahmed remembers the camp?" I ask her.

"I don't know," she replies. "I think he has a feeling. But not the words for it yet. Not the questions."

Amina lights a stick of incense and waves it in one hand as she sings a song of few but potent words. The coffee beans smoke and chuckle their way from green to brown, transforming this cramped, windowless room on the ground floor of a house in a desperate London borough into a more comprehensible world. A familiar world where the smell of coffee draws women together, an olfactory call throughout a neighbourhood luring women from their homes to gather, to chatter, to solve the mysteries and miseries of the universe, or at least of their domestic lives.

—

Amina and I started talking about this organization in 1982; we were sensing the increasing need for an office in London where people could exchange names in the hopes of locating family members. But much as we talked about it, we didn't act. We said it was because we were too busy: daily life traps you with its demands. We offer some relief to each other in this regard: every Sunday we cook together, making a week's worth of injera and preparing and freezing containers of wat. I often babysit, and I'm always available to help with homework, while Amina stops by the market for fresh vegetables on her way home from work and has an unfathomable love of ironing, a passion I encourage by turning up in wrinkled shirts.

"Give me that, Lilly," she'll tsk, tugging at my sleeve. "Honestly, you are shameful."

I'll unbutton my shirt and she'll tsk again. "I know," I'll say, rolling my eyes, "too skinny."

She teases me about this all the time. "Too many cigarettes," she chastises. "And never enough food!" She happily slaps her own belly. My body is a whisper where hers is a shout.

"My husband loves this—" she hesitates, looking for a word, "this duba!"

"Pumpkin," I remind her.

"Yes, my pumpikin!" She laughs infectiously.

Amina and I live in separate flats, though we share domestic responsibilities, including the children, tease each other, bicker occasionally and compare appearances that are nothing alike. We are co-wives, though we lack the common tie of a husband.

What we share is rooted in the past. I grew up in Morocco at the shrine of the great Ethiopian saint Bilal al Habash, while Amina grew up beyond the walls of the ancient city where the saint was born and served as patron. We both made our way to Harar: me by way of pilgrimage when I was sixteen years old, Amina by way of assimilation at about the same age. For both of us, Harar became home, the place we came of age, fell in love, the place we were forced to flee.

The more we disclose over the years, the easier it becomes to weave the severed threads together. We make sense of our lives by reconstructing them as linear stories that carry us from African childhoods to London streets. Mine begins in Morocco, under the tutelage of the Great Abdal. He showed me the way of Islam through the Qur'an and the saints and the stable of mystical seekers who gathered round him. Although he and Muhammed Bruce agreed my education would be more orthodox, the Great Abdal hoped that one day this would lead me into the more esoteric world of Sufism. Among the Sufis who lived at the shrine I found a brother in Hussein. It was Hussein who accompanied me on the pilgrimage to Harar, though once there, the differences between us became acutely apparent, differences that would eventually lead me, alone, to London.

Amina's journey is no less remarkable. She was the youngest child of Oromo tenants who farmed green fields beyond the city, and the only one in her family to attend school. When her older brothers were imprisoned for smuggling arms into the Sudan, her mother took the money the police had failed to find, sewed the bills into the hem of Amina's dress and sent her to live with cousins in the city. Amina became educated in the urban ways, adopting the language and culture of the Hararis as many Oromo did, aspiring to become Harari, for to be Harari is to be cultured and rich. She found a like-minded man in Yusuf, married him and bore a son, before the three of them were forced to flee to Kenya.

Amina and I did not know each other in Harar, though we shared the outsider's struggle to assert a place there and the euphoric, if fleeting, sense of peace in finding one. We know each other now, as refugees in the aftermath of the revolution, re-enacting rituals, keeping the traditions of home alive in our council flats.

But there are some threads that hang loose, out of place. These are the love stories. The best we can do is knot these threads at the ends so they won't unravel any further. In truth, I think this is why we delayed starting the organization. Not because we were too busy, but because we were in some ways afraid of the answers our work might bring.

But then came 1984, the year that half a million

people died of starvation and half a million more fled the country. Every evening for weeks, Amina and the several other Ethiopians who lived in the building by then crowded into my flat to watch in horror as a parade of bodies on the verge of crumbling into dust crawled across the screen. We were sickened with ourselves for being riveted by the spectacle of this death march. We were ashes-to-ashes fascinated by this movement, heaven-bound invariably, for there is no hell any more when it has arrived here on earth.

We established the community association that year, anticipating an influx of refugees. We knew that there would be thousands—tens becoming hundreds—of people on the move, families fractured and scattered. Those who did not die would be internally displaced or spend years in refugee camps in Somalia, Djibouti, Kenya and Sudan. But it is not these people who would make it to Rome or London. It would be the urban, the educated, the ones who had the means to pay their smugglers to make it this far. The minority, most of them men, most of them alone. People like Amina. From Dire Dawa to Nairobi in the back of a truck, from Nairobi to London by plane.

A similar office had been established in Rome a year earlier. Italy is the point of entry into Europe for most Ethiopians. They come by boat or they come by plane; they come illegally or they come with coveted papers as Convention-status refugees. However they come, they arrive with mixed emotion:

hope, despondency, relief, want and fear. And guilt. The unrelenting guilt that burbles in the bowels; the magma at the core.

Every month the office in Rome sends us a list of recent arrivals in the hope that we might be able to match them with relatives in London. Our mission is family reunification. The matches are few because we are still a relatively small community here, but one reunion between brothers spreads a fire of hope among the rest. Amina and I play a small part in rebuilding if not families, at least spirits, and after reviewing each list, we make a copy for our files and send the original on to North America, where, eventually, a great many more matches will be made.

Our work is not as altruistic as it sounds. We are each looking for someone. Amina's husband Yusuf. My friend Aziz. (Such a weak word, *friend*. In Harari he is kuday, "my liver," he is like rrata, a piece of meat stuck between my teeth, but English does not allow for such possibilities.)

Every month we try not to appear hopeful, but we are. Every month we try not to appear disappointed, but we are. The truth is, reuniting people as we do is bittersweet. And the more time that passes, the more bitter the sweetness. It can overwhelm. The names can become indistinguishable, impossible to grasp. Like the spectre of him: the way he can appear in the bubbled old glass of the windows of a pub, in the fog of reluctant mornings, his image distorted and fleeting.

It is Amina's hope that keeps me buoyed, keeps it bearable in those moments when the names slip

like water through my fingers. She places a bucket
in my hands and together we begin again, pulling
out one name at a time. We compare the names
from Rome with the ever-expanding list of names
of the family members of all those who pass
through the doors of our small office in London.

In each case we begin by drawing a family tree.
It's necessary because Ethiopians do not share
family names—one's last name is the first name of
one's father. Amina Mergessa is the daughter of
Mergessa Largassom. Sitta is Sitta Yusuf, as
Ahmed is Ahmed Yusuf, just as Hussein and I took
the name Abdal.

It has a striking effect, this mapping of relations.
We offer coffee and a seat across the desk from us to
each new visitor. Pull out a fresh sheet of A4 and
align it horizontally. Begin the questions: date
of birth (almost always an approximation), place of
origin, ethnic background. And then the painful
drawing forth of names. Spouse and children first,
then working back—siblings, parents, grandparents—and across—grandparents' siblings, uncles
and aunts, cousins. Question marks beside those
who are also believed missing, and subtle, lowercase
*d*s next to those who have died.

When we finish, we spin the paper around. Most
people are speechless. They see their own names at
the centre of this complex web and they no longer
feel quite as alone or displaced. They have a family,
a place they belong, here is the proof. We give them
a copy to take with them. To fold into the back of
their Qur'an or Bible, place under a mattress in a

room of like mattresses in a temporary shelter, tape to the mirror in their bedsit or tack to the inside of a kitchen cupboard door in their first council flat.

Amina has encouraged me to map my own family in this way, but the one time I tried it proved dispiriting: it looked like a rubble-strewn field. At the far left of the page I positioned the Great Abdal as father to Hussein and me. Next to him, Muhammed Bruce Mahmoud. I drew a dotted line across the paper, as if marking footsteps west to east across the Sahara. At the far right-hand side I wrote "Nouria"—the name of the poor Oromo woman with whom I lived in Harar. I connected her to me on the page as older sister, as I did her cousin Gishta. I wrote the names of Nouria's children beneath hers, precious to me, children I cared for and taught.

But then what of the man I love? I could think of no way of representing this relationship on paper. I left Aziz hanging in the middle of the page, as if he were a lone cloud hovering somewhere over the desert.

"Wait!" Amina exclaimed, picking up the pencil as soon as I threw it down.

I watched as she added her own name somewhere in the blank middle.

"Your co-wife," she declared. "And your co-wife's children." She added Sitta's and Ahmed's names.

"But there's not an ounce of blood shared between me and anyone," I said.

Amina sighed. "Sometimes you are exhausting, Lilly, honestly. Okay, so yours is not a map of blood. But can't you see? This is a map of love."

—

Amina and I copy the names from each new family tree into binders arranged alphabetically by first name. Perhaps one day we will have a computer, but for now, our resources are limited; most of what we do we do by hand and we're grateful for the things we have. This office, for instance. It's an old pantry, complete with shelves lined with paper in the 1920s and a hidden stash of tinned war rations. Beyond a battered and bolted wooden door, Amina grows onions and garlic in a tiny garden she has planted between crumbling bricks.

The building belongs to Mr. Jahangir, who did so well operating a grocery out of the front that he was able to buy the entire building. He and his wife moved off the estate and into the first-floor flat. They offer us this room at the back of the building, behind the grocery, without condition. This is in part because, Mr. Jahangir says (and only half-jokingly), that it is thanks to the crisis in Ethiopia that he has become a rich man.

When Mrs. Jahangir first introduced Amina to her husband's grocery, she filled Amina's hands with garlic, ginger and chili peppers and put fenugreek on her tongue. Amina, taste buds deadened by plain pasta and potatoes, was overjoyed at the revival in her mouth, but when Mr. J presented her with a mango, her face froze as if her entire life were flashing before her eyes. Inhaling the skin, she broke down.

Every Ethiopian who has arrived on the estate since has undergone a variation of this ritual.

For the most part this stretch of road is good to us. Mr. J sells halal meat, and two doors down there is the Mecca Hair Salon, with its special enclosed room at the back where hijab-wearing women can reveal themselves without shame. Volunteers offer Qur'anic classes at the back of the church on Saturdays, and while the Brixton Mosque, which draws us to Friday prayers, is only a bus ride away, the Refugee Referral Service just down the road offers a place in the neighbourhood for daily worship, clearing out its reception room at dusk every day to receive the knees, foreheads, palms and prayers of men and women of all colours.

This is where we are reassured of our place in the world. Our place in the eyes of God. The sound of communal prayer—its growling honesty, its rhythm as relentless and essential as heartbeats—moves me with its direction and makes me believe that distance can be overcome. It is the only thing that offers me hope that where borders and wars and revolutions divide and scatter us, something singular and true unites us. It tames this English soil.

There are rooms being similarly transformed, senses being reoriented, everywhere on earth. I know from experience that you can remap a city like this, orient yourself in its strange geography, strew your own trail of breadcrumbs between salient markers—mosques, restaurants, markets and grocers—and diminish the alien power of the spaces in between. You can find your way. You grapple with language, navigate your way on the underground, stretch your meagre allowance, adapt unfamiliar provisions to make familiar food, and find people from back home in queues at government offices, which at once invests you with a new sense of possibility and devastates you with the reminder of all the people you have left.

Ten years ago Ethiopians had no word for diaspora, nor emigration. There was only the word for pilgrimage, a journey with an implicit return—to Mecca or the shrines of beloved Ethiopian saints—but the idea of leaving your country, except for a very educated few who sought higher degrees abroad, was incomprehensible. A betrayal, even.

Amina is an anchor in this small but growing community. While the others moan their longing for injera, Amina sets about making the Ethiopian bread using millet instead of teff. The women are grateful for the instruction, even though the injera lacks the critical bitterness that distinguishes it. But taste ultimately comes to matter less than resourcefulness. Amina locates a Yemeni merchant in Brixton who smuggles in qat from Djibouti twice a week. The men are jubilant. Bread and stimulants. The stuff of life.

Amina is not a spectre in this landscape; she is unusual in putting down roots. She began by washing dishes in the kitchen of a Punjabi restaurant, which she did while taking advanced English for foreigners at Brixton College at night. She soon began taking secretarial courses as well. Now she works from Monday to Friday in the legal aid department of the Refugee Referral Service alongside well-meaning English women with solid names like Marion and Patricia.

While other refugees dream of mountains and hyenas and rivers, Amina takes Sitta and Ahmed to the zoo in Regent's Park and introduces them to lizards and giraffes. She fashions paper boats out of pages of tabloids for Ahmed to float on the Thames near the foot of Lambeth Bridge. Old England looms large on the other side. Big Ben and the Houses of Parliament would cast shadows over his tiny paper boat if it were to cross the river, but a paper boat cannot span the distance, and we are both alienated by and grateful for the divide.

We know plenty of Ethiopians in London who do not even furnish their flats. What possessions they acquire sit in their cardboard boxes ready for transport. The tower of boxes holding televisions, toaster ovens, microwaves, electric heaters teeters to the left of the door, ready to be shipped at a moment's notice. They commit to nothing. They float on the myth of return.

—

When the coffee beans are nearly black, Amina tips them from the plate into a mortar. She brought that mortar with her. Showed up at Heathrow with nothing but Ahmed, a man's wallet and that mortar, Sitta still in utero. She unwraps a ball of waxed paper pulled from the pocket of her skirt and shakes two cardamom pods into her hand. She rubs these briskly between her palms, adding their silken ashes and brown seeds to the mix, and then passes the mortar to me.

Sitta places her hand over mine as if to help. A twist of the wrist brings a distant yet familiar sting. The suddenly charged senses and the near-primal urge to follow. Everything lifts. The dull hangover of nightmares about bodies ripped from houses and dragged through streets; bodies jailed in terror and left to sleep in their own excrement; bodies stripped of fingernails, expressions and will; bodies raped with rifles, sodomized with sticks, lacerated and mutilated and broken.

Everything lifts with the twist of a wrist. Everything comes alive.

Part Two.

—

ʜɑɾɑɾ, ᴇᴛʜɪᴏᴘɪɑ

1970–72

Al-Hijrah.

—

It was a still night in November 1969, the air thick
with the smell of overripe fruit and woodsmoke,
when Hussein and I disembarked in Harar's main
square. We stepped out of the Mercedes in which
we'd travelled from the capital and skulked away.
The extravagance of having spent three days winding up and down the miles of scrub-covered mountains in the back of a chauffeured car, complete with
an ashtray full of chocolates wrapped in gold foil,
had somewhat sullied our arrival. Not only did it
seem contradictory to the spirit of pilgrimage, it
was hardly representative of the rest of our journey,
an arduous overland odyssey of months spent blis-
tered and parched and subsisting on little else than
the gritty bread our Tuareg guide baked in sand.

We would repent, we told ourselves, as we stood
in the muddy shadow of a mosque and looked up at
the stars. Soon, we would be kneeling to pray
before the entombed remains of our beloved saint.

We could hear the patter of drums in the near
distance, and Hussein gripped my arm. I nudged

him on, following him downhill through dark and narrow streets littered with vegetable matter and animal waste. Cats feasting on carcasses scattered as we grasped the walls on each side of us for balance. Before us, we saw a green archway framing the entrance to the compound surrounding the shrine. Through that archway, the movement of hundreds of people sparkled like sunlight on the crests of waves.

I was used to the slow, quiet, uniform ways of the Sufis at the shrine in Morocco, but here, worship was far more colourful: urban Hararis, the men in their starched white galabayas and white knit skullcaps, their wives, daughters and sisters glittering in bright head scarves and beaded shawls; the people of the countryside, Oromo peasants who work the Harari lands, darker skinned and wearing duller hues than the Hararis, and the herders, sinewy Somalis and their butter-scented wives draped in long diaphanous veils. Landlords, serfs and nomads. Conspicuous wealth, backbreaking servitude and drifting poverty—secular distinctions all erased in the presence of God.

In front of the shrine, a small, white, cupola-capped building buttressed against the city wall, a semicircle of men pounded taut-skinned drums with heavy sticks, throwing sweat from their bodies with each beat. The saint's descendant and disciple, Sheikh Jami Abdullah Rahman, stood in the middle of them, his white turban the only thing visible at this distance, but his huge voice audible over the crowd. He was leading the heaving mass through a series of dhikr, religious chants, some recognizable to me in Arabic, others offered in a foreign tongue.

Women were clacking wooden blocks together high above their heads as they repeated the dhikr over and over. Stalks of qat were being passed from hand to hand, their leaves washed down with water drunk from a hollowed gourd. Mouths were green, lips spittle caked, sweat flying as people bounced from foot to foot. They were too entranced to take any particular notice of Hussein and me. We leaned left and right with the crowd, and stalks of green leaves were passed into our hands. We hadn't known qat in Morocco, and it was tough and bitter upon first taste; I spat it out onto the dirt at my feet.

The qat fuelled devotion, allowing people to sustain their energy over the hours and taking them to a point of near ecstasy where they began hissing through their teeth and their eyes rolled so far back their pupils disappeared and they spun around in blind circles. When they lost their balance, they were pushed gently back upright by the crowd.

"Like whirling dervishes!" Hussein marvelled.

At some point in the early hours of the morning, the sheikh's voice suddenly vaporized and people's movements began to slow, until their feet were leaden, still, and they took deep breaths and began to drift homeward. I looked at Hussein and implored him. Speak to the sheikh. It's time.

—

We had come to Harar to honour Saint Bilal al Habash and seek his blessing and protection, for this is the city that houses the original shrine in a series of shrines in his honour strung like pearls on a necklace across the sands of North Africa. The shrine in Morocco where we lived and studied with the Great Abdal lay farthest west. The Great Abdal had once made this pilgrimage, and like all his students, Hussein and I had been raised to believe in this journey as our duty, and our desire.

"You will go when God wills it," the Great Abdal used to say to us.

But first, Hussein had to fully recover. I never knew exactly what ailed him, only that he had spent some time in a cave in the desert and returned a broken man. When I first arrived at the shrine I noticed him because he sat apart from all the other Sufis. He hid under his woollen cloak clutching a string of prayer beads and remained still for days at a time.

But one day, while the Great Abdal and I were having our morning lessons, something compelled Hussein to look up. His expression was utterly blank. His teeth were black, the whites of his eyes yellow, and his hair a mop of greasy black strings. He looked so old to me, though he was probably only in his early twenties. So old and so sad.

From that day on, Hussein made feeble attempts to move. By the time the Great Abdal and I had reached the twentieth chapter of the Qur'an, several months later, Hussein had managed to push himself upright onto thin, quivering legs. He was a white spider, all limbs poking out of a brown wool sack. He stood staring at his dirty feet, his face contorted with the effort of considering what he should next do. I worried he was going to topple over and asked the Great Abdal if I should help. "Go on, then," the Great Abdal encouraged.

Much to my surprise, Hussein let me take his limp, bony hand and place it upon my shoulder. He then slowly raised his leg, but he couldn't put it down. I suggested he try stepping backwards, the way my mother used to do whenever she'd lost something. A key, her cigarette lighter, me.

Hussein looked up at the sky and considered this, taking a long, deep breath through his nostrils. He leaned his bony weight deeper into my shoulder and raised his leg again. "Steady me," he said weakly.

Then a dog barked in the distance, and Hussein's foot came down and touched the ground behind him. The Great Abdal gasped. So did Hussein. "Subhaanallah," he said. Glory be to God. "It *is* easier when I cannot see where my foot will land."

"You have to concentrate more when you don't have your eyes," I offered.

"Yes. Vision is a distraction," Hussein agreed, and with that, he closed his eyes.

For Hussein it was a question of retreating backwards to where he had lost his way; for me it was a question of moving on from the loss of my parents. I suppose we met somewhere in the middle. Took each other by the hand and stepped forward into a life of prayer and learning and companionship.

My Qur'anic study with the Great Abdal was supplemented by monthly visits from Muhammed Bruce Mahmoud. He would bring me volumes from the library he slowly dismantled over the years. He was rather peculiar and certainly very pompous, but I adored him. "For your edification, mademoiselle," he would announce, bowing dramatically and presenting me with a new stack.

Muhammed Bruce told me stories about Bilal al Habash's homeland, where he boasted having long-standing connections. He was particularly proud of his association with a man named Sir Richard Burton. He claimed the famous British explorer, who had been the first European to visit the city of Harar, was his great-great-uncle. Muhammed Bruce also knew the emperor of Ethiopia, Haile Selassie, the King of Kings, Conquering Lion of the Tribe of Judah. He told me they'd played polo together.

Ours was a rich and good life in a small and peaceful place, a self-contained universe hooked up to its own generator. But after seven years of devotion—measuring the weight of every word, savouring the hard edges, feeling them dissolve in my mouth as I stood, as I kneeled, as I pressed my forehead to the ground—the insularity of our bubble burst.

In the late 1960s a new king came to power. He felt the shrines and brotherhoods had grown too powerful; they were a challenge to the way he wanted to govern now that the French had let go of the reins. The king's army soon broke down the doors of the shrine in the nearby town of Tamegroute, sending its brothers into flight. Some of them landed on our doorstep, seeking protection from the Great Abdal.

He worried our shrine would be next, since we received funds from the brotherhood in Tamegroute for taking in the local poor. We were dependent to a large extent upon them, just as they were dependent upon a larger brotherhood in the north, the leader of which had unfortunately tried to assassinate the king. Our beloved sheikh suggested that perhaps it was time for Hussein and me to make the journey to Harar. And then suggestion became insistence. Suddenly it became *now* rather than *when*, hijrah as well as haj: as much a flight as a pilgrimage. He would follow with the rest of the Sufis, he promised, if the situation necessitated it.

So in February of 1969, Qur'an in hand, and a letter of introduction from Muhammed Bruce to the emperor of Ethiopia (signed: "Your supplicant, Your servant"), our haj and hijrah began. The Great Abdal drained the coffers in order to send us across the Sahara in search of refuge in Ethiopia, just as the Prophet had sent his family and followers to what was then Abyssinia thirteen centuries before. I was sixteen years old.

It made a noble and self-sacrificing story if you omitted the fact that we had spent just over a week living in luxury at the emperor's palace in Addis Ababa, courtesy of an introduction by our friend and my guardian, Muhammed Bruce Mahmoud. From there, at the emperor's insistence, we had been driven to Harar by a member of the palace guard. And omit, Hussein did, for it was a crime for a Sufi, meant to fulfill himself on a diet of devotion, to have indulged.

Hussein returned from his conference with Sheikh Jami to find me sitting in the bark folds of a giant tree. He was glowing with rare giddiness, and smiled sheepishly, gesturing for me to follow him through the tall carved wooden doors of the first in a row of three identical whitewashed buildings.

Inside, a weary and sweat-stained crew of the sheikh's friends and relations were strewn across the red-earth platforms of a large room with shiny turquoise walls adorned with baskets and wooden bowls and tin plates from China and gold-lettered Arabic proverbs hanging in frames. Fatima, the sheikh's senior wife, somewhat taciturn but gracious, offered us a seat in a corner. We leaned back against silk-covered pillows and huddled under a blanket, and I soon fell asleep against the pitter-pat of women's conversation and the hearty bass notes of men's snores.

It was just after sunrise when Sheikh Jami's full figure nearly filled the doorway. My head snapped from the platform as his booming voice pounded the muted din. It was a terrifying sight: he was huge and ugly. His blue eyes were swimming in protruding ochre bubbles, his tobacco-stained teeth hung from his mouth like stalactites, his red hair cascaded from his turban to his shoulders, and his beard was so sharp it could have sliced bread.

At first sight of me, Sheikh Jami bellowed angrily: "*Yee min khowraja? Farenji?*" Terms of insult in an unintelligible tongue.

Hussein leapt forward, threw himself at the sheikh's feet, grasped him by the ankles and begged his understanding.

"Yes, of course!" bellowed the sheikh, switching to Arabic. "You, fine, but what is *she* doing here? A European! In my house!"

I reached up gingerly and tried to recover the veil that had slipped to my shoulders while I'd been asleep.

"The Great Abdal has sent us both," Hussein said.

Sheikh Jami's barrel of a chest subsided at the mention of the name. "My brother," he said. (Or rather, as we would figure out later, his third cousin, some dozen times removed.)

Hussein continued: "She is the charge of a friend who once visited your greatness, a man named Muhammed Bruce Mahmoud—"

"Stop!" the giant sheikh roared. "That man is the last farenji I had the misfortune to encounter! A charlatan!" he shouted, and spat on the floor just next to Hussein's knee.

I wondered what Muhammed Bruce could possibly have done to cause such a reaction. He had claimed to love Harar and its people.

For all his usual timidity, though, Hussein offered a Sufi proverb as if asking the sheikh to excuse Muhammed Bruce. Or me. "Enlightenment must come little by little, or else it would overwhelm," he said.

Sheikh Jami pursed his lips as if he were sucking a lemon. Slowly, he spread his arms, inviting

Hussein to stand up and come and join him in his breakfast, an enormous platter of meat and rice topped with fried onions that Fatima had just set down on one of the platforms.

Gishta, the sheikh's plump and dimpled youngest wife, held a bowl in one hand and poured a slow stream of water from a jug over her husband's hands with her other. He rubbed his palms together vigorously and mumbled something to her. She nodded and stepped over to Hussein, and poured water over his hands as well. She handed the bowl to a young girl at her side and then reached for my forearm, though not to wash.

"Where are we going?" I stammered in Arabic as she pulled me to my feet.

She led me wordlessly to the door.

"But why?" I pleaded.

"It is just a small confusion, Lilly," said Hussein quietly, as if something might break. "Everything will be fine, insha'Allah."

Gishta led me across the threshold. I clutched the outside wall of Fatima's house. Hussein and I had come all this way together through hostile lands in search of refuge. He had been my shadow for years, my brother, beholden to me for his recovery. I couldn't ask him not to stay; it was what he had always wanted. Tears spilled down my face, but Gishta only nudged me on with her knuckles pressed into the small of my back.

## Call to Prayer.

—

I wanted to disappear, to blend into the stench in the air, melt into the high white walls of the compounds that flanked us on each side, be an observer, not the observed. My life was now in the hands of a woman who was leading me left and right and right and left through tangled streets until I was sure we had come full circle.

It was early, but the city was already in second gear. We passed toothless old women and shrunken old men and expressionless Sufis clinging to the edges of their wool blankets, and neatly groomed men with short beards and knit skullcaps, and clusters of veiled teenaged girls with fits of the giggles, and snotty-nosed children who ran up and touched me, shouting "Farenji! Farenji!" and round, oily mothers standing in doorways with babies on their hips shouting at Gishta, who offered answers incomprehensible to me that made everyone except me laugh. I fingered the amulet the Great Abdal had given me, which I wore tied on a string around my neck. The small leather pouch contained a verse from the Qur'an to ward off the bad jinn, evil spirits.

There was some relief once Gishta and I passed over the main road and climbed down a hill on the other side. We came to a less congested part of town, a rundown neighbourhood where the compound walls were crumbling and dust coloured. Makeshift shacks made of tin siding and wood scraps had been erected between broken walls. The streets reeked of urine, and there were people missing limbs who could not even be bothered remarking at the sight of me.

We slipped through a narrow passage, where a runny-nosed girl sat alone on the ground eating dirt. "Bortucan!" Gishta snapped at the girl, hauling her up onto her feet. "Nouria!" she called, pulling back one of the rough pieces of corrugated tin that formed a fence at the end of the passage.

A dark woman emerged from a dark kitchen, a grease stain on her face, her dress sewn together clumsily with thick string. She stood at a defensive distance, wringing her hands. The little girl clung to the backs of her knees.

Gishta pointed at me; Nouria shook her head. Gishta shook her head; Nouria pointed at me. Gishta grabbed the woman's hands and shook them and yelled, the rolls of fat around her middle trembling, the gold in her mouth flashing, until Nouria bowed her head and gave an exasperated sigh.

Gishta, I suddenly realized, looked at me as a source of income for this woman, her cousin, expecting me to pay rent, and pay well. I would soon discover that rumour of the farenji who had arrived in Harar in a Mercedes was spreading as quickly as a cloud of locusts tears through a field. Rumour that seemed to neglect the fact that Hussein had arrived this way as well. But he was an Arab, a man and a Sufi, whereas I was an enigma and a threat.

I surrendered to my new landlady a portion of the money the Great Abdal had given us for the journey. Nouria rolled the bills together and pushed the bundle down between her breasts. She did not look pleased.

Nouria's compound was nothing like the sheikh's with its whitewashed buildings arranged around a treed courtyard. This was little more than a few square yards of dirt containing a small mud-walled building with a grass roof. To the left of the doorway stood a single Wellington boot, home to a battered-looking plant. The kitchen, with walls of mud and metal scraps, narrow as a closet and blackened with soot, leaned over precariously in one corner. A cat licked the flies from an open wound, an emaciated goat bleated in a corner, and the air smelled of sour milk and the oil Nouria had obviously left burning on the kitchen fire. A balloon of grey smoke drifted out the kitchen door to greet us, and Nouria threw up her arms and cursed me before ducking into the haze.

Two boys whom I guessed to be Nouria's sons, about seven and eight years old, had been staring at me through the parting in the fence, and now they pushed their other sister into the yard to get a closer look at me. She had the same wide eyes and nest of matted curls as the dirt-eater. All four of the children were dulled by a matte finish of dust and scabbed on elbows and knees.

"What's your name?" I asked the girl in Arabic.

"Bah!" she shrieked, and disappeared back through the fence to cower in her brothers' shadow. They pushed her through the fence again.

This time I pointed at her sister, who was ignoring me as she stabbed a mound of dirt with a stick. "Bortucane?" I asked.

"Bortucan," the older girl corrected.

"And you?" I pointed.

"Rahile." Hesitantly, she pointed at me.

"Lilly," I replied.

This sent the boys behind the fence into hysterics, and they started banging their palms against the tin, which dragged their mother yelling from the kitchen. Her threats quieted them down, but they continued to stare through the fence. I closed my eyes and recited in silence, taking up a position I would occupy for much of the day. Learning Qur'an had taught me how to be engaged while perfectly still. It had also taught me patience, something I didn't naturally possess.

When the sky burned orange and dusk descended, Nouria set down a bowl of red water and called the children to supper. Come, the boy named Anwar gestured, holding out a stale piece of bread. The sky darkened with each bite, and it was black by the time we retired to the windowless mud-walled building. Nouria and her four children crawled onto a single foam mattress that covered the dirt floor against one wall; I wrapped myself in a blanket she reluctantly tossed my way against the opposite.

I lay awake, alert to the hyenas whooping their strange way through the city streets, the children's rib cages rattling as they coughed, the flying cockroaches batting their wings against the walls and the sound of what must have been rats foraging in the corners. I curled up in a ball, afraid I would lose my toes. But for all the discomfort, for all the distress at being dismissed by Sheikh Jami and separated from Hussein, I did feel some sense of relief. Hussein and I had come through hell. It was not just Morocco but all of North Africa that was on fire. Borders and whole populations were in flux as people, in the absence of a colonial enemy, turned weapons on each other and themselves. In these troubled lands we'd welcomed the appearance of occasional towns only to feel the tensions and suspicions of their people and rush back into the relentlessness and safety of more desert.

Our Tuareg guide hadn't spoken Arabic or French or English, but we'd prayed together after performing our ablutions with desert dust, and slept side by side on the ground like mummies wrapped in sheets under night's mist of sand. Islam unites us, where language and borders do not.

But then came the Sudan, where the Muslims of the north were imposing Islamic law throughout the land, killing the people in the south:

Africans, animists, Christians. Three days into the Sudan, somewhere south of Khartoum, Hussein and I had left our camp to gather water from an oasis in the distance. Our guide had remained behind, burying bread dough in the sand, when we heard the explosion. The northern army had apparently marked the divide between north and south with landmines.

For the first time in my life, I was made aware of the angry possibilities of Islam.

That night Hussein had reached, uncharacteristically, for my hand. "This is not the true meaning of jihad," he spoke into the starless dark. "Jihad is the holy war we have within ourselves. *That* is the meaning below the surface. Our internal struggle for purity," he said with emphasis, pressing his forefinger into his chest. "It is the war of ascendance over our basal instincts. It has absolutely nothing to do with others. The only thing we can have control over is ourselves."

It was a relief to find myself in a peaceful place again, no matter how unwelcome. In this city of saints, encircled by a protective wall. In a country that was not fighting these post-colonial wars, because it, alone in Africa, had maintained its independence.

—

I awoke my first morning in Harar to a sky crackling with a staggered chorus of muezzins. The *Allahu akbar*s rippled in waves down my spine. I reached for the rusty water can so I could perform my ablutions before prayer, but Nouria grabbed the can from my hands.

"But how am I supposed to pray?" I snapped.

She shrugged, not understanding, so I pointed at my chest, I pointed to the minaret in the sky above us, I raised my hands as if to bow down in prayer.

She looked at me curiously and muttered: "Masha'Allah."

"Yes! Allahu akbar!" I cried. "God is the greatest!"

She handed the rusty can back to me and nodded, as if to say: *All right, then. Prove it to me.*

Later that morning, Gishta arrived carrying a sack of mangoes and bananas for her cousin. She was dressed elaborately in a voluminous red dress embroidered with gold silk across the chest and a clashing fuchsia veil. She was the embodiment of Harari wealth, complete with arms laden with the fruits of her husband's lands.

Nouria, too, had made an effort: her dress was only a simple one of light blue cotton, but it was clean and well made.

As they were about to squeeze through the tin fence, I grabbed Gishta by the elbow. "Masjid?" I asked.

Gishta nodded and looked at me defiantly, as if to say: *Yes, the mosque. What of it?*

I pointed at my chest and raised my palms as I had done with Nouria earlier that morning. Gishta turned to her cousin and chattered away for a good minute, pointing at me and then the sky and waving her hands about, ending her speech with what sounded like a question mark.

To me she said one word: "Fohdah." She tugged at her veil.

"Yes, yes," I said excitedly, raising a finger, asking them to wait a minute. I went into the dark room and pulled my one veil from my rucksack. Navy, plain, a little rough around the edges.

Gishta made a sucking noise and shook her head.

"What's wrong with it?" I asked.

"Ginee?" she replied.

I frowned, not understanding.

She rubbed her thumb and forefinger together.

I had a bit of money left, though not much. I patted my pocket in reply, and Gishta nodded and strode out of the compound, which I took as an invitation to follow.

The three of us walked single file up the hill to the Faras Magala, the main market. It was barely recognizable as the square where Hussein and I had disembarked; by day it was a cacophonous junction where taxi drivers and qat sellers and merchants bartered at the tops of their lungs fighting to be heard over the bells of the Medhane Alem, the turn-of-the-century church, ringing overhead.

We made our way through the market and down the street on the far side, a steep, rocky slope lined with men rattling away on ancient sewing machines. We stopped at one of the fabric shops partway down the hill where several bright veils were displayed on hooks on the inside of the door.

Gishta pointed at one, but I shook my head. *Too gaudy.*

I pointed at another, but Gishta shook her head. *Too plain?*

Nouria pulled an elegant but simple veil of swirling soft greens and blues off a hook, at which Gishta and I nodded our approval in unison. Nouria threw it loosely over my head and draped the end over my left shoulder, Harari-style. Gishta boldly dug into my pocket, acquainting herself with just how much money I had left, before handing over a couple of greasy bills to the amused merchant.

—

Hussein came to visit me at Nouria's compound after our visit to the mosque that day, possessed with a confidence I had not seen in all the years I had known him: an aura of calm, as if overnight, he'd outgrown the insecurities of an extended adolescence and become a man. His adolescence had begun with steps backwards leading to steps forward, which ultimately led to steps beyond. Our first walk outside the walls of the Great Abdal's compound had been to the small shrine of a nameless saint nestled in a cluster of palms on the other side of Tamegroute. Hussein had had to bend in half to fit through the door. I followed him in, but even I could barely stand up. It was very dark, but I could make out an old man sitting cross-legged in the corner of the room. He was swaying back and forth as he recited Qur'an.

Hussein approached him mid-recitation, took the man's hand from his lap and kissed the back of it. He then untied the incense crystals he had bought from a blind Berber woman in the market from the knot in the corner of his wool cloak and laid them at the man's feet. The man picked up the incense and threw it with dramatic flourish into a small clay pot of coals, engulfing us in a sweet, sticky cloud so thick and grey that I could see nothing any more.

"Hussein?" I said tentatively. "Hussein?" I said a little louder when he failed to answer.

"What do you see, Lilly?" he asked.

"I don't see anything."

"Exactly." He sighed. "The presence of God. Isn't it beautiful?"

In the presence of God, nothing particularly extraordinary had happened, but perhaps that was the point. I had not sensed God in that moment, but I had seen Hussein's awe and desire. That's all I was: his witness. But to be seen in the dark is to be reborn.

He had been superstitious, connecting the path to wellness with my presence, keeping me by his side even though it conflicted with his aspirations as a Sufi. "Earthly love is a distraction," he'd told me long ago when I'd tried to talk to him about my parents. "All our love should be for Allah. This is the Sufi way. It is good to be freed from earthly love. It is good for a Muslim. It is good for Allah.

It is good for you. Do not worry. Allah will fill your heart. You mustn't grieve. It is as Rumi said: 'Anything you lose comes round in another form.'"

It was clear that Hussein was ready to dispense with earthly love and go blank to the world. He had pulled out the tent pegs nailing the corners of his woollen cloak to the ground and was moving in the slow way of all mystical seekers along the road to transcendence. He looked, as far as I could detect in the glazed, monotonous expression of a Sufi, content.

My needs, meanwhile, were as basic and worldly as they come: food and shelter, some way of earning my keep. I didn't have the option of going blank.

# A Single Wellington Boot.

—

I contributed to Nouria's household in the ways that I could. I took the broom from her hands, swept away the dead insects and the cat and goat feces and sprinkled water over the dirt to settle the dust, leaving Nouria free to take in more laundry. She rubbed her hands raw washing richer women's clothes in a big tub filled with water that her oldest boy, Anwar, carried by the jerry can each morning from the river beyond the city wall. Later, we used the pinkish brown laundry water to wash our faces, hands and feet, then our dishes and our own clothes. When the water was black, we threw it into the street, where it trickled downhill and eventually seeped into the parched ground.

The boys spent most of the day lingering in the market, selling peanuts or, when there were no customers or peanuts, begging. They kept their eyes glued to the fruit and vegetable stands, ready to pounce on anything rolling away from its seller. At the end of the day they scavenged for anything spoiled and discarded, returning home with the soft, battered remnants of what had once passed as food.

Nouria's twin girls, meanwhile, spent most of their time playing—shoeless and filthy—in the streets. I would often find the smaller one, Bortucan, sitting alone in the road eating dirt. Seeking nutrients where she could.

The birth of the twins had changed Nouria's fortune, not that her prospects, coming from the poor Oromo background that she did, had ever looked particularly bright. Like her cousin Gishta, though, Nouria aspired to belong among the Harari—their wealth and privilege powerful aphrodisiacs—and had made the language, the food and the customs her own.

When her husband died—of some mysterious illness called "ground disease," people said— Gishta had encouraged Nouria to find a Harari man just as she had. Nouria did her best: for several years she had been a Harari man's mistress, and although he had given her an allowance that enabled her to send her two boys to school, he did not ask her to marry him. When she got pregnant, he cut off relations altogether.

The boys were forced to drop out of school and go back to the streets; Nouria was forced to beg rich Harari women to let her do their laundry. She would not go back to being a household servant, as she had been as a child. She would not surrender her own home. Rahile gave up mother's milk for water and stale bread and the black flesh of overripe bananas. Bortucan, however, still refused to let go of her mother's breast, whether milk was forthcoming or not.

Dinner, which I would help Nouria prepare, was a modest meal, a stew made of onions and lentils and chili peppers sopped up with stale injera, or sometimes injera and ground red chili pepper alone.

We relieved ourselves on a patch of ground behind the kitchen, wiping with the left hand, pouring water over the left with the right. We tiptoed in flip-flops—mine hand-me-downs from Gishta—across this patch of earth, its slippery brown sheen no doubt caused by ingesting these foul-smelling thin stews made from poisonous water.

Nouria didn't deny my help because it allowed her to earn more income, but there was no easiness between us as we settled into our reluctant arrangement. I knew this was not simply due to the limitations of language.

The children, on the other hand, were proving to be a blessing. The boys soon got over the giggle-inducing, wide-staring curiosity of having a foreigner in their midst, though they would still drag people to have a look at me over the corrugated tin fence and then beg to be paid for providing entertainment. I simply waved at the women and children who peered over, which would send them into flight. I hoped that the novelty would eventually wear off, though thousands of people lived within the city's walls.

I felt immediately protective of Bortucan because she was in much greater need of attention than her sister. I was surprised to learn they were twins, both four years old, because Bortucan, unlike Rahile, hadn't started speaking and never played with other children. She was sullen, where Rahile was perennially bright. Perhaps, in her wordlessness, her isolation, there was something I recognized and understood.

During the heat of the afternoon I sat on a mat in a shaded corner of the yard, fanning the flies away, making vocabulary lists, diligently recording each new Harari word I learned and doing my best to make some sense of the grammar. Many of the words seemed very close to Arabic, derived from the same root, though they were strung together in unfamiliar ways. And Arabic, I discovered, went far with some people. Amongst the more educated, the ones who were well versed in Qur'an, as were some of Nouria's wealthier neighbours, Arabic was familiar. Nouria didn't know Arabic per se, but she had a number of Arabic proverbs on the tip of her tongue.

Anwar spoke some, which he'd learned during his few years at the madrasa. I would point at something in the compound—a cockroach, a sack of grain, a dress hanging from the washing line— and Anwar would give me the Harari word. The last thing he named for me in the compound was the plant growing out of the rubber boot, but he didn't have a word for the boot itself.

"Where's the other one?" I asked him.

"What other one?"

"The pair to this one."

"There is only this one," he said.

What was a single Wellington boot doing sitting in this compound in a remote Muslim city in Africa?

"And the plant. What's it for?" I asked Anwar.

He shrugged. "It's for nothing," he replied.

"It's not used as a spice or a medicine?"

"It's just for being a plant."

*For nothing. For being a plant.* In this impoverished world where everything had its use, I found this one frivolous gesture reassuring.

Once he'd named everything in the compound for me, we moved inside the mud-walled house and named its meagre contents. Armed with the word for foam mattress, I asked him where I might buy one of my own. He seemed proud to be able to escort me by hand to the market, where a man cut a piece of foam according to Anwar's instruction.

"But Anwar, that's far too big," I objected, once the man had cut the piece.

"No, no, it's good!" he said, and placed the thick tube of foam on his head.

"All right," I sighed, and dug into my pocket.

As I thought, the tube was too wide to fit through the door of the mud house.

"No problem," said Anwar and unrolled it on the ground. He went into the kitchen, returned with a knife and drew a clean line down the middle of the mattress with the blade. He carried each piece into the house separately and placed his clothes at the head of the second mattress.

My vocabulary grew over the months with words picked up from Nouria, from Gishta when she came to visit, as she did almost every other afternoon, and from the other women in the neighbourhood who would gather in the courtyard on the occasional Saturday for what they called a bercha. They would spread a blanket on the ground and sit in a circle and share a little gossip and qat. They snacked on popcorn, roasted on a flat pan over an open flame, threw crystals of incense onto dying embers, drank tea and smoked the hookah, which here was the sole preserve of women. The qat, the tobacco, the popcorn and the gossip were the only extravagances in Nouria's poor life, gifts brought by more affluent neighbours.

I sat on the edge of their circle, Bortucan often in my lap, me wiping her perpetually running nose with a rag. Some of the women wove threads of straw while they chatted, making baskets to adorn the interior walls of houses richer than Nouria's. Bortucan often tugged at my breast, and inevitably crawled in frustration from my lap to her mother's where, although she could not always be assured feeding, there was comfort.

I learned from listening, from being corrected when I attempted to interact, from sheer exposure and immersion, through the days come weeks come months of hearing little else, from the knowledge that I had no choice.

In return for my new vocabulary, I offered to teach the boys some more Arabic. After dinner, we would sit by the dying light of the fire in the cramped kitchen and practise the alphabet together, writing the letters on slate with chalk.

One morning Anwar came to me carrying a book

in his hands—my Qur'an, the one the Great Abdal had given me.

"Anwar, where did you get this?" I chastised.

"From your bag," he said, pointing at the house.

"You shouldn't go rummaging through my things," I said, immediately shamed by the possessiveness in my voice. "Do you want me to read to you, is that it?" I asked more gently.

He nodded vigorously.

"Well, first we have to wash our hands. Then we have to state our intention—"

"Wait!" he said, and ran to get his brother.

Each morning after that we sat in the doorway of the dark room we all shared and recited quietly for an hour against the rhythmic sounds of Nouria on her knees scrubbing clothes in a big metal basin. Over the weeks, the two boys revealed their knowledge of verse after verse, then chapter after chapter. They ground to a halt at the last verse of chapter five. So it was here that we began in earnest. Listen and repeat. Listen and repeat. Line by line, verse by verse, just the way the Great Abdal had taught me.

The Great Abdal had taken me by the hand and said this is a flower and this is a rock and this is a tree. Under his guidance I put down roots word by word. Each utterance prefaced by *bismillah al-rahman al-rahim*, in the name of God, the merciful, the compassionate. The world within the book was whole, and there was an order, a process, a logical sequence of steps. It was the antithesis of the peripatetic life I'd lived with my parents; it was the antidote to their death. There was always a safe landing, even when I made a mistake. If I stumbled over a sentence, I could just retreat to the one before. I could always go back to what I knew.

This is the way of Islam; it is passed like a gift through generations. It connects us through time. Through this process these children would be connected to the Great Abdal, to his father and teacher before him and his father and teacher before him all the way back through the generations to the saint himself. In a fatherless world, I was a link in a chain that connected God's Prophet (peace be upon him) with two dusty Ethiopian boys.

## Purity and Danger.

—

Nouria and I sorted through a sack of sorghum as she'd taught me—shaking the grains over a mesh screen, getting rid of the loose chaff and picking out the grit and small stones. When we finished, we would grind the grain in a mortar, mix it with water and then leave it in a bucket to ferment. We would use that sour, hissing puddle in a few days to make enough injera to feed us all for a couple of weeks.

Rahile was standing at her mother's side that morning, tugging her sleeve. Nouria tried to quiet her: "Hush. Soon, Rahu, soon. Do not bother your mother. Go and play."

But Rahile started crying and stomping her feet. Bortucan, in the spirit of twinhood perhaps, burst out in the same manner; eyes squeezed shut, little fists scrunched into balls, she punched at the air and let out a strange moan while her sister's crying escalated.

"Good God! What is the fuss all about?" Gishta yelled as she entered the compound. She was carrying a qat-stuffed leather satchel over her shoulder and a gourd of camel's milk in her hand. "Did a stone fall on your head, Rahu? Are you possessed by the jinn?"

"I want absuma! Ab-su-ma! Ab-su-ma!" she wailed each syllable.

"What is this absuma she wants?" I asked.

"It's expensive, that's what it is," Nouria said, deftly tossing the grain up and down.

"She wants a party, like her little friends in the neighbourhood," Gishta elaborated, squatting down with us. "So people will come and say, Oh, aren't you a good girl, here, have some sweeties, here is some money, have some more honey."

For her birthday? I wondered, though no one seemed to know exactly how old they were. *Maybe I am this many years*, they would say with a shrug. *What does it matter?* Or, *Four droughts have passed in my lifetime*.

"But Nouria is right, this party is very expensive," Gishta explained. "You have to kill some chickens, maybe even a goat, and feed everybody. And then, of course, you have to pay the midwife."

"Why the midwife?" I asked.

"Because she makes the party happen, Lilly!" Gishta shouted, incredulous. "It's not a party without the midwife. Don't you know anything? She doesn't know anything, Nouria!"

"Well, I'm not her mother!" Nouria hissed.

Had my mother not taught me anything? She'd shown me how to do simple crocheting and how to join my letters together. She'd taught me card games, including strip poker, telling me that nakedness was not cause for shame. I'd wondered about that at the time, though, because while they lay about with little or nothing on smoking marijuana and giving each other sponge baths, the rest of the world had been very much dressed.

She'd taught me where babies came from but not where they go when they die. It was the Great Abdal who taught me about heaven.

Both of the women were staring at me.

"What?" I demanded.

"You know that you must always cover your hair outside the compound," Gishta said.

"And that you must never be alone with a man, because the devil will be your third companion," Nouria added, the first in her arsenal of Arabic proverbs, most of which seemed to concern relations between men and women.

"And you know that when you have the monthly blood, you must never visit the mosque or prepare food, for this is a hurt and a pollution," Gishta said gravely.

I didn't know what any of this had to do with Rahile's party, but I wanted to help, and so I later pressed a small amount of money into Nouria's hand.

Nouria smiled at me for perhaps the first time, and said: "For both Rahile and Bortucan. You cannot do one and not the other."

—

Rahile boasted about the forthcoming party for weeks, telling anyone who would listen. People on the street patted her on the head and told her she was a good girl. Even Bortucan appeared to bubble with anticipation.

Gishta had matching dresses made for the girls for the occasion, and even though Bortucan had managed to rub dirt into the front of hers within half an hour of putting it on, they both looked uncharacteristically neat. And happy.

Rahile perched herself on a small wooden bench that had been moved into the courtyard, sitting straight-backed and waving her legs with excitement as women from the neighbourhood flooded in through the parted fence. The women had marigolds and aromatic herbs tucked behind their ears and they carried shiny packages of sweets that they placed on the ground before sitting themselves down in a circle around Rahile. Gishta passed around a tray with small clay cups of tea made from coffee husks boiled in milk and water.

Most of the women ignored me as I hung back by the kitchen, keeping an eye on another pot of milk and water about to boil on the fire. Two sisters from down the road, who clearly found me amusing, shouted: "Tell us, what new Harari words have you learned lately?"

"Absuma gar," I replied plainly, wanting to keep the attention on Rahile who was looking a little put out.

They roared and raised their hands above their heads.

"Absuma gar! Allahu akbar!" cried one.

"Allahu akbar!" repeated the others one after another, until the ripple of a whisper threaded its way through the crowd and the women fell silent. A large elderly woman with drooping eyelids and deep lines etched into her sagging face entered the compound, followed by a young Oromo girl gripping the creped legs of two upside-down chickens.

"Abai Taoduda," Nouria fawned, rushing forward, dropping to her knees and kissing the fleshy part of the woman's hand where the thumb and forefinger meet. Abai Taoduda exchanged greetings of peace with the women while the young Oromo girl handed the two chickens by the legs to Anwar, who was standing far back by the fence with his brother. Anwar held them proudly, talking to them as they protested this change of hands.

The elderly woman made her way into the centre of the circle and raised her palms in praise of Allah. A chorus of praise shuttled through the air. She approached Rahile on the bench, pulled her to her feet and kissed her on the forehead before sitting down precisely where Rahile had been sitting and pulling the girl down onto her generous lap.

"Uma Sherifa!" called the midwife. Sherifa, a blind woman who lived in the neighbourhood and had a reputation as a wonderful singer, rose to her feet. She was often paid to perform at weddings, but having never been invited to such an event, this was the first time I'd heard her sing. Her eyes were clouded by a white film, but her voice was so clear that I could hear the river of sweet water cascading down the mountainside, I could see the wall being built around the city inch by inch, I could feel the bittersweet joy of being ge kahat, a "daughter of the city," one whose protection serves the community as a whole.

The midwife lifted up her skirt and spread her plump, dimpled legs. She pulled up Rahile's dress as well and tied the girl's thighs to the soft insides of her own with two long black scarves. Then she put a cloth in Rahile's mouth, told her to bite hard, tugged at the folds of skin between Rahile's legs and swiftly ran a metal blade down over them.

"What is she doing?" I couldn't help but cry out.

"Uss!" the women closest to me chastised.

I stood with my hand over my mouth as the midwife made several quick slices with the blade, removing thin bits of skin. All the colour drained from Rahile's face. A tremor rippled throughout her body as a thick pool of blood grew between her legs. I lost all sensation in the lower half of me, watching in horror as the blood began to creep over the side of the bench. Rahile caught sight of it as it lurched toward the ground and she let out an agonized cry.

In the background, one of the chickens, which Anwar had beheaded with the last downward pull of the midwife's blade, ran amok around the compound. The women raised their heads and cupped their hands over their mouths: a celebratory chorus of epiglottises as they ululated heavenward. I wanted to catch Rahile's blood in my hands and give the colour back to her. She was whimpering, her lips trembling, her eyelashes fluttering over her glazed eyes.

Nouria blotted her daughter's wound with a rag, and then the midwife tugged the scarves loose and scooped the girl up under the arms. Nouria grabbed the deadened heap of her daughter by the ankles, and the two women lay her down on the bench. The midwife pinched together the two remaining flaps of skin between Rahile's legs and began piercing them perfunctorily with a row of six sharp thorns. I bit my knuckle so hard I drew blood. The midwife inserted a matchstick in the space between the last two thorns, and Rahile's whimpering slowed and deepened. She breathed heavily, as if through a blanket.

Abai Taoduda dragged her by the underarms and held her over a small smouldering pit of aromatic wood so that the smoke washed up over the wound. She held out her callused hand, and Nouria passed her warm ashes from the fire, which she patted up and down between the thorns with her flat fingers. Two women held Rahile by the shoulders as the midwife wrapped a bandage round and round her legs, binding her immobile from her hips to her feet. They carried her into the hut and lay her on the foam mattress.

I couldn't bear it: Nouria was pulling Bortucan forward.

"She's too young!" I protested.

Rabid whispers all around me.

Nouria said, "She is old enough to remember the pain."

I had to turn away. I had to push my way through the crowd of women and stand alone in the street. I heard nothing from Bortucan, only the jubilant chorus of ululating women. A manic, headless chicken brushed my calf as it ran down the street. Anwar chased it a few feet before throwing himself upon it and stifling it with his chest.

This was the party Rahile had been waiting for.

# The Doctor.

—

The girls were instructed to lie bound for forty days, long enough for scar tissue to form, and to drink as little as possible so as not to have to remove the matchsticks to let their urine pass. Rahile—though she mewled when she had to urinate—told me she felt special, she felt loved.

The women had lined up single file and entered the room one by one to congratulate the girls and offer them sweets and money and kisses on the forehead.

"Now they will grow up to be respectable women," Gishta told me with pride. "This is the greatest occasion in a girl's life, Lilly—next to her marriage, of course."

And the latter depended on the former, according to Gishta: no one would dare marry an uncircumcised girl, a sharmuta, a girl wild with heat. Such a girl could only bring fitna—chaos—and shame to her family.

Bortucan, however, did not appear to be faring as well as her sister. She moaned in a most unholy way. I gathered she'd lost consciousness during the operation, and although she awoke and took a few small sips of sugary tea the day after, her bandages were soaked in blood. I helped Nouria unravel and change the bandages, trying not to reveal my horror, lest I should alarm Bortucan even more.

Her legs were stone cold and her teeth chattered while we wrapped her in fresh cloth. We covered her with blankets and every article of clothing we had. She drifted in and out of sleep, muttered as though delirious, and by the end of the second day Nouria was concerned enough to call for the faith healer.

The old man came with his ink and quill. He sat in the doorway of the hut, and I watched over his shoulder as he wrote a few verses from the Qur'an onto a tiny square of paper that he rolled up and placed in a thin red leather cylinder. He strung a piece of thread through the open ends of the cylinder and handed it to Nouria, who tied it around Bortucan's neck.

I fingered my own amulet. To ward off the bad jinn, the Great Abdal had told me. But this situation was not the work of evil spirits. It was the work of a midwife, with the full support of every woman in the neighbourhood. It was the outcome of a little girl demanding: "Ab-su-ma!"

On the third day, Nouria called for the herbalist. The tattooed woman with the henna-bright hair stewed a sulphurous concoction over the fire until it thickened into a clay-like paste. She applied this mixture to all of Bortucan's orifices—her mouth,

her ears, her eyes, the spaces between the thorns—
and dragged her out into the sun on a blanket so
that the paste would harden and crumble.

Bortucan awoke the fourth day, her bandages
once again soaked in blood. Now, Nouria
lamented, we would have to call for the doctor.
Nouria had never called for a doctor in all the
months that I'd been here, though she and the children were often sick, their bodies unwitting hosts
to parasites, tormenting them with diarrhea,
inflating their bellies into hardened balloons. The
doctor was the last resort in a community where
midwives and faith healers and herbalists ruled.

———

I lay between the girls in the dark corner, trying to
distract them with the story of the Arab missionaries who had come to Abyssinia and heard the call of
Islam's first muezzin while passing through the
eastern mountains. They had prayed to God, for it
was a miracle, asking him if this was a sign that it
was here that they should settle. Their answer came
when a great wind swept down from the sky and
created a fertile valley before them fed by rivers as
sweet as those of Mecca. Some stayed to build a city
in the heart of the valley—a labyrinthine maze of
intersecting lanes, some of which are so narrow that
a man must lift the jerry cans from the side of a
donkey to let the animal proceed—while others continued westward, spreading news of the miracle of
Bilal al Habash's voice across North Africa.

The neighbourhood women suddenly scurried out of the compound. A man bent down and stepped over the threshold into our home, a room I was quite sure no man had ever entered. Nouria was at his heels.

I had expected an old man, a grandfather wrapped in white layers, not a young, tall, handsome man with butter-soft dark skin and bright teeth, wearing a jacket and matching trousers.

Dr. Aziz Abdulnasser had clearly not expected me either. He did a double take, squinting in the dark, then turned to Nouria.

"Did the midwife at least disinfect the blade?" he asked, not masking his anger.

Nouria replied in a quiet whisper, her eyes cast downward.

He turned to me. "Perhaps you could describe what happened," he said in perfect English

But I didn't have the words in any language. All I could say was that I thought Bortucan might have lost consciousness while it was happening.

"Shock and hemorrhaging, I imagine." He nodded, biting the pink at the centre of his bottom lip.

He cradled Bortucan in one arm and unwrapped the bandages with his other hand. I held a candle for him while he inspected her, but it was only seconds before he straightened his back. "We *must* get her to hospital," he said.

Nouria tugged at his sleeve with both hands. "Please, I beg you. Tell us how to take care of her here, but please, not the hospital, anything but that."

"They hate the hospital," he said to me in English. "They think it's a place where people go to die."

"And is it?" I asked him.

"Often," he said, "but only because they come to us when it's too late."

Ignoring Nouria, he picked the little girl up, threw her over his shoulder, bent through the door-way and walked straight out into the sunlight of the courtyard, leaving a faint trail of sweet cologne behind him. His black curls glistened in the sun, and he stood unapologetically tall.

"Go with her," Nouria urged me. "Please."

I stepped into the courtyard. "Wait!" I called out to the doctor. "I'll come with you."

"Fine," he said, "get your shoes, then."

I hesitated. I had only what I was wearing on my feet, the flip-flops everyone wore: national dress. I looked down at his bright white socks and newly shined lace-up shoes and I suddenly felt ashamed.

# Blood.

—

The Ras Makonnen Hospital lay just beyond the wall, along the eucalyptus-lined road that led into the city from the west. The yellow-brick building stood far bigger and grander than anything inside the city walls, intimidating all but the beggars who were strewn across the front steps, displaying their third-degree burns and waving their imaginary limbs in a bid for sympathy—preferably expressed in the form of cash. The farther up the stairs they crawled, the closer the beggars came to being poked in the ribs with the barrel of a guard's gun or kicked down the steps to begin again their agonizing climb.

It was not only the hospital's reputation as a morgue that the Hararis feared but the neighbourhood. To the north, south and east of the city lay their farmlands. This was why the people of the city were rich by Ethiopian standards: the Hararis owned the land and controlled the lucrative trade of the waxy, intoxicating leaves and the crisp green beans that grew upon it. They rented the land to peasant farmers, all Oromo, who tilled and tended the gardens in return for a 10 per cent share of the harvest. While there was the occasional threat of hyenas or banditry, these lands were theirs: neatly ordered plots passed down through the generations.

But on the west side lay a new city, a largely Christian Amhara neighbourhood that had evolved since the time of Harar's annexation into the Ethiopian empire. In 1887, the Muslim city at the heart of an expansive kingdom became a regional capital in a Christian empire. One jewel in somebody else's imperial crown. A royal residence stood across the road from the hospital, home to the duke and duchess of the province.

Hararis thought of this neighbourhood as a site of sin and depravity, a haven for buda, the evil eye, and forbade their children to enter these parts. But one had to pass through the area to leave the city for destinations west, like Dire Dawa, the market town an hour away, or the capital, Addis Ababa, three days away over winding roads. Hararis shut the windows of minibuses and held their noses when they passed through, alleging the stench of brothels and beer.

*Outsider* is what they smelled; contamination is what they feared.

I did not see sin and depravity. I saw a wide boulevard where the austerity of buildings and asphalt was interrupted by the velvet trunks of eucalyptus trees and the occasional burst of colour from a flame tree. I saw people swinging their arms freely because they were not funnelled between

compound walls. I saw the whites of people's eyes
because the road was flat and dry and did not
demand their complete attention. I saw Dr. Aziz's
back and Bortucan's chubby cheek mashed against
his shoulder, her eyes closed, drool sliding from the
corner of her mouth. I saw the sun bouncing off
Dr. Aziz's shoes.

Inside the hospital, people leaned against the
peeling green paint of the corridor walls or held
their heads in their hands as they slumped over on
hard wooden benches. Men and women in white
coats strode down the halls with clipboards in their
hands, ignoring the pleas of "Yaa docture! Yaa
docture!" from the leaners and the slumpers.

"Assalaamu alaykum," Dr. Aziz greeted one of
his colleagues; "Good morning," he greeted the
next; "Ciao, ragazza," a third; and to a fourth,
"Have you finished with that book yet, Mouna?"

"What have you got here?" asked a young man
with a stethoscope hanging around his neck, stopping to rub Bortucan's cheek.

"Another botched infibulation," Dr. Aziz groaned.

"You're a hero, Aziz," said the other doctor, slap-
ping him on the arm. His English was equally as
good. He was just about to move on when he caught
sight of me. "Who is this?" he asked his colleague.

Dr. Aziz appeared unable to answer.

I said plainly: "I'm her sister."

"Masha'Allah," said the man, savouring each
syllable. "A farenji-speaking Harari! I've never
seen such a thing in my life! Where, dear God, did
you find her?"

"Goodbye, Munir," Dr. Aziz said sternly.

I pulled my veil closer, lowered my head and carried on down the corridor, staring at the heels of Dr. Aziz's shoes, which seemed to squeak in protest with each step.

Moments later, I was watching the doctor thread a needle into Bortucan's arm. The needle was attached to a tube that ran from two plastic sacs hanging from a hook on the wall.

"If you *must* circumcise, we try to tell them," he said as he squeezed one of the sacs, "make a cut in the clitoris, but do not remove it. And do not in any circumstance infibulate."

Fluid dripped down from both bags, disappearing into Bortucan's arm. Her eyelids fluttered closed. Dr. Aziz helped a nurse unwrap the bandages, sponge away the blood and clean the wound, and then he pulled out the thorns. I could not watch, although he was swift and efficient and there was no more blood than what I had already seen each morning. He restitched the wound with surgical thread, leaving a hole much bigger than the size of a matchstick at the end.

"At least this way she'll be able to urinate and menstruate properly." He sighed. "You get terrible infections otherwise."

I watched his large hands do their work, thinking how different he was from anyone I'd ever met. So plainspoken. No awkwardness, no metaphors, no proverbs or quotations and the assumption that I understood, though he was using words I'd never heard before. Words in English.

"There is a great deal of resistance," he said. "The mothers *want* to see their daughters suffer. They believe that girls must pay this price to be guaranteed the reward of marriage. They fear that no man will want to marry their daughters otherwise, and they'll remain a burden on their parents for the rest of their lives."

"And is that true? Does that happen?"

"Well, yes," he admitted. "But it's largely the midwives who perpetuate this idea. As soon as they deliver a girl they start pressing her mother, saying, 'Oh, I'm so sorry for this burden of a girl that has been delivered to you. Don't worry, I will return when she is old enough to make sure she remains pure.' This is their livelihood," Dr. Aziz said with a dismissive wave. "They make considerable money this way, and the more radical absuma pays much more than the simple removal of the clitoris, so of course they have a vested interest in continuing the practice."

"But they say you are not a true Muslim if you don't have absuma," I said hesitantly.

"Yes, they say a lot of things, but it is custom, local custom, which they attribute to Islam in order to justify it. There is nothing in the Qur'an that suggests this is necessary. Or even desirable."

Perhaps he was right: I had never heard of anything like absuma happening in Morocco. I had had a flicker of worry that perhaps this business was alluded to in some section of the Qur'an the Great Abdal and I had neglected to explore in serious depth. There were certain parts he was more comfortable skimming over—the whole matter of women's courses, for instance.

The first time I'd had bleeding, I told the Great Abdal. He sent me to the Berber woman in the village who washed our clothes, and she bleached my skirt with lemon juice and left it to dry in the sun. She gave me a cup of green tea and tore a cotton sheet into strips. She said I was to return the used cloths to her and she would boil them in a special pot so they would be ready for the next month.

When I returned to the shrine from the Berber woman's house, the Great Abdal told me that I needed to study the fourth chapter again, Al Nisa', "The Women," but I could not touch the book until the bleeding stopped and I was clean. It was then that I understood the implications.

There was no suggestion of absuma in the holy book as far as I knew, though might it just be a matter of certain words being interpreted differently here? "It's not just the words," I said to Dr. Aziz, "it's how you read them. Sometimes there is more than literal meaning. You can go beneath them to discover batin."

"Batin?"

"Hidden meaning. Inner meaning."

"I'm not familiar with this," he said, looking at me directly.

"Perhaps it is a Sufi philosophy," I said, looking down self-consciously.

"Are you a Sufi?"

"Not in practice. But I have been influenced by the thinking. My teacher, the Great Abdal, was both a great scholar in the orthodox tradition and a Sufi philosopher. He showed me that if you probe beneath the words you can often illuminate truths that are not apparent when you simply read them."

"I admire your scholarship, but I suppose you could say I am more literally minded," said Dr. Aziz. "Forgive me, but I'm a scientist. I look at what's presented to me."

"But no," it occurred to me, "you also look beneath. A patient comes to you with certain symptoms. You can diagnose their origin, what disease might be at the root. How else could you know what the cure should be?"

He nodded slowly and rubbed his chin, before bending down to release the brake on the wheels of Bortucan's bed. He unhooked the bags from the wall and asked if I'd mind holding them while he pushed the bed out of the room.

I walked beside the bed with the bags held high, down the corridor to the children's ward, which trembled with the quiet din of women praying at their children's bedsides. I stared at the doctor's broad back as he hung the bags on a hook and willed him to continue the conversation. I hadn't spoken like this since Hussein and I had lain in the desert and contemplated the true meaning of jihad; since the Great Abdal and I had discussed the mental fasting that works in tandem with the physical.

He was different, this man, this Dr. Aziz. He made me feel different: stirred, compelled, vaguely anxious.

The colour in Bortucan's face was already returning to brown from chalky grey. Dr. Aziz reached for
her forearm to take her pulse and her eyelids fluttered open to reveal a mute wildness. I stroked her
hair and offered a few words of prayer.

"I think she'll be fine," said Dr. Aziz.

"Insha'Allah," I said, to which he surprisingly
did not offer any refrain. I turned to him and
asked: "Are you a Muslim, Dr. Aziz?"

"Yes, of course," he said. "Did you think I was
not?"

"Do you discount the power of religion to heal?"

"I do not discount belief in a general sense.
Particularly the role of optimism."

"You're different from most Muslims I know," I
said.

"Because I look for a cure in science rather than
God?" He leaned down then and whispered in
Bortucan's ear. "She calls me different, Bortucan.
Can you imagine? The white Muslim of Harar is
calling *me* different!"

I had to laugh.

"I know *they* think of me in this way," he said.
"I'm still trying to prove to them that I'm worthy
despite my mixed blood. That I am actually a
Harari, born and raised, despite the fact that my
father was Sudanese. Both my parents, I might
add, are *very* Muslim."

"My father was English," I told him. "Not a
Muslim. But I was brought up as a Muslim in
Morocco."

"So I hear," he said.

"Really? What exactly have you heard?"

"Mmm, let me see. I've heard that you are English, Italian, French. I've heard that you are a Catholic missionary sent here to infiltrate and convert, even that you are a spy sent by Haile Selassie to report back to him on the very insular ways of the Harari. Of course, it's just gossip," he tried to reassure me. "You should hear what they call me. Black savage, African, slave, barbarian, pagan. I have even heard it said that I was sent to medical school as a *specimen*, not a student, but that I somehow managed to slip away from the table just as they were lowering the blade to dissect."

When Dr. Aziz came to check on Bortucan later that afternoon, he pointed at the red bag suspended over her head. Blood was scarce because people would not donate, he told me; they feared losing some essence of their souls. The doctors and nurses routinely donated, and apparently it was common practice in the West. "The way farenjis give alms, I suppose," he said, before asking me if I might.

But I didn't know if my blood would work. Mixed, he'd called his own. What did that make mine?

He laughed. "We all have the same blood types, Lilly. Even the Sudanese, even farenjis."

"Forgive me," I said, "but I'm not a scientist."

"I apologize." He hung his head. "There are four blood types. Yours might not be compatible with Bortucan's, but it will be right for some other patient. It could save another life."

Put that way, I could hardly not agree to do it. It felt like a challenge. I offered my arm as alms.

"Perhaps you should not tell the little girl's mother, though," he suggested, swabbing my forearm. "She might think I'm trying to steal your soul."

But how do I know you're not? I wondered as he drew blood. And if you are, where are you taking it? And will part of my soul be given to someone else in this exchange?

"Now," he said, putting a plaster on my arm, "I'll get the orderly to bring you both some food, but this," he said, pulling a cardboard package from his pocket and unwrapping it to reveal a piece of honeycomb, "just rub some on her lips if she refuses to eat."

I lay down next to Bortucan, who was sleeping soundly now, her nose whistling, a mucus bubble inflating and deflating at the corner of her mouth. "Little girl," I whispered, and closed my eyes.

A dream in English. The first dream in English in years. In Bilal al Habash's shrine, where the frightening form of Sheikh Jami dominated, I stood pegged to a wall while the sheikh read off a list of my sins from a giant scroll. "Friend to unbelievers! Doubter of holy words! Perpetrator of lewdness! Audience of Satan!"

I awoke as a woman threw the first stone. *I must repent, I must repent*, my heart pounded in panic. "Verily, Allah doth forgive those who repent," I said aloud, picking at a hair stuck to my lip. My lips were sticky. Honey sweet.

# The Education of Girls.

—

Nouria had started to listen, even allow herself the odd smile. As Fathi and Anwar progressed further through the holy book, their fluency evident in greater speed and precision, their mother unconsciously slowed down. Her strokes, *swoosh swoosh* against the side of the metal tub, became an accompaniment of brush and brown water.

As she softened, I found myself warming to her. It was hard not to: she was not inherently dour, she just had a very difficult life raising four children on her own. When she asked me if I would begin teaching the girls as well, though, I hesitated. Bortucan had recovered fairly quickly after her stay in hospital, though she had still to begin speaking. But then, elements of this education are wordless. Bortucan could hear the rhythm; it was obvious from the way she sometimes swayed from side to side when the boys and I recited. So lessons with the girls began, Bortucan in my lap, the two of us swaying together, Rahile repeating each line after me, swelling with the pride of someone who, though new to water, instinctively floats.

There was something remarkable about Rahile. She had a self-confidence there was no earthly reason for her to possess. She exerted a subtle influence on the family that in any other environment might have been construed as manipulation. She'd had her absuma exactly when she wanted it, and I'd seen her weasel a new dress out of Gishta with flattery and a reasoned argument—she had aspirations, this girl, even at five years old.

It was Rahile who took my hand one Thursday night and insisted I come with them to the shrine.

"But I can't, Rahile," I objected. She grabbed my wrist with both hands, dug her heels into the ground and tugged. "The sheikh doesn't like me very much," I said, not knowing how else to explain it to her.

"Rahu! Leave Lilly alone," Nouria chastised.

But Rahile wouldn't take no for an answer. "If you love God, you will come," she said.

People moved through the streets: small groups merging, individuals being swallowed up by the dark cloud that rolled through the market and down the steep road on the other side where drumbeats, thumping with the rhythm of a human heart, became audible, and the pace quickened, and one mass of humanity squeezed itself through the green arch into the compound surrounding the shrine.

I was well covered for this outing, but still, people commented. I heard the whispers: "The farenji, the farenji."

"How can they see me when it's so dark?" I asked Nouria.

"It's your skin," she said. "White shines."

I wondered if I should turn around, for surely the sheikh would notice me, but fortunately he had not yet made his entrance. Hundreds of people were already crammed into the courtyard and still more were streaming in. And there was Hussein, standing where the sheikh would soon stand, his apprentice, his proxy, keeping his place warm. I resisted the urge to wave and hung my head instead. I left Nouria and wound my way to the far back of the crowd, past the murmurs about the farenji in their midst.

The drummers announced the sheikh's impending arrival with a dramatic crescendo, followed by abrupt silence as they muffled the resonating skins with their chests. With the sheikh's entrance I sank, my spine compacting, my guts crushed. Now nobody commented on my presence; they had much more important business to attend to. They clapped and offered the refrain after the sheikh bellowed the chorus, and they passed qat my way. I accepted politely, plucking a few leaves and grinding them between my teeth, sticking the masticated green into my cheek. I was doing my best, but it was an acquired taste. Even the best qat leaves were bitter and had to be chewed for hours.

I scanned the crowd for Dr. Aziz, though knowing how unlikely it was that I might find him there. I suspected he who preferred intellectual to spiritual reasoning wasn't much one for saints and their shrines.

I'd seen him twice since Bortucan had left hospital. The first time, all he needed was one quick look beneath her bandages to declare her healing well. The second time, I held a candle for him in the dark room while he removed her stitches. Nouria hovered in the doorway, wringing her hands. She didn't have the courage to challenge the doctor, but she'd confided her disappointment to me. "The hole is too big," she'd complained. "She has a hole like a sharmuta."

"Dr. Aziz said it would be better, less chance of infection—"

"Lilly!" Nouria had said gruffly. "Who knows best? A mother, that is who."

In his presence, though, she said nothing.

"I want you to continue to wash this whole area with water and soap every day and then apply this cream," the doctor said. "It's not enough just to pray. And I want you only to use this cream, okay? No more butter, no more of that herbalist's oil, just this, and not too much."

He stood up, but he was too tall for the room. He crouched through the doorway and into the courtyard. He must have known he'd just insulted us both, dismissing the things in which we believed, particularly prayer, but I couldn't help admiring his certainty, how it even seemed manifest in the fullness of his height as he stood there in the sun, his white shirt so bright against the mud of our surroundings, against the velvet darkness of his face.

I caught myself staring and blushed. It felt like a swarm of bees had just been let loose in my stomach. Perhaps he could hear them buzzing, because he looked at me, and for no reason at all, he smiled. For all his self-assurance it was such a humble smile, with a hint of sadness around the edges: it was a smile to cup in one's hands. He was looking at me, looking for something, though I couldn't imagine what it was he was after.

"I have to thank you," he finally said, breaking this strange spell that had had us staring at each other.

"Thank me? For what?" I asked.

"I've been thinking about something you said at the hospital. About how we as doctors can diagnose an underlying illness. You were right, it's not unlike this search for batin that you explained. But you know, we don't really have that luxury. Not here. We don't have the resources to test all that we might, or to analyze the results. You saw how it was—we barely have a blood supply—so all we end up doing is treating the symptoms, never the cause. We forget we can do anything more."

"That's a shame," I said.

"That might be, but it's the reality. Still, I am grateful to be reminded of the possibility of something deeper, even if we are too poor to do anything about it."

His presence lingered far longer than his visit had lasted, like the smell of incense in a closed room, the residue crystallizing on the ceiling. It lingered in me as I wondered about the distance between all his conviction and his faintly troubled smile. I fed every piece of injera I dipped into the stew that night into Bortucan's willing mouth, thinking about his provocative statements. I couldn't bring myself to eat a single bite.

"She is much better," Nouria observed as Bortucan reached for the piece of injera in my hand. "But that farenji medicine has no power. She is better because God wills it, not because the doctor wills it." The previous morning the faith healer had come and written a verse for Bortucan on a slate. He'd washed the slate and collected the chalky water in a cup, which Nouria had put to Bortucan's lips throughout the day. By evening, her appetite had returned.

—

I scanned the hundreds of faces that night at the shrine, but none of them were his. I could imagine him saying of what we did there: it is culture, local culture, which people attribute to Islam. Orthodox imams were known to say such things, dismissing our traditions as rooted in superstition, but if you look deeply for the inner meanings in the book you will find God's friends, the saints, hidden there.

Whenever I tried to meditate beyond the page these days, though, an image of Dr. Aziz came to mind. Of his brown eyes made clear in sunlight. Of the uncertain corner of his mouth. Then the bees would awaken, rush into my throat and dance on the tip of my tongue, depositing pollen between my teeth, making it difficult to recite anything at all. Nothing in my life up to that point—not grief, not illness, not dislocation—had ever interrupted my religious practice. But then no one had ever challenged it.

## Affliction.

—

I now taught Fathi and Anwar just after breakfast and Rahile and Bortucan just before lunch. Between these two sets of lessons I tended the stew over the slow fire and helped Nouria with some of the larger pieces of clothing, twisting one end while she held the other, squeezing out all the water we could before heaving it over the washing line to drip, drip and eventually dry.

Except during the rainy season. For two months it was cold and the clothes would not dry, but the qat was so soft and plentiful and cheap that people complained less than they might have and simply chewed a great deal more. For two months we did not see the sun, and qat lifted the malaise caused by the thick, dull, grey blanket of low cloud that did not move and shed little rain despite the name of the season.

But the euphoria we should have felt the morning the sun reappeared was stolen. Nouria awoke with a rash of red blisters running across her chest and down her arms.

"An allergy?" I suggested. "Maybe spiders?"

She shook her head with conviction. "Somebody," she said, wagging a finger, "has cursed me with the evil eye."

Throughout the day, the rash crept up her neck, itching, biting at her jaw line. She anointed herself with a poultice of sour milk and ash from the fireplace while I introduced Rahile and Bortucan to the next chapter of the Qur'an.

After five days of itching and many variations of poultices, Nouria consulted a diviner, a toothless woman with several white hairs growing out of her chin. They sat together in the courtyard, the diviner drinking tea and consulting the entrails of a chicken laid out on the ground before her.

"*That* is your problem," she eventually hissed into Nouria's ear. She was pointing across the courtyard at me.

I glared at the woman. I'd worked hard for my place here: I taught Nouria's children, helped her with the housework, the cooking, the shopping, went to the shrine on Thursdays and the mosque on Fridays, and sat for berchas with her on Saturdays. How dare this woman try to unsettle this hard-won balance.

The old woman cracked three eggs and rubbed the whites over Nouria's rash. For this privilege, Nouria had to give her the chicken whose entrails pointed in my direction, payment she certainly could not afford.

The next day, one of Nouria's neighbours brought her ragged-looking daughter and son into the courtyard. "Will you teach them Qur'an?" she pleaded.

I'd made such progress with Nouria's children that I didn't really want to have to start all over again. "Maybe when I get through with Rahile and Bortucan," I tried to say politely, though that would be years, and the woman knew it.

As soon as the woman shuffled dejectedly out of the courtyard, Nouria threw herself on the ground and grabbed the tops of my feet.

"What is it? What's wrong?" I asked.

"Please, Lilly. I beg you. You *must* teach her children."

"But why is it so urgent?"

"The women are jealous," Nouria cried. "They will curse me again."

Suddenly it made sense. I was teaching her children and not theirs. I was the cause of Nouria's rash. Nouria would have to share the good fortune, correct the imbalance, regain parity with her sisters. I would have to teach their children.

And so it was that one by one, the poorer families in the neighbourhood began bringing their sons and daughters to Nouria's compound in the mornings to join in what seemed to be emerging as a local school. I sat the children in three circles on the ground based on the knowledge they brought with them. The two new children, who had had some schooling and could read, joined Nouria's boys. That group of four had the tools to progress with the book shared between them, and could, to some extent, lead the several others who, though they could not read, had the first few chapters memorized. Rahile joined that second group even though they were much further ahead, but Bortucan would remain with the youngest, the easiest group in some ways, because they brought to it nothing but their open hearts and mouths.

Eventually, I would begin drawing the letters that give shape to the words for the younger ones, etch them into dirt if we had no other option. I would establish a routine that would allow the three groups to make progress simultaneously. It is how we'd learned when I was child at the madrasa in Tamegroute: not just three groups, but ten, verses bouncing off walls and greeting us from every side.

Within a couple of weeks, my class had settled at eleven students, seven of them girls. In addition to Nouria's four, there were five other poor and dusty Oromo children, and two Hararis, scrubbed and much better dressed than their classmates. In addition to these regulars, there was the occasional, irregular appearance of two Somali boys from the countryside who turned up whenever their mother had something to sell in the market.

It was good for Nouria; the parents agreed to pay a small fee—the Hararis in cash, the Oromo in kind—and they did so not a moment too soon. One morning we'd lost an entire washing line of clothes to a hungry goat, causing Nouria to pull a chunk of her hair out and rub dirt into her eyes.

"If you take me for the lover of Satan then so be it! Kill me now!" she wailed.

I came up with a solution. Between the cash and the money Nouria made by selling the qat brought by the Oromo parents, we were able to replace the clothes within a month, not only placating four irate co-wives but leaving us with enough material to have new dresses made for ourselves.

The first time I tried on my new dress, I ran my hands over the silky sheen, thinking it the neatest I'd looked since once, a long time ago, when Muhammed Bruce had taken me to Marrakech. That had happened twice. Eight hours on a bus stinking of cooking oil and petrol and cigarette smoke. Did he really make this journey once a month just to visit me? Perhaps I should dissuade him in future, I remember thinking. He seemed very happy in Marrakech, after all. He owned a flat in an old French building on a wide boulevard outside the medina, with a lift man and big marble ashtrays in all the hallways. A young Arab boy cooked all his food and washed his feet with warm water and slept like a cat at the foot of his bed. The flat was full of birdcages, and in the evenings, Muhammed Bruce let me close the balcony shutters and open all their cages so that they could flutter about the rooms. He didn't seem to mind them dropping white splorges onto the sofas, but it was the Arab boy who had to follow the birds from room to room cleaning up after them. I could tell *he* was looking forward to the end of my visit.

Muhammed Bruce took me to restaurants where we ate crepes, and we went shopping, not in the suq but in a glass-fronted shop with a French name, where he bought me a pinafore and a pair of shoes, which were very nice but didn't alleviate my feeling of homesickness.

I was about twelve the next time. On that occasion, too, we went to a French restaurant and he bought me a new dress. The old Arab boy had been replaced by a new one, and Muhammed Bruce took us both for a ride on a Ferris wheel and then we had ice cream, but although I was older than the last time, I still missed the shrine the whole time.

He could tell I wasn't happy. "I just wanted to make sure you were aware there were alternatives," he said. "To help you make an informed decision."

I didn't ask what decision I was supposed to be informed about.

—

I was enjoying the feel of the blue silk against my thighs while I moved around the courtyard arranging my students when the fence parted. Dr. Aziz cleared his throat and I lost all memory of who should be sitting where and what the little girl with the plaits was called, and "You, you," I said, "sit over there beside Rahile," trying to regain composure, when he asked: "Do you have room for one more student?"

He stood with his large palms on the shoulders of a black girl in front of him. His father's cousin's daughter, he said.

"Will you teach her?" he asked, rephrasing the question when I failed to answer.

"But how did you hear about our lessons?" I stammered.

"I live just over there." He pointed. "You know the house beside Sheikh Khalef's shrine? That is where I live with my mother."

My heart plunged into my stomach, bobbed in that morning's tea. I was dizzy with the sudden self-consciousness that he might have seen me en route to the market or the mosque, witnessed the shouts of "Farenji!" as I traipsed along the broken streets in flip-flops, with my dirty hair peeking out from under my veil, quite possibly muttering some new vocabulary to myself.

"Yes, of course I'll teach her," I said, recovering. "Has she had any schooling at all?"

"Just the verses her father has taught her. He doesn't read so he can only share with her what he remembers."

"We're only doing Qur'an," I thought I should clarify, "nothing more. Not any math or science like some of the madrasas."

"Of course," he said, matter-of-factly. "It is just the beginning."

It was a beginning, but not just. Perhaps one day there would be an occasion for me to show him the science in the Qur'an. And the math in its numbers. I had heard it said that the wall surrounding the city was 6,666 arms' lengths long—the exact number of verses of the Qur'an. There was as much spirit in the architecture of this place as there was science. Perhaps that is true of anywhere if you look deep enough.

At lunch that day, when I was quite sure Dr. Aziz was far away at the hospital beyond the city wall, I went to the market to fetch a cone of salt. I passed a set of metal doors I had passed nearly every day, this time counting the footsteps between his compound and mine. One hundred and two. So close. He must fall asleep to the same sounds, I realized. Metal doors being scraped shut, babies crying and hyenas whooping as they roam the neighbourhood scavenging for scraps. And if he were to listen closer: Bortucan blubbing, Nouria comforting her, Fathi's mouth falling open, catching flies, and me lying awake with a pounding heart wondering if that was him I could hear breathing in the distance.

In the Blue Glow.

—

Dr. Aziz's father's cousin's daughter proved to be an extremely bright girl. Not only did she memorize without apparent effort, she asked surprisingly perceptive questions. Why does this chapter end here? she asked. Why does the voice in this chapter feel so far away? I could not afford to risk alienating the rest of the class by veering off into exegesis, so I tried to steer her back to the text, to get her to open herself to it, to trust in it. You will come to understand in time, I told her, if you just focus on repetition and memorization.

I did not have answers for all her questions. I was not a Sufi philosopher like the Great Abdal or Sheikh Jami: I did not possess the wisdom and gifts that they both did as descendants of saints. I was nothing more than a dedicated student who, through sheer necessity, had been forced to become a teacher. But I relished this new role. And I was enchanted by this new student with her keen curiosity and her vague resemblance to her father's cousin's son.

"If you want me to try and answer some of your questions, you'll have to ask your father's permission to stay after class tomorrow," I told Zemzem. "But during class try and stop your mind from interrupting the rhythm. Do not think, experience."

Rahile was not about to let me offer a private lesson to the new girl. She began interrupting at the end of every verse with questions that were far less relevant than Zemzem's.

"I have questions too," she declared when Zemzem remained behind after class the following day.

"You'll have to take turns, then," I said. "So why don't we begin with the question about revelation that Zemzem brought up yesterday."

"Because I don't want to begin there," Rahile said.

"Who is the teacher, Rahile?"

"You are the teacher."

"That's right. And the teacher says where we begin."

I spoke about revelation, how the verses were revealed to the Prophet Muhammed, peace be upon him, through the angel Gabriel over a period of twenty-three years. This is why some of the verses feel different from others.

"Why twenty-three years?" Rahile asked.

"Because God had a lot to impart," I said, growing impatient with her.

Just then, a man pulled back the fence and entered the courtyard, and Zemzem leapt to her feet.

"Zemzem!" he said gruffly. "What do you think you are doing?"

Her father, I assumed. I introduced myself, apologized for delaying her.

"You are the teacher?" He blinked repeatedly as he stood before me, his legs apart, his hands on his hips.

"I am. And your daughter is my best student," I said truthfully, hoping to flatter.

Rahile harrumphed and kicked the ground.

"She has to work, she knows she has to work!" the man exploded. "I agreed with Aziz she can come for this class in the mornings, but now she is late. Who is going to clean the house? Who is going to go to market and do the cooking? Should we live in dirt and starve?"

Bortucan, as she always did whenever she heard a man yelling, burst into tears. I pulled her into my thigh. "I'm sorry," I said to Zemzem's father. "She had some questions which were a bit too advanced for the rest of the class, so I offered to answer them after the other children left."

"Oh, paah, paah, don't tell me this! It is a curse to have a girl who is advanced." He yanked her by the arm, wrenched back the fence and pushed Zemzem ahead of him into the street.

"What about my turn?" Rahile bleated, tugging at my sleeve.

"School's finished for today, Rahile."

"It's not fair! You gave a turn to the black one but the red one is better," she said, pointing at herself.

Poor Dr. Aziz, I thought. He will never prove to them that he is worthy. Even a child sees only darkness. A poor child who is relatively dark herself.

—

I stepped out of the compound and slipped out of my flip-flops. I had bought a pair of shoes in the market, but I was trying to keep this from Nouria lest she think I was developing pretensions. I pulled them from my rucksack and put them on. The shoes felt clumsy, but I ventured forth determined, counting to one hundred and two.

I immediately regretted being so bold. I peeked into his mother's compound, found him out of uniform, wearing a loose white galabaya, shaving his chin with a straight razor, eyes wide and boyish as he peered at his reflection in a broken mirror.

"Good morning," he said with surprise, dropping his razor into the bowl at his feet.

"I'm sorry to bother you," I said, gripping the edge of the metal door.

"No, no," he said. "It's a nice surprise. Come in. My mother will give you tea."

"No, thank you," I said. "It's just that Zemzem didn't come to class yesterday. It's my fault—the day before I kept her late and then her father was angry. I wondered if you could speak to him. I won't keep her late again, but she's very bright and it would be such a shame if she didn't continue."

"I see." He nodded. "She is the only child, so it is difficult for him to spare her for school."

"I appreciate that, but it's essential to learn Qur'an."

"Essential," he repeated. "Making sure you have enough food to feed your family is essential."

It was no use trying to explain it to him. "I'm sorry for interrupting you. Insha'Allah, Zemzem will return to class," I said, stepping back into the lane.

"Wait," he said, and came up to the doorway. "I will speak to him. It's no problem. I was the one who insisted it was important she have some schooling in the first place."

He of the near-perfect English carried on, stumbling a bit, backtracking—something about how difficult it can be to see the importance of other things when one lives hand to mouth—then asked if I might like to come to his uncle's house that Saturday for a bercha. Berchas were how all Hararis and Oromo in the city took their leisure, from the time they were adolescents until the time they were toothless and mashing their qat leaves with a pestle. On the Saturday afternoons that neighbourhood women did not gather in Nouria's compound, she went elsewhere, often taking me with her, to do the same in the whitewashed clay houses of wealthier women with their red floors and raised red clay platforms and shining Meccan souvenirs.

"I don't know," I said. I was taken aback: men and women did not sit for berchas together.

"I'll draw you a map." Dr. Aziz bent down and grabbed a stick.

I smiled while he etched the shape of the wall into the ground, rubbing out sections with his palm, correcting himself, striving to convey its irregular shape accurately. He suggested the road adjacent to but outside the circumference of the wall and then he erased all evidence of the map from the ground.

"I bought some shoes," I said, still looking down.

"I noticed," he laughed.

—

On Saturday the women from the neighbourhood arrived with qat and hookahs and set down their blankets on the ground in front of Nouria's house. I was squatting in the kitchen stirring coffee leaves into hot salted milk. Coffee beans were too expensive and mainly reserved for export, but nothing was wasted, not the husks nor the leaves. I stared into the eddy of hot milk, thinking it impossible, a trip to the market, perhaps, but I couldn't justify an absence from the compound of any longer than half an hour.

A young woman I had never seen before stepped through the parting in the fence. She wore footless striped leggings, a modern variation of the trousers her mother's generation wore, under a short dress of purple silk. A veil of loose lavender chiffon floated about her delicate face. She was flower fresh and about my age.

"Sadia!" the women greeted her. "How is your mother? My, how you have grown. So beautiful like your mother. Have you come for bercha? Lilly, is qutti qahwah ready?"

"Thank you, Aunties," said Sadia, bowing politely, "but today I'm taking Lilly for bercha."

"Lilly?" Nouria asked curiously.

I stood stunned in the doorway of the grim kitchen holding a wooden spoon.

"Every girl needs girlfriends, no?" Sadia said brightly to the women. "Lilly and I were chatting at the market and I told her this: why do you have no girlfriends? Even a farenji must have girl-friends. So I made a promise and here I am!"

"Yes, yes, of course," they all agreed. "Go!" they shouted at me. Murmurs of approval all round. *Such a good girl. And from such a good family.* They were clearly surprised I was able to make such respectable friends.

Nouria nodded. "Go!"

I smiled at Nouria. She was wearing my shoes.

Sadia and I slipped out the gate at the bottom of the hill and walked in silence, travelling left for a quarter of a mile along the dusty road that runs adjacent to the city wall. Only Oromo and Somalis travel this road: men leading animals by thick rope, women bent double under the weight of firewood, children carrying water from the river—people, in other words, for whom there is no day of rest.

We slipped back into the city through the next of the five gates in the city wall. This was the route Aziz had scratched into the dirt. The key, appar-ently, to moving around the city undetected. Aziz's uncle's house was right there, immediately to the left of the gate.

We entered the compound and Sadia waved at an old man sitting cross-legged inside the main room with the Qur'an in his hands. "Good afternoon, Uncle."

"And good afternoon to you," he mumbled toothlessly. There followed a series of inquiries about his health, each of which he answered, "Thanks to God."

I nodded politely and followed Sadia up a wooden staircase to a narrow balcony. It was a very old Harari house, one with an upper floor traditionally used for storing firewood and tobacco leaves. From the balcony there was a stunning view of the farmlands in one direction, the dense matrix of the city in the other.

We took off our shoes and entered the last room, a place of discretion, dark and small, without windows. I felt burlap beneath my feet and could barely make out faces, but I could see the forms of several people, both young men and women, reclining against pillows lining the walls. In the middle of the room was an enormous pile of qat amassed on a scarf, and beside it, a tray with two thermoses of tea, a jug of cold water, plastic cups with daisies printed on them and the ubiquitous clay pot for burning incense.

Dr. Aziz greeted me from the floor, patting the pillow beside him, but he did not introduce me. I sat beside him as he recited a du'a, distributing the qat as he did this, passing a bundle of fresh twigs to each of us in the room and keeping a tenth aside—the Prophet's share, it was called.

"These are the best leaves, the sweetest," he said, passing me a few pale stalks.

Once the qat had been passed round, he threw incense onto the coals in the clay burner and we said our thanks to God. Now chewing could officially begin.

The men were all wearing sarongs, leisure wear, and sat with their left arms balanced on their left knees while they stripped the twigs quickly from top to bottom between their thumbs and forefingers. Their cheeks grew as they stuffed more and more leaves into the sides of their mouths. They chatted away in a mixture of Harari and English. I thought this must be for my benefit, even though nobody but Dr. Aziz addressed me directly. I didn't want to change the language of this or any other room. *It's okay*, I wanted to tell them, *I even dream in Harari now. And Harari dreams are not like Arabic or English dreams: there are always a great many more people involved.*

I listened to the men talk about waterborne diseases and some recent decision made by the council of elders concerning alcohol. They talked about pollution in the river from a factory in the nearby town of Babile, about the price of electronics on the black market, about a musical group that was using an electronic keyboard. Their talk was alien to me. If they had relayed legends of the saints or debated the best method to teach Qur'an I would have had much to say. If they had discussed how best to sort grains, how to diagnose affliction with the evil eye or how to keep flies at bay I could have contributed.

Even the girls offered occasional comments, and while mostly spoken quietly to the men they sat beside, they clearly had their own opinions about whether the elders should be allowed to ban the electronic keyboard, about alleged banditry in the foothills of some nearby mountain, about water, about a corrupt imam, about the inflated prices of imported goods.

How strange it all seemed. Men and women in the same room, people speaking English. And then, when the conversation subsided, Dr. Aziz making great ceremony out of getting up and unveiling a sacred object in the corner of the room. *A television.* I hadn't known there were neighbourhoods with electricity.

A small white dot in the centre of the screen ballooned into a picture, not of a football match, as I expected, but of the emperor greeting the officers of the Imperial Guard. He was a tiny man packaged in a neat suit with a regal robe hanging from his shoulders. His head, with its trim salt-and-pepper beard, appeared to sit apart; a distinguished face, like that of a statue, perched atop the neatly packaged body of a boy.

The palace loomed behind him, though the small black-and-white picture did not do it justice. Standing before those gates, Muhammed Bruce's letter in hand, I'd felt utterly daunted by the begging mass of humanity there, the women wailing as they waved notes at the stern row of guards. Ours was but one of a thousand letters, I'd realized, crushing the paper in my hand.

"You go," Hussein had said, nudging me forward. He insisted I had a much better chance of attracting the guards' attention since the emperor had a notorious love of foreigners, especially the English. "And besides, my English is terrible," he said.

"But look at me!" I'd said, fed up with his excuses. "I might look like a foreigner, but I'm filthy." I'd been wearing the same dress for months. We'd done our best at a public bath, but the unmistakable smell of camel had worked its way deep into our skin.

In Ethiopia, television seemed to be devoted nearly exclusively to broadcasting the events of the emperor's day. We watched a convoy of cars push through crowds of people. A royal hand passed bills out of the window of a Rolls-Royce and people kissed the bonnet in gratitude. We watched the emperor emerge from the car and tour a school.

"That's where we studied medicine," Dr. Aziz told me, nodding at the screen. "Haile Selassie I University. Me and Munir and Tawfiq were in the same class," he said, indicating two of the other men in the room. "And Tajuddin and Amir"—he pointed at the others—"were one and two years ahead of us."

"We still are," Amir ribbed.

"Not forever, my friend!" Munir answered back.

"We're hoping to continue eventually, Munir and I," Dr. Aziz said. "But to continue we must go to Cairo. And to get to Cairo we must study and pass the university's entrance exams. The difficulty is, in order to study, we need textbooks from abroad, and more times than not they are lost in the post."

"People steal them," Munir said.

I recognized him then—the doctor who had stopped us in the hall of the hospital that day.

"They don't steal them," Dr. Aziz said. "Why would they steal books in English?"

"I don't know," Munir said with a shrug. "Perhaps they make good pillows, or excellent flames."

"Will the exams be in English?" I asked.

"Yes, it's all in English—the textbooks, the medicines, the curriculum—all of it comes from the West. Even some of our teachers at medical school were farenjis. From the London School of Hygiene and Tropical Medicine. And from Johns Hopkins University in America. That's partly why people resist the hospitals, particularly the older people. They prefer their traditional practices, the things they know. They feel insulted by the suggestion of alternatives, especially Western ones."

"But these things can work," I said, "the amulets and the herbs."

"Because they want to believe they work."

"I've seen them work."

"Have you heard of spontaneous remission? The mind is a very powerful thing." He pointed at the television. "The drama is about to begin."

The program, like the news of the emperor's day, was broadcast in Amharic—the national language, the language of education and state and, because it was state owned, television and radio—a language of which I knew only half a dozen words.

Dr. Aziz translated in whispers for my benefit.

We watched a line of people dancing in white, their shoulders moving swiftly up and down, their eyes thickly kohl-lined and wide, a hissing sound coming from between their clenched teeth.

"Amharas," Dr. Aziz said.

"As if they are the only ones who dance," Munir mumbled.

The music was abrasive, and the room had grown quiet. Qat leads one through animation into mirqana, a mood of quiet reflection. All I was conscious of then was Dr. Aziz. I could hear him inhale and exhale as he sat cross-legged beside me in the blue glow of an otherwise entirely dark room. It *was* his breathing I heard at night; now I knew this for certain.

Introducing Custard.

—

Zemzem not only returned to class but brought with her a piece of paper folded into a small square. Inside, I found a silver necklace and a note from Dr. Aziz.

It seems it is Zemzem's father's pride that is the real issue. He does not wish to be seen taking charity—especially charity from a farenji—but he does want the girl to learn. It is my fault, I hope you can forgive me. I neglected to tell him you were a farenji, because it did not seem relevant. So when he came to find Zemzem that day he was shocked to find you. He offers you this necklace that belonged to his late wife as payment for her lessons.

He wishes you peace, as do I.

Later, I waved the necklace before Nouria's eyes.

"Perhaps we could have meat for lunch after the mosque on Friday," she said, glowing.

"With rice," I added.

"And fried onions."

Nouria's affection toward me increased exponentially. She sold the silver necklace to Abai Taoduda, the midwife, and with that money safely stored between her breasts we walked to the market on Thursday morning, arm in arm, passing the beggars pleading "baksheesh" and "have mercy," the goats bleating like bruised infants, the men bartering with the qat sellers—"If your skin is as tough as this qat, God has no mercy for your husband"—the merchants elbowing and outbidding each other—"Lady, lady, look here, this is real Indian silk," "This mango is much much sweeter" —and the shouts of "Farenji! Farenji!" at which Nouria hissed in my defence.

We bought not only beef, rice and onions but cucumbers, tomatoes, chilies, eggs, sugar and all the spices we would need to make berbere. We shared our extravagant lunch with Gishta and several women from the neighbourhood. Rahile poured water over the hands of each woman in turn before we said our bismillahs and tucked in.

"So delicious, Nouria."

"Yes, but how could you afford this meat?"

"And not goat, but cow!"

"Is it a special occasion?"

"You can thank Lilly," said Nouria.

"Ah, so the farenji has more money after all," said the neighbourhood cynic.

"She earned it," Nouria clarified.

I had even improvised a pudding my mother used to make when I was a child. Here we never ate pudding, apart from dates and sweet potatoes, which in season were so abundant that merchants had to give them away.

I offered the women spoons borrowed from Gishta and placed the bowl in the middle of the circle. "Eat!" I encouraged, as they stared at the bowl.

"What is it?" one woman whispered.

"Farenji food," her neighbour replied.

"It's good!" I exclaimed. "It's called custard."

"Cus-tard," Gishta said, trying the word out. "Okay." She inhaled before tentatively prodding the skin with her spoon.

"Here," I said, taking the spoon from her hand and scooping up a generous amount.

She opened her mouth and we all looked on with expectation. She swallowed. "I don't know," she said, shaking her head.

One of the women leaned forward. "What does it taste like?"

Gishta grimaced. "You try it," she said.

The woman took a small spoonful, looked heavenward and pulled a piece of skin from her mouth, holding it between her fingers for inspection. "What is this?" she said, sticking out her tongue.

"The skin. Like the skin you get on milk."

"This is some kind of farenji milk?"

"It's made with milk, eggs and sugar."

"What a ridiculous thing to do to eggs," she muttered to her friends.

Later that afternoon, after Bortucan and I had licked the bowl clean, I helped Nouria and Gishta lay out chili peppers to dry in the sun, transforming the entire courtyard into a bright red carpet. It would be three days before the peppers were properly baked. "Any moisture, you get rot and your berbere is finished in two weeks," Gishta explained, smacking her palms together.

Nouria would sell batches of this fiery cocktail in the Amhara market beyond the city wall. We did not eat it ourselves, but Amharas could not taste anything without it. It was a compromise to sell to them, but given Nouria's poverty, one that she was accustomed to making. We'd spent money in order to make more money.

While we waited for the peppers to dry, we prepared the rest of the spices, bouncing cardamom, fenugreek and coriander seeds with a hiss and pop, the buds of cloves and black pepper, the allspice berries, the cinnamon bark, the nutmeg and the shaved ginger root in sequence over the fire. It was hot, repetitive and tedious work, and while Nouria and Gishta sang to relieve the boredom, I thought about Dr. Aziz. "Your friend Aziz," he'd signed the note Zemzem had carried. My friend Aziz, I thought, pressing my pocket to check if his words were still there.

"Lilly!" Nouria snapped.

"Mmm?" I turned to her.

"I thought you wanted to help!"

"I do."

"Well, grind then, you lazy girl," Gishta shouted, pushing the mortar and pestle toward me. "The spices are not going to disintegrate on their own!"

Big Fashion.

—

Gishta's acceptance of me was gradual: hard-won but mighty. Though she was Sheikh Jami's favourite wife, as an Oromo she had once been on the outside herself. And it was for that very reason that her resistance to me had been far greater than that of many of the other women. When you've fought long and hard for it, belonging can come to mean despising those who don't.

Gishta began life as a servant in a Harari household like most Oromo girls in the vicinity of the city. Her employer was unusually kindly disposed to her. As a lonely widow whose only son had made the pilgrimage to Mecca some years before, where he'd married a Saudi woman and set up shop, the woman loved her little Oromo servant like a daughter. She gave her gifts of boxed dates and gold thread sent from Mecca by the son she resented. And she sent Gishta to school for half a day until she was sixteen. She even gave her a Harari name—Gishta, meaning custard apple.

Gishta grew up with dreams of belonging in the city, but unlike most Oromo, she was given access, not only through education but also by virtue of being left a small inheritance by her employer. Gishta adopted the language, the manner, the dress and the customs of the Harari and took up the age-old Harari profession of selling qat in the market.

Once you step inside, history has to be rewritten to include you. A fiction develops, a story that weaves you into the social fabric, giving you roots and a local identity. You are assimilated, and in erasing your differences and making you one of their own, the community can maintain belief in its wholeness and purity. After two or three generations, nobody remembers the story is fiction. It has become fact. And this is how history is made.

In keeping me at a distance, Gishta had continued to refuse to believe Bortucan's progress. "It's just not possible!" she would say to Nouria quite deliberately when I was within earshot. Bortucan, who could still barely mumble the word for mother, was now able to recite the Fatihah, the first chapter of the Qur'an. These were actually Bortucan's first words, as if she had the confidence to speak God's words but not her own.

"It's Lilly," said Nouria. "I keep telling you, she just knows, somehow, how to teach her. And the other children as well."

"Tell me," Gishta would say, "how is it that a farenji can know Qur'an this well?"

Every time she asked, I told her the same story of being raised at the Moroccan shrine. "It was actually one of your husband's distant relatives who taught me," I said. "The Great Abdal. He was Hussein's teacher as well."

"Yes, yes, you and your famous story," she would say dismissively. But then one day, the day after the second hidden bercha, she really listened. It seemed Gishta only began to believe me once I started keeping secrets.

—

I had spent every day of the week after the first bercha with Aziz hoping that I might be invited to join him and his friends again. I fought off the disappointment when Saturday arrived without a sign. After lunch, the neighbourhood women were gathering to carve meat in the compound next to ours. All the families had contributed toward the purchase of a cow that had been ritually slaughtered that morning. Large pieces now sat on burlap sacks in Ikhista Aini's courtyard. Nouria was demonstrating proper technique to me, gripping a large knife between her feet. She rolled up her sleeves and moved a large piece of meat up and down against the blade.

I was just getting ready to help her when Sadia arrived, greeting the women with questions about their health, their well-being, their happiness.

"Stay," the women insisted, "at least until we have carved up these ribs—you must take some home to your mother."

Sadia protested but the women were insistent. The women insisted but Sadia protested. Then the women insisted a third time, which meant Sadia was now obliged to wait while Ikhista Aini carved up part of the rib cage and wrapped it in burlap.

"You are too kind." Sadia bowed. "Jazakallahu khayran." May Allah reward you for the good.

Sadia had nothing to say to me. She made no effort to conceal her dislike of me. We walked in silence round the wall, she several feet ahead, nose turned up, proud, me vaguely nauseous with anticipation.

When we arrived at Aziz's uncle's house, the room was bristling with conversation. Aziz and Munir were questioning the legitimacy of a Palestinian organization under a man named Arafat, not convinced by his justification for recent attacks on Israel. Tawfiq was in complete disagreement.

"Welcome," said Aziz, patting the pillow beside him. He passed qat into my hand, and Tawfiq resumed, punching the air with his finger to make his point, which was lost on me. I sucked on the bitter leaves while the conversation digressed into an exchange of opinions about whether Abebe Bikila, who had been the first African to ever win a gold medal at the Olympics, was too old to compete in the upcoming games in Munich.

I might not have had much knowledge of secular affairs, but where was their concern for religion? I wondered. That was the source of this Palestinian situation they'd been discussing, was it not?

"It is an issue of imperialism and economics," said Munir, answering a question it had taken me so long to formulate that they were already well onto another topic. His answer only left me feeling confused and uncertain. My questions not only came at the wrong time; they seemed to be the wrong questions, at least as far as the men were concerned. I was good at learning languages—why did theirs seem so foreign?

When the relief of mirqana descended over the room, Aziz leaned back and joined me in silence. I felt his presence beside me like one feels the day's heat radiating from stones.

"See you next Saturday," he said at the end of that afternoon, and suddenly the week ahead looked very long.

—

"So that story is true?" Gishta asked the next day, raising one eyebrow.

I bit my tongue hard. "What other story is there, Gishta?" I asked with calculated calm.

I knew she wouldn't repeat the rumours—that I was a spy, an anti-Muslim agent, a sharmuta here to lead their sons astray. In the year that I'd been here, I'd still not provided any evidence in support of these allegations. The women in the neighbourhood had gradually come to accept my presence: those who knew me in the day-to-day, those whose children now uttered holy words. They even referred to me differently as a teacher—as Bint Abdal, daughter of Abdal.

"Call me Gish," Nouria's cousin said a few days after that second bercha.

"I made you these," she said the following week, holding out an expensive-looking pair of trousers, the ones the wealthy Harari women wore under their long skirts, striped silk with colourful embroidered cuffs.

I told her it would take an eternity before I earned enough to pay her back. She scoffed and insisted I try them on right away. The cuffs were tight by design, so tight that I had to oil my feet before I could begin.

"Now no one will inflict you with the evil eye because they are jealous of the sight of your skin!" Gishta shrieked once I'd pulled them on, nodding wildly with approval.

So the trousers were not simply a fashion statement. I had been gently chastised; conformity is induced through gifts. Through flattery. And gossip. Once I was wearing these trousers, the remaining rumours seemed to subside. I was now fully dressed. And thus began another sort of apprenticeship, becoming a young woman of Harar— Gish, self-appointed as my guide.

—

I'd never given much thought to my appearance until meeting Sadia and her friends. At the Moroccan shrine our rituals concerned cleanliness, not appearance per se. After I lost my mother, I'd simply let my hair grow because she wasn't around to chop it off with a blunt pair of scissors any more. My nails grew and broke of their own accord. And my clothes? In the past, I'd had to rely on the gifts of others and now I wore one of the dresses that Nouria and I had had made.

Clothes had always served a utilitarian purpose, and shoes hadn't even been necessary. Until recently. Until the growing insecurity that Aziz, who was so neat and smartly dressed in his white pressed shirts, must think me a gypsy. Until these past few Saturdays of listening to Sadia and her friends, Warda and Titune, the two other girls who came to the berchas, admiring each other's nails and calling this and that helwa (sweet) and fashinn gidir (big fashion).

Perhaps the reason Sadia disliked me had something to do with the lack of concern I showed for my appearance. They compared forearms and agreed it was time to strip them with honey, and they favoured something called Roxy rather than henna for colouring their hair. It came from a fashinn gidir boutique in Mecca, brought back by relatives returning from the haj. It turned their hair an alarming shade of orange. Sometimes they even dyed their eyebrows to match.

I thought of the Ka'bah when I thought of Mecca, not clothes shops. I was not like Sadia and her friends. What I did best, perhaps, was pray, recite Qur'an, teach. There were a few other women in the city who had made religion their profession: teachers at madrasas, Sufis, religious scholars or disciples of saints, but the thing was, all of these women were old.

I was shocked when Sadia told me she didn't even fast during Ramadan, she even seemed proud of the fact. And when the subject of marriage came up one Saturday, she shrugged: "Not yet." She nodded coyly in Munir's direction. "Nineteen, even twenty, this is the best time for marriage," she said. "Not fourteen like my mother—"

"Or thirteen like mine," Warda piped in.

"*After* high school," said Titune.

The vital ingredient, they agreed, was love. Love first, then marriage, reversing the order of generations before.

—

Gishta applied a thick henna paste to my hair, dying my ashen blonde a deep red. She combed my hair with oil, flattening it against my scalp, and draped a loose, lime-green chiffon scarf over my head. She trimmed my nails and painted them with henna as well. Nouria boiled honey in the kitchen, and she and Gishta applied it hot to my arms and legs. They ripped every single hair off my limbs with deft painful swipes. It tingled and itched and turned my skin bright pink, which sent them into hysterics.

Another afternoon, Gishta brought a woman with a leather pouch full of different-sized needles to Nouria's compound. The woman did piercing and tattooing for both healing and aesthetic purposes. She could cure a sinus infection by punching two blue dots between the eyebrows; a kidney infection by tattooing a circle on the lower back.

Quick shocks ran down my spine as the needle burst through my earlobes. The woman had surreptitiously pushed gold hoops through before I'd even had a chance to recover. Then, much more painful, she did the same through the cartilage at the tops of my ears, which yielded with a distinctive pop.

She pulled out a third needle, a small stone and a pot of black ink.

"What's that for?"

All three women pulled their lips away from their teeth to show off their bluish-black gums.

I cringed. "No way."

"You don't think it's beautiful?" asked Gishta with an exaggerated pout.

"On you, yes," I tried diplomatically. "I just don't think it's for me."

Nouria tsked-tsked. "But it will make your teeth look so white."

Long, long ago I'd used toothpaste. I knew there were gentler alternatives.

When I asked Sadia about it later, she waved her hand dismissively. "It was fashinn gidir maybe until twenty years ago. The mothers still think it is beautiful, but it is just fashinn qadim now." And then she cocked her head and commented that my hair looked very pretty.

—

As my apprenticeship advanced, Gishta told me it was time that I had a special dress of pink and purple silk made to wear to weddings, a fuchsia veil woven through with gold threads to match. A traditional Harari dress. The dress was deliberately cumbersome, ostentatious. And it was, of course, expensive, made from silk imported from India, sewn by one local tailor and embroidered by another. I could not possibly afford it, but Gishta generously assumed the cost. Conveniently, the dress was reversible so that I might turn it inside out to reveal black should I need to attend a funeral. No matter that I had never been invited to either event.

"You will be sick of weddings in one year from now," Gishta assured me. "You will say: I cannot possibly eat any more stomach lining and sausages. Insha'Allah, you will become fat!"

There were also skills for me to develop, primarily domestic: special foods to prepare, rituals to enact, techniques to perfect. At one of Nouria's wealthier neighbour's houses one afternoon, Gishta pushed some coloured straw into my hands. The back wall of the room was adorned with baskets, each with a specific name and purpose—some large and flat, designed to hold injera, others neat packages with lids to hold jewellery, veils or incense. All were tightly woven pieces made with dyed straw, rimmed with leather and adorned with cowry shells from the distant Red Sea.

"After a girl's beauty and virtuousness, it is this skill that makes her attractive as a bride," Nouria said with a giggle.

Gishta laughed. "Yes, even an ugly girl can become beautiful if she makes baskets well enough!"

"Are you suggesting I'm ugly, Gish?" I asked, eyebrows raised.

"No, no, Lilly, you are okay. I mean, for a skinny farenji with pink gums."

"Not to worry," Nouria said, "you will be sure to attract a wonderful man once we've taught you this!"

I blushed. I could not help but wonder if Aziz was looking for a girl who could weave baskets and embroider pillowcases, if he was looking for someone who could make pumpkin stew and knew how to carve up a cow with a knife between her feet and not waste a single piece, even cleaning out its intestines with ashes so she could make sausages. If he was looking at all.

It was politics that seemed to concern him most. While the girls increasingly included me in their conversations during Saturday berchas, I kept one ear tuned to the men. Their conversations were often heated—fierce debates about the war in Eritrea and even fiercer debates about corruption in Saudi Arabia—and didn't leave a lot of room for me to interrupt as much as I might have. When I did, they tended to dismiss it if I raised the spiritual side of an argument.

"Even if the Saudis see the haj primarily as a money-making venture, this is irrelevant to a pilgrim in a spiritual sense," I argued. "He has accomplished his duty by fulfilling this pillar of faith, whether he has been gouged along the way or not. It's not the money that matters."

"Well, you wouldn't see me making the haj," said Munir.

I sank back against the pillows in shock.

Aziz leaned back beside me, his arm touching mine and my skin glowed red.

"I see the point about corruption," I said quietly. "But I think you are only harming yourself if you choose not to fulfill your religious duties because you think someone else is taking advantage of you. You end up denying yourself the chance to have what could be rightfully yours—the rewards of the afterlife."

"I admire your conviction," said Aziz. "I suppose we are just as much concerned with this life as the one after." He took my hand then and squeezed it. He kept my hand in his and began drawing circles with his thumb. I don't know which shocked me more, what Munir had said or what Aziz was now doing, but where I could argue with Munir's comment, I couldn't refute the feeling of Aziz's touch. It was too seductive. I stared straight ahead without breathing. The room was totally silent and I glanced around to see whether anyone had noticed Aziz take my hand. I suddenly felt slow and heavy. Mud filled my mouth. Munir and Sadia were also holding hands. And so were Warda and Tawfiq and Tajuddin and Titune. How haram it was. And how naive I had been.

Part Three.

—

# London, England

## 1986–87

Encounters with the Jinn.

—

More rain falls in a winter here than in two decades in Ethiopia. How quickly the novelty wears off. It's been pissing down for months. "Greedy," Amina calls England. The greedy green English earth.

The summer of 1986 brings not just rain but a thick and continuous stream of refugees. People camp out on the doorstep of our office, shivering with a cold they have never known before, awaiting our arrival on Saturday mornings. Those who are Muslim kiss our hands and pepper their speech with religious phrases, asking the time because they haven't a watch and kneeling down on the brown acrylic carpet to pray. Those who are Christian kiss our cheeks and bow as low as they can in gratitude. Those Oromo who have managed to resist all the proselytizers thank Waqaa, their traditional God.

Amina and I thank God the Harari way. Once a month, we burn crystals of incense over coals in a flowerpot in her kitchen garden. We raise our palms to the English sky and offer special prayers in honour of Bilal al Habash, which the smoke carries heavenward.

This month Amina declines to accompany me outside on the grounds that it's too wet. Last month she declared it too cold. For all her conviction that her children should know where they come from, she seems increasingly less interested in maintaining the rituals of the past. It's more than weather: she is impressed by the words of the imams at the mosque and the teachers at Ahmed's madrasa who preach what they call the official, the orthodox, the *only* version of Islam. In this version, saints are called false gods, and to honour them is to commit the crime of shirk: association, elevation, worshipping something other than God.

For the second month in a row, I make my way out to the garden without her. Sitta lingers in the open doorway, observing as always. "Do you want to throw in the incense?" I ask, holding out my hand.

She immediately throws the handful of dusty crystals in her palm into the air. They scatter like chicken feed on the ground.

"Come closer," I gesture, and she thumps down the peeling steps in Ahmed's big yellow rubber boots. She huddles beside me under the umbrella, one hand between my legs, gripping my inner thigh. I pull the paper bag out of my coat pocket again, sprinkle incense into her other hand and tell her to drop it this time, pour it gently over the dying coals, do it with intention, as the Great Abdal taught me.

Sitta laughs and jumps back as the smoke rises.

"Bismillah al-rahman, al-rahim," I begin singing, before invoking the name of the saint and asking him to protect the people of Harar and their descendants. "Do you know who Bilal is?" I ask Sitta.

She shakes her head, though I've repeated the story a thousand times. In a couple of months Sitta will begin taking Saturday classes at the madrasa like her brother, at which point I fear she'll also abandon me in the kitchen garden for a more orthodox education where the only history is that of the Arabs and traditions like this become heresy.

"Do you remember how I told you that nobody believed the Prophet Muhammed when he began spreading the message of God?" I ask. "Well, Bilal was this poor Ethiopian man who had been sold as a slave to an Arabian family. He had no power, no influence, but when he heard the man who claimed to be a prophet speak, he was so convinced of the purity of the message that he was willing to risk his life by standing up and telling people they must listen. He believed that the Prophet's word was as he claimed—the word of God.

"Of course, Bilal's owner punished him severely, but when the Prophet learned of this, he sent one of his companions to pay whatever was required to set the poor slave free. The Prophet rewarded him for his courage and devotion, and Bilal, in turn, became one of the Prophet's most trusted companions. He continued to work loyally in the face of opposition, walking through the streets of Mecca and calling the believers to come to prayer."

"The muezzin," says Sitta.

"Absolutely right," I smile. *Alhamdullilah. It's finally sinking in.* "Islam's first muezzin."

———

Amina asks me if I wouldn't mind looking after the children. She doesn't tell me where she's going. I'm dreading a day when Amina gets knocked about by one of those lager louts standing outside the tube station. Those men standing there for the sole purpose of menace in their skin-tight jeans and boots and leather vests, arms bare in winter, exposing their aging tattoos, shouting, "Oi! Nig nog!"

She dons a heavier, darker veil, and even though she says she feels more protected, I fear it also draws more attention. She kisses the children goodnight, leaving lipstick on their foreheads and a trail of Chanel No. 5.

Later, Ahmed and I are working with Bristol board on my kitchen floor, trying to outline the countries of Western Europe without aid of an atlas.

I could draw North and East Africa without a map. I could show him Tuareg caravan routes across the Sahara, the route I followed, the paths of pilgrims, and draw the dotted lines of shifting sands and contested borders, but when it comes to Western Europe, it's admittedly a bit of a white blur.

"Did Ayo tell you where she was going?" I attempt casually.

"Just visiting." Ahmed traces over the pencilled outline of the British Isles with black marker.

We've managed to get this far courtesy of a map in the telephone directory, but beyond this, I fear we're in trouble.

Sitta is concentrating hard throughout all this, biting her bottom lip while she adds rows of numbers. The pencil looks as big and dangerous as a bread knife, poised in her tiny hand. She has a tiny face too, like a doll's, topped by a halo of loose ringlets, and she's dressed in her pink fuzzy pyjamas, ready for bed.

"Finished!" she announces triumphantly.

"That's a good girl. Maybe you can help Ahmed and me finish Europe," I joke.

She pouts. "But it's story time."

Ahmed looks helplessly at the Bristol board.

"I'll tell you what. I'll take you by Mr. Jahangir's shop on the way to school tomorrow. He'll be able to help us. Like he always says, he's a very educated man. All right? Now, teeth-brushing, both of you, then story time."

Tonight's story will be the story of every night when we crawl into bed together: that of Hussein, the Sufi crippled by spiritual failure, and Lilly, the orphaned girl who relights the fire in his ailing heart.

—

"Lilly?" I hear Amina whispering.

Sitta is curled against me, her head nestled under my arm, drooling on my shirt, and Ahmed is clinging to the edge of the narrow bed. Amina gently shakes my thigh, waking me up.

"Is everything all right?" I ask.

"Mmm-hmm." She stands at the foot of the bed, fingering the bedspread.

"What is it, Amina?"

She puts her finger to her lips, gestures for me to disentangle myself from the children and follow her into the kitchen.

She puts the kettle on and liberates herself from her veil, coat and cardigan. The wind rattles against the thin windowpane. I open it up a crack and light a cigarette.

"Where were you?" I ask.

"Just shir shir," she says—visiting.

"Oh," I say.

She shrugs. "I just went to see someone, but it was useless. Why should I tell you something that is nothing?"

I've been known to make a great deal of something out of nothing. About a year ago we had a visit from an Oromo man whose wife had encouraged him to come and see us because he was desperate to find his brother. The man and his brother had been imprisoned together in barracks in southwestern Ethiopia, where even the guards were starving. Once a day, the guards and those prisoners who were lucky were given a cup of stew made from onionskins. Those less fortunate were forced to eat the rubber soles of their shoes and dirt from the prison yard once the patches of grass were all gone.

But those who weren't dying of starvation were dying of some disease that was spreading through the prison. "Finally, they brought in a doctor with some pills to save us," the Oromo man told us. "He had only maybe one hundred pills and there were more than six hundred of us. So the guards said to him, forget the ones who are starving and pick out the few of them who although sick are still standing.

"The doctor put the pill on my tongue and truly, thanks to God, it saved my life. Bedri, my brother, was lucky too. We who had swallowed the medicine became better, and to prevent us from catching the sickness again, the doctor convinced the guards that we had to be moved to another prison.

"They blindfolded us and threw us like potatoes into the back of a truck. And there was an ambush on the second day and suddenly we are staggering into the night and there is shooting all around and I fall to the ground and crawl as far as I can. When I stopped from exhaustion, I heard breathing near me in the dark and I was so terrified I tried not to make a sound. But I hear breathing on the right and on the left and behind me. There were people like me crawling and no one would speak because the night was so dark and we did not know if we were surrounded by enemies or friends. Finally, this one takes the risk and speaks. It is my brother Bedri, alhamdullilah. He tells us that the Harari doctor told him it is only about twelve miles south to the Kenyan border. And when the sun rises in the morning? Alhamdullilah we know the direction to go."

"The doctor was Harari?" I asked. I couldn't help myself.

"Yes. The one who saved my life. Many lives."

"Do you remember his name?"

"I don't know this," the man said. "I only remember he didn't look like a Harari because he was very black. In any case, my brother . . ."

I was convinced it had to be him: there weren't many Harari doctors, I knew them all, and Aziz was certainly the blackest. But how on earth do you go about locating someone when all you know is that he was somewhere close to the Kenyan border about four years ago? All you can do is pray. And wait. And go a little crazy. I developed a fever and had terrible dreams and when I woke up after a week I found that all the cupboard doors in my kitchen had been torn off their hinges.

"Do you think I'm losing my mind?" I asked Amina, as I stood there stunned by the destruction. My hands were scratched and bruised, but I had only a vague recollection of having been frustrated by a vain search through all the cupboards for some tea.

"Perhaps you have just had a little encounter with the jinn," she said sympathetically.

The zar, the worst of the jinn, can take possession of one's mind and body. I saw it happen a few times in Ethiopia. Always to women. Women who had reached their limits.

"I called your work," Amina said, sweeping splintered wood from the floor.

"You didn't—"

"I had to, Lilly!"

"What did you tell them?"

"Just that you had family business to attend to," she said. "I spoke to a very nice man called Dr. Gupta."

"Oh shit," I groaned.

"He seemed very nice."

One of the doctors often on duty on my ward. Tall and arrogant. Good looking and altogether too aware of it.

I'd missed five shifts in all and had to pay the price of undergoing a probationary hearing with a board of three doctors, including, much to my humiliation, Dr. Gupta.

They asked me questions about depression and drug use, and I said, rather angrily, that this really had nothing to do with my mental health. I was dealing with family matters, and when you come from a family of refugees things can be unpredictable.

"A family of refugees?" the chief of staff asked, as if amused.

"Yes."

"That must be complicated."

I nodded and looked away.

"And do you think this will continue to interfere with your work?"

"No, I don't," I said firmly. "The matter's been dealt with. It's over."

I would not be blindsided like that again. Aziz was somewhere in southern Ethiopia, close to the Kenyan border. I was braced now: it was just a matter of time.

The best we could do was try to get a message to

the main UNHCR camp outside Nairobi, where Amina and her husband had spent time. I left my name, phone number and address with a Christian charity that distributes second-hand clothes among refugees in the camp, branding thin African men with slogans like "Let's Boogie," "Sex Appeal—Give Generously," "Save the Whale."

No one from the charity or the camp has ever made contact.

I topped up Amina's tea. "So this something that turned out to be nothing—"

"Lilly! Why do you do this to yourself, eh? It is nothing, I tell you."

"Please," I asked, pouting like a child.

Amina sighed. "I just heard about this doctor, he is called Dr. Berhanu, Berhanu Wondemariam, and they say he was very very famous, he used to be head of the medical school in Addis—"

"Aha. So you were thinking maybe he was there when Aziz was a student."

"I thought there was no harm to try and ask. I heard from this lady at my work that he was here, that he came for some conference and declared asylum and that he was living with his friends in Camden Town. She made an arrangement for me to go and meet him."

"You know I would have gone with you," I say.

"That is *exactly* why I didn't tell you, Lilly. In any case, this Dr. Berhanu is not well. He has had some trauma, it is clear in his eyes. It will be some time before he is ready to speak about the past."

I preferred it when she used to blame things on

the jinn or the evil eye. She's taking a psychology class at night school once a week. The refugee organization she works for is paying for it. The effects are beginning to show.

"I asked him, 'do you remember this student Aziz Abdulnasser?'" Amina continues. "But the doctor just shook his head and apologized. His friend said, 'Look, Mrs. Amina, Dr. Berhanu and I have taught hundreds of students over the years. I'm very sorry, but you can't expect us to remember the name of every one, can you?'"

"I suppose not," I agree.

Amina admits it was pushy but she told them it would be helpful to our office if he could make a list of those students he did remember. I suppose she hoped that there'd be a name we might recognize amongst Aziz's classmates.

"You're sweet," I say, squeezing her hand in gratitude.

Of course, Dr. Berhanu's friend said they couldn't possibly. It would be far too painful. "But sometimes I am suspicious of ones like these," Amina says, wagging a finger. "Sometimes those who don't remember are refusing because they are guilty of some crime. In psychology it is called denial."

But each of us is guilty in someone's eyes. If you are an Amhara you are guilty of supporting a brutal dictatorship; if you are Oromo you are guilty of counter-revolutionary sentiment; if you are Harari you are guilty of harbouring wealth and exploiting peasants. If you are a refugee you are guilty of the worst crimes of all: deserting your homeland and abandoning those you love. In every case, it's a matter of perception: in the last case, self-perception, the most damning of all.

Amina is suspicious of this doctor because of his Amhara name. In exile, the wars between us are not erased.

"Now forget this, okay?" Amina says.

"Sure," I say. "It's nothing."

# A Bitter Habit.

—

I am seeking a little respite in the cafeteria while an eighteen-year-old boy lies dying upstairs, the result of a drug-motivated swan dive off a twelfth-floor balcony. I've just cranked up his dose of morphine: he'll be dead within the hour. I'm fairly immune, given that I've done this so many times over what will soon be a decade, but sometimes, where dying is the result of something needless and senseless, like a fight or a beating or a head injury sustained by people who refuse to wear helmets, I have to battle the impulse to judge. When you live among people who have endured unimaginable tortures, who have sacrificed everything in order to give their children better lives, you lose sympathy for those who would throw it all away because of ego.

It's my job to help the dying on their way; it is humane and merciful, I remind myself, listlessly spooning tapioca into my mouth.

Someone slides an orange-coloured tray into view as I stare blankly at the table. Brown hands, short, trim nails, a few stray black hairs between the knuckles.

"Hello, Lilly," says a deep voice.

I look up. "Dr. Gupta."

"Rabindranath. Robin." He smiles. His teeth are very white. Suspiciously so.

"Rabindranath," I repeat. I would prefer to stew in silence.

"It's a Hindu name," he says, "Bengali." I watch him pull a bottle of Tabasco sauce out of his pocket and cover his mashed potatoes in red polka dots. "What about your name?"

"English, I guess."

"Lilly, but not Abdal."

"No," I concede.

"And your accent's not very English."

I laugh, taken aback. "No, it's a mess." People aren't usually so rude as to draw attention to it.

"More like a fruit cocktail," he says.

I shrug, hoping this will be the end of it. Doctors normally sit with doctors, just as nurses sit with nurses and orderlies sit with orderlies. Residents don't even sit with doctors or surgeons, and nurses, they're the worst—the senior nurses, charge nurses and nurse specialists make a strict point of sitting apart from those of us who are simply staff nurses, stupid or unambitious or lazy or incapable or whatever it must be that keeps us in our lowly station.

"I was intrigued when you said you come from a family of refugees," Dr. Gupta says, putting his fork down.

"Were you?" That was ages ago. I look at him curiously. I've never noticed this before but one of his eyes is slightly sleepy, like only half of him is awake. I wonder if he was teased about it at school.

"I'm not entirely sure what you meant by it, but it nevertheless struck a chord in me," he says. "I mean, very few members of my family are here. We're all scattered about. My parents in Calcutta, family in Delhi, some in Manchester, cousins in Birmingham, Melbourne, Vancouver."

It's not the same thing at all, I want to tell him. Your family left by choice. You know where each of them is. You can pick up the phone.

I excuse myself, scraping back my chair, saying I must get back to my rounds.

—

Ramadan begins at midnight. Sitta wears her white cotton veil and Ahmed fidgets with his knit skullcap as we take the bus to Brixton. I'm defiantly more colourful, wearing a bright veil like the Harari women do and a gold shawl draped over my burgundy dress. The bus is crowded with people from the estate who greet us, stroke the children's cheeks affectionately, ask after Amina. She has her psychology class this evening but she will join us for supper at home.

Many of us don't attend the mosque as often as we might. In Harar, we visited the shrines more often than the mosques because they were where we felt closest to God. Ahmed's Qur'an teacher insists that parents take their children to the mosque at least once a week. Good practices must be instilled before puberty. Between us, Amina and I seem to manage about once a month.

Tonight, the imam speaks about the particular difficulties of fasting in a world of twenty-four-hour take-aways, about the vigilance required to fight the temptations of tea and coffee and vending machines full of Mars bars, of having the discipline to say no to lunch in the school cafeteria when everyone else is tucking in. "When your schoolmates ask you why it is you are not eating, you must use this as an opportunity to educate them about Islam," he says. "And if any of them tease you or abuse you, do not react in anger. Use fasting as your shield."

On our way home, we stop to pick up fish and chips. The kids unwrap theirs in their laps in front of the telly. They won't be fasting, but Amina and I will. The fish and chips are a treat for us all. The hardest thing for me to give up is smoking. It's the most English thing about me, this love of Silk Cuts.

"Oh good, I'm starving," Amina moans when she finally gets home, dropping her textbook on the kitchen table. She pulls open the oven door without even taking off her coat and tears at the newspaper. In between mouthfuls she asks me about my day.

I relate my conversation with Dr. Gupta, Rabindranath, Robin, which is still bothering me. He might also be from elsewhere, but he comes from a wealthy family and studied medicine at

Cambridge. He has relatives in England, no doubt goes back to India to visit his family and friends once every two years and has a special rate plan that allows him to spend hours on the phone with people in Bombay on the weekends. It's not the same thing at all.

Amina tsks and wipes oil from her lips with the back of her hand. "You sound so bitter sometimes."

"Do I?"

"You don't hear yourself? He's just trying to establish some common ground with you. He's not trying to compete, or I don't know, whatever it is you're thinking . . ."

"Belittle my experience."

"Lilly, I'm sure this is not his intention. He doesn't know your experience, does he? And besides, why would he bother? It sounds like he was trying to make friends. And it would be good for you to make some friends."

"You sound like a parent," I scoff.

"I am a parent."

"Not my parent."

"Ooph, Lilly." She rolls her eyes.

"Well, I didn't ask you to be," I say.

She stands up, rubbing the salt from her palms. "You have to pull this dagger out of your heart!" she yells, complete with dramatic gesture. "You behave as if life is finished. You remember when you asked me if I thought you were losing your mind? You did not lose your mind, but you did lose something. You lost hope. Ever since that man told us about the doctor who saved his life you have had no hope. You have no dream for the future any more."

She stuffs the greasy paper into the rubbish bin.

She leaves me sitting at the kitchen table long enough for me to understand the point she's making. In a few hours Ramadan will begin. Ramadan teaches us patience and restraint, and it is the time for each of us to wage jihad against the destructive habits we have acquired. Smoking is the least of mine.

## Eid el Fitr.

—

Aziz's image is shimmering in the yellow and purple rainbow of oily residue as I thaw tubs of dorro
wat in hot water. I wonder if he has fasted this
Ramadan. I hope he had the choice.

There are those who do not swallow their saliva
all month: a discipline far greater than mine. Then
there are those who beg off fasting more than
most, like the women Amina and I know who claim
to menstruate twice in thirty days. Most of us
linger somewhere in the middle, erring once or
twice, which we can make up by fasting sometime
later during the year. Regardless of our personal
success or failure, though, Eid el Fitr is the biggest
celebration of the year.

Amina returns from the shop with coriander,
and I reluctantly pull the plug in the kitchen sink.
Aziz becomes a circle and spirals down the drain.

At night, a parade of colour approaches from
left and right. Women stream down the concrete
corridors leaving punishing echoes in their wake;
the piercing squeals of delighted children bounce

mercilessly off the walls. En route, they bear the condemnation of unsympathetic white neighbours who stick their heads out into the hallway and ask them to keep the bloody racket down.

A perfumed cloud wafts through the door of Amina's flat. The guests are mostly Oromo, but we have also invited Mr. and Mrs. Jahangir and a few neighbours, Eritrean, Kenyan and Sudanese. The two Harari women who live on the floor below arrive in true Harari style, wearing all their silkiest finery, shining from their teeth to their ankles. Even here, in exile, they look rich.

Mrs. Jahangir arrives with a small mountain of samosas heaped on a plate balanced over a curry of okra and peas. The Oromo women balance injera—which can now be purchased at the newsagent's in soggy stacks of six—on platters on their heads, carry plates of sweets and bowls of popcorn in their hands and tow multiple children in their wake.

The men are off celebrating in more subdued fashion. The Oromo brothers took up a collection to buy qat from the Yemeni merchant in Brixton who charges more at this time of year for a small bunch of dry green leaves than it would cost to buy a cow in Ethiopia.

While the men get high, we spend the night singing. One of the Harari women accompanies us on the drum as we sing dhikr, religious praises, known to all the Muslims in the room. We take turns singing our traditional songs, during which the children grow bored and tug at their mothers' skirts until the women give them permission to go and play It in the corridor rather than listen to these moral tales and songs of ethnic pride in which we wish they'd take more interest.

Finally we eat.

—

The following morning, hoarse from all the singing and still inflated from all the food, Amina and I drag our bodies to the community association office. We're suffering from the Muslim version of a hangover, complete with a slight feeling of sadness and regret: one that comes from realizing that for all our disciplined reflection throughout the month, there has been no permanent shift in consciousness, no profound alteration of ourselves or the world around us.

I smoke my tenth cigarette of the morning, sucking with a fury after a month of abstinence, while drafting a letter to Amnesty. I do this routinely, this time because the dictatorship is forcibly relocating civilians again, taking hundreds of thousands of them from the famine-stricken north and depositing them in government-controlled villages farther south. They say it is the only solution because the north is on the brink of environmental collapse, but we know that it has nothing to do with famine relief. We've seen this happen twice already in the last three years. It's an aggressive counter-insurgency measure designed to disperse ethnic concentrations, propelled by the dictatorship's fear of rebel fronts in the north, guerillas who refuse to die, no matter how much Mengistu's government tries to starve them through another famine of its own engineering. A famine that, in turn, allows Mengistu to fatten his army and make his officers rich with food aid sent by the governments and Bob Geldofs of the world, fuelling the dictatorship to reach new heights of horror.

Amina is sitting in the squeaky orange office chair with a stack of envelopes in her lap, scanning the names on the list on the table in front of her. She is wearing my old patent-leather shoes, ones I bought in a momentary lapse of judgment. Sitta is sticking her finger into the sugar lurking at the bottom of my coffee cup and humming the theme to *Blue Peter*.

Amina suddenly stands up, sending the tower of envelopes onto the floor. Sitta giggles as the envelopes spill, but abruptly stops, caught by the look on her mother's face. Amina is a photograph of agony: utterly still.

I move toward her as if walking through water. "What is it, Amina?" I venture quietly, my hand on her shoulder.

She shakes the list in her hand. "Yusuf," she can barely manage, bursting into sobs.

She leans into me. I put my arm around her neck, pull her forehead to my shoulder. Water rises to the height of my chest. "Alhamdullilah," I manage to whisper in her ear, a bubble floating to the surface.

"Alhamdullilah," she chokes. She grabs my hand and pulls it to her heart. "Can you feel?" she asks.

I can. I can almost hear it.

"One day you will feel this," she offers.

We both know how unlikely that is. It's now been twelve years. But there is a lesson in this. I stopped hoping. Amina was absolutely right. A dagger. She has tried to keep hope alive for both of us, and for that, she is being rewarded.

## Phantom Limbs.

—

Sitta has never been more talkative—the existence of a father she has never known seems to have given her language: questions and ideas. Ahmed, on the other hand, has gone rather quiet; missing his mother, I expect, during these weeks that she's with Yusuf in Rome. He reads comic books, can't get enough of them, grunting from the sagging brown sofa when I ask him if he's ready for tea.

"Macaroni?" I ask him.

"Yes, please, macaroni cheese," Sitta answers for the two of them, clapping her hands together with each syllable.

I put a pot of water on to boil. Sitta is stuck to my thigh in the tiny kitchen, nattering on like a talking doll with someone pulling repeatedly at the string in her back. "When did you get to be such a chatterbox?" I ask her.

She ignores that, busy fiddling with the dial on the radio.

"I wonder what your mother is up to at the moment," I say.

"Eating a pizza with Baba!" Ahmed shouts from the other room—selective hearing, apparently.

"Eating a pizza with Baba!" Sitta repeats.

"What do you remember about your baba?" I call out to Ahmed.

"What do you remember about your baba?" Sitta repeats, as if it were a game.

A few things, I could tell her, though most of them rather vague. Swimming with him in the Mediterranean, him playing the guitar on the street with the case open, a few coins sparkling against the blue velvet. My mother and father naked and lazy in Tangier, where we lived in a decaying white hotel in the medina with a broken banister and stairs so rickety we couldn't have two feet on one step at the same time. I seem to recall my father offering to fix the stairs and Haji Mustafa being so humbled by the offer that he said we could have the room for free, but I have no recollection of my father ever actually doing the work. They got far on charm and promises.

"What about Ethiopia—do you remember anything about Ethiopia?" I call out to Ahmed, who hasn't replied.

"Do you?" he shouts back.

"Yes, as a matter of fact I do."

"What do you remember?" he shouts. He gets up from the sofa and stands in the doorway of the kitchen with his comic book in one hand. "What do you remember?" he demands. He wants stories now not of ailing Sufis and orphaned girls but of the place he comes from. His people.

It's difficult for me to answer. It is not simply what one remembers, but why. There are sites of amputation where the past is severed from the body of the present. Remembering only encourages the growth of phantom limbs. And it is not simply what one remembers, or why, but what to do with what one remembers, which of the scattered pieces to carry forward, what to protect and preserve, what to leave behind. "It's complicated," I tell Ahmed.

He skulks back to the sofa with his comic book.

Sitta watches while I pour macaroni into the pot. Bing Crosby sings "White Christmas" on the radio.

"We have a Christmas tree at school," Sitta tells me.

"Do you, love?" My memories, I could tell Ahmed, are at once too powerful and not nearly enough.

"It's sparkly and it has a star this big," Sitta carries on, arms spread wide.

"That's not very Muslim, is it," I remark. At least a third of the children in her class must be Muslim.

"It's pretty," she says.

Fair enough. She's a girl who likes pretty things. Christmas ornaments and the framed gold-lettered Arabic proverbs that hang on the walls of her mother's flat. Barbie, whom she often wraps up and puts to bed in her mother's purple silk veil. And Ahmed is a boy who reads comic books and listens to Prince. Posters of Mecca and Michael

Jackson hang side by side on their bedroom wall. Both of them are looking forward to the Christmas hols even though there will be no pudding, no tree, no photos of them on the fat man's knee.

For all the differences between them, the missionized Ethiopians—Lutherans, Seventh-day Adventists and Pentecostals—take up a collection every year to give a Christmas present to each of the Ethiopian children on the estate. But we look upon these gifts with some suspicion. Not only did these people adopt farenji religions brought to Ethiopia by earnest Swedes and Norwegians and Canadians (why always the coldest countries? I wonder), they adopted a bit of the missionizing spirit as well. Pamphlets are surreptitiously left behind in the wake of presents.

For Sitta and Ahmed none of these things is a contradiction. Nor is this—a white Muslim woman who grew up in Africa making macaroni cheese for them in a council flat in London. The world beyond is, of course, full of alien encounters, contradictions that people cannot or do not wish to reconcile.

When Amina is dropping the children off at school.

*Oi, nig nog! We've already got too many fu'in for'ners. We don't need the likes of you adding more bloody monkeys to the earf!*

Friday prayers, the one time a week I wear a veil.

*Would you look at 'is cunt! A white fu'in Paki!*

A lout with a lager can mock-triggered to his head.

*Master race. Go' it?*

—

On Saturday morning, Ahmed is keen to have a little lie-in on the sofa even though he knows he has
his Qur'anic class.

"But why do I have to go?" he whines.

"Because it's important, Ahmed. Come along."

"But hardly anybody else at my school has to go
to another school on Saturdays."

I know that's not true.

"It's not fair," he bleats.

I was desperate to go to school when I was a
child. My father's "school of life" involved so
many lazy mornings that I was sick of it by the
time I was six years old. I would have traded anything I owned—my toothbrush, my rucksack, my
rag doll—to go to a real school where I could wear
a uniform and have a pencil box and friends. But
my parents refused to subject me to what they
referred to as the stifling confines of institutional
life. Thank God for the Great Abdal. When I told
him I wanted to attend the madrasa in
Tamegroute he was very pleased. My entire day
was then ordered by lessons: mornings at the
madrasa, afternoon study with the Great Abdal,
and nights spent reading books from Muhammed
Bruce by candlelight. "Are you eating the candles?" the Great Abdal used to tease. "It is a lucky
thing the pilgrims are so generous."

But we all want what we don't have, don't we?
Ahmed wants to lie in, and I want him to go to
school.

"I'll tell you what, Ahmed," I say. "You can't stay in bed because I need to get to the office, but you can miss the madrasa just this once."

He's suddenly bolt upright, about to leap out of bed.

"I haven't finished. On one condition, all right?"

"Mmm-hmm."

"You'll recite chapter seven to me later."

He groans. "Okay."

Porridge for the kids for breakfast, and for me, a cup of tea and a cigarette—puffing with my head out the window. I'm dreading going through the new list from Rome this morning without Amina.

"Ahmed?" I ask, tossing the fag end into the dustbin.

"Mmm?" he asks between gummy lips.

"Listen, if you get to miss the madrasa today, does that mean I get to miss the office?"

"And do what?" he asks. Not an unreasonable question.

"Whatever you'd like to do."

"Make Christmas biscuits," says Sitta. "Like the ones we have at school."

*Except that.* "Eat your porridge, Sitta. What about you, Ahmed?"

"Watch cricket."

"I'm not sure there's any cricket on at the moment. Shall I ask Mr. Jahangir?" How difficult it is to please everyone. How does Amina do it?

Mr. Jahangir is more than pleased to have the young Ahmed by his side at the Kennington Oval.

"I'm very grateful to you, Mr. J. It's not easy having two children."

"Try having seven, my dear."

Even if I wanted to, I'm afraid time's rather running out.

This leaves Sitta and me with a whole day ahead of us. I should take her on an outing, something educational; that would please Amina. I'm being completely irresponsible—I should at least make the day worthwhile.

Sitta is keen to go to Kensington Palace. She's developed a bit of an obsession with Lady Di since a school outing to the palace a couple of months ago.

"Let's go somewhere you haven't been before," I suggest. Somewhere colourful, alive, multicultural.

It's all very grown up of me to suggest going into the city when I leave our neighbourhood so rarely. I'm not terribly good with the buses but it's too sunny a day to waste underground. Sitta is content dressing and undressing her Barbie beside me on the red plastic seat, oblivious as I pick at my cuticles.

We spill out onto the pavement in the midst of Camden Market and I stand and squint in every direction, trying to orient myself while we're jostled left and right. I've been here twice before, both times with Mrs. Jahangir, who comes to buy fabric, but it's a shifting landscape, fluctuating monthly depending on who can pay their rent.

Sitta swings Barbie in one hand and puts her other hand in mine as we wander down a street

closed to traffic. Reggae blares from the entrance
of a shop framed with pictures of Bob Marley and
battles the soundtrack of a Hindi film across the
road. Racks of clothes line the pavement. Women
finger the fabric as they pass, and men try on hats
and sunglasses and bend down to see their reflec-
tions in small mirrors held by squat Eastern
European women. Farther down the road people
haggle over great mountains of undergarments,
and Nigerian men throw open duffle bags offering
selections of watches and perfumes.

There are punks with Mohawks and white kids
with dreadlocks and I wonder, just for a minute,
why it is we don't live here, why we live in
benighted parts of the city with no street life, on
estates built in the 1960s, in heartless high-rise
buildings, half of which have no central heating,
that have been deteriorating since the very
moment they were conceived.

"I'm hungry," says Sitta.

I scan the shop fronts, looking for a restaurant,
somewhere sufficiently neutral, unintimidating.
Sandwiched between a laundrette and a shop selling synthetic clothes and drug paraphernalia
stands a café no wider than a bus with Amharic
letters stencilled onto its window. I drag Sitta and
Barbie across the road and through the entrance
into the narrow space. Incense burns, Aster Aweke
strains through cheap speakers, and the few men
who are seated along the wall look up, look surprised, look away.

I help Sitta out of her coat and into a seat. "I

want McDonald's," she says. "Mama always lets us have McDonald's when we go on an outing."

I sigh and unbutton my coat. "Can I just have coffee?"

She pouts, and a waitress with bright red lipstick and long lacquered nails approaches.

"Hello, little one," she says to Sitta in Amharic. "Why do you look sad?"

"She doesn't speak Amharic," I reply in Amharic.

"But you do?" she asks in English. "You are missionary?"

"No," I laugh.

"You want something?"

"Buna, please."

She hesitates. "Nescafé?"

"No, *buna*," I say, getting irritated.

She shrugs. "*Ishi*, okay. And for you?" she asks Sitta in Amharic.

"Sitta, do you want something?"

"McDonald's," Sitta says petulantly, swinging her feet.

My coffee is delivered on the heels of laughter between the two waitresses. The waitress sets down a tiny ceramic cup.

"Pretty," Sitta comments, touching her nails.

"You like?" the waitress smiles. "It is called Strawberry Kisses."

Sitta giggles.

This must be why I live on a blighted housing estate in a distant borough. That is where I belong.

I knock back the coffee. The bitter residue lingers in my mouth.

—

Sitta gets McDonald's on her way home. She's pulling chips from the bag when a sign catches her eye through the window of the bus. She jumps up and sends the paper bag and its contents cascading to the floor. "It says palace! Palace!"

Everyone on the bus turns round to look, amused by the African girl's enthusiasm for the monarchy.

I'm reaching down to pick up chips off the floor when I hear my name. Dr. Gupta waves, his scrubs visible under his coat. He takes the seat in front of us and sits sideways.

"Fancy running into you," he says. "Normally, I take the underground to work, but it was too nice a day. Who's this?" he asks.

"This is Sitta. Sitta, this is Dr. Gupta."

"Robin," he says, though she doesn't turn from the window. "Is she a relative?"

"My best friend's daughter."

"She's charming," he says. "Where are you two off to, then? You're not working today, are you?"

"No, we just went on a bit of an outing. Took her to Camden Market, though it appears she's much more interested in British royalty."

You can neither see Buckingham Palace from here, nor is it the palace where Lady Di lives, but Sitta nevertheless remains with her face pressed to the glass.

"You know, there's a palace in Ethiopia," I try to interest her.

"You've been to Ethiopia?" Dr. Gupta asks.

"Mmm." I nod. "It's quite something, Sitta. It sits in a lush jungle, and there are all sorts of birds flying about, and there's a zoo of exotic animals all moaning and groaning in golden cages."

"Is there a princess like Lady Di?" Sitta asks over her shoulder.

"There was a princess once, but she wasn't very beautiful."

Her Royal Highness Princess Tenagneworq. Hardly the stuff of fairy tales. In her photograph she looked very plump and very old, and I distinctly remember thinking she had a round red face like a pomegranate crossed with the unfortunate wartiness of a toad.

"Did she have blond hair?" Sitta asks.

"No, she didn't have blond hair," I reply. "Not all princesses are blond."

"Sounds like my sister's children," Robin laughs. "The girl won't eat anything my sister cooks because she says ghee makes her fat—she's all of seven stone. And the boy came home with a crew cut the other day—his father's a Sikh, he's never cut his hair in his life, I gather he just about had a cardiac arrest. They only moved to Los Angeles six months ago."

"Have you met Barbie?" I ask, sneering at the doll on the seat.

"Amazing how quickly they pick it up. Like sponges, really. In any case," Dr. Gupta says, "I'd love to hear about your adventures in Ethiopia some time."

*Adventures?* Ethiopia wasn't some gap year experience. I tug at Sitta's arm. "Come on," I say, standing up.

"Getting off here?" he asks with surprise. "Where are you heading?"

"Home."

"Oh." He hesitates. "I had no idea."

"That I live in council housing?"

The look on my face sends him rushing to clarify what he means. "No. That you live so close to the hospital. I don't want to be anywhere near it on my days off, you know? I like to keep some separation between my life and my work."

Me too, I think, taking Sitta's hand and stepping off the bus. Sitta looks back over her shoulder and waves. I am determined not to turn around.

—

I recite chapter seven with Ahmed after tea, have him backtrack and repeat certain words and discuss their meanings. I miss teaching, but at our local madrasa, the Qur'anic teachers are all men. Things are stricter here, much more orthodox on the whole.

I call Amina to check in. Her voice is light, ethereal, outer-spacey. She tells me I'm trying too hard. All I have to do is let Sitta be Sitta.

"Even if that means Barbies and hamburgers?"

"Especially if that means Barbies and hamburgers."

Instinct.

—

Amina arrived home after three weeks in Rome carrying a suitcase full of presents for the children and radiating with an unmistakable glow. It is the woman in me, not the nurse. Yusuf's papers are being processed in Rome while another baby grows in Amina's stomach; everything is growing round for her, round and buoyant. I have to try to make something else work in my life, something separate and apart from her, I tell myself, determined to find a way to care about nursing again.

It actually doesn't prove all that difficult to ignore the sting of the fluorescent lights, to let go of the cynicism as I increase the flow of someone's morphine, to talk to mothers, tell them to stay. "He needs you here. Do you see the way his eyelids flutter when you talk?" It doesn't prove all that difficult, admittedly, because of Dr. Gupta.

I bumped into him a couple of weeks after Amina returned. Ward rotation brought him into my orbit. I saw him coming down the hall and tried my best to avoid him, staring intently at my clipboard as he approached, keen to engage.

"I'm so glad to run into you," he said, gripping my wrist. "I've been worrying that we might have started off on the wrong foot."

I stood there stupidly, not knowing how to respond.

"Look," he said, lowering his voice as we flattened ourselves against the wall to prevent a collision between two stretchers. "It's just, I'd like to be friends, but every time I talk to you I feel like I've said something offensive. Or idiotic."

I shook my head lamely.

"There's nothing I should be apologizing for?" he asked.

"No, it's my fault," I said.

"How so?" he asked gently, leaning in.

"I'm rather shy," I said, though that wasn't quite it. "Slow to get to know."

"Slow is good," he said. "It brings out the full strength of the flavours."

I didn't know where to look. I opted for the name tag on his chest.

"Listen." He cleared his throat. "I'd better get on with my rounds, but I wanted to ask you— there's a lecture series I attend once a month at the London School of Tropical Hygiene and Medicine. Next week they have an Anglo-Egyptian team presenting some of their findings on Nile parasites. Epidemic in Egypt. I just wondered whether you might have any interest."

"I wonder if they affect the Sudan and Ethiopia as well," I said.

"Good question. Perhaps you can ask."

—

Amina is painting her flat—an expense, an extravagance; no one else in the building would bother. My flat has not been painted in all the years I've lived here. I've not even hung a picture. But Amina is a mother; she knows how to make a home. She buys a new rug and a framed poster of lion cubs and whacks a nail into a freshly painted white wall.

Her housekeeping extends to our office, an impossibly crowded room at the best of times. She's all about reorganization and increased productivity—terms borrowed from her work with the government-funded Refugee Referral Service—but our office has an internal logic, one governed by heart. We prioritize the things that move us, we fall behind on bookkeeping and other administrative tasks, we do not pride ourselves on efficiency. Imagine telling one of our visitors: your tears are not productive; this is a waste of resources; your search is a hopeless case. We offer something no other organization does: familiarity, affection, and a good strong cup of buna, and if a story takes eight hours to tell? It takes eight hours to tell.

"If we were a registered charity, perhaps someone would donate a computer," Amina says, transferring files from one drawer to another.

I think headache. I think lawyers and accountants. And the miles of data entry. "We'd need a secretary then."

"Yes," Amina says with a nod, slamming a drawer shut.

"But we can't afford a secretary."

"But if we are a proper charity—" She stops herself, sees me shaking my head. "Lilly, every organization must grow and change. Move with the times, no?"

—

Robin and I sit side by side in the dark, staring at the road ahead as we drive back to Lambeth. The lecture was even more compelling than I'd imagined. I'd heard of bilharziasis, knew it vaguely as a disease caused by parasites, but not the grisly details: nasty, madly copulating worms laying hundreds of spiny eggs a day, eggs that wander the dark corridors of the intestines, bladder, kidneys, lungs, tearing tracks through the body, feasting on red blood cells, causing anemia, infection and disease. There is a treatment, though it's expensive and hardly available in Africa, where this is the most devastating parasitic disease after malaria. I think of a hundred children I once knew who were probably suffering from internal bleeding without any of us realizing it. Who are probably still suffering.

The Egyptian doctors are trying to work on a vaccine, but a major hurdle lies in how to isolate these parasites when they dress themselves in the host's cells. Camouflage warfare.

Robin must have sensed that I didn't have the
courage to put up my hand in that audience—men,
mainly doctors with white hair—because the last
question of the evening was mine coming from his
mouth. About the Blue and White Niles. He
remembers everything, it seems.

Our mood is sober as we talk about cutbacks
to the NHS, and how the hospital is responding to
the increase in HIV-related infections. I tell him
about the work Amina and I do on Saturdays, the
refugees we encounter, my certainty that if there is
no anonymous HIV testing you'll never have people like this taking the test.

He understands my concerns, sees a real argument, but I feel I'm talking far too much, giving
up a layer of skin.

"How did you become interested in medicine in
the first place?" he asks as he pulls up to the curb.

"Long story," I reply. "For another time. I
should get home now, anyway," I say, reaching for
the door handle.

Robin laughs. "I only stopped here because you
haven't told me where you live. All I know is that
it's somewhere in the vicinity of this bus stop."

I hesitate.

"Can I at least drive you to your door?" he asks.

"Thank you, but I can walk from here."

"Okay. Well, thank you for coming with me."

"Thank *you*. It was extremely informative," I
say, retreating to workplace formality.

Part Four.

—

# Harar, Ethiopia

1972–74

## The Emperor.

—

Moments of solitude were rare in a city like Harar, privacy an incomprehensible notion. Even sick, where the farenji way was to cocoon you in quiet and dark, the Harari way was to entertain you with music and song, never leave your side, for there was always the fear that you might have been possessed by the zar, the darkest of the jinn spirits.

Berchas offered a compromise: a way of being alone in the company of others, solitude sanctioned and contained by witness, but in a city so overflowing with people and animals and their noise, needs and waste, transcendence was required, and for that, qat was the key.

I came, through sheer persistence, to find its hidden pleasure. I discovered how to grind the leaves to a pulp between my teeth and patiently extract their gentle power, to rise like a balloon and float in a slow, dull sky. People said it aided concentration, freed the mind from the cumbersome body, helping one persist through the monotony of prayer on Thursday nights, helping students pass their exams. It seemed to take me through a cloud and down a rabbit hole where I was a child and two people named Alice and Philip dressed up in funny costumes and spoke in riddles for my amusement and theirs. I visited their world, and if ever I was disoriented, they simply pointed me in the direction of up. I rather liked being able to visit but I wouldn't have wanted to live there. I was different from them. It was here that I belonged: in this dark room alive with conversation, at Aziz's side, feeling the heat radiating from his skin, feeling my own temperature rise.

I looked forward to Saturdays with an eagerness I did my best to conceal from Nouria. I brushed my teeth with a stick whittled from the wood of a special tree, the bark of which tasted like licorice. I rubbed used cooking oil into the soles of my feet in the dark of the kitchen at night.

I made my way to Aziz's uncle's house alone now, slipping out one gate and back through the next, first stopping at the market to buy qat. I'd learned how to choose the best leaves and bargain the sellers down. *This looks like yesterday's qat. Are you trying to swindle me because I am a farenji? Don't you think I can tell the difference? I would not even give you one birr for qat with such rough edges.* Or another tack: *Oh, Mouna, that is such a pretty dress you're wearing. You must have had to sell a lot of qat to purchase such beautiful cloth. You are so hardworking, and so generous, your co-wives are so lucky they have you among them. And your daughter, my, she looks just like you, she is so lucky to have you for a mother, to inherit such beauty, no doubt you will have such a difficult time choosing between all her suitors. Oh, you are so sweet, you saved this bundle of young leaves just for me? But I'm afraid I have only one birr with me today.* It could take half an hour.

Exchanging greetings with Aziz's uncle could take another half an hour. He would greet me in Arabic, wishing me an afternoon full of light, and I would wish him an afternoon full of cream. He would greet me in Harari, asking if I had peace, then greet me in Oromiffa, Somali and occasionally Amharic. It amused us both. Invariably I stammered. Unlike the Hararis, I didn't seem to have the capacity for more languages. They switched between them as easily as if they were changing veils. My inability to do so seemed to be the thing that amused Aziz's uncle most of all.

There was always much discussion about the events of the week at these berchas, discussions in which I began to engage more fully as I learned more about the secular world that concerned them. I brought a notebook with me, to record new words. The men often talked about the world beyond our walls, a world that seemed so unsettled in comparison to the peace and order of life in our city. One week it was Palestine, the next, Algeria or Uganda.

Tajuddin was stripping qat leaves off their stalks as fast as a goat when he told us that the Ugandan president, Idi Amin, had announced the expulsion of all the Asians in the country.

"But how can he do that?" I asked.

"The Asians control the marketplace," Aziz said. "They have most of the wealth in Uganda."

"A dictator can do anything he wants," added Munir.

"He'll destroy the economy," Tajuddin said, shaking his head.

"Haile Selassie is apparently very angry about it," said Aziz.

"Why's that?" I asked.

"It's part of Idi Amin's efforts to strengthen ties with certain Arab countries," he replied.

"Haile Selassie feels lonely," Munir said. "We have Muslims in the north—in Egypt and in Eritrea—and in Djibouti and Somalia, and on the other side, in the Sudan, so, you see, he feels Ethiopia is this small island of Christianity floating in this Muslim sea."

"But his own mother was a Muslim," I said. In fact, I remembered the man who had driven Hussein and me to Harar from the capital telling me that the emperor's mother was a Muslim from Harar. The emperor loves Harar, the driver had said, describing it as a place where Muslims and Christians are locked together in an embrace.

Munir raised his eyebrows in surprise. "Well," he said, clearing his throat, "his mother died when he was small. And besides, it doesn't matter who your mother was, it matters only who your father was, and his father was Ras Makonnen, the last emperor. No father could matter more among the Christians."

When mirqana had descended, Aziz rose, and at

the push of a button the white dot exploded to reveal a familiar picture. The emperor's convoy approached the palace. A thousand people prostrated themselves before the gates in anticipation of the arrival of the King of Kings.

The golden gates only hinted at the extraordinary wealth beyond. The north wing, where Hussein and I had spent a week, boasted a series of rooms off a long corridor of speckled marble, closed off from the rest of the palace by a set of double doors the height of trees. Hussein had cowered behind me, peeking over my shoulder while I opened the first of those doors along the corridor.

Gilt-edged mirrors and ornate furniture painted white and gold filled the rooms.

"Look at this," I remember marvelling as I ran a finger over the silk bedspread in the master bedroom. "Have you ever seen anything like it, Hussein?"

"The Gardens of Eternity," he said dreamily. "The righteous shall be adorned therein with bracelets of gold and pearls; and their garments there will be of silk."

"They will recline therein on raised thrones," I quoted in reply.

I left Hussein and explored what lay behind the rest of the closed doors. When I reached the drawing room I threw open the shutters to let in the glow of the late-afternoon sun. I stared out the window at a pond where pink flamingos were being pink flamingos—perched on single legs, pecking at fleas under their wings.

Miriam, the woman the palace secretary had assigned to look after us, entered the room then, carrying a wide tray.

"Buna," she said firmly, placing the tray on the table.

"Buna," I said in reply, thinking it must mean hello in Amharic.

Miriam lifted the white cloth to reveal tiny white coffee cups and a black clay coffee pot.

"Buna," she said again, pointing at the tray, and then went over to the window to close the shutters. "No good," she said, shaking her head.

"But it is good," I protested, opening the shutters again.

Miriam put her hands on her hips and sighed. She left the room, returning a few minutes later with a small hibachi full of coals. I watched as she kneeled on the floor and shook a large flat pan of green coffee beans over the heat. They spat and smouldered as they browned, and the stream of rich smoke enticed Hussein into the room.

Miriam scraped the beans off the pan into a mortar and began to grind them with a wooden pestle. She threw in a cardamom pod, and when she'd ground it all into a rich black dust, she lifted it by the spoonful and slid it delicately down the narrow neck of the clay coffee pot.

We kneeled on cushions Miriam had placed on the floor, and she handed us each a cup. I glared at Hussein, afraid he was about to refuse. Miriam offered us popcorn to accompany the coffee, producing it magically from inside her skirt. It was a

strange combination, but I, who had not seen popcorn since attending a fair in southern France with
my parents a lifetime ago, grabbed white kernels
by the fistful.

We drank three small cups and then she
rearranged everything neatly on the tray and carried it away. We sat in silence, unsure of what we
should be doing. But Miriam returned immediately and drew a bath. She asked for our laundry
as well. I dumped out the contents of my rucksack
and handed over every one of my few articles of
clothing. Miriam looked for more—suitcases,
valises, hatboxes and trunks, the luggage of previous farenjis.

We sat down to dinner, just Hussein and I, at a
table covered in white cloth laid with silver knives
and forks, salt and pepper shakers, wine glasses
and silver serving dishes under gleaming silver
lids. Hussein flinched at the display on the table.
The desert had made us so serious, placed us under
so much strain. I gladly relished the pleasures we
were being offered, while Hussein seemed determined to remain joyless.

"Could you at least remove *that*," he said, pointing at the bottle of wine.

I set the offending object on the floor.

"Bismillah," said Hussein, reluctantly lifting
the alien fork and knife to sample the feast before
us: quail swimming in sweet juices flavoured with
onions and apples and walnuts, accompanied by
some soft green vegetable soaked in garlic and oil.
And under the third silver lid, a mountain of chips,

cut by hand into long thin strips, glistening with oil and salt. It was the best meal I'd ever eaten.

Here in a dark storage room, perched above a congested city where disease moves far more freely and easily than people, it was difficult to believe I was in the same country. That this was the city where the emperor was born.

"The drama is about to begin," Aziz said. He reached for my hand and began outlining the plot of the show in whispers. "This man is devoted to serving the emperor, and you see this woman? His wife? She has some scheme with her husband's brother to steal a small medallion that the emperor gave her husband in recognition of his service."

I couldn't distinguish between the episodes from week to week. There were always schemers, usually women, trying to sabotage a loyal servant of the emperor. The schemers always came to ruin in the end, and while a man might have lost his wife, his children, his brothers, his limbs, he never lost his loyalty, and for that he was ultimately rewarded.

The music of the finale blared and the picture sizzled to a stop. Aziz did not let go of my hand even though the others were standing up, brushing qat debris off their clothes as they commented on the story's predictable end.

He leaned close to my ear. "Stay," he whispered before standing up to say goodbye to his friends. I sat in the corner of the humid room, examining the henna on my nails, and muttered "Masalaama" to each one of the group.

"See you next Saturday," they each said.

Aziz closed the door, shutting us back into a room smelling of incense and sweat.

"Don't worry," he said, adjusting his sarong at the waist and sitting down.

"I should leave, Aziz. It is too haram." They say that when a man and woman are alone together the devil is their third companion.

"You are a very good Muslim," he said. "I admire this about you."

"Even if you don't agree with the importance I place on it."

"It's not a question of whether I agree or not. I think what I admire is the inner strength this conviction gives you. This is not an easy place for an outsider, but you have this certainty about you, because of your faith, perhaps, and it has allowed you to fight for a place here."

"It's the only certainty I have."

"I don't even have that," he said, taking both my hands in his. "My point is only that I don't want you to lose your place."

"What do you mean?"

"You are earning a good reputation as a teacher," he said. "You need to be more careful. You've worked hard to earn the community's respect. You don't need the rumours to start again."

He was right: I shouldn't come here any more. It was far too risky. The women would call me a sharmuta, withdraw their children from my class, banish and condemn me to hell if they had any idea of my flirtation with the devil on Saturdays, of the daydreams that polluted an otherwise pious life.

"It is best if you don't suggest any familiarity with the emperor," he continued.

"What does the emperor have to do with it?"

"This fact of his mother being a Muslim."

"But doesn't everybody know that?"

"Maybe, but still, it invites curiosity to speak of him with any familiarity. Do you know this English expression, the walls have ears?"

I didn't. All I knew was that God sees everything. God saw this: Aziz bowing his head and kissing my right hand in that fleshy triangle where thumb meets forefinger. The way a pilgrim kisses the hand of a disciple. "It is not religious transgression you have to worry about," he said, "it is political."

## The Inner Sanctum.

—

It was my determination that made my reputation as a good teacher, but there were limits to what I could accomplish with one Qur'an, my Qur'an with its faded green leather cover, leaving gold dust on all who touched it. When one group of students had memorized a chapter by repeating line by line, verse by verse, I took the book in my hands and read them the entirety of the next chapter before we began again, line by line, giving song to each word.

The older ones had the advantage of being able to write each line down on the two slates Fathi and Anwar had once used at the madrasa, giving them a visual association that helped them build a picture of a chapter in their minds. They were doing well, had progressed as far as the twelfth chapter, but to memorize each chapter individually is not to know the Qur'an. The Great Abdal had taught me that the relationships between chapters are just as vital.

To know the Qur'an is to hold the book in your hands at a distance, too far to read the actual words but familiar enough with their patterns on the page that the book is less text than compass. If you have simply memorized the text in sequence you have no words when someone asks you to recite chapter forty. Unless you are one of those rare geniuses who can see the book laid out in his mind, you have to run through thirty-nine chapters in your head before you can speak.

I needed more copies of the holy book. It occurred to me that Hussein might be able to help. I asked Gishta to ask him if he would come and visit me at Nouria's compound.

She shook her head. "That one does not leave the compound, not ever. You will have to go to him."

But that was impossible. She knew that.

"This Sunday," she raised her finger and said coyly, "our dear sheikh makes his monthly visit to his mother in Dire Dawa."

I was astonished to hear the sheikh had a mother. He struck me as so old. "Why is she not here with him?" I asked.

"She prefers Dire Dawa because there is no Fatima there."

"You mean Fatima your co-wife?"

"Exactly," said Gishta, forming claws with her hands.

And so, that Sunday morning, after brief lessons with my students, I threw my darkest veil over my head and made a hasty exit into the street. I walked through the meat section of the market, where the halal offerings of the butchers hung with bulging eyes off giant hooks, past the fruit sellers hidden behind their yellow and orange pyramids, through swarms of flies and the grey stench of diesel and down the steep street on the far side of the market where the tailors hemmed away against the open blue metal doors of their shops.

I passed Oromo girls carrying more than their body weight in firewood, lepers on street corners waving their begging stumps, and Harari men with white knit skullcaps making their way to work in the shops lining the one paved road through the centre of town. These merchants sold cheap imported goods from China and India—textiles, electronics and dinnerware—and dry goods, medicines and tobacco. The main street was a symphony of screeching metal doors and boisterous greetings shouted over tins of vegetable oil and bolts of cloth.

People greeted me en route, I them. "Have you peace this morning?" "Peace, thanks to God," we each asked and replied as we moved through the narrow, rubble-strewn lanes of the city, lanes so narrow they have names like "Meeting and Reconciliation," for you may be forced to make peace with an enemy—and there are always enemies—in order to pass.

My presence seemed as ordinary as the smells of donkey dung, rancid butter and frankincense. I felt relieved, in the wake of Aziz's cautioning, that I was finally unremarkable.

—

Sheikh Jami's compound was an entirely different place without visitors, an oasis of calm, with aromatic herbs ringing its perimeter and fruit trees full of birds. The courtyard was largely empty. Fatima, Zehtahoun and Gishta had left early for the fields, as they did every morning, carrying great leather satchels on their backs, flat as deflated lungs.

Uncle Jami's farmlands were close to the city, beginning just beyond the river. They grew stimulants and fruit—qat, coffee, mangoes, oranges, bananas. The qat had to be picked fresh every day, for the softer and greener the leaves, the more intoxicating their effect and the higher the price consumers (both the addicts and the ordinary) were willing to pay. The fruit didn't have to be picked as often, the coffee even less often than that.

When their satchels were half full, the women would take a break, squatting on their haunches in the shade of an orange tree to share tea. Later, once they'd collected the day's fill, they made their way back to the city, climbing uphill to relieve their burden in the market.

Uncle Jami was so rich that his wives sold the qat in bulk to brokers who in turn employed girls to sell to customers throughout the day. Women who were less well off sat down on their skirts and sold qat straight out of their satchels. They sold to the wild-eyed man who preferred the green leaves to food and waited nervously in the marketplace from the first crack of morning, to the merchant who, like every other merchant in this city, purchased a generous amount after lunch to chew throughout the afternoon in the back of his shop, to the middle-aged woman who chewed the leaves of a few stalks with her friends as they weaved baskets and sorted grains throughout the afternoon, to the pious old man who had no teeth any longer and had to grind his qat with a pestle, adding sugar and water to form a thick paste, and to everyone who was paying a visit to a shrine—the adolescent and the ancient—for it was an essential component of any offering in a city of saints.

At the end of the day, any remaining qat was sold to dealers who shrink-wrapped and transported it to Djibouti and beyond.

It was a drug, the basis of an economy, a spiritual lubricant, a way of life.

I smelled petrol and heard the swish of a broom being used behind one of the buildings. Each of the sheikh's wives had her own house. The large wooden doors of these buildings opened onto the common courtyard, at the far side of which was the separate building Sheikh Jami shared with his sons.

Each of the wives also had a servant, an Oromo girl—child, really—plucked from the countryside where her parents were tenant farmers on Harari lands. The girls swept the courtyard every morning, sprinkling water over the earth behind them to settle any dust. They brushed away goat feces and dead cockroaches and poured petrol over thresholds to deter flies.

They resurrected a fire in the shared kitchen, a blackened hut where they reheated a giant cauldron that cradled an endless stew. They added more contaminated water, more garlic, more chili and fenugreek, leaving it there to simmer until the women's return from the fields.

Once a week, the girls would grind sorghum, for Hararis sopped up their stew with injera made from sorghum rather than the bitter teff used elsewhere in Ethiopia. It made them fatter, and the fatter they were, the wealthier they appeared. I was the antithesis of the Harari ideal: long and thin like a poor Somali nomad.

Gishta was constantly complaining about the servants. Every week, one of them would run away because she'd been beaten by one of the wives or fondled by one of the sheikh's many sons, denied her wages because of some misdemeanor, or simply because she missed her family, missed a world where she was loved, for beyond its borders they called her people the Galla, "the uncivilized."

Gishta was just as likely to administer a beating as the others. It was one of the privileges she enjoyed for the hard work spent erasing her origins, work that had paid off with the ultimate coup— marrying a Harari man, and such a distinguished one at that. Here was the cement that had solidified all the foundations she had spent years laying down.

"For you too," she'd begun to say to me. "*Especially* for you. It will be the only way."

I passed a number of the sheikh's children, too young and too absorbed in their stone-throwing game to remark as I walked across the courtyard toward the small white domed building clinging to the far wall. Through the arched doorway, I peeked into the dark cave-like interior of the shrine for the first time. I stepped gingerly over the threshold into a cloud of incense and paused as I adjusted to the dim.

This was the inner sanctum. It was here that Sheikh Jami spent most of his time, and on Thursdays where he received visitors, people of the city and the surrounding countryside, and occasionally pilgrims from afar. One by one, visitors would fall to their knees before him, kissing the back of his giant hand. They would present offerings of qat, milk, money and crystals of incense or grains wrapped in newspaper cones. They would whisper their requests into his ear and breathe gratitude as he threw incense into a pot of burning coals, releasing their prayers into the sweet smoke that rose to form a great sticky cloud above the congregation. Thus blessed, each visitor would take a seat against the walls of the shrine, lean back and begin stuffing their cheeks with qat, slowly grinding the leaves between their molars to extract their hypnotic power.

At sunset, the drumming would begin, calling the rest of the faithful to the shrine. Only then, once darkness had fallen and the courtyard had filled with people, would I normally arrive.

Today, the grey mist of incense cleared to reveal Hussein sitting alone: Idris, Sheikh Jami's other apprentice, taught at the Bilal al Habash Madrasa in the centre of the city in the mornings.

"Lilly," Hussein said vaguely, looking somewhere over my shoulder.

"Yes, it's me."

"I thought you were the jinn."

"Me?"

"To see you here. So, you have heard, then."

"Heard what?"

"That our Great Abdal has passed."

I bent to my knees before him and covered my face with my hands as the weight of this news sank like a stone in my stomach.

Someone had sent news of the Great Abdal's death to Sheikh Jami. According to Hussein, he had died "the ordinary way"—of old age. He had remained at the shrine, steadfast through the political changes. He had not been killed. At least there was that.

"Innalillahi wa inna ilayhi raji'un," we both whispered. We are from Allah and to him we are returning.

I put my head against Hussein's shoulder. He didn't move. "Maybe we shouldn't have left him," I said after a few minutes.

"We didn't leave him," Hussein said calmly. "He is in you, he is in me, he is in Uncle Jami."

"I'm trying to carry on his good work," I told Hussein. "I'm teaching Qur'an to the children in Gishta's cousin's neighbourhood."

"So I hear."

"You know?"

"Bint Abdal. I am always listening with one ear."

So he had not altogether abandoned the profane world where I lived. The rumbling low tone of the muezzin's call began then, and I straightened. Idris would be returning at lunchtime. I wiped my eyes with the edge of Hussein's rough wool and rushed to tell him about my class, how limited we were by the use of only one Qur'an. Surely there were others here? Surely I might borrow one without it going noticed?

He looked at me blankly.

"No?" I ventured.

He picked up a bunch of qat stalks and offered them in lieu of saying there was nothing he could do to help me. The sky above was now filled with the chorus of the muezzins of all the nearby mosques—I really did have to move.

"It's okay," I said, standing up quickly. "I'll sort it out. Peace be upon you." I bent down to hurry out the door, but as soon as I stepped across the threshold I smacked straight into Idris's chest. He hissed and shuddered as though he had just been doused with cold water and he jumped back to let me pass. I bolted across the courtyard and out into the street.

—

I found Bortucan alone at home, scratching her ear with one hand, jabbing a stick into the dirt with the other. I picked her up and carried her around on my hip while I nattered away and paced the courtyard. "How am I going to sort it out, Bee? Too many students, not enough books. All the willingness in the world, but so many obstacles."

Bortucan was distracted by her itchy scalp. I pulled her hand away to find her fingers covered in blood. "Oh, Bee," I groaned. It was obvious a mess lay under her hair. Since Nouria wasn't around, I didn't have to consult. I carried her up the paved road and out the main gate.

Bortucan whimpered at the sight of the hospital, clearly remembering it. I held her firmly with both arms and climbed up the steps.

We passed several doctors and nurses before seeing someone I recognized.

"Hey! It's the Harari-speaking farenji and her sister," Munir joked as he came toward us.

"Her scalp's bleeding."

"Shall we have a look?" he asked, stroking Bortucan's cheek.

"If you'd like," I said.

"Ahh. I will go and find your doctor," he said with a wink.

Aziz rounded the corner a few minutes later, breaking into a smile. "Munir told me that a beautiful girl was asking for me."

"It's Bortucan," I blurted out.

"I can see that," he said. "Her scalp."

I followed him into a green room, where I sat Bortucan down in a chair and he gingerly parted her hair. As he shaved around the bloody area he found several raised red patches. In the end, all her hair had to come off. She held her curls between her fingertips, looking at them as if they did not belong to her.

"It's a type of worm," Aziz explained. "It burrows

under the skin and lays its eggs there. This one here? She broke the surface with her nails and the eggs were released. I'm going to have to break the others."

"Ouch."

"We'll give her something to make her sleepy."

When he returned, I held Bortucan while Aziz slipped a needle into her arm. She made a noise like a wounded cat. I felt the warmth of Aziz's breath on my neck and the sudden heaviness of Bortucan going limp in my arms.

I laid her down and Aziz made small incisions in her scalp, applying hot towels and pressure to the four other nests. He finished by painting her scalp purple.

"Come, we'll have a cup of tea," he said. "She won't wake for another half-hour."

We sat in a small courtyard behind the hospital where several other men and women in white and green were seated together. The laws of separation did not appear to apply here. Aziz bought two tin cups of tea from the hospital canteen, set them down and pulled a bag of white powder out of his pocket.

"Powdered milk," he explained, offering me some. "I don't drink any other kind. Is Bortucan learning anything in your class?"

"A little."

"Zemzem's father seems to be very impressed with his daughter."

"She's exceptional. By far the brightest. Trouble is, there's only so much I can do with one Qur'an.

I can't exactly tear out the pages so they can each study the part they need to work on."

"I know everything about having only limited resources to do your work. I wish there was something I could do to help."

"Do you have a Qur'an we could use?"

"I do," he said, raising his eyebrows. "And I'll ask Munir."

The next day Zemzem brought a piece of injera to class for me. Folded into it was a note from Aziz: "I have a solution for your problem. If you can meet me half an hour earlier at my uncle's house on Saturday, I can show you." This time it was signed not "Your friend" but "Your servant."

I met him in his uncle's courtyard just after noon that Saturday and followed him into the main room. His uncle opened a wooden chest in a corner, revealing dozens of thin leather-bound booklets. Each one contained a juz, the text of a thirtieth of the Qur'an. These were used on only one occasion, during the month of Safar, the dangerous month when people must not marry or travel, one juz for each day of the month. Aziz's uncle was a member of a council of elders who met each night of Safar to read through one booklet and keep the danger at bay.

"For the children," said his uncle.

I looked at Aziz. What a gift.

"He just needs them back for Safar. For the rest of the year they're yours."

We kneeled together and counted out two full dusty sets, which we wrapped in an old leather satchel used for carrying qat. I was speechless throughout, aware only of the soft worn leather passing through my hands and the desire to touch Aziz's skin.

"From Hussein," I lied to Nouria, stacking the booklets in the corner of our room.

The Book of Lies.

—

Several different chapters being recited simultaneously produced a blissful blur of holy words that echoed throughout the city: my students reciting while Sufis sat in shrines and recited the ninety-nine names of God, and holy men like Sheikh Jami recounted Hadiths and imams sat in mosques and spoke to God and qadis filled their courtrooms with words of holy law and muezzins flooded the sky with their invitations.

With aid of the booklets, my older students could address their own weaknesses, working on the chapters they knew least well. I tapped a stick against the wall, encouraging them to keep a measured and consistent pace. At the madrasas the teachers used a whip, which they lashed against the floor and, not infrequently, across the palms and backs of their students.

When the older children had managed to repeat an entire chapter as a group, without interruption, without falter or hesitation, I'd tap them into the next. With the younger students, more guidance was required. They would listen and repeat each line of a verse. I would correct their pronunciation, offer a line to jog their memories when they began to falter, encourage them to sway from side to side and find the rhythm of each verse in their bodies. She hadn't gone beyond the first chapter, but Bortucan served as a metronome for the others.

Once the eldest six could recite the entire first third of the Qur'an together, we deemed it time for a celebration. Nouria and I invited the students' parents over one Friday morning. Gishta made a huge tray of sweets and provided milk and sugar for tea. All the children were instructed to wear their very best clothes, even though for some of them this simply meant a laundered version of the clothes they wore every day.

The six children stood in a row facing east, Fathi and Anwar among them. I wore the traditional dress Gishta had had made for me and stood before them and recited the first line of a randomly selected chapter from the first third of the book. They repeated that line and then carried on through the rest of the chapter without me. I then turned the pages of the book and read out the first line of another chapter.

The parents stood stone still, mesmerized.

"Do they know which chapters you are going to select?" asked one father just as I was poised to choose a third.

"No. Here." I held out the book to him. "You choose."

He approached hesitantly and looked at the book over my shoulder. I turned the pages for him and invited him to tell me where to stop.

"Yes, there, there is good," he said.

"Please, go ahead," I encouraged him, nodding at the expectant children.

He cleared his throat and sang the first line of the third chapter. He had a beautiful voice, but the page before us showed the beginning of chapter five.

As the children finished the chapter, he burst into applause. More than one mother cried, and Nouria's expression was one of rapture, as if she had never before been this close to God.

"They are as good as the rich children at the madrasas!" declared Zemzem's father.

There were murmurs of agreement all round.

"We shall bring them to Uncle Jami," said Gishta.

I glared at her. *What was she thinking?* The parents, too, murmured with uncertainty. Sheikh Jami was an imposing figure.

"All the Harari children do this," Gishta said with a wave of her arm.

"True, true," the parents agreed. The madrasas brought their students to the shrine once a year so that they could demonstrate their learning and receive the saint's blessing for continued success.

"But those children are wealthy and well dressed," one mother said.

"Shame on you," Gishta chastised. "We are all equal in the eyes of God."

—

I warmed to the idea that Gishta seemed to have adopted as something of a mission. My students deserved the sheikh's recognition as much as any other students and he could not, at least, fault me as a teacher.

"He *hates* farenjis!" Gishta delighted in telling me. "The tourists are one thing, but the worst ones are those who come here and say they are on a spiritual mission. Ooh, this makes him so mad!"

"But does that really happen?"

"Oh, maybe once every five or so years. They say they are Sufis. One came from England, another from a place called Florida. I like this word, *Florida*, it sounds like a girl's name. One from Pakistan. And one from California, another girl's name. Why do farenjis call their cities after girls?"

"My father was from a place called Basingstoke," I offered.

"*That*," she said, "is a ridiculous name."

The sheikh apparently treated the arrival of any foreigner claiming to be on a spiritual journey with a suspicion bordering on contempt. *You want to learn the Sufi way?* he would demand of them. *Then you must live as an ascetic, renounce all worldliness, all mortal concerns, walk barefoot in the hot sand, live off scraps, refuse, have one thought and one thought only—that of eliminating the self, erasing the ego through devotion, seeking grace, seeking unity with the divine.*

And they begged, *Oh yes, yes, please, my master,*

*that is exactly what I want,* and threw themselves at his feet, saying they would do anything, anything at all.

It wasn't his job to test the limits of their devotion; the test was of their own making. But the conviction of the foreigner inevitably proved as thin as his reedy voice. Gishta's husband did not believe a foreigner was capable of giving up mortal pleasures, no matter how much of a Sufi he claimed to be. Each and every one of them eventually proved himself a hypocrite. There was the one who came with chocolate that he hid under a blanket. There was the one who took farenji medicine that made him have violent dreams while awake. There was a particularly terrible one who'd kept a change of clothes in a post office box just in case he ever felt the need for a break—a binge where he could dress in a suit and stay at the Ras Hotel in Dire Dawa, drink beer and pay a sharmuta for company.

But this would be different, Gishta insisted. Because I was a farenji doing good by teaching the poor children of Harar.

—

We were a shining bunch with nervous smiles. Nouria had had new shirts made for her boys out of one of her long-ago deceased husband's shirts, which appeared magically, as if it had been lying in wait for just such an occasion. The mothers of three of the four female students had hennaed their daughters' hands and given them new white

veils like the children of the formal madrasas wear;
the boys wore white knit skullcaps. I had dressed
Zemzem myself.

Gishta met us in the laneway, pulling strands of
silver beads from her pocket and looping them
around the astonished girls' necks. She showered
all the children with perfume before leading us
through the green archway.

Her co-wives, Fatima and Zehtahoun, had left
for the fields that morning without her—though
not before Fatima had cursed her with the ultimate Harari insult, calling her a lazy wife. A servant girl stopped sweeping, surprised by the sight
of us, and Sheikh Jami's voice floated through the
door of the shrine. He and Hussein were reading
together as they did every morning—esoteric texts
with accounts of miraculous events, and some of
the more obscure Hadiths, records of the actions
and sayings of the Prophet made by his companions and descendants.

We hovered at the entrance to the shrine, the
children fidgeting. Most of them had been here in
the compound among the hundreds one Thursday
night or another, but never had they entered the
shrine and stood before the sheikh and asked for
his attention. Anwar's grin wavered. He started
when I put my hand on his shoulder.

Gishta held me by the arm. "It would be best if
you stayed back," she whispered. She nudged the
children through the door, and they filed inside.

"Bismillah al-rahman al-rahim," the eldest boy
began singing after a moment, leading the group

into their recitation of a section of the Qur'an particularly favoured in Harar because it refers to seeking refuge in sympathetic lands.

I stood holding my breath, one hand on the wall of the shrine, one hand on my heart. I had Aziz to thank for this moment.

"Very good," I heard the sheikh say, though not congratulating them with any particular vigour. "But I don't understand. Which madrasa are you from?"

"Bint Abdal's," said the oldest boy.

"Bint Abdal," the sheikh grumbled. "Who is this Bint Abdal?"

"Our teacher," answered the boy.

"Yes, yes, but who is she?"

Gishta nudged me forward. I ducked through the entrance and stood beside my students.

The sheikh stared, utterly silent, Hussein kneeling beside him. "Masha'Allah," the sheikh eventually muttered, shaking his massive head. Hussein opened his mouth as if he were about to speak. Anwar, still wearing that petrified grin, reached for my hand.

"Ya'Allah," the sheikh said dramatically, clasping his meaty hands together in front of his face. He inhaled deeply, eyes closed.

One of the girls stepped backwards, and the rest of the children followed her lead.

Suddenly the sheikh looked up, his eyes brimming yellow. He threw his arms wide and bellowed: "Farenji!" He roared something that roughly translated meant bastard child of a charlatan.

Then he named Muhammed Bruce Mahmoud. The booming bass notes coming from his mouth would have shaken the foundations had there been any, but instead they fell dead against the soft clay walls, the ratty rugs and dirt floor.

One of the children began to blub, and Gishta's hands suddenly appeared through the doorway, tugging at the children's clothes, pulling them out into the light.

"Gishta!" the sheikh shouted. "What is this?"

She spoke timidly through the door. "The students have come for blessing," she said.

"But with a farenji? We do not learn our Islam from farenjis! These people are useless! Liars! Thieves!" he shouted.

"How dare you judge me," I said, staring into the oily puddles in his eyes.

He was fuming, about to erupt.

"Only God can judge what is in another person's heart," I said into the dim. "Peace be upon you." I ducked out through the door to join my students.

—

"Do you remember this man Muhammed Bruce?" I asked Gishta once we'd made our humbled way back to Nouria's compound. She nodded vigorously. Muhammed Bruce Mahmoud, she told me, was legendary as one of the most dangerous pilgrims who had ever set foot on Harari soil. He, who had claimed to be an albino Pakistani raised in poverty in Lahore, had been taken in by the sheikh, but made the rather great mistake of hiding his secrets inside the hollow of one of the trees in the compound.

Shortly after Muhammed Bruce's arrival, Sheikh Jami had thrown some burning coals inside that very hollow followed by a few lumps of incense, as he did once a month in honour of Bilal al Habash's mother. That month he was met not by a sweet spiral of smoke billowing forth from the tree but rather by a smell decidedly more toxic. He was forced to throw a can of water into the hollow, dousing the smouldering fire.

Bewildered, he reached inside the tree and pulled out a soaked and partially burned satchel. Inside, he found a roll of banknotes, a passport of the man who called himself Muhammed identifying him as Bruce Mac-something of the United Kingdom, a flask of alcohol, a book about Harar and a set of playing cards depicting naked boys.

Sheikh Jami had sent Bruce and his burned satchel full of poison packing. "A less peaceful man would have killed you," the sheikh had said. "But *that*, I'll leave up to God."

The one thing the sheikh had kept was the book, because books were revered, words were power. "A farenji book of lies about Harar," Gishta told me with a shudder. "You will see! You will see!" she exclaimed. "I will bring it and you will see."

The next afternoon she dropped a battered volume onto the ground at my feet. It was *First Footsteps in East Africa: A Journey to Harar*, by Sir Richard Burton, the famous explorer Muhammed

Bruce had boasted was his great-great-uncle.

The sheikh could not read the book, but one of his scholarly friends had underlined certain passages and written Arabic translations in the margins.

Gishta looked over my shoulder as I read the underlined passages. Burton called the place "a paradise inhabited by asses." He denounced the people as "religious fanatics," "bigoted," "barbarous," "coarse and debauched," "disfigured by disease," with ugly voices: "the men's loud and rude," "the women's harsh and screaming."

He boasted of being the one to break the guardian spell said to protect the city and its people. He had sought to tear away the shroud of Islam and render the Harari people naked, vulnerable, beholden. To subjugate through contamination.

"But he didn't break the guardian spell," I said, turning to look at Gishta. Burton or no Burton, Islam was within and all around us. And Sheikh Jami, as descendant of the greatest of all the saints of Harar, was the fulcrum of this world; he was its heartbeat.

"But after this man, the farenjis started coming," said Gishta.

"Even if they'd come and destroyed all the mosques and all the shrines, Islam would not have been broken," I said.

"Maybe one day you will write another farenji book and tell the truth," Nouria said.

"Insha'Allah," I replied.

"My husband is a blind man if he cannot see what is in your heart," said Gishta.

## Kissing in English.

—

Nouria and I took turns pouring water for each other to perform our ablutions each morning.

*Allahu akbar*—our necks, nostrils and mouths were washed clean.

*Allahu akbar*—our hands, forearms, head, feet and ankles.

Night's sins were washed away, fell in droplets to the ground, and thus purified, we kneeled together and prayed.

I'd taken to returning to bed for another hour, even though such behaviour wasn't encouraged. Nouria indulged me to a certain extent because, as she and Gishta had taken to reminding me, I would soon enough have to take on all the responsibilities of the adult world. Not only was laziness not a virtue but being by yourself, they said, left your soul susceptible to the invasion of evil spirits. I'd developed a terrible suspicion they might be right. In my solitude, I couldn't help but indulge secret longing. While I could discipline my brain to maintain purity of thought, my senses betrayed me.

They had independent will, their own memories.

The warmth of his pink palms. The faint smell of sweat ironed deeply, repeatedly, into a cotton shirt. The chocolate brown of his irises. The butter-soft of his skin. The solid wholeness of his presence: not heavy, but bearing remarkable weight.

Our stolen moments, late on Saturday afternoons in a dark room once used for storing tobacco leaves; the secret world we shared with our friends.

—

Sadia had started to visit me after school for English lessons because she wanted to impress Munir. Our lessons were rather limited; she was interested in only one subject.

"I would be," our first lesson began, with me exaggerating each word.

"I would be," Sadia repeated.

"Honoured . . ."

"Unnerred . . ."

"To be . . ."

"To be . . ."

"Your wife."

"Your wife!" Sadia squealed.

"Uss!" I had to quiet her as Nouria and Gishta looked up from where they were squatting on the other side of the compound, dipping straw into dyes, one bucket of bright pink, one bucket of the Prophet's favoured green.

We burst out laughing and grabbed each other by the shoulders. Gishta looked over at us with amusement, a certain fondness, pleased to see the two of us being ordinary teenagers. They were delighted that Sadia and I were friends. *Such a good girl*, they always said. *From such a good family. Her father has made the haj seven times. And she herself made the haj at such a young age.*

But little do they know what good girls from good families get up to on Saturdays. It is more than just holding hands, Sadia was keen to tell me once the women had left the compound to take the dyed straw to Ikhista Aini's next door. She and Munir might leave Aziz's uncle's house separately, but only to reconvene ten minutes later behind one of the thatched roundhouses that sit in a cluster beyond the closest gate.

"The leper colony?"

"Exactly. We hide behind the far one so no one sees us. If the lepers saw us, they wouldn't care. They won't speak to our parents, and God knows, no one would believe anything they say anyway."

"But aren't you afraid of catching it?"

"It's not so easy to catch, Munir says. And besides, I would cut off my leg to be with him. I have another. God was very kind to give us two of everything. Well, almost everything!"

"Sadia!" I gasped. "What do you get up to there?"

"Kissing," she whispered conspiratorially.

It was one thing to hold hands in our closed room, but to take the risk of showing affection beyond those walls was quite another. The women would call her something worse than a sharmuta if she were ever caught. They would say no man would ever want her. Perhaps her family would even send her away to Dire Dawa to be rid of the shame.

But Munir did want Sadia for his wife, and the campaign to seduce Sadia's mother into believing she had chosen him for her daughter had already begun. First, Munir went to her family's compound to introduce himself, saying he was available to the family should they ever require the services of a doctor. Next, he took a keen interest in Sadia's brother, who excelled at science, and asked him whether he would be interested in going to medical school. Then, he'd involved his mother, sending her over on what would be the first of several goodwill missions. Although it was fathers who had to give approval, it was mothers who brought forth the candidates; it was mothers who were really in charge.

"Okay, Sadia, now let's be serious," I said. "When Munir tells you that your father has given his approval?"

"I say: I would be unnerred to be wife."

"I would be honoured to be . . ."

"I would be honoured—"

"Sadia?" I interrupted, lowering my voice. "Has Aziz ever had a girlfriend?"

"Mmm . . ." She looked skyward. "Not girlfriend, really, just, I don't know . . . Munir tells me there was one girl in Addis Ababa but she was Amhara."

"A Christian?" I immediately wished I hadn't asked.

"Oh, Lilly, no," she said. "She is Amhara, she cannot be his girlfriend. And besides, whose hand is he holding, hmm?"

—

*My hand*, I tried to reassure myself as I walked along the dusty exterior wall the following Saturday. *My hand in his hand.*

Qat and chatter and television in the dark, the elements of that Saturday's bercha were indistinguishable. I felt sick, wondering if he'd ever kissed the Amhara girl.

Aziz asked me to stay at the end of the bercha as he did every week now. The desire to remain in his company overwhelmed common sense; I would pick up my good Muslim self on the way home. He closed the door after his friends, and it was dark and still again, the sweat of bodies in the air, qat debris strewn about us on the floor. He lifted his sarong slightly and sat cross-legged in front of me. He took my hands from my lap, both my hands in one of his. And then his other hand reached up and cupped my chin.

I swallowed the ball of wool in my throat as he traced the outline of my face with his thumb. My face felt tiny in his hand, like a mango he was holding up to admire.

I raised my hand and put my palm on his cheek. I ran my fingers over his eyebrows, down his nose. Then he caught my finger between his teeth and closed his full lips. He tugged my entire body forward.

This is why the Sufis try to erase the body, I realized in that moment. Not because it is a host for parasites, not because it demands food and water and sleep, but because one mouth to one finger can override the most sacred sentiment, the most pious intention. One mouth to one finger can lead to a kiss and that kiss can change the world.

He released my finger from his mouth and leaned into me, his mouth at my neck. His lips searched my face, grazed my cheek, my eyebrows, my forehead as if he was touching the raised letters of an old gravestone, trying to read the story of a life from its beginning. He wrote the future onto my face with his lips.

"I hear that you silenced the sheikh," he whispered between kisses.

"That wasn't my intention."

"No Harari girl would ever have been so bold."

"I was angry."

"You fight for what you believe in. That is something beautiful and rare."

Obstacles in the Path of Righteousness.

—

The residue of guilt coated my skin like egg white.
One false expression and I feared the sheen would
crack. I prayed for forgiveness every Thursday
night. The sheikh's rejection of me and my students had not deterred me from joining the heaving crowd that gathered round the squat shrine
once a week to celebrate the saint and his miracles.

I bounced from my left foot to my right, whispering prayers. I asked Bilal al Habash to pay special attention to Bortucan, whose mind was not
right, to ensure the Great Abdal was safe in
heaven, to bring good fortune to Nouria, to recognize Hussein's efforts, to help Aziz pass his exams,
to forgive me my flirtation with the devil. I never
mentioned my parents or Muhammed Bruce in my
prayers because I feared they had gone to that
other place, a burning pit Bilal al Habash would
never have occasion to visit.

Hussein stood tall beside Sheikh Jami at the front
of the crowd as the sheikh led us through the dhikr.
I lingered at the back, clapping and dancing and

chewing qat like everybody else. Well, almost like everyone else. Part of me, admittedly, could no longer surrender on these occasions and resisted mirqana. While everybody else's mind loosened and expanded, my focus seemed to telescope to the singular image of a tall and handsome boyish man with a compelling bittersweet smile and a soft voice that contradicted his size.

It was not worship of him, for that would be a crime, the greatest crime a Muslim can commit: idolatry. We who believed in saints were sometimes accused of such a thing. Not everyone condoned our practices; many of the clerics in the cities dismissed our beliefs and rituals. They believed the roots of our devotion lay in the pagan practices that existed here before Islam rolled like a wave over our part of Africa in the ninth century. They called this ignorance, backwardness, African.

Beyond the critics were those who condemned, those who said we were engaged in practices hostile to Islam, saw our beliefs as heretical, our actions as criminal, and would have us imprisoned, even killed. In Saudi Arabia beliefs like ours were seen as a deadly plague. Hararis making the pilgrimage to Mecca had to suppress the names of the saints on their lips, but as soon as they returned home, they headed straight to the shrine of Bilal al Habash to secure his blessing for having fulfilled this pillar of faith.

We felt safe here, under the protection of more than three hundred saints, Bilal supreme among them, in a country with an emperor who was said to love his Muslim subjects as much as his Christian.

But then I had also heard Aziz say that the emperor feared his Ethiopia was a lonely Christian island floating in a Muslim sea. He needn't have worried. Unlike Morocco, we did not have brotherhoods here, nor proselytizing disciples, simply a proliferation of local saints, their shrines cared for and memory kept alive by their descendants and the people under their care.

Our practices were gentle, diffuse, apolitical.

While I did my best to lose myself in the sway of the Thursday-night crowd, I imagined Aziz in his mother's compound, wearing a sarong knotted at the waist, his hospital clothes hanging on a nail in the wall, making pencil marks by candlelight in the margins of a textbook. Closing the book and repeating entire paragraphs in English about the central nervous system.

I was glad to have the excuse of taking Nouria's girls home and putting them to bed. This left their mother free to remain at the shrine and twist and turn and hiss and bounce into the dawn of the next day. And it left me alone, my susceptible soul leading me to imagine the kisses in the dark over and over, to carry the watery sensation of them with me into the early morning. It was not worship. It was more that distraction Hussein had always warned about: earthly love.

## Terms of Endearment.

—

I sat cross-legged on a straw mat in the courtyard, taking advantage of the last light of the day. I was working on my new project, a Harari–English dictionary, an endeavour people encouraged because Emperor Haile Selassie had long been preaching the virtues of learning English, reforming the education system to reflect this and insisting it was the way to go forward as a nation.

Islam teaches us that education is the means to enlightenment, and that discipline is the only way to get there. But while Haile Selassie's educational reforms might have been celebrated, they appeared to benefit very few. Except for the richest people in the cities, no one could spare their child for an hour, let alone half a day for school. The Hararis were that exception, ensuring all their children, girls included, got some education—at a minimum, in Qur'an.

I took great pleasure in working on the dictionary, though I occasionally annoyed people with my questions. "Precocious," my mother used to say. "Curious Lilly-George," my father called me, "monkey." He too had loved language. He gave me a notebook when I was six, and it was soon after that that I began collecting words. Arabic words and later Harari, and even the occasional English word, usually to do with medicine or politics.

"Tell me the name of every plant you know," I asked Gishta. "Tell me every single word you can think of that has to do with the sky," I asked Nouria.

Sometimes they indulged me; other times they said they were too busy for my games. They liked it least of all when I asked about abstract entities—"I don't know, Lilly. How would I know? Happy, sad, there is no in-between"—and obscure technical terms—"I'm not a farmer, Lilly. I don't know what they call that thing. Why does it matter? It's only a peasant's word, after all."

—

We were surrounded by the debris of another bercha, but instead of whispering and drawing close in the dark as we usually did after everyone left, Aziz rose and threw open the shutters. He had something he wanted to show me: a new medical textbook he had just picked up from the post office in Dire Dawa.

I admired its hard, shiny white cover and the colour photographs of internal organs on its slippery pages.

"Do you know why I am showing you this?" he asked, looking over my shoulder as I flipped through its lurid pages. "Because this is the last one I need to study."

"And then you'll be ready to write your exams," I said, realizing the significance.

"In six months time, at the end of August, that is when they are scheduling the next exams. I will have to go to Cairo to write them."

I wasn't sure how far away that was, but however far, it was away. "For how long?"

"I will probably only stay for one week. But there is the journey to Addis and back, so maybe I will be gone for two. Have you ever been on a plane?" he asked.

"Yes. A long time ago."

"I have always wanted to go on a plane," he said.

"What happens after you write the exams?"

"I wait for the results. I have to get top marks to be awarded a scholarship. I can't afford the tuition otherwise. I've been saving money, but you know, this is Ethiopia, where even the doctors are poor."

"Well, I know you'll get the scholarship."

"Insha'Allah," said Aziz. "And if I do? You know this means I will be in Cairo for four years."

"That's a long time."

"Then I will return and serve the community. I want to develop expertise that we don't have here. Internal medicine—especially for children."

He will be able to save a generation of children, I thought. He'll rescue children like Bortucan from the dirt.

"Insha'Allah, we will have berchas together again after that. That is, if you are still here."

Still here? "This is my home, Aziz."

"You won't return someday to Morocco?"

"Not now," I said. Not since the Great Abdal died. Not since I started teaching the children. Not since knowing you.

"But then, of course, berchas will not exactly be possible because your husband will object."

"My husband?"

"The ladies will find a husband for you," he said. "Perhaps they have done so already. It is what ladies do."

—

Gishta had come to refer to me using favoured terms of endearment: kuday, kulayay, "my liver," "my kidney." "If only you were circumcised," she lamented. "You would be almost perfect. Are you quite sure you don't want to be circumcised? It's never too late."

"Quite sure," I insisted.

"Well, maybe your gums . . ."

"I told you I wasn't having that done."

"Just like a teenager," she sighed. "So stubborn. So hot-blooded."

"It is a mother's job to extinguish the flames," Gishta would warn Nouria. But Nouria had never treated me like a parent. I tried to dampen the fire that Gishta rightfully suspected burned inside, but Aziz invariably rose from the ashes, his lips moving, his conversation endless, his words making me feel heavy and slow as if there would never be enough time before he left for Cairo to finish what we had to say.

Since the first day that Aziz had held my hand, I'd been discovering that nothing was quite as it first appeared. But then, this is where we begin in every new world: first we read the manual. We practise the laws as they are laid out, and it is only when we become literate through living them that we find the contradictions, the subtext, the spaces in between. There were signs everywhere: evidence of a current flowing beneath the strict rules of engagement that governed the relationships between men and women. Like the placement of the water jug in the small niche to the right of the main doors inside Gishta's house. "Normally, the jug sits on the floor," Gishta explained, "but if it appears in the niche, then it is my turn."

This meant that most Tuesdays Gishta sent her two children over to her co-wife Zehtahoun's house after the last call to prayer, leaving her alone to line her eyes with kohl, anoint her hair and body with oils and perfume, and dress in a sheer diri, a Somali nightdress, pulled over her bulging breasts and plump thighs.

"He comes to surprise me in the night" was how Gishta described it. I wanted to press her for details, but I knew my curiosity would alarm her. I was meant to be passive. To wait until I was chosen by a suitor—a Harari suitor, my passport to full acceptance within the community, a man who would marry me, then teach me.

If she knew that I had kissed Aziz. That I

craved being in the dark with this man, that I day-dreamed him into the pauses between sentences. That I would wait four years for his return. That I was compromising the one thing, the only thing I had always believed mattered, to be near him.

People were not supposed to marry for love, they were supposed to marry to secure alliances between families: for lineage, for wealth, for status. And darkness like Aziz's offered none of those things. Hararis turned away from the dark even when it ran in their own blood: they preferred to look east, not to Africa, for their origins. They pre-ferred to think of Arabs—the Prophet and his com-panions, the saints—as their ancestors, rather than slaves. It was a fiction that was complicated by dark skin.

I was meant to wait for a suitor, but I was nine-teen now. The wait was not meant to last too long.

"Life is short in Africa," Gishta often said, "too short to waste time. You don't want to stay on the tree for too long, Lilly. Eventually you will lose your grip, drop to the ground, splatter, go rotten. No one wants to eat the fruit that has fallen—that is for the beggars and the birds. They will only want to step on you."

# Part Five.

—

# London, England

## 1987–88

Reunion.

—

Ten women have been cooking in ten flats all day in anticipation of Yusuf's arrival, each woman behaving as if it is her own husband coming home. Those who have already been reunited with their husbands want to share their good fortune, those who have yet to hear anything fantasize that this reunion is their own, and those who know their husbands have been killed live vicariously for a night, while I battle envy and berate myself for selfishness.

Amina, a giant duba, waddles away, off to collect her husband at Heathrow, while I supervise the rest of the preparations. We arrange the food on the table, and the Oromo brothers from down the hall bring roses, the scentless variety wrapped in cellophane that come from a petrol station, and carry a bucket of beer that's been fermenting for weeks in their loo. It is thick and cloudy, sweet and yellow: honey-rich, Ethiopian-style. We stick a cassette into the tape deck and a warped chorus of faraway voices fills the room.

Soon enough, Yusuf is waving his hand and bowing his head at the ululating crowd standing before him who shower him and Amina with rose petals and words of welcome. Amina waves to Sitta and Ahmed, who are both lurking on the periphery. "Come and greet Baba."

Sitta sticks her thumb in her mouth. I take her by the other hand and suggest we go and get the picture she has drawn for her father at school that day. She shakes her head and stares at the small bearded man with the scar on his cheek.

Ahmed strides forth wearing a suit he'll be able to wear for the next three years. He breaks into an unabashed grin.

"Masha'Allah," his father rumbles. "Such a big boy." Yusuf pulls his son awkwardly into his stomach.

One woman then another bursts into song. Attention gradually shifts away from Ahmed and Yusuf toward the table of food. I introduce Sitta to her father.

"Sitta?" Yusuf whispers gently, squatting on the floor so that they are eye level. "Beautiful Sitta?"

She nods, thumb still in her mouth. She pulls it out just long enough to ask: "Did you bring me a present?"

Yusuf smiles sympathetically and looks knowingly at me. How simple it can be. To let Sitta be Sitta, an English girl.

Yusuf moves through the room, chatting quietly, nursing a heavy glass of beer. I can tell he is trying to keep his mood light for his family's sake, but he is preoccupied, not entirely present. Insomnia and depression have been his devoted companions for the last seven years, taking place of his wife and son after they were separated in the refugee camp at Thika, outside Nairobi.

There were thousands in the camp, housed in tents and buildings, lining up for food, sharing a communal well. There were Ugandans and Sudanese, Eritreans and Ethiopians. Men separated from women and children, families split apart. Yusuf's roommates, three Amharas, were disgusted by the presence of an Oromo among them. They made trouble for him right away, reporting him to the camp manager, an officer with the Kenyan security forces. They said he wasn't a genuine refugee but a member of an Oromo nationalist movement, an agitator communicating with other Oromo in the camp in order to plan their attack on the Dergue, Mengistu's government, from bases in Kenya.

Yusuf was arrested by the Kenyan police, handed over to Mengistu's agents and taken by helicopter to Addis, where he was jailed and tortured for years. He had no idea his wife was pregnant with Sitta when he was spirited away. Because she wasn't. This is the secret Amina has kept from him and only recently confided in me.

After Yusuf was taken they began interrogating all the Oromo in the camp. Amina, as the wife of an alleged Oromo agitator, was immediately regarded with suspicion. How could she convince them of her innocence? The only way to protect her son was to yield to their demands. She lay down, spread her legs and let the first officer charge into her. The second officer, dismissing her as a prostitute because she was not infibulated, and demanding a tighter hole, heaved himself into her anus.

She was ruptured, she was pregnant, she was free. A man in a police uniform scares her far more than some drunken neo-Nazi bigot on a tear.

The first officer packed Amina and her son into his vehicle and drove them to the airport, where he threw them out onto the dirt. "See if the farenjis will have anything to do with a Galla whore," he spat before careening off.

She picked up her son from the cloud of dust and ran. She'd had the temerity to steal the officer's wallet, stuffed with American dollars and Ethiopian birr he'd stripped off refugees in the camp—stealing their savings and destroying all means of escape—enough to feed and keep her and Ahmed sheltered in the months it took to secure the forged documents she needed to get them on a plane.

"He must have been afraid that I, this dirty Galla, would give birth to someone who looked like him," she told me. "But it was the end of Africa for me, in any case," she said, wiping her hands across the Formica table as if to obliterate the past. "I would have died and gone to hell rather than stay."

And then came Sitta, with that mole like a continent stamped on her cheek. And the fact that Amina chose to see that mark as Africa.

—

"It will get easier. It does, eventually" is all I can think of to say to Yusuf as I make my way to the kitchen, though I wonder as soon as I say it if it would be kinder to say nothing. I'm not even sure I believe it. It's more that the emphasis eventually shifts.

When the celebration goes quiet and the kids reluctantly go to bed, Amina and I wash up, while Yusuf sits cross-legged on the floor with the holy book open in front of him, tears streaming down his face. Amina and I pretend not to notice, but it is agonizing to bear witness to the moment when the dams in a man's river collapse. One of the cruelties Yusuf endured in prison was lack of access to the Qur'an. The only thing that is certain is the Qur'an. Precise and uncompromising—exactly as it was delivered to the Prophet Muhammed as he sat in a cave and received the words of God through the angel Gabriel more than thirteen hundred years ago.

To read the Qur'an with your family around you is to be home.

—

Daily life does not cease in honour of Yusuf's arrival. All evidence of celebration is washed up and tidied away.

"I'll be fine," Yusuf says when I pop my head in on my way to work. Amina has left a giant pot of soup on the cooker for him, and the smells of garlic and kohlrabi fill the flat. I offer him a stack of the day's papers, which he politely accepts. We of all people should understand that Yusuf has no appetite, no interest in the news or ability to concentrate, but we nevertheless offer him things that you would ordinarily give someone with the flu.

To some degree we feel helpless, but to a larger degree, perhaps, it's that we forget, or rather, that we want to. I remember feeling like a Galla when I first arrived here, uncivilized in the ways of this place, like a Falasha: an exile, a landless one, treading on alien soil, tiptoeing so as not to leave footprints. It's ghostlike, not a feeling one aspires to recapture. Attending to the ordinary demands of our English lives prevents us from joining Yusuf in the void he now inhabits. A place so close we can see it through a thin veil of gauze; a pit that reeks of mud, rancid butter and the bitter metal of spilled blood.

The hospital, by contrast, is over-illuminated, a pristine assault on the senses, a rude awakening. Robin stands out for me in this whitewashed, anodyne world. His brown skin, the timbre of his voice, his slightly wonky eye—for all his Cambridge education and upper-class accent, there is a vulnerability about him that I had failed to notice at first.

I see it most acutely a few weeks later, when we attend another lecture together at the London School. Two Californian researchers have isolated a new strain of hepatitis they're calling C. Robin is fighting to be heard over a cluster of white-haired men who have sequestered the Americans for themselves. Robin has genuine questions, which, unlike those of the white-haired men, have nothing to do with patents.

He does not seem thwarted, however; he has the enthusiasm of a golden retriever, he waves his hand with tail-wagging earnestness.

"Robin, I'm going to need to get back," I say, moving to rescue him.

"Oh. Yes, yes, of course." He turns to me, disengaging from the crowd surrounding the Americans.

We're both struck by the similarities between this new virus and HIV—its mode of transmission, the populations it seems to affect—though from what these researchers had to say, hep C is caused by an entirely different type of virus, one belonging to the same family that causes yellow and dengue fevers, tropical diseases largely found in Africa. I can already see the implications.

"Do you know, Robin?" I turn to him as he drives. "I won't name names, but I've seen some of the most intelligent nurses at the hospital avoiding Africans in their care. They're subtle about it, they just reorganize their rounds so that it's the more junior nurses who have to care for them."

He unnerves me by abruptly pulling off to the side of the road and stopping the car. He's nodding, lost in thought.

"You know, I'm so used to this sort of thing that I don't even see it any more," he finally says.

"Depressing, isn't it," I say.

"Among other things. Listen, shall we talk about it over dinner?"

"Tonight?" I ask, taken by surprise.

"A quick bite?"

"I should really get home."

"Perhaps another time, then," he says more politely than I deserve. He reaches over and squeezes my hand before putting the car into gear.

—

The lift is broken again. I climb eleven flights of poorly lit concrete stairs. These halls can be dangerous, though most of the violence that occurs is man-on-man, drug related. My heart is about to slip out of my mouth by the time I put my key into the door of Amina's flat. There's a trail of flour from the sofa to the kitchen. Sitta is standing there with her sleeves rolled up, flour in her hair, rolling pin held at the height of her underarms as Mrs. Jahangir instructs her in the rolling of chapatti dough on the cracked kitchen counter.

Mrs. Jahangir has come over to look after the children. Amina is at her class this evening, and Yusuf is just not ready. His awakening is proving a slow thaw, ice retreating inward from the edges of a frozen lake. Since the initial relief of reunion he's grown inert. He hides in the dark, lights off, away from windows, while his wife and children are away. He returns the newspapers to me unread.

Amina almost wishes Yusuf would get angry, even though, as we have seen time and time again among

men emasculated by their helplessness and depend-
ence, that anger is usually directed at women. "At
least he wouldn't feel powerless," she laments.

Money is an issue, though Amina does not push.
Yusuf once held a senior position in the faculty of
agriculture at Alemaya University, outside Harar.
He researched the adaptation of American farming
methods to teff cultivation and taught agricultural economics. It is hard to imagine a place for
Yusuf in this dense concrete world where the only
green is that of moss clinging to damp brickwork,
and weeds making tenacious gestures through
broken pavement. My gift to him is a window box
of geraniums, but it is Amina who waters them.

This evening he stands in the doorway of the
kitchen and watches as I brush the flour from
Sitta's hair. His face has softened. The crease
between his eyebrows is fading. Even the scar on
his cheek looks less prominent.

"Did you enjoy your lecture?" he asks. It is his
first real initiative at conversation.

"Yes, I did. I mean, *enjoy* might not be the word.
It was informative, certainly. Where's Ahmed?"

"He is in the bed. Reading Qur'an. We were
reading together." Another good sign.

The following morning, his fifty-fifth morning
in London, Yusuf is left on his own once again.

## Check Mates.

—

Yusuf must know in his heart that he is not Sitta's father, for it is only when Tariq is born that the solid mass at his centre begins to melt. I slip him some money so that he doesn't have to ask. He gives it to one of the Oromo brothers down the hall, asking him to buy a small used black-and-white television he can give to his wife to keep her entertained during those forty idle days of ulma at home.

But Amina does not rest this time. "How can I?" she shouts. "It's totally unrealistic. I have to work!" She looks at Yusuf and me as if we are a pair of idiots.

It's not just practicality influencing her decisions. She scoffs at my suggestion that we bury the placenta in Kennington Park. "It's just a silly superstition," she says. "There is no need."

Somewhere in the last seven years need became superstition, tradition became voluntary, and then ritual further degenerated into a subject of some embarrassment.

"But we must at a very minimum see that he is blessed," Yusuf confides in the wake of her derision. He appeals to me, knowing somehow that part of me still remains in the old world, unwilling to let go, while Amina is "moving with the times."

Amina returns to work, dropping off her fourteen-day-old son and a supply of breast milk at the Jahangirs' shop. Mrs. J has generously agreed to look after Tariq during the days just as she looks after her two youngest grandchildren. Either Amina or I pick him on the way home, his breath smelling of milk, the scent of garam masala radiating from his thick, black hair.

On the fortieth day of Tariq's life, Yusuf meets me at the shop. It is one of the first times he has left the flat, certainly the first time he has ventured out alone. He has shaved his beard for the occasion, revealing more scars. He arrives carrying a frozen chicken wrapped in plastic, which he presents with a rather helpless shrug. This is what he brings by way of an offering. Mrs. Jahangir relieves him of the frozen bird, placing Tariq in his arms instead.

I make my way through the shop, down the narrow hall and into the community association office at the back. Yusuf follows and surveys the cramped room with its bookshelf overflowing with black binders and manila files. He fingers the red, gold and green of the polyester flag bought from a Jamaican woman in the market for three pounds fifty.

I wave my hand. "This is where it all happens." Where reunions are facilitated, hearts are broken, hope is restored. "That is exactly where Amina was sitting the day she finally saw your name," I say, pointing at the orange chair.

He stares at the chair as if it is in some way responsible. "I'm afraid she is disappointed in me," he says quietly.

"Yusuf? She waited years to see your name. It was all she wanted."

"Like you are waiting."

"Insha'Allah."

Mrs. Jahangir comes through the door then, holding a tin plate of coals with an oven glove, pushing past us, sliding the bolt of the back door open and pouring the coals into the flowerpot. Yusuf descends the few steps with Tariq in his arms, and I pull the incense from my pocket and throw it onto the coals. Yusuf passes Tariq to me and kneels down in the dirt. He raises his palm upwards and silently whispers prayers into the fragrant cloud. I rock Tariq back and forth as his fingers grope the air above his head and his father asks the saint to ensure the protection of his son through these vulnerable first years during which, in Ethiopia, every other baby seems to die.

Mrs. Jahangir has prepared sweet cardamom-flavoured tea. We sit on overturned crates by the fridge at the back of the shop and she offers us English biscuits from a tin. There's a monumental wail as one of her grandchildren bites hard into the forearm of the other. She moves quickly to muzzle the offender and then comforts the victim while the cash register ka-chings at the front of the shop.

Yusuf notices the chessboard perched on a case of tinned tomatoes and rises with interest. He studies the pieces and brightens.

"Who is playing?" he asks Mrs. Jahangir.

"My husband is playing my husband," she says, laughing with a slight roll of her eyes. "The match is very uneven."

"Mr. Jahangir!" I call out. He approaches in his Tower of London apron, carrying the till drawer. "Maybe Yusuf would like a game."

Mr. Jahangir immediately puts the drawer down into his wife's lap. "Count this," he commands and unties his apron. "You are a serious player?" he asks Yusuf with great intensity, his eyes popping.

Mrs. J pinches my elbow, amused by how seriously her husband takes this. Nobody will play with him any more. He says it's because his opponents are intimidated, but I've heard more than one person say that he's argumentative and given to reinterpreting certain rules for his own convenience.

"Well, I—"

"Perhaps you recognize this board?" Mr. Jahangir says. "From the eighth game of the great match between Fischer and Spassky."

"I had a chess partner in prison," Yusuf says quietly. "Although it was months before I knew who he was."

Everyone falls silent, even the children. It's the first time Yusuf has offered anything about his time in prison.

"We had fifteen minutes in the open air every

day," he says, staring blankly ahead. "They release us in shifts into this square yard of only dirt and stones. One day I find this pattern of stones of different sizes on the ground, and I recognize it as a chess game. It is something amazing to me. And I see the next move so clearly that I cannot help myself. I move the stone. And the next day? Someone has moved a piece on the other side. Day by day, one stone at a time, my silent partner and I play this game."

Mr. Jahangir admits that he cannot figure out the game from here, that he's been stuck with this board for months. He's even willing to give over the side that eventually wins. "You be stars and stripes," he says. "I am hammer and sickle."

Yusuf stares at the board and considers the options.

—

I think of Yusuf when I'm at work.

"Who was your silent partner?" I'd asked him later.

"The day I won the match, I found the door to my cell unlocked. It was the major. I know because he turned his head as if not to see me pass."

He continues to relay small anecdotes about prison. He meditates on the meaning of things. Meanings below the surface, like a mystical seeker looking for the truth beneath the words.

"It's all you have when they destroy your body," he tells me, tapping his temple.

Sufis deny their bodies, victims of torture

detach from theirs: both seek transcendence in their own way.

"You look lost in space," Robin says, sitting down across from me at a table in the cafeteria.

"Just thinking."

He looks eagerly for more; I dare an attempt to offer it.

"You see all these people plagued with psychosomatic illnesses, but then you get people who have experienced the most extreme physical trauma who manage somehow to bear the pain. Even more than that—they maintain a fundamental optimism which the psychosomatic types don't even seem capable of."

"Big thoughts to have before lunch."

I laugh. "Sorry. You asked."

"I agree, it's interesting," he says, spooning an alarming amount of sugar into his coffee. "There's no physiological difference in what we feel. People's pain thresholds seem to be influenced by any number of things. Culture, personality, childhood experience . . ."

"You've never told me how you became interested in medicine," I remark.

"Me?" he asks, raising his eyebrows and pushing his coffee cup aside. "I really wasn't given much of a choice. I think I knew I was going to be a doctor by the time I was ten years old. So many people kept telling me that I was going to be a doctor, and study in England—Cambridge, of course—that I suppose I began to believe it was who I was destined to be."

So mapped out. So certain. Such a straight line. Knowing exactly how your life would unfold. How could someone like him and someone like me end up in the same place?

"You?" Robin asks.

"Well, until I came to England and studied nursing, my education was mainly religious: Qur'an, Hadiths." I am not really sure how to answer. "I'd read quite a few Western books. There was a man, British originally but he'd converted to Islam, who was a friend of my parents' in Morocco—where I grew up. It's rather a long story. This man, Muhammed Bruce, was sort of like my guardian because my parents, they didn't really, well, you know, last."

"I'm so sorry," Robin says, reaching for my hand.

"It's fine." I shake my head, withdraw my hand. "Anyway, Muhammed Bruce was a bit odd and quite pompous. He claimed he was the great-great-nephew of this famous explorer, Sir Richard Burton—"

"The one who wrote *Arabian Nights*?"

"Exactly."

"I'm afraid ours was a rather sanitized, illustrated version for children, read to us at bedtime between Enid Blytons. But that's fascinating. A descendant of Burton's."

"Claimed to be. Claimed many things, but in any case, he was quite sincere, devoted to me, and I was enormously fond of him. He would visit me once a month with a stack of books and dump them into my arms. He was very insistent.

'Well-roundedness is the goal of a British education,' he used to say."

I hear the subtext now. *In contrast to this rather
exclusive education you receive at the shrine, where
the Qur'an is your only book, Arabic your only language, God your only subject. Submission your only
posture.*

"That sounds familiar," says Robin.

—

I pass the old Lambeth Hospital on my way home,
as I do every day. I stop and pull a cigarette from
my purse. This is where Sitta was born, right here
on this pavement, six and a half years ago. Though
it looks much the same, Tariq has been born into a
much different world. His mother's orientation has
shifted from east to west between the births of her
two youngest children.

As west as Amina leans, though, those books I
mentioned to Robin, these points of reference that
Muhammed Bruce introduced me to would be foreign to her. They're not part of the vocabulary we
share. I remember reading Dickens and Jane Austen,
verse by Rumi, an illustrated version of *Alice's
Adventures in Wonderland,* and of course *The Arabian
Nights* (the original, quite brutal and salacious),
Anne Frank's diary (I wanted to know her; I thought
she knew me) and Robinson Crusoe and *Gulliver's
Travels* and most of the work of Jules Verne.

Muhammed Bruce's choices were more deliber-
ate than I've ever realized. He supplemented my

diet of Islam with doses of other realities. He must have envisioned a time when I would have to make my way in the wider world; the books he presented offered lessons about war and morality and disease and love and betrayal and, perhaps most important, survival. Under the sea, at the centre of the earth, on another planet, alone on a desert island, as a person hunted, in war, as a giant among little people, in the future, in a world upside down, a world through a looking glass, a world gone mad.

A world like the one we live in. A world like the one we left.

Yusuf describes Ethiopia as a field of fire: an infernal blaze leaving a trail of charred bodies and scorched earth. The civil war with Eritrea has continued to worsen, the Tigrayans are waging guerilla war in the north, the Somalis have invaded the Ogaden again, and the Oromo continue to operate underground in their fight for independence. Local insurgencies flare up routinely, and military camps form armed rings around every city.

The Dergue needs all the men it can to fight these wars. Enforced conscription began in the early 1980s. Soon they'd closed all the universities, forcing students to enlist. We're hearing rumours now that they are using food aid as incentive, and bribing and kidnapping schoolchildren, forcing boys as young as nine to take up arms.

Imagine Ahmed armed and dangerous. He could be leading a commando unit at his age. Imagine Fathi and Anwar forced to surrender their adolescence to war.

—

"I'm reading about your city," Robin says proudly. He has a copy of Burton's *First Footsteps in East Africa* in the pocket of his white coat.

The sight of it provokes a pang of possessiveness. "You know, Hararis find Burton's portrayal of them very insulting," I tell him.

"Mmm, it's fantastically romantic and condescending," he agrees. "It reminds me of much of the colonial literature about India. I should lend you the book he wrote about the Sindh."

I've just insulted Robin. I don't have to put it in context for him; it's a history he knows all too well.

"So was your guardian also a traveller?"

"Not really, at least not by the time I knew him. He'd lived in Morocco for decades. Tangier then Marrakech. I think he'd travelled a great deal when he was younger. He even boasted that he'd played polo with the emperor of Ethiopia. I used to wonder how the king's crown stayed on his head while he was waving a mallet about."

Robin laughs. And I think of how things changed. In 1969 King Hassan II began inflating the Moroccan army to rid the country of remaining colonials. Spain had just handed back the coastal town of Sidi Ifni, but the Spanish remained entrenched in the western Saharan provinces. This would be the final battle.

Even Muhammed Bruce had grown despondent by then. He had lived in Morocco for more than thirty years. He had witnessed the country gain independence from France. He'd known plenty of foreigners who'd been murdered in the cities during those years, my parents included. But he'd stayed in Morocco despite all of this.

"Perhaps it's time to leave," he had said wistfully.

It felt like betrayal, but in truth it was simply Muhammed Bruce's lament for the passing of an era. A time when Europeans had roamed the earth in pursuit of adventure, largely oblivious to the lives and laws of the people in the countries they picked through like cherries. Spitting out the pits. Just like my parents. They had stomped on the world like the Burtons of their era, only worse somehow because they did not think that their shoes left marks.

"Do you know what happened to him?" Robin asks.

"Vaguely." Several years ago I'd read an obituary. He had returned to England, been diagnosed with Alzheimer's and died of a stroke in a private hospital in Guildford as Bruce MacDonald. I didn't keep the paper. I prefer to remember him for the loveable enigma that he was: Muhammed Bruce Mahmoud, in his element in North Africa, surrounded by books and boys and birds.

"You stayed in touch?" he asks—one question too many.

Prosthetics.

—

Yusuf is at home with Tariq all day now, and longs for a bit of adult conversation by the late afternoon. He prefers my company because I don't ask questions. Since he started playing chess with Mr. J once a week, Amina has been pestering him about how he's spent the day, when he might be ready to start looking for work, whether she should enrol him in some classes.

Yusuf and I have taken to watching television together and I've been teaching him how to cook. He resisted at first: I had to work hard to convince him that this would not be yet another assault on his manhood. Hard enough that his wife is the one working. Harder still that he enacted a woman's ritual by taking the baby to a shrine and that he is now at home with Tariq because Mrs. Jahangir's been landed with another grandson. You'd never find a man in a kitchen in Ethiopia. And even among the poorest, this is a servant's job. In Ethiopia, there is always someone poorer than you. Even Nouria was able to procure a servant eventually.

I tell him my friend Robin likes to cook and he's a doctor. Robin has told me he likes to grind his own spices and follow his mother's recipes. He likes to scour second-hand bookshops and watch cricket on his days off. It made me realize I have no hobbies at all.

Yusuf lifts the lid and stares into the pot. "Lilly, it's burnt. I burnt the rice again," he says, shaking his head in dismay.

I have a look in the pot. "It's not a total disaster. We can salvage what's on top." I scrape the rice into a bowl. "Pass me the bin," I say.

"We can't throw it in there," Yusuf says. "Amina will be furious if she sees the waste."

"All right. Put it in another bag, I'll take it to my flat."

"Thank you, Lilly."

"Robin was asking me about my guardian today," I say. Yusuf has heard most of the stories by now.

"Is this good or bad?" he asks, poking at the rice left in the pot.

"A bit awkward, I guess."

"Too personal?"

"Well, yes."

"I've noticed this about farenjis. You give them one piece of information and then they have ten questions. And they don't think this is at all rude."

"I know. I'm still not used to it. But in Robin's case it's not just invasive but a bit off somehow. Like he's asking the wrong question."

"And what is the right question?" Yusuf asks.

"I don't really know."

"Ahh. A typical Harari woman," Yusuf teases, a rare smile upon his face. "You want the man to read your mind."

———

Unfortunately, the one time Yusuf accompanied us to the community association office, we had to deal with a man in a fury over the fact that his wife had enlisted a friend to help her circumcise their daughter. He wanted this woman hung. "She is preying on our women!" he shouted. "She is twisting their minds and stealing our money!"

Amina and I assured him we would try to get a community health nurse to offer a seminar on harmful cultural practices, but we already knew it wouldn't be well attended.

Yusuf remained silent in the corner, embarrassed to hear a man talking so explicitly about women's business.

Then a woman we call the Sky Queen turned up. She used to work for Ethiopian Airlines and she treats us as if we are her servants. Neither of us can stand her. Amina, perhaps wanting to impress Yusuf, lost patience with her that day. She swore at the woman and told her to stop wasting our time with these ridiculous, selfish demands of hers for "enquiries" and "investigations."

"Bloody hell!" Amina shouted, much to my amazement. "We are dealing with crises here! We are not your team of private investigators!"

Yusuf has declined to accompany us ever since, despite our reassurances that not every week is quite so dramatic or loud. He spends Saturday mornings with his new friends, Oromo he met at the mosque, whom he joins for coffee and a game of chess at a little Ethiopian café that has opened in Brixton.

We have Tariq with us in the office now, just as we used to have Sitta. He squirms in the little nest we've made for him in a chair; he wriggles like a rasher of bacon in a pan. I've just picked him up to try to distract him from his own bodily discomfort when the door opens.

"I hope you don't mind me dropping in like this." Robin hesitates in the doorway. He holds a cardboard box in his hands, tied with a pink bow.

"No, come in," I say, quickly recovering. I introduce him to Amina. He offers her the cardboard box—baklava, from a Lebanese bakery. Amina is charmed and offers Robin the orange chair and asks if he would like coffee. She excuses herself to fill the kettle from the squeaky tap in the hall.

There is no apparent reason for his visit. He sits with us and sips Ethiopian coffee from a tiny porcelain cup. It looks like a thimble in his hand. He compliments Amina on the coffee and says it's nice to see where we do our work. When he was a student he did volunteer work for an organization that sent used prosthetics to India. Our office reminds him of the one they had in Cambridge.

But you were not missing an arm or a leg, I

think while Amina smiles at him coquettishly and asks him how the organization was funded.

"Donations," he replies, then asks if we need any office supplies. He knows someone with a stationery shop who offers discounts to charities.

Amina says "How wonderful" at exactly the same moment as I say, "I think we're fine, thank you."

Robin looks between us and laughs. "All right then, let me know when you're running low," he says and bids us goodbye.

"He just wants to help," Amina insists once I've shut the door behind him.

"But our business here doesn't concern him," I say.

"Let him help, Lilly. Men like to feel useful. Particularly when they fancy someone."

## Chalk Outlines.

—

It is a rare bright Sunday morning, sunlight flooding the tiny strip of Amina's kitchen. Amina pours a thin stream of batter in a circle onto the underside of a large frying pan and presses me again about Robin. She's convinced I'm keeping something from her.

"I hate to disappoint you, Amina. We've gone to a few lectures together, that's all. There's really nothing else to tell," I say for a second time.

On the way home from the last lecture he asked if I knew how to drive. He placed my hand on the gear stick, covering it with his own, and guided me from first through fourth. The order, the pattern, appealed to me. I wondered why I'd never imagined driving. It was more than the expense of a car.

Amina sighs. "He's such a nice man."

I have to agree. So cheerful all the time, but almost a bit too enthusiastic. "You would fancy any man who gave you baklava," I tease.

"You think I am some kind of sharmuta for sweets?"

"Well, did you share them with anyone? Did you even bring them home?"

"Never mind," she says.

"Shall I take them to the park later?" I suggest.

"Make Yusuf go too," she pleads. "Maybe he will come today because of the sunshine."

The park is full of frenetic children. Women with various types of headdresses sit clustered together on benches, so engrossed in conversation that they don't notice the older children pushing the younger ones out of the way. Most are not familiar enough with English to know that "poof" and "wanker" are words that should concern them.

"Play nicely!" I shout at Ahmed periodically. "Help your sister reach that, Ahmed!"

Yusuf does not yell. He stares straight ahead at this noisy, colourful scene of children clambering on climbing structures, turning manic circles on rusted roundabouts, fights breaking out over bicycles shared between too many siblings and acrobatic, attention-seeking feats that inevitably end up in tears.

Yusuf is one of very few fathers in the park and the only father who is neither smoking nor sitting with another man. I wonder if he has always been an exception to the rules, whether this is what makes him special. I resist the urge to take his hand.

"Why don't you play chess anymore with Mr. Jahangir?" I ask.

"He is fed up."

"Oh dear. He wants you to change sides?"

"No. He wants me to pretend that I don't see him cheating."

The music of an ice cream van works its way like an electric current though the crowd. "Can we, Baba?" The children are suddenly before him.

"You don't like this ice cream, do you?" Yusuf says, stalling. "Ooh, but it's so cold." He pretends to shiver.

I lean forward and coins spill from my pocket. Yusuf has no money.

"If you can find enough on the ground for two ice creams, then you can have them."

They're immediately on all fours, elbowing each other out of the way.

"I saw that one first!" shrieks Sitta, grabbing Ahmed's fist with both hands.

Ahmed elbows her. "You did not, you Paki!"

"Ahmed!" I shout.

He looks up, startled.

"Don't you *ever*, *ever* say that again. To anyone. All right?"

"Sorry," he mumbles, uncertain whether it's all right to resume.

"How much do you have now?" his father asks.

Ahmed begins to count the coins in his palm.

—

You'd think Sitta had spent the day trudging through the Sahara the way she drags her feet on the way home. We encourage her to practise counting in Arabic, hoping to distract her. Ahmed plays along, but Sitta continues whining behind us. As Ahmed reaches thirty-five, we hear the distant, plaintive wail of a siren coming our way. Yusuf stiffens at the sound, grabs hold of both of the children by the hands and yanks them down the next alleyway. He flattens his back against a brick wall. I can see the pulse pounding in his neck.

"It's an ambulance," I say calmly.

He squeezes his eyes shut and his Adam's apple plunges as he swallows. In another second, the siren passes.

"Maybe someone had a heart attack," says Ahmed weakly. He will grow up like many of the children in the playground today: reading the landscape and detonating the mines for the generation before.

—

There's a message waiting for me the following morning at the nurse's station. I've been called upon to assuage the fears of infibulated women in labour, to explain to a doctor that the scars on someone's back are not the result of abuse but the well-intended evidence of leeching or cupping, to help bedridden folk perform ablutions before prayer, even to read from the Qur'an while someone slips away. Such requests are not unusual.

The bed, though, is empty by the time I get there. All evidence of Mr. Tadesse has been laundered away. He died slowly in the night, his lungs punctured by a shattered rib cage, the impact of falling ten storeys from a building on the estate. He's a recent arrival and there appears to be no next of kin.

People never actually say suicide, but it happens more often than any of us like to admit. No one uses the word for fear of contagion; we speak of accidents and noncommunicable diseases. It is a crime against God to kill oneself. No one wants to believe that things can get so despairing that one would abandon God. The streets around us would be awash in chalk outlines.

I probe Amina for information when she comes by that evening to study at my kitchen table. She's well plugged-in to the dramas, good and bad. "They accused Tadesse of being a Dergue officer." *They* are his Ethiopian neighbours. "They threaten they will tell the authorities that he is not a legitimate refugee. He says, please, no, my whole family has been killed by the Dergue. And they say, no, *you* are the killer."

Not only are the wars between us not erased, they are exaggerated, because here, people are allowed to speak. They can express their hatred of the Dergue without fear they will be wrenched from their beds at gunpoint in the middle of the night, forced to watch their wives being gang-raped, shot in the stomach and left to die in the street. Here they can even seek revenge.

—

I offer Robin half my cheddar and pickle sandwich. I'm writing up notes, and when I pause, pen in hand, Robin taps my knuckles playfully, as if they are the keys of a piano.

He persuades me to stay for another cup of tea.

His attention is flattering, even if he does ask too many questions. His perseverance grates against my exterior wall, somewhat gentler than sandblasting but not quite as gentle as wind weathering paint.

"Have you ever heard from anyone you knew in Ethiopia?" he asks. "I mean, through your work with the association?"

"Not exactly," I reply.

He puts up with my evasiveness, being determined despite, or perhaps, even because of it. But I am slower than slow, glacial, an ice age.

He rings me the evening of my day off, the first time he's ever contacted me at home. He's at a phone box, keen to chat. I can barely hear him over the traffic. It's not a good moment: Amina is at her evening class, I've got Tariq clinging to my leg while trying to prepare supper, and Ahmed has just managed to pull a cupboard door off its hinges by swinging on it. I'm not a terribly good disciplinarian, and Yusuf is that much worse. Where the hell is he?

"Yusuf!" I shout into Robin's ear. "Sorry, Robin."

"I thought you lived alone," he remarks casually.

"I do. I mean, yes and no." It would be too difficult to explain that Amina and I are like co-wives.

We used to joke that all we lacked was the common tie of a husband, but even that's not quite true any more. I seem to spend more time with Yusuf than she does.

"I can fix it," Yusuf mouths at me as he investigates the cupboard door.

There's an almighty wail just then, and Ahmed chases his sister through the kitchen with a fork.

"Dear God," Robin says.

"Sorry, I've got to go," I say, ringing off.

Restricted Access.

—

We've dressed up so the children can feel just as proud of us as we do of them. Yusuf is wearing a silk tie he bought from a car boot sale and the new navy blue pea coat Amina picked up for him for twenty-nine pounds because the lining was slightly torn. His hair glistens with Afro Sheen.

The three of us file into the school gymnasium, and Amina throws our coats down on the seat beside me. "Reserved," she says confidently. She scans the audience, then waves both her arms wildly. "Up here, up here!" She lifts the coats and buries Yusuf. Robin slides into the seat beside me.

"I was afraid I'd be late," he whispers as the lights dim. He's still wearing his scrubs, though he's changed his shoes. I can't believe Amina invited him without telling me, without asking me. I pinch her elbow. She pulls her arm away and smiles coyly, raising her finger to her lips.

A young woman stands on stage, her bottle-blond hair pulled back in a ponytail. The microphone squeals and she recoils, wincing. She taps the microphone once she's recovered and welcomes us all in her thick Kiwi accent to Kennington Road Primary's annual pageant.

As soon as the children fill the stage, Amina is shaking her hands above her head. Sitta smiles and waves back from the stage while Ahmed stares down at his bare feet. They're dressed up as Maoris, wearing paper outfits painted red, black and white. It's both endearing and absurd. Their blond teacher plucks a ukulele, and the children make waves with their hands.

Robin puts his hand on my knee and keeps it there. I feel the heat of his palm tempting its way up my leg until an hour of performances later when the audience erupts with applause and everyone stands up and his hand falls away.

Sitta and Ahmed jump up and down in front of their parents.

"Was I good, Mama?" Ahmed asks, his arms around her waist.

"You were the best," she says, kissing the top of his head.

"What about me?" Sitta cries, squirming out from her father's embrace.

"I could hear your voice singing like an angel above all the others!"

This exchange is echoed throughout the room in twenty-four different languages. It's an audience full of saris and hijabs and kente cloth, a United Nations of proud mothers. The men are few and far between— at evening classes, on assembly lines, driving taxis, frying fish, or behind bars in faraway prisons.

The conversation spills out onto the street. But here the noise of the crowd subsides, and the voice of one man dominates. A beefy English man with a shaved head is poking a small Nigerian man in the shoulder.

When the Nigerian man steps backwards, several other men rush forward. Punches and accusations start to fly, and Amina and I pull the children back.

"Come on, kids." We tug as they stare.

But Yusuf remains standing there. Immobile at the edge of a fight in which all men in the vicinity are now engaged with their fists.

"Yusuf!" Amina calls, but he is fixated on the spectacle of falling bodies, unable to move or speak.

Robin takes him by the elbow. Yusuf allows himself to be led away.

—

I thank Robin for escorting Yusuf back and say goodnight.

"Look, I've seen the building now, if that's what you were worried about," he says, no doubt fishing for an invitation up for a cup of tea.

I've tried to picture him inside—walking down the concrete corridor, entering my flat, sitting down on the sofa and sipping tea, putting his cup down on the floor, reaching to take my hand, pulling me close, kissing my mouth—and it all works for about a second but then I open my eyes. It's the wrong man. At the wrong moment. In the wrong place.

This building is for men like Yusuf, easing their way back into the world, and men like Aziz whose absences haunt the halls, and the women who love them. It's the only place we can define as our own, where we can give up the language, the reserve, the protocol, the niceties that England requires. Where we are protected.

"But how can I get to know you if you won't even let me see where you live?" Robin asks, and quickly apologizes, reaching out and gently squeezing the back of my neck. "I just want to get to know you better," he says.

It sounds so simple. To want. To want what is before you in the here and now.

"I really like you."

But you know so little about me, I think, overwhelmed by his directness. He must look at me and imagine something whole.

"I like you too, Robin," I manage to say.

I do and it feels absolutely terrible.

—

Yusuf retreats inward again. I'm not sure he is a man who would use his fists; rather, it's the loss of his voice that seems to have broken him. And he has a beautiful voice: lilting and mellifluous. I have no doubt he was a poet in the world of agricultural economics. He was renowned as a teacher, Amina tells me, and while the primary language of instruction at the college was English, Yusuf joined the campaign to codify Oromiffa in the

early 1970s, giving a script to an oral language
with more than thirty million speakers. He even
produced a couple of pamphlets about pesticides in
Oromiffa, but with its liberal definition of propa-
ganda the Dergue condemned these as incendiary
tracts designed to rouse counter-revolutionary sentiment amongst those who tilled the land.

It became clear fairly early on that the relations
of power in Ethiopia had not fundamentally
changed with the revolution. The Dergue is dominated by Amharas, just as Haile Selassie's empire
was. Adopting their language and culture remains
the only way to get ahead.

I wonder if Yusuf will teach his children to write
in Oromiffa one day, but right now he can't even
tell them bedtime stories. Amina is losing patience.
She tells me that the other day a car backfired in
the street below and Yusuf hurled himself on the
floor and tried to crawl under the sofa. The children had laughed.

Amina has boundless empathy for everyone but
her husband, it seems. How is it that disappointment arrives as soon as what you have desired for
so long steps over the threshold? It's like finding
the end of your wedding train dragging behind
in the mud.

—

Yusuf is watching children's television with the
curtains drawn. He holds a cold cup of tea in his
hands. I should get to work, but I take the cup

from his hands and place it on the kitchen counter. I wash my hands and cover my hair, take the Qur'an from the shelf, kneel down on the floor and begin the story of the child Moses—Musa, as we know him—raised in exile amongst the pharaohs.

The message I mean to impart, of the many messages the story of Musa offers, is that God sometimes puts us in alien and difficult situations, and in time, the adversity of our situation may be revealed to be a blessing in disguise. It occurs to me I should remind myself of this more often.

Yusuf takes the book from my hands, about to continue from where I left off.

"The children are good with the Qur'an, aren't they?" he says bittersweetly.

I nod. "They are."

"I'm grateful to you, Lilly. It is as if you are doing my job in my absence."

Part Six.

—

# Harar, Ethiopia

March–July 1974

## A Crack in the Holy Armour.

—

There was comfort in the order and predictability of our world. Ours was a city of ninety-nine mosques and more than three hundred saints, their shrines organized along seven concentric circles. There were five gates punctuating the city wall and five raised clay platforms in Harari houses, just as our days revolved around five daily prayers and our lives were governed by the five pillars of faith.

The certainty of our world was reinforced at the beginning of every new day as we woke with the call to prayer. Every day, that is, but one. One strange Wednesday in March of 1974, Sheikh Jami Abdullah Rahman, feared and revered community leader and spiritual guide, descendant and disciple of the city's patron saint, mentor of generations of men pursuing the mystical path, all-powerful patriarch and husband of Fatima, Zehtahoun and Gishta, father of twenty-two children and grandfather of nearly fifty, did not wake up for the first time in sixty-seven years.

The sheikh was attuned to waking to a particular chorus, the certain density of a hundred voices less one, but that morning one less muezzin made the call to prayer. Sheikh Jami did not rise, and as a consequence, no one else in the household did either.

Gishta told us she awoke to a silence so eerie she wondered if Judgment Day was upon us. She put her ear to her door, listening for the sound of the sheikh sliding the thick bolt across the adjoining wooden doors that separated him and his sons from the women and their daughters in their houses on the other side of the courtyard.

Gishta listened for the sound of her husband relieving himself in an empty bucket behind the woodshed, the familiar ting of his urine pelting metal. She braced herself for the blistering screech of the sheikh shifting the heavy lid that covered the oil drum before he scooped out water for his ablutions. She waited for the sounds of her husband snorting and spitting as he washed, but there was nothing that morning, only silence.

None of the wives opened their doors, for it was customary for them to do so only after Sheikh Jami and his apprentices, Hussein and Idris, had finished. But by the time the women finally heard the sheikh, it was too late for them to make the trek to the farmlands. The waxy qat leaves would have already lost their early-morning tenderness. To pick them that late in the morning would have been to waste them, to leave them wilting in their hands while brokers and customers made snide remarks and handed their money to others.

The Oromo farmers who awaited the sheikh's wives every morning eventually realized the women weren't coming, for rumour had it that they decided to chew the equivalent of a day's haul between them, getting so high that they forgot to weed and water instead, and spent the day engaged in their second-favourite pastime: discussing their fantasies of peasant revolt. The brokers who usually distributed the sheikh's wives' qat to the sellers stomped their feet and threatened never to do business with these three women again. The girls who sold for these brokers suffered the brunt of this, being harassed by the increasingly wild-eyed and squirrelly addicts who had been waiting for their qat all morning.

Because the women did not go to market that morning, they didn't buy any meat or vegetables for dinner. They watered down the remains of the stew from the day before, and the children complained they were still hungry. The women, who were never restrained about meting out physical punishment, gave more than one child a few rough slaps to stop their whining.

But not everyone could be silenced with a slap. There was nothing to leave out for the hyenas that night. The hyenas were used to being fed well in the laneway in front of the shrine. Feeding the hyenas was incumbent upon each of us. This was an unspoken and highly ritualized agreement. The hyenas paced back and forth all night, refusing to disappear. No one in the compound enjoyed the relief of the retreat of their anguished cries as the sun rose the next morning. Gishta said she could hear them circling, their breathing thick with anger.

She and her co-wives were afraid to leave the compound. Their fears were confirmed by the discovery that the Somali girl who brought them fresh camel's milk early each day had been mauled to death and devoured in the laneway.

Gishta's failure to turn up at our compound was one of several clues that something was not right. Three of my students did not show up for class for a second day in a row. Anwar came back empty handed from the market where we'd sent him to buy some milk from the Somali women. And then that Thursday night, en route to the shrine, we didn't hear drumbeats. Some people stayed home, sensing it as a bad omen; others, Nouria and I among them, carried on, only to find the door to the compound locked. We heard rumours that the shrine had been closed all day—the first time this had happened in living memory. We turned back and headed for home.

When Gishta finally turned up at our compound on Friday, she told us of the mother who had brought her sickly newborn to be blessed the day before. The woman had interpreted the locked door as a sign that the child was possessed by the jinn and' had taken him to a spiritual healer to be exorcised. There were stories of pilgrims who had walked thirty-six miles from the countryside and had had no choice but to walk, unblessed, the thirty-six miles back home. There was a rumour that a young man had come seeking a blessing because he had lost an eye in an accident. He went home believing he was destined to be blind and poked out his other eye with a stick. Every visitor that day had been forced to question whether they had offended the saint, whether they had fallen out of God's favour.

Rumours spread from Sheikh Jami's compound to neighbouring compounds, from muezzin to muezzin, from the peasants who worked Uncle Jami's land to the peasants on neighbouring lands, from the qat sellers who normally sold qat brought by Sheikh Jami's wives to all the other sellers in the Faras Magala, from the pilgrims who returned unsatisfied from Bilal al Habash's shrine to their families and neighbours, and in a town where there were only two degrees of separation between the most beautiful girl and the ugliest man, the current of whispers had washed over the entire city in a mere three days.

When Gishta finally came to see us, our suspicions were confirmed. Somehow, over the course of those few days in March of 1974, in a city that had survived for centuries, enduring war, famine, pestilence, foreign invasion, destruction of an emirate and incorporation into a Christian empire, everything had begun to unravel.

It was if the guardian spell had finally been broken; there was a crack in the holy armour that protected us.

### The Shrunken Heads of Enemy Invaders.

—

The events of the week did not prevent us from
holding our bercha, though we were all unsettled.
But where I was concerned about the kink in the
holy armour that surrounded the city, Aziz and
Munir appeared, as usual, to have more secular
concerns.

Munir was all nervous energy. He and Aziz had
heard of protests in the capital, university students leading demonstrations, people raising their
voices in anger against the emperor.

"But people worship him like a God," I said,
thinking of the images we saw on television every
Saturday: people throwing themselves on the
ground and kissing his feet. Kissing the pavement
he had walked upon. Kissing the tracks left in the
dirt by his passing convoy.

"They've made him into a God," said Munir.

"Come on, Munir," Aziz objected. "You make it
sound like it is the people who have given him this
power."

"Well, haven't they?" Munir asked.

"He's created this mythology around himself in order to instill fear," said Aziz. "The Conquering Lion of the Tribe of Judah, God's Elect, the King of Kings, Might of the Trinity, all this business."

I had certainly been afraid of the emperor: his reputation inspires it. The palace was a shrine to his greatness, with his coronation robes, his military uniforms, his wall of medals, orders and decorations, and the shrunken heads of ancient enemy invaders all on display in glass cases. His greatness was reinforced by all that surrounded him, including a veritable solar system of ministers and servants. To request an audience to offer him a simple thank you, I had been forced to make an appointment with the venerable minister of the pen.

"You have a matter of business you would like to discuss with His Most Beneficent Majesty?" a tall man with a long, sad face had asked with all the gravity in the world.

"Well, not exactly business . . ."

"A matter of a personal nature?"

"I just wanted to say thank you, really. I wondered whether there might be a convenient time for me to do that."

"Well," the minister had said, clearing his throat. "After breakfast the emperor does his calisthenics and then he takes his walk through the zoological gardens. Then he goes to his office at the Jubilee Palace. He takes some requests from the soliciting masses at the gates en route to the Audience Hall where his ministers await him for nine o'clock. Nine to ten a.m. is the Hour of

Assignments. When the hour is finished and all the assignments have been handed out, he moves on to the Golden Hall for the Hour of the Cashbox, where His August Majesty considers the requests of his subjects. At eleven, the Hour of the Ministers begins, and the emperor turns his most brilliant mind to imperial matters. At noon, the emperor dons his judge's robes and opens the Hour of Supreme Court of Final Appeal. Then at one, the emperor returns here for a brief dinner with his family before resuming his station in the afternoon to preside over the Hours of Improvement, Corrections, Relations and Commissions. Then, after a light supper, he retires."

"I see," I responded, slightly concerned that the minister had not taken a breath. "So you're telling me there is no good time?"

"I am telling you that unless you are a minister or a general, a family member, a zoological specimen, a subject or a criminal, there is no hour into which you fit. Unless, of course, you are a visiting dignatory."

As a concession the minister agreed to convey our thanks, though I have no assurance that he ever did. I have no certainty the emperor ever knew of our presence in the palace, whether the letter from Muhammed Bruce had ever even reached his hands. It had been passed from guard to guard and ended up on the desk of the palace secretary. He had escorted us into Miriam's care. In any case, the next day, the minister delivered notice of our travel arrangements. We would be

leaving for Harar the following morning in one of
the twenty-seven cars of the imperial fleet.

I had been struck by the driver's comment that
the Muslims and Christians of Harar were linked
in an embrace. I had grown up with the sense that
Christians were not enemies but rather people who
had missed the last word of God. People more to be
pitied and educated than condemned. We were all
believers in the book, Christians, Muslims and
Jews, but our version carried on for six more
centuries. We had a responsibility to share this
information with others.

But in Sudan we'd witnessed a Muslim government killing its fellow Christian citizens. And here,
our city was surrounded by armed Amharas living
in the corrugated-tin settlements on the nearby
hills. If this was an embrace, rather than the circle
of love I had imagined, it looked more like a
barbed wire fence. Perhaps this is why Aziz had
suggested I not imply any connection to the
emperor: the words didn't quite match the pictures. Like the Christian church in the centre of
the city. It was hardly a gift to the people of
Harar; it was a garish reminder of conquest standing in aggressive opposition to its surroundings.
What else can it mean when the tallest building in
a city of Muslims is a church?

Munir's shoulders slackened. "It works both
ways, I suppose. People invest him with power
but he certainly has his own . . . I don't know the
word exactly, maybe magic. Part of it is legend,
myth, whatever you want to call it, but part of it

is definitely his personality. Especially the way he handles the West. He has completely charmed them. I just don't see who has the personality to succeed him after his death."

Certainly not his son, Asfa Wossen, who I gathered from what Tawfiq was saying had tried to overthrow his father a few years ago. Apparently the prince had recruited people directly from the palace, members of Haile Selassie's very own Imperial Guard, decrying his father's regime as one governed by ego and nepotism. He said his father had no real interest in developing the country and alleviating poverty, only in increasing the wealth and privilege of the aristocracy by keeping ordinary civilians destitute.

"But nothing came of that. The plot was discovered before they could overthrow the emperor," said Munir.

"Not nothing," Aziz said quietly, staring at the floor.

"Okay, sure. Now suddenly people saw a weakness in the mighty empire."

Aziz threw down the stalk in his hand. "Hundreds of people died, Munir."

The emperor had had all the members of the Imperial Guard executed. And virtually everybody else in the palace. He did spare his son, though he happened to be permanently disabled now and living in a hospital in Switzerland.

"So were these allegations his son made true?" I asked.

Munir glanced sideways at Aziz. "Well, the

answer depends upon whether you are an aristo-
crat or just a poor ordinary citizen. Look at Harar.
There really is no in-between."

"There is a small in-between," Aziz interjected.

Munir grinned. "Yes, agitators. This is the
problem with education—you create people with
opinions. It's better if you don't educate the peasants, because then they might start demanding
rights. Stick to educating boys like me: sons of
wealthy landowners, people who do well under this
feudal system."

"This educational reform is a sham," Aziz said,
rolling his eyes.

"Or you make sure you recruit all the best grad-
uates from the secondary schools around the country for your army," Munir continued. "That way
you force the educated to be loyal to you by making them dependent upon you for their livelihood.
They educate most of them right here, in the military academy just beyond the wall."

"Oh, here we go again. Chew this, Professor
Munir," Sadia said, passing him a stalk. "Hurry up
and get mirqana so you'll be quiet!"

Sadia came to sit beside me while the men
talked on. As much as I wanted to be part of their
conversation, Sadia was intent on dividing the
room into male and female, and the men were quite
happy to barge on without us. She leaned against
my shoulder and lifted the notebook out of my lap.
She flipped to a blank page near the back and
began sketching a picture of a woman in a wedding
dress. "Sadia," she wrote above the image. She

drew her bridesmaids: her sisters, Orit and Huda, as well as Titune, Warda, and me. I was distinguishable only by my height.

We amused ourselves, taking turns with the pencil, adding details to the scene. She drew the cow that would be slaughtered. I wrote the name of Gishta's mean wife Fatima above the cow. Sadia gave herself hoop earrings and drew a silver chain around her forehead, and I added a curl to the corner of her mouth to give her a mischievous smile. I pictured myself in Sadia's place. I would do more than wait for Aziz to return from Cairo. I would go with him if he asked.

But that afternoon there was no invitation of any kind. Aziz and Munir were still engaged in serious conversation when Sadia rose and said goodbye. Their conversation faltered.

"It's getting late," Aziz said to me.

"I'd best be going too," I said, standing up and brushing the qat debris off my skirt.

"Ciao," they both said, "masalaama," neither of them rising from the floor.

## Calling All Saints.

—

Nature added her voice. The sky was thick with cloud but there was no rain. We still had water brought by the bucketful from the river, but the tops of the boulders that sat midstream had been dry for weeks.

Sheikh Jami had made a pilgrimage to the disciple of the saint who can communicate with the hyenas. He and this disciple had sat in a field at night and offered the hyenas a special bowl of buttered porridge and meat. Now the women were embarking on ritual reparation, making weekly pilgrimages to a saint with the power to bring rain. But the rainy season passed without delivery. We applied more perfume. We burned more incense. We found lice in the children's hair once again.

Our yard was parched and dusty and swarming with flies, though curiously, the once-battered plant in the Wellington boot had perked up considerably. In the middle of a drought, where not a drop of water could be spared, somehow an exception had been made: a plant that was good for nothing had been fed.

Gishta siphoned off what she could from the supplies in her storeroom—a little sorghum, a little oil, a little butter, anything that we might be able to use. But without water, Nouria had no income. There was no way for her to wash clothes. But Gishta had her own problems. Fatima apparently became a monster when there was no water, bossy as only a senior wife can be, with her strict rationing, and her *ussing* and commands. "I'd like to stick her head in a bucket of water and make her shut up," Gishta sneered, handing me a gourd of sour milk.

Not only was life short in Africa, as Gishta frequently reminded me, it was often difficult.

We began to hear rumours that a terrible famine was sweeping the north of the country. But all we saw on Aziz's television were His Majesty's speeches about the country's development, and the shining-medalled officers of his Imperial Army surveying scenes of progress—a new well, the successful harvest of a new hybridized crop, a school for the blind, a textile factory employing amputees.

"There has always been famine," Amir said dismissively. "It has been this way for thousands of years."

"Ah, yes, but this time, the rest of the world has noticed," Munir said, waving his finger. "It would not be such a problem if this famine were caused by drought and crop failure. That would be nature at work. But when you force the peasants to harvest the same amount in a year when the crops are suffering and then they have to give all of it to the landlords, they are left with nothing to eat. *That* is why there is famine."

"Not always," said Aziz. "It's different up north. There the problem is the war with Eritrea. They burn the fields so there is no harvest, and the peasants are forced to buy guns instead of feeding themselves. *That* is why there is famine."

"It's terrible," Sadia muttered, shaking her head.

"Oh, don't be so naive," Aziz snapped. "Do you think it doesn't happen in Harar?"

"It's just hard to picture," I said in Sadia's defence. Even though I had no difficulty believing in the unseen because God manifests his being in so many hidden ways, I couldn't imagine what famine looked like.

Munir said, "We're not at war and we don't get those terrible droughts. This thing we have been going through recently doesn't even compare."

"No, but if it did? Do you think it would be any different? Do you think the Hararis would say to the Oromo: Oh no, keep some food for yourselves. You are our friends, our Muslim brothers, and after all, you harvest the food we eat, so we couldn't possibly let you starve."

His mocking tone rang in the dead air. There was an uncomfortable silence. Aziz stood up, pulled his sarong tightly at the waist and left the room.

—

He turned up at Nouria's compound the following afternoon. It would have been too revealing for me to be overly familiar, so I buried my head and busied myself with my dictionary while he paid his respects to Nouria. She offered him tea, despite having so little water, and because he was polite he did not refuse, but when the cup was in his hand he tipped the contents into Bortucan's willing mouth.

Nouria was intimidated by the doctor; she must have been wondering what warranted this unexpected visit. So was I. But when he picked up Bortucan and the girl giggled, Nouria broke into a smile.

"I was just wondering how she was," he said to Nouria. "She looks good. Has she had any more of those lumps under her hair?"

Nouria mumbled something and excused herself in order to stoke the fire.

"They come and go," I said, approaching.

"That we can treat," he said. "But this, I'm afraid," he said, pointing at her temple, "we cannot."

Not even farenji medicine had an answer.

"I really came to apologize for getting so angry yesterday," he said, lowering his voice and switching to English. "You must just ignore me when I'm like that."

"But I want to understand."

"I wondered if you would come to the farmlands with me next Saturday."

I hesitated.

"There's something I want to show you."

I nodded.

He passed Bortucan to me and pulled a sweet out of his pocket for her. He poked his head into the kitchen to bid Nouria goodbye.

"What was he saying?" she asked me as soon as he had gone.

"He is studying for exams and his books are in English. He asked me the meaning of some words."

I was amazed at how easily the lie came.

—

My students were cautious and slow. Their reserve must have had something to do with the strain in their households because of the drought, but I couldn't help worrying that I was at fault. I must repent for my secrecy and lies, I told myself, but then I drifted off to see his palm raised before my eyes. I stared at the lines, wondering if he was trying to show me a map of some part of the world.

—

Aziz and I huddled together in a horse-drawn calèche, hidden under the awning of the low cart as the driver led us north of the city into green fields by way of a well-worn track. We passed acres of qat shrubs, herds of goats and the occasional farmer with a gun slung over his shoulder.

"Why do they need guns?" I asked.

"Protection," Aziz replied.

"Hyenas?"

"Mostly."

We followed a shallow creek toward a cluster of short palms bearing bunches of small green bananas. The breeze was sweet: an aromatic cocktail. It was here that we disembarked.

Aziz carried a sack in one hand and took my hand in his other. He obviously felt much freer here. It was so open and so lush, so unlike our tight, walled existence within the city, but I felt awkward about holding hands in this naked light.

"My mother's land," he said wistfully, unfolding a blanket at the edge of the stream.

I admired the beauty of this place as we sat on wool laid over a grassy bed in the shade. A thin silver current ran past our feet. I wondered if this was the world I'd seen mapped on his palm.

"It has belonged to my mother's brother for decades now."

"Because she married a Sudanese man?"

He nodded. "Disinherited."

He poured sweet tea from a thermos and unwrapped squares of fatira, a thin pastry stuffed with scrambled egg. He told me he was glad to be able to share this place with me. It was where he came whenever he received a new textbook—where he first opened it, a ritual of his own.

"Somehow being here allows me to imagine things are possible," he said. "You are like this air to me, Lilly: something fresh, something hopeful. You and your batin." He reached for my cheek but then his hand fell away. "It's hard to maintain your resolve, your determination to do good in a

country where there is so much poverty. You hear
our frustration—the inadequate supplies, the
chronic illness, the people's reluctance to seek our
intervention until it is too late. It wears you down
and then you hate yourself for giving up."

I wished there was a way I could help him, just
as he had found a way to give me what I needed to
teach my class.

"We have a right to be angry," he said, wiping
crumbs from his lips. "Particularly with the injus-
tice. We have this pride in the fact that we are a
country that was never colonized, but what people
don't want to admit is that we live under a colonial
regime of our own making. We call other Africans
Barya—slaves. We call the Ethiopians in the south
Shankilla. It means something like dirty blacks.
We call the Oromo Galla. They would use all three
insults to abuse me if they could, but I am an
enigma to them. A black man with a Harari
mother. A black man with a good education. They
don't know where to place me."

"Perhaps you are just a new kind of Ethiopian,"
I offered. "A modern Ethiopian."

"Well, the modern Ethiopian is an angry
Ethiopian, then," Aziz said.

We rose from the bank and in his silence he took
my hand again, leading me through banana trees,
across a field of qat shrubs, toward a wooden
shack. The children playing in the dirt in front of
the shack saw us coming and ran squealing toward
us. "Farenji! Farenji!" they cried, stroking my
arms, touching my clothes.

"Uss!" Aziz quieted them, pulling sweets from his pocket. He said something in Oromiffa that sent all but one of them scurrying back home. Aziz lifted the straggler over his head and sat him down on his shoulders. The snotty-nosed boy laughed and ran his dirty fingers through Aziz's hair.

Aziz set the boy down at the entrance to the shack where chickens clucked away. We followed him in. The dark room was full of stinging smoke coming from a charred pot bubbling away on a small kerosene stove in the corner. It was so dark it took several minutes for my eyes to adjust, and even then, all I could really see were the whites of eyes—at least ten sets of them—peering sullenly from all four sides of the room.

Aziz approached an old man lying on a cot. I couldn't make out his eyes, and he moaned in response to Aziz's touch.

"The owner pulled out his eyes," Aziz said to me. "Last year he only beat him with barbed wire."

I shuddered.

"The harvest wasn't as big as he'd expected. For two years running now we've had less rain." Aziz pulled a pair of scissors from his sack and doused them with alcohol. He was removing stitches from the man's face. "I had to sew the holes shut," he explained. "There was nothing else I could do."

But what kind of harvest would this man reap next year, I wondered, without his eyes?

"Can you take this?" he asked, holding the bottle of alcohol out behind him.

I moved in closer to take the bottle from his hand. I could see then that the man wasn't lying on a cot. He was reclining on a mountain of guns.

Shame.

—

There was disaster all around. No one seemed to know why things were so, but people agreed that it had all started that morning the one muezzin failed to call. Although he had been replaced within a day, the pitch of the new voice was different, slightly off key, tainted by the mystery of where the original muezzin had gone and why. That day in March that had simply not begun had led to weeks and then months of false starts and less hidden bouts of anger. Farmers were now stockpiling guns in the countryside, poor women were being possessed by the spirits of the zar, young men like Aziz and Munir were agitated and angry, children were frightened and forgetting what they learned in their classes, and wives were inflicting cruelties on co-wives.

In the absence of much water, people became parsimonious and mean, looking over each other's shoulders, calling one another greedy, screaming if a drop fell needlessly to the ground. Gishta showed up bearing the evidence: a split lip, a blue cheek.

"That Fatima is a monster," she said, rubbing her jaw as we squatted in the kitchen making tea. "She used to beat me all the time. The first year of marriage is supposed to be a honeymoon. What did I get? Punched in the stomach and kicked in the head."

Gishta had struggled to get through that savage initiation without tears; Hararis hated tears, hated such displays of weakness.

This latest battering was a result of Gishta's having dared, in the dead of night, to wash her hair. But a senior wife's ears are impossibly tuned, particularly during a period of drought. Fatima appeared around the corner as if she had been waiting to pounce the whole time, wrenched the bowl from her co-wife's hands and threw it against the wall. "You selfish, selfish girl!" Fatima screamed as the bowl rolled away.

Fatima boxed Gishta on both ears, held Gishta's head between her hands and shook it back and forth as if she was rattling the last stubborn seeds from a gourd. Gishta tore at Fatima's hands with her nails.

"I should cut off your breasts!" Fatima had hissed before shoving Gishta to the ground. "You are only taking, taking, taking! Stealing from the kitchen for this lazy Galla cousin of yours and that farenji!"

Gishta remained with us for a couple of days, helping us make berbere to sell in the Amhara market. Her lip only got worse when she rubbed ash into it to dry up the oozing pus.

"Let me call the doctor," I insisted several times. When she refused dinner, it was obvious that her lip was causing her more pain than she wanted to admit. "I'm going to call the doctor," I said firmly. Strangely, she burst into tears.

Within an hour, Aziz was pushing Gishta's chin upwards with two fingers. I played nurse, holding on to his medical bag.

"I can't stitch it with this infection," he said. "We'll have to clear that up first." He cleaned the cut with hydrogen peroxide and applied antibiotic ointment. "And take one of these twice a day, just in case," he instructed Gishta.

She stared with distrust at the white pills in the paper packet.

"He's a good man," Gishta said after he left. "It's a shame he is so black."

"So Shankilla," Nouria agreed.

—

We made berbere in lieu of washing clothes. For three days, the yard had been covered in a red blanket of chili peppers drying in the sun. We had just begun picking up the crisp skins when Nouria looked up and asked, "Did you feel that?"

"I did," I marvelled, wiping my forehead.

"Alhamdullilah!"

"Rain!" Fathi shouted.

"Quick!" Nouria shrieked. "We have to get this inside! It will be ruined if it gets wet!"

But the rain suddenly came pelting down, and

though the children were helping us drag the tarps toward the door of the house, we couldn't move fast enough. Nouria looked as if she was about to cry but she burst into hysterical laughter instead. This would be a disastrous waste, but we were so over-joyed that we threw up our arms and surrendered as the ground instantly turned to mud.

—

Anwar led us through the Fatihah, the first chap-ter, that night, but when he began, Bortucan did not follow.

"What's wrong, Bee?" I asked, pulling her into my lap.

Nouria shrugged. "She forgets."

"But she knew this chapter."

"Her mind is small. Twins are not good. Bad luck. One steals from the other."

"But she'd made such progress."

"Allah giveth and Allah taketh away," Nouria said with resignation. "He gave Uncle Jami and then he took him away, after all."

I looked at her.

"Their father," she whispered.

I gasped. "Sheikh Jami?"

"Five years," she said, holding up her hand. His mistress for five years. She spoke in signs: a preg-nant belly, the end of the affair.

This from a man who called farenjis hypocrites and liars.

"Does Gishta know?"

Nouria laughed. "Of course she knows. It was her idea. He is a good Harari man. She was thinking maybe he would take me for the fourth wife."

"So why didn't he?"

She shuddered. "Ohh, that Fatima. She doesn't like Oromo. Two Harari wives, two Oromo wives? No, she didn't like the balance tipping. She is too old to have more children. She did not want these half-breeds running around and growing up to gain some inheritance she wanted for her own."

"But she accepted Gishta."

"Ooph! She tried to kill Gishta! She put the most evil of evil eyes on her. Gishta lost the first baby and the third baby and the fifth. She has had a very, very hard time."

And so had Nouria. Without marriage, a father would not recognize children as his own. Because paternity, as Aziz had said, was everything. Your liberation, your death sentence, your legitimacy or lack thereof in the world.

# A Mother's Job.

—

Munir took on the job of distributing the qat that Saturday because Aziz was nowhere to be found. He separated the stalks, passed them round the circle and set the Prophet's share aside, threw some incense onto the coals and said a du'a before inviting us to begin chewing. I never knew what happened to the Prophet's share.

"But where is he?" I asked, listlessly placing leaves between my molars and my cheek.

"Probably a woman in labour," offered Tawfiq, throwing down a stalk he'd already stripped clean. "The rain comes and suddenly women go into labour. It happens, though I cannot offer you a medical explanation for it."

But a doctor was rarely called upon to deliver a baby. A midwife first, a spiritual healer if there was a problem, but a doctor only if the situation was truly desperate.

"It's more likely he's stuck in Dire Dawa," said Munir. "No taxis."

"No taxis?" Sadia looked shattered. There was a

new boutique in Dire Dawa she was hoping to visit.

"On strike," said Munir. "The emperor doubled the petrol prices."

"Just like that?" I asked.

Munir shrugged. "He's the emperor."

"Perhaps if he realized he was going to interrupt your shopping he would have waited," said Tawfiq, but despite his teasing Sadia, the group lacked energy. It was not just the absence of the sparks that flew when Aziz and Munir sparred, but some other, intangible quality. My body felt limp, sluggish, abandoned in a room where I was used to feeling every fibre of me pulled taut with expectation.

The next day Nouria returned from the market empty handed save for an onion and two tomatoes. How were we going to make the injera for the week without sorghum?

"Sometimes it happens. I don't know, Lilly."

"What do you mean, you don't know?"

"I mean, suddenly it would take one month of what we earn to buy just the smallest handful. I don't know why, but every one was the same. That lady with the silver teeth, she had some which was a little cheaper, but it was riddled with mould, I could smell it."

"What about rice?"

"Ooph. You should have seen it. I saw the Saudi lady—you know, she is married to the man with the glass shop?—and she was saying to Ikhista Aini, 'Sure, I can sell you rice, just give me that gold ring on your fourth finger.'"

We made do with the onion and the tomatoes, making a watery stew into which we threw some scraps of dry injera. Rahile searched in vain for a piece of meat. She said she didn't like old injera. Her mother grimaced at me as if to say: just look at how spoiled she has become! Ever since I had been teaching we'd been eating better, and Rahile had taken to the good life as if it were her birthright. She'd procured her first veil recently by telling Gishta that when she grew up she would like to dress exactly like her. "I wish I was grown up already," she said, pouting, "grown up and beautiful like you."

"That one will never be poor," said Nouria, watching her daughter parade around the yard in my shoes and her new veil.

But that was before the cost of fabric soared—the fabric that came from India from which our veils and dresses were made. Gishta flounced into our courtyard, irritated, having just had a fight with the fabric merchant she most often frequented. "He's trying to sell me this cotton for the price of silk. Who does he think he is all of a sudden? I bet his wife has forced him. She's a greedy woman."

"I remember when his wife was a girl," Nouria said. "She was greedy then, even stealing apricots from the market . . ."

The women gossiped away while I retrieved my shoes from where Rahile had abandoned them. I smacked their soles together to get rid of the dust and wondered what to make of all the price increases and how we would cope if this continued. Aziz would know, I would ask him, but then what if he didn't turn up again on Saturday?

I donned my veil and told the women I was going to the market to see if all the cloth merchants had raised their prices or just this particular one.

"And see if you can smile a little when you speak to the cloth man," Gishta said.

"And remind that Somali woman that her boys are lucky to have you as their teacher," said Nouria.

I knocked on the metal door of Aziz's mother's compound and he answered right away, wearing his loose white galabaya and sandals, holding a notebook in his hand. I slipped into the courtyard at his invitation. He was alone, his mother was doing shir shir, visiting, I could sit with him on a platform in the main room if I'd like and share a fizzy drink.

I preferred to remain standing in the courtyard, too nervous that his mother might return and find us sitting together. He said he'd missed me on Saturday but that he'd had a family obligation to fulfill. It was an explanation that offered no comfort. Something called envy fermented in my stomach as he spoke. Apparently his mother had claimed she had found the ideal girl for him and sent him off to introduce himself. Finding suitable matches for one's children was a mother's job. In some senses, it was what success as a mother depended upon. It was the second time since he'd returned from medical school that she'd done this.

What was ideal? I wanted to know.

"Obedient, good at housework, skilled at handicrafts, light skinned, beautiful and from a good lineage," Aziz replied without hesitation. "Though not necessarily in that order."

Light skinned, I thought. One out of six.

"It's like a game," Aziz said, trying to lessen the significance of it. "I go to introduce myself to the girl's mother and say that I'm available if the family needs the services of a doctor. She offers me a seat facing the wooden doors so that I can see the girl as she passes across the courtyard. It makes me very uncomfortable. It is a game where I am supposed to be a hunter and the girl the prey. In any case, my mother is furious now because I left long before it was polite to do so. I should have stayed and prayed with her father and eaten dinner with her brothers. But I just couldn't."

I wondered if the girl was pretty. I wondered if I could bear it if this happened again. I felt slightly nauseated.

As soon as I returned home Nouria asked me if I was sick.

"No. Why?"

"Rahile says you went to visit the doctor."

"I thought maybe his mother could tell me where to buy affordable cloth. She wears such nice clothes."

"And did she?" Nouria asked, her eyes full of warning.

—

That was not enough to stop me from walking to the hospital at lunch the next day. I was feeling something new and awful. What if one of these days his mother introduced him to the ideal girl, or a girl whose beauty swept him away? And for that matter, what about the nurses? The hospital was a world, after all, where girls were much freer to interact with men.

The front entrance of the hospital was blocked by a crowd of women shouting and waving placards. I found a way in through the back of the building.

"What's going on out there?" I asked as soon as I found Aziz in the dull green corridors.

He led me out to the back courtyard. "The nurses are on strike," he said as we sat down on a bench. "The doctors are taking extra shifts in order to deal with emergencies."

He insisted I share the bread and tomatoes he had brought for his lunch and he bought me a cup of tea in a tin cup from the canteen. He offered me powdered milk from the bag in his pocket.

"Are you worried?" I asked him.

"It's always worrying. In any case, Lilly, I'm glad you came. I wanted you to know that yesterday, when my mother came home, I told her that I will choose for myself when I am good and ready. Of course she objects because it is not the traditional way. She is quite sure that only a woman can honestly judge another woman's character. It is always best to leave it to your mother, she says."

"Is the girl pretty?" I asked, despite my best intentions.

Aziz sighed. "My mother is doing this because she wants me to be married into a good Harari family. People rarely marry for love. They believe the heart leads you astray, leads you to make choices that will harm you in the end. Look at my mother—she's still paying the price. She doesn't want me to suffer the alienation she did. And honestly? I think she believes she can elevate her social standing through forming an alliance with an old established family. Gain her place back. And she probably can. Could."

"Through you."

"Through me."

"Isn't it enough that you went to university, that you have this respected job with a title and an income?"

"This isn't a democracy, Lilly." He looked lost in thought while he stirred his tea.

"What about the girl in Addis Ababa?"

"Ah, I see there has been gossip," he said, looking down. "Mintiwab. She was at medical school with us."

My skin bristled at the sound of her name.

"She did not love me back," he said without apparent emotion.

Envy rolled over me and spilled to the ground.

"You know, before I met her—you'll have to forgive me—but I used to think girls were rather silly. And then here we were at medical school and I see this girl who has no problem suturing a wound, or dissecting a cadaver, and I realize: girls are not passive by nature. They are only so because the culture demands they be.

"One day I approached her and asked if maybe she would like to come to a small party Munir and I were going to have. But do you know what she said?"

"That she couldn't date a Muslim?"

"No. She actually said she was not interested in anything other than her studies. She'd seen far too many girls abandon university when they met a man and she had no intention of not completing her studies and becoming a doctor. And the funny thing is, I think that is why I loved her," Aziz said, sounding surprised. "I realized that given the opportunity, a woman could be a man's equal. It made me wonder if perhaps this is the real reason why they keep men and women apart in Islam."

I didn't have a moment to think about that. Aziz gripped both my wrists, his knees pressed into mine. "The fact is, my mother would like me to meet a nice Harari girl, but medical school ruined me for traditional marriage. None of them are like Minti. And then there is you, farenji, with such independence and conviction, with your desire to change the lives of poor children. Not just a desire—a plan and an effect. What am I supposed to do?"

I stared at the impression of his fingerprints on my skin.

## To Hold a Girl.

—

The Faras Magala still fluttered. Qat addicts pleading with qat sellers, city folk bartering with peasants, tailors humming away on their old machines, goats and donkeys farting and dumping, children whining and grovelling, and lepers begging without arms and legs and noses. Produce had become fresh and plentiful again with the end of the drought. This was lucky: the qat addicts had become abusive during the drought, as they do whenever their drug is costly or unavailable, hurling insults and stones at passersby.

There was only one communal taxi to Dire Dawa these days. The minibus was already full when I slipped on board, with several Oromo returning to smaller towns outside the city and two Harari women off to spend the day shopping or visiting relatives from whom I deliberately concealed my face.

Over the years, many Hararis had gone to live in Dire Dawa. The French had built a railway from Djibouti to Addis Ababa at the turn of the century, and Dire Dawa was one of the only stops along the five-hundred-mile route. Imported goods, most from India and China, were cheaper there, where they were offloaded straight from the train.

Hararis would move as far as Addis Ababa to make money, and prospered in trade wherever they went. But the majority of them still remained in the old city, and none of them left the country, except to make the haj. Ethiopians as a whole did not leave their country. A few students had made their way west to pursue further education, which they planned to put to use back in their own country, but there was no emigration, there was no such thing as a diaspora; the words for these things would not even come into existence until sometime later in history.

I paid a huge sum of money for the trip and as the bus pulled out of the main square I waved behind me, a tear rolling down my face.

"Why are you crying, dear?" a toothless Oromo woman with a chicken in her lap asked me in Harari.

I was grateful she assumed this to be my language. It was in my dress and the way I carried myself. It helped that her eyes were clouded with a white film.

"Because I'm leaving my mother," I replied, looking backwards again, lying because I didn't really know the answer. Conflicted? Partly. Lies were becoming more frequent. And easier. Nouria and Gishta had given me their blessing, believing I was on my way to meet Sadia in Dire Dawa, where we would stay with some relatives of hers and spend the weekend shopping for items that Munir and his family were obliged to provide for their eventual new home.

It was not implausible; we were planning to do this soon enough, just not yet. Sadia happily colluded in my risky adventure, saying she would cover my tracks if I might, in return, please try to visit the new boutique with its fashinn gidir imports from India and memorize everything on its shelves.

"You are a good daughter," said the old Oromo woman, stroking her chicken.

After an hour of twisting mountain roads, we reached the desert floor. I had to fight my way off the bus as returning passengers attempted to cram their package-laden bodies on board. I lifted my head to see him, an obelisk standing strong and solid in the middle of the teeming square.

"This way," he said, leading me by the elbow through the crowd, past fruit stalls piled high with mangoes, goats scavenging for vegetables, a storefront displaying plastic buckets in primary colours, a boy shining shoes though he himself was not wearing any.

We turned into a beautiful street lined with acacia trees bursting red and purple, speckling the street with colour and shade. The buildings, modern and spacious, were cheerful pinks and yellows and crisp, clean whites. Vines spilled suggestively over their compound walls, saying: There is life here and life is good. It was so much cleaner and brighter than Harar. And so much hotter. The air was unwhispering, utterly still, and the sun blazed white even though it was already late afternoon.

We slipped through an alleyway between two buildings, at the end of which shone a bright blue metal gate, and I followed Aziz into a small, shady, meticulous courtyard made up of yellow and blue ceramic tiles, an ornate fountain standing at its centre. The house belonged to Munir's grandfather, and Aziz stayed here whenever he came to Dire Dawa, as he occasionally did to collect books or pick up medical supplies.

"Let me introduce you," Aziz said, climbing the three steps to the main room. "Prepare yourself," he warned me. "Grandfather Ibrahim!" he yelled.

A wrinkled little Harari man with flaming red hennaed hair was sitting on a pillow, a cup of water on one side of him, the Qur'an on the other.

"This is the girl I was telling you about!" shouted Aziz. "The Arab girl!"

The old man's eyesight was obviously worse than his hearing, but what he lacked in senses he made up for in strength. "Ahlan wa sahlan!" he said surprisingly loudly. Welcome. "Have you ever met anybody who is ninety-eight years old?" he asked in Arabic.

I laughed and told him no, I never had. He pulled out his false teeth then, and I couldn't help but shriek, causing him to laugh so hard that his entire body shook. Suddenly, the old man leapt to his feet.

"I might not have my teeth, but I can still

dance!" he shouted. He jumped off the platform onto the floor and ran into the courtyard. "Look at me!" he shouted with a snort, running around in circles, his red curls bouncing. "I have the energy of a man half my age! All my wives died!" he yelled. "None of them could keep up with me!"

"It's true," said Aziz. "He's alone here now. Most of his children are dead. He's got only his grandchildren and great-grandchildren now."

"You're incredible," I said.

"I'm ninety-eight!" he shouted again, before running back into the main room and hopping onto the platform to resume his seated position. He immediately closed his eyes and began to snore.

I stifled my laughter.

"He has a medical condition," Aziz whispered. "Narcolepsy. He drops off to sleep in the middle of things. I honestly think it's what's kept him so young. He must have slept through half his life. He's really only forty-nine!"

I tiptoed out of the room and followed Aziz up a narrow staircase. The balcony overlooking the courtyard ran the entire length of the first floor. Aziz showed me to my room at one end. It was simply furnished, but it had a bed. I hadn't slept on a bed since being at the palace. The edge of the mattress sunk under my weight.

"I thought only royalty slept in beds in Ethiopia," I said.

"Grandfather's second wife was Italian," said Aziz, "and she insisted on beds. With Egyptian cotton sheets. And good chocolate. She had it sent from Rome. I'll leave you now, shall I? I'll come back and fetch you for dinner."

I stretched out on the bed, leaving the door open so I could enjoy the late-afternoon sun, and stared at the dust dancing above my head. How strange to be here, free of prying eyes, liberated from cramped quarters. I thought about the grandfather and his Italian wife. Wondered how they'd met and whether the Italian woman had learned Arabic or Harari and converted to Islam, and whether they'd had children who were half black and half white and whether those children were despised because of their mixed blood. I wondered if the grandfather had ever been to Italy, skied the Alps. I envied his narcolepsy and drifted off to sleep.

—

Aziz was standing at my door. He was wearing a navy blue suit, the arms of which looked a bit too short.

"I thought I could take you somewhere European for dinner," he said somewhat self-consciously.

"I didn't know there were any Europeans living here," I said.

"The Europeans are gone, but their food isn't. There's a very special Italian restaurant here. You can have anything you want—spaghetti, risotto, lasagna. They make all of it in their kitchen."

I grimaced. "I'm afraid I don't have any nice clothes."

He pulled a scarf from behind his back and held it out to me—a loose and beautiful pink and purple chiffon. "Grandfather's Italian wife used to wear this," he said, pressing it into my hands.

"It's beautiful." I ran its soft length through my fingers. "But won't he be upset if he sees me wearing it?"

"He told me to give it to you."

I put one hand on his shoulder and stood on my toes to kiss his cheek. As I leaned into him he cupped the back of my head and pulled me in.

"I'm so glad you came," he whispered in my ear. I could feel his heart beating through his jacket. He smelled like burned matches and cologne. I closed my eyes and breathed him in before stepping back and draping the scarf over my head.

—

He linked arms with me as we walked down the dark street. It was a lot less conservative in Dire Dawa, he assured me. "Harar is so old-fashioned. It makes me crazy sometimes," he said.

We passed through a pair of red curtains into a small courtyard where a wooden shack sheltered a single long table covered in red-and-white checkered cloth under an awning. The table was lit with candles and lanterns hung from the beams. It was magical. It reminded me of sitting in a café with my parents somewhere in Europe. But such scenes were always noisy and crowded. Here a lone couple sat huddled together at one end of the table, too lost in each other to spare us a glance.

A man stepped out of the shadows and shook Aziz's hand roughly.

"Ciao, Girma," Aziz said. "It's good to see you." They gripped each other by the shoulders. "How are you? How is your family—that mischievous brother of yours?"

"I've got Ibsaa with me at the moment," Girma said, lowering his voice.

"I haven't seen him in years!"

"Since they closed the university."

Aziz stepped back in surprise. "When did they do that?"

"Beginning of last week. The students were demonstrating outside the palace."

"Because of the inflation?" Aziz asked.

"It started when they raised the petrol prices. The students came out in support of the taxi drivers; they even started setting the emperor's buses on fire, but the police put an end to that with their batons. Of course, this only made the students more determined. But you know it, Aziz, they make trouble for themselves, they are too young to know that they are not invincible."

"But they are right to act on their principles. I envy them what they don't know," Aziz said.

Girma sighed. "What is to envy? This time some of the students managed to get past the palace gates and, well . . . poof." Girma raised his arms as if hefting a rifle.

Aziz encouraged his friend to continue, though

he gripped my shoulder in a way that suggested he could sense my growing horror.

"So now they've prohibited public gatherings of any kind," Girma continued. "You stand with four of your friends in the street talking about the weather and they can arrest you."

"But we never see any of this on the television," I blurted out.

"The emperor owns the television station," Girma said. "We didn't see the garbage collectors go on strike either. Or the civil servants. Or the journalists. Anyway," he said, cupping Aziz's shoulder, "this is enough talk of politics. You and your friend have come here for dinner. Let me not spoil it."

Aziz was silent for a moment after we sat down. He stared at his hands in his lap.

"Why do we never hear any of this?" I asked him.

"We're very cut off in Harar," he finally said to the tablecloth. "We hear only bits and pieces. An uprising over here, a protest over there. People keep calling these things isolated incidents because most of them happen in small towns, but if this is what is happening in the capital, I really doubt . . ."

"What do you doubt?"

"No." He shook his head. "It's best I don't let my imagination start," he said, sweeping his palm across the table.

Girma handed Aziz a menu and set down two small glasses. "Grappa," he announced.

"It's a lot less conservative here," Aziz assured me for the second time that night. "I don't think it hurts anyone to have a drink now and then. In the right circumstances. And only if you don't make it a habit and neglect your responsibilities."

I smirked. "You're very practical. The most practical Muslim I've ever met."

"I think true discipline comes through exercising moderation. I see the rules as simply guidelines for those times when we lack the strength or wisdom to decide for ourselves."

But that must take such courage, I thought. It is harder in many ways to live in the middle than at the edges. Much harder to interpret as you see fit, because then you have no assurance you are doing right in the eyes of God, no confidence you will be rewarded in the afterlife.

Aziz ordered veal, and I asked for something called gnocchi because Girma described it as "every bite having completion." Girma laid down napkins and knives and forks. I picked up the fork and turned it over.

"Do you miss eating with a knife and fork?" Aziz asked.

"I like eating with my hands."

"But it's not very hygienic."

"It's much more sociable, though. There's something uncharitable about having your own plate, something wrong about stabbing your food with a piece of metal. Food tastes right from the hand."

He raised his eyebrows. "Where did you get this open spirit from? Did your parents teach you this?"

I stared at him and found my reflection in his twinkling eyes. "In a way, I suppose," I answered, having only just considered it. No one had ever asked me such a thing. Under the Great Abdal's tutelage I was asked to look forward, never back, as if my life before was the Jahiliyya—the time of ignorance before the arrival of Islam. My memories of my parents were tainted. Predicated by questions. Were they fundamentally immoral? Did they deserve to die? It was easier somehow to believe that the answer to both questions was yes.

"They were very adventurous," I struggled, not knowing how to put them into words. "Passionate and curious about life, but those same things often led them to be rather careless and irresponsible."

Our food arrived, but neither of us touched it while I attempted to pull something concrete out of the hazy pre-Islamic times spent wandering Europe with my parents. Moments of joy were brief and isolated, lived out against a backdrop of uncertainty and not infrequent loneliness.

"I can see why Islam had such appeal," said Aziz, offering me a first bite—a bit of veal from the end of his fork. "Here we are born to Islam," he said. "We are not asked to choose between one life and another. The problem, I imagine, is what you do with the other life once you have chosen this one."

"What, indeed," I said. You ignore it. Or you condemn it. You think of non-Muslims, including, quite possibly and perhaps especially your parents, as hedonists. You call them selfish and unethical because it is easier than having to reconcile it all. And you strive to be good in your new life. You strive to be a very good Muslim. But then you meet a man who says it is possible to have a much more liberal interpretation—to have the occasional drink, to be alone with a girl. And you are that girl. And you are alone with that man. And you find yourself compromising everything you thought you believed in to be here with him. And ironically, though things feel even more uncertain in many ways than they did when your life was a nameless existence governed by the whims of your parents, you cannot resist being here.

I snapped out of it, boldly raised my glass of grappa. "In French they say: to your health."

The fire tore down my throat.

Hours later, we stumbled together along the nearly deserted street with bellies full of cake and heads full of grappa. Aziz recounted a tale about his grandmother, a blind woman who was said to have healing power in her touch.

"She was a great believer in the saints," he said, "a frequent visitor to the shrines of Ay Kulleeyay, the patron saint of broken pots, and Aw Warika, the saint who can make warts disappear—especially the very big ones with black hairs growing from them."

I laughed in disbelief, but Aziz insisted he was serious. "Really, there's a saint for just about every problem you can imagine. If it is only a little wart you can visit Sidi Abou."

I grabbed his cuff and stopped him in the street. "You don't believe in them, do you?"

"I believe people believe," he said, looking away as he considered the question. "They need to believe in something closer than God, because God often feels too distant."

He was right: the saints offer us a ladder to reach Him more easily. "And they bring people together," I contributed.

He nodded. "They do. Or at least belief in them does."

"One and the same," I said, sounding much more certain than I felt.

—

It was a hot night, a night of memories visited against the backdrop of the old man snoring boisterously below. I was a reluctant spectator, watching my parents crawl up through the rabbit hole and throw off their costumes. They usually remained underground. Under our feet where the jinn live.

It was so much easier to keep them separate, to divide the world in two: male and female, dead and alive, black and white, misguided and Muslim. It was easier to be bitter and condemn, deny the relationship and keep the distance, because without judgment, Aziz was leading me to discover, there lurked longing.

Philip from Basingstoke and Alice from Dublin, two people who died in search of different lives. And the daughter who was perhaps living that life that eluded them. Alice, through the looking glass, had become Lilly . . . and Lilly, in the presence of Aziz, was unveiled.

He stood angelic in the doorway, his feet bare, moonlight electrifying his hair. He inhaled and stepped gingerly into the room, and sat on the edge of my bed. He said my hair felt strange: slippery, almost wet. He touched my cheek.

"What's this?" he asked, wiping a tear from my chin. "Why, Lilly? What's the matter?"

"I don't know," I whispered. "I was just thinking about my father."

"I'm sorry," Aziz said. "Now you are missing him."

"I was just thinking about a time . . . a time we were on the beach outside Tangier. There was a cluster of women sitting huddled in black under an umbrella who were pointing fingers at us and shaking their heads. I asked my father why they wore all those clothes, even at the beach, and he said they do it in the name of religion. But aren't they hot? I asked him, and he said: I'm sure they are, but maybe other things matter more to them.

"Like what? I wanted to know. We were drying off, getting ready to leave, and he said: Maybe one day you'll have a chance to ask them. It was odd— like he knew somehow that I would. That this would become my world. But at the time I said: They scare me. And as he pointed out, they seemed to be scared of us too."

Aziz stretched out on his back beside me, his head sharing my pillow, his arms rigid at his sides. I pulled his right arm underneath my head and lay my cheek on his chest. His chest was warm and solid, his heart loud, and he smelled faintly of sweat, like pepper and the woodsmoke of Girma's kitchen. He clasped his hands together to hold me there.

—

I watched his soft face as the muezzins woke the world. Propped on my elbow, I leaned across his smooth, bare chest and lingered, eyes shining, lips hesitant and falling. His lips parted, pulled me in, filling my mouth with the sugar and warmth of his tongue. A bubble of silence carried us upward, where we floated on a sea of holy voices. He gripped the back of my neck and rolled his body lazily toward me, his eyes closed, as if in sleep.

He pressed his lean body into mine, his tongue still deep in my mouth, his hand slowly circling my back through the thin fabric of my diri, lulling me into something as tingling and drifting as mirqana. The movement of his hand kept me afloat as we rocked back and forth. He rolled me over, my back to his front. His fingertips circled my navel and he breathed heavily into my neck. I shivered and felt the hardness of him against the small of my back.

"Aziz! Why aren't you awake, you lazy boy?" the old man hollered from the courtyard below.

Aziz wrapped his entire body around mine like a shell and squeezed me, the snail.

"I'm ninety-eight years old and I've got more energy than you!" he continued.

"Distract him, will you, Lilly?" Aziz whispered.

I straightened my diri, then slipped out the door and poked my head over the balcony. "Good morning, sir," I called over the railing. "Shall I knock on his door?" I made a great performance of doing so. "No answer," I shouted over the balcony. "Didn't he say he had to run an errand early this morning? You don't remember? Well, perhaps you had fallen asleep."

"Perhaps," the old man conceded. "Will you come and have breakfast with me, then? I've been waiting for some company for over an hour."

"Of course," I replied, hitching up my diri in one hand and making my way down the wooden staircase. But how could an hour have passed since the call to prayer?

I sat with Grandfather Ibrahim in the main room, breaking pieces of injera to lift lentils, but I could barely bring myself to eat.

"Where did Aziz tell me you were from?" the old man asked.

"Yemen," I replied without hesitation.

"Ah yes, the *real* home of the great Queen of Sheba." He nodded. "I don't believe this Amhara story that she was one of theirs. I think they just invented this myth to convince themselves they were some kind of God-chosen master race. In any case . . . don't get me started . . . Aziz says you're visiting family here?"

"In Harar."

"Pah," he said with a dismissive wave. "I can't see why Munir and Aziz are so intent on working there. We have a much better hospital here, and people aren't so superstitious about it. I can't stand all that nonsense—saints and miracles and that thing they do to little girls. It's all folklore, not Islam. A pack of lies," he said. "Believe me, I was married to an Italian woman for years. She was lovely and pure. Nothing dirty or dangerous about her."

Aziz joined us, dressed and clean-shaven. He looked straight at me and smiled. I felt my burning red skin of guilt.

"There you are, my boy!" shouted the old man. "A good thing, too. If I'd spent any more time alone here with this charming girl I might have started to believe I'd finally found a wife young enough to keep up with me!"

## Eyes Peek over the Wall.

—

We returned to a different city. The Imperial Army had always stayed out, letting Hararis run their own affairs, but suddenly we could see fingertips, followed by the whites of eyes, as soldiers began peeking over the wall.

Two ragged-looking soldiers had stopped the minibus I took back from Dire Dawa and interrogated the driver. He was forced to slip them some money before they let the bus pass through the city gate. The driver rolled up the window.

"They have caught the Negele flu," one of the passengers finally said.

"I heard that the soldiers are sick," I said to Aziz when we next met for bercha, "with Negele flu."

"Who said this?" Munir asked abruptly.

"I overheard a man saying it."

Negele was a town in Sidamo province, it turned out. Soldiers there had staged a mutiny after inflation had made it impossible for them to buy teff or rice. They were living on mouldy potato skins and

water, demanding raises, while their officers continued stuffing themselves with meat and injera
and beer. The soldiers put their guns to the
temples of their senior officers, saying they were
doing this in the name of the emperor, weeding out
corruption and disloyalty in the imperial ranks
and rewarding those who actually serve the imperial regime.

"This flu is very contagious," said Aziz.

"It's about time," said Munir.

I didn't know what Munir meant, because this
Negele flu made it increasingly difficult for us
women when we went to market. The soldiers now
loitered there, resting on their guns, reaching out
to touch women as they passed. Men got angry
with their wives because they were reluctant to go
to market, then got angry at their wives for going
to market and being accosted. Nouria and I braved
it as we had to, but I was "the farenji" again.
Nouria could see how angry it was making me, so
she told me not to worry, she would go alone. She
came home from the market disgusted, washing
thoroughly after being touched by these men who
were dirty and stank of Christian meat and urine
and beer.

—

The television showed Haile Selassie smiling, greeting dignitaries from foreign countries, taking a trip
to the southern provinces where thousands of his
subjects in tribal costumes appeared enraptured

and lay prostrate on the ground before him. Entire villages dancing, singing, "Long live the emperor, the King of Kings."

We watched footage of a trip to Jamaica, where jubilant, long-haired masses shouted, "Jah Rastafari!" and waved placards that read "Selassie is Christ." He was Ras Tafari until 1930, the year he was crowned Negusa Negast, or King of Kings, and adopted the name Haile Selassie, meaning "Might of the Trinity." God, the Son and the Holy Ghost.

"Look at that," Aziz exclaimed, "they're recycling old news! This is from years ago!"

"And do you know the joke of this, Lilly?" Munir pointed at the tiny medalled man on the screen. "While these Jamaicans see him as a great symbol of African independence, the emperor denies Ethiopians are Africans at all! Ethiopians are the sons of King Solomon of Jerusalem, they claim. At least the Amharas are."

"Certainly not the Oromo," said Aziz. "They would never include the Galla—"

"—or the Shankilla."

"—or the Falasha."

"—or the Barya."

"They have a term of insult for everyone but themselves," said Aziz.

"And the Harari," Munir added. "They don't have a name for us."

"No, they just call you greedy, self-interested misers who would sell your children to make money. You are the real Jews of Ethiopia."

"That includes you, Aziz," said Munir.

"Does it?" Aziz snapped.

They both sighed with exasperation and turned away.

—

The soldiers came closer, daring to approach the mosque: they were standing guard outside the women's gate as we flooded through for Friday prayers, mocking with lewd insults and rude gestures. Women collapsed on the stairs at the entrance of the mosque, contaminated and unable to enter.

Once the imam realized a good portion of his congregation was missing, he himself came to see what was the matter. He had his assistants bring buckets of water so the women could wash the defilement away, and together, as a community, we recovered and kneeled down to pray.

The following Friday, the men of the council of elders, distinguished men with skullcaps and trim white beards, formed a human fence between us and the soldiers as we filed in through the women's gate. The soldiers did not dare spew their evil over the heads of the leaders of our community. They stood in mocking silence instead as they watched us pass.

But our imam was not present that day, and it appeared no one had been appointed to take his place. Whispers rippled throughout the congregation. Perhaps he has disappeared like the muezzin, people were saying—speculation that struck fear in the hearts of everyone, for if a muezzin and an imam were not safe, was anyone?

Sheikh Jami called for peace and order, the stilling of hearts, belief in faith as our guide.

Afterwards, I pressed Gishta for information. "Has the sheikh said anything, said whether it is true that the imam has disappeared?"

"He does not speak of these things to me," said Gishta. "But on Tuesday nights I can extract from him anything I want, so give me until then, I will see what I can find out."

But before Tuesday, the council of elders met to discuss the situation. They sent messengers into the neighbourhoods to tell people it was a time for caution, for taking smaller footsteps, for observing the curfew that had just been imposed by the army prohibiting people being in the street after six o'clock at night.

Everyone was silent, uncertain what it all meant. Reasons had not been given, implications not spelled out. For a day or so people remained closed in their compounds, as if no one had work to do, a shop to keep, a stall to man, homework to complete, vegetables to buy, food to prepare, children to feed.

"Commission" was the word on Gishta's lips on Wednesday. Some commission organized by a newly formed council of officers from the military and the police force, appointed to investigate corruption on the emperor's behalf. Sheikh Jami told Gishta they had charged the imam with being disloyal to the emperor, though on what basis, he did not know, for this commission did not offer explanations. And it was they who had been responsible for the disappearance of the muezzin as well as several less notable others over the last couple of months.

"Have faith" was Sheikh Jami's message. "The righteous will be rewarded; the perpetrators condemned."

I did have faith, but I also had a desire for more information. I headed to the hospital after lunch, taking the road outside the wall to avoid the soldiers at the main gate. But the wide boulevard where the hospital stands was deserted, and the front doors of the hospital were closed, not a guard in sight. I looked up and down the street, growing increasingly anxious, for there was no one, no movement save for a couple of oblivious goats biting the fleas at their ankles. And then I noticed that the gates of the usually guarded and concealed royal residence across the road from the hospital were splayed wide open. I took a few steps forward and I could see they were ravaged like a face scarred by smallpox.

I ran, lost a shoe but kept running down the middle of the deserted boulevard to the closest point of entry—the main gate, where two soldiers stood guard. One stopped me and said something in Amharic, but all I understood was "Miss Farenji." "Capisce questo?" he then asked, grabbing the front of his trousers. The other soldier laughed and whacked him on the arm with his gun.

I bolted through the door of one of the shops near the gate.

At first I thought the shop was empty, but the owner slowly rose from the back room where he was chewing qat, pulled the curtain and stared at me.

"Haji Mahfouz," I said, relieved to see a familiar face from the neighbourhood.

"What do you want?" he asked, failing to greet me.

"The soldiers," I panted, pointing toward the street.

"I don't want problems being brought into my shop." He stepped round from behind his counter and opened the door.

Again, I ran.

Aziz was at home, Munir with him, both of them still wearing their hospital clothes, when I arrived, completely out of breath, veil around my shoulders, unable to get out the words.

"Try and breathe first," said Aziz, bringing me a glass of water. I put my head in my hands, trying to recover.

"What's happening?" I finally asked. "I came to find you at the hospital—"

"That was very risky," said Munir.

"But how was I to know?"

"You heard the message from the elders—it's not safe at the moment, especially outside the walls."

"I just wanted to ask you something, something I heard about a commission."

"It's not even safe to be asking questions now, Lilly," Aziz said. "Why don't you listen to your sheikh who is preaching for stronger religious observance?"

He's patronizing me, I realized. He doesn't believe faith is the answer, at least not the answer for him. He's sending me to a corner like a child. Or a woman.

—

It was the commission that was responsible for barging into the royal residence and spiriting the duke and duchess back to the capital. The army then took over the residence. And where was the emperor in all this? Nodding his head in support, apparently. But why was the emperor advocating the arrest of members of his own family? And why did I have to rely on Gishta for information charmed from Sheikh Jami on Tuesday nights when Aziz and Munir clearly knew what was going on? Their conversations on Saturdays were hushed, though they obviously had much to say. They were not stunned and paralyzed like so many people I knew, but buoyed, with great urgency to their exchange. I didn't dare interrupt them with questions; I'd been warned.

Apart from Sadia, the other girls stopped attending berchas, preferring to remain closer to home. The other men felt excluded by Aziz and Munir and convened at Tawfiq's house for berchas, at which he was very sorry, it would be impossible to have girls.

One Saturday that summer, I turned up at Aziz's uncle's house as usual. The old man greeted me as he always did, gesturing welcome, proceed, but the room was empty. I found the usual thermos of tea and jug of water on the floor as well as a small pile of qat, but no one else until Sadia arrived a few minutes later, saying, "Munir says they have business today." She either could not or would not elaborate.

"You want qat?" she asked listlessly, waving a stalk.

I shrugged. "Not really." The point of it was the company. His company.

We turned on the television. It was raining in the capital. Except for one or two members of the Imperial Guard, the emperor stood alone on his balcony, poised to make a speech. He stood in the rain and addressed the nation, speaking compassionately about famine in the north. I was sure we had never heard him use the word *famine* before. He stressed the progress being made in economic development and praised the army and police for their fierce, undying loyalty, for guiding the commission that was ridding the country of corruption.

But was he crying as he spoke? Perhaps it was the rain, but for years afterwards, people, regardless of whether they actually saw the broadcast or not, would say they had witnessed the exact moment when the lion began to die. With that throne speech it became apparent: a two-thousand-year-old dynasty was disintegrating before our eyes.

## A Beach, a Bridge.

—

Nouria and I had taken a job sewing cowry shells onto the rims of finished baskets. The tedium of our chores worked to offset some of the uncertainty that surrounded us. We sang songs while we worked, folk songs Gishta had taught me about Harari children lost in the wilderness brought home on the backs of hyenas, about Noah and the animals and about girls who mistakenly marry for love.

My voice faltered as the fence parted one afternoon and Aziz stepped through. The urgency of his expression pulled me upright, shells spilling from my lap onto the ground. He greeted Nouria and Gishta, who remained seated, and affected a smile before addressing me in English.

He wasted no time. He apologized for his absence the Saturday before but said he needed to be elsewhere in his free time, with a different group of people, thus officially putting an end to our berchas. I felt numb.

"Meetings," he said, when I pressed him for more. "About what is happening."

"But what is happening?"

"Changes," he said quietly.

"But can't I be involved?"

"Not with this group, I'm afraid. We meet outside the city."

"But I've left the city with you before, Aziz," I pointed out, wondering if this had anything to do with an arsenal of guns lying underneath a man with no eyes.

"This meeting is only for men."

I was stunned. "But you said you believed men and women to be equal, at least given the chance. *Minti*. Remember?"

"Right now there is no time to give people a chance."

I looked at him coldly.

"Look, Lilly, not everybody is like Munir and me. Some people are more conservative and prefer to keep those lines between men and women strictly drawn, particularly where politics are concerned. It's a question of priorities."

He was choosing this over me. It reminded me somehow of the women on the Moroccan beach. Draped in black. Not feeling the heat, my father suggested, because other things mattered more to them. But I'd shed my black in order to be near him.

"Why, Aziz?" I pleaded.

"Because the needs of the collective have to take precedence over self-interest," he stated, sounding nothing like himself.

"But what about your exams next month?"

"That will have to wait."

"You would choose to stay here rather than pursue your education in Cairo?"

"Right now, if it came to that, yes. Yes, I would."

"But I thought you wanted that advanced medical training so you could help more people. That would benefit the collective."

"That's a very Western way of looking at it," he said.

It was as if a bridge between us had just collapsed. Or rather, he'd just detonated it.

I didn't have a moment to survey the destruction. As soon as he left, Gishta leaned over and patted my hand.

"It's for the best," Nouria said.

I was too upset to reply.

"He has to marry a Harari girl," Gishta said. "If he were pure Harari, then maybe he would have a choice. Men have less choice about these things than women."

They obviously knew Aziz and I had some kind of relationship, but my relief that they were not angrier was fleeting. Gishta meant that our parts would never add up to make a Harari whole. I was furious that she had to reduce it all, once again, to marriage when there were much bigger things at work.

"It's got nothing to do with that!" I shouted, but immediately regretted having snapped at her. If women were truly kept away from politics, then I could hardly blame them. These were their politics. The affairs of the heart.

Part Seven.

—

# London, England

1988

## Butchering the Stems.

—

"Wow" is all I can say.

"You don't like it?" Amina asks, stretching her neck to take a look at the back of the skirt.

"It's just, you know, a rather unusual choice." Tartan, just above the knees, second-hand and smelling of mothballs and patchouli, like the shop.

"It is fashinn gidir!" she says.

That might be. I just wouldn't have pictured her in it, *can't* picture her in it even now that she's got it on.

She jerks the curtain closed, pulls off the skirt and nearly tears the curtain from the rail as she re-emerges and stomps past me to slap the skirt down on the counter, where a teenager with a pierced lip gladly takes her money. Thirteen pounds fifty for a mouldy skirt.

But it's an occasion—the first anniversary of Yusuf's arrival in London. He's insisted he doesn't want a big party, just the family and Mr. and Mrs. Jahangir, and though it isn't our way not to share any celebration as widely as possible, we defer.

We've spent the last three nights preparing a feast of special foods, dishes normally reserved for weddings and people's return from the haj. There is mulukhiya, a thick, green turgid soup we adopted from the Egyptians during their brief occupation of Harar in the last century; sambusas, small samosas introduced by Indian merchants; misr wat, stewed lentils we borrowed from the Sudanese; spaghetti Bolognese, introduced into our diet by the Italians; ruz bi laiban, rice pudding courtesy of the Arabs by way of the English; and ankhar mahtab, tripe stew, possibly the most unpalatable of all the dishes but the only one of them we can rightfully call our own.

Amina burns incense to mask the dominant smell of fried onions and we sing folk songs while we knock elbows in this impossibly small space. We complain now where we once created such miracles out of brown river water, battered produce and unrefrigerated meat, which we cooked over wood fires, smoke in our eyes and black smudges on our faces, wiping our brows from the staggering heat with the corners of our skirts during droughts when we couldn't even bathe or wash our clothes.

I cover the table with a cloth Amina bought at a bargain shop—reindeer and holly, discounted in July—and arrange her fancy bowls and plates with the gold trim so that people can serve themselves. Amina lays down another plate.

"We have enough," I say.

"Better one too many than one too few," she says, twirling round in her new skirt. I can still smell the mothballs.

Our honoured guest arrives at six, ready to break the mirqana he has achieved with the Oromo brothers down the hall with a can of lager. He admires his wife's outfit. "Very chic," he says, eyes glimmering as he stares at her knees.

"Masha'Allah," I mutter and look away. It's been a year since Yusuf arrived, but it is only now that he is returning to his wife.

Mrs. Jahangir brings the children. Sitta and Ahmed have bright red tongues and lips though Mrs. J swears she did not ruin their appetites with sweets. Mr. Jahangir follows, huffing dramatically with the weight of his generosity—a gift for Yusuf, a heavy chess set made of brass, accompanied by an apology for the way their last game ended.

Now that everyone has arrived and removed their shoes, Amina presses Play on the tape deck. Yusuf beams as the voice of his favourite singer fills the room.

"Where did you find this?" he asks her.

"He lives in Norway now. I sent him a letter."

Imagine. Someone who was so famous in Ethiopia that he had a band of bodyguards, an army of servants, a harem of women throwing themselves at his feet is now a man who lives alone in a small subsidized flat on the outskirts of Oslo, eating pickled herring on dry toast for supper, receiving a letter and penning a reply in his own hand.

Amina is about to fetch the letter to prove it when there is a knock at the door.

"We're not expecting anyone else, are we?" I ask.

She brushes by me, swings the door open, and

there stands Robin, two massive bunches of flowers wrapped in purple paper in his arms.

I could kill her—wait, I take that back—I could damn well near throttle her.

Robin places one bouquet in her arms and offers the other over her shoulder to me. He brings the perfect flowers: pink and yellow roses for Amina, white lilies for me. I stare at their orange stamens. Family, Amina, remember?

He's also brought a jar for Amina, peach chutney he claims he made himself, following a recipe of his mother's. And where do you find the small tart peaches that make a perfect peach chutney, Mrs. Jahangir wonders, holding the jar up to the light, and "Forgive me, this is Dr. Gupta," Amina introduces him, "Lilly's friend."

"Robin, please," he says as he shakes Mr. and Mrs. Jahangir's hands.

Yusuf offers him a lager, Amina says, "Come, come and eat, we have a feast," and the whole time I am standing there, flowers in my arms, feeling decidedly unlike celebrating.

I put the flowers down on the kitchen counter, return to the sitting room and proceed to pile food high on two plates for Ahmed and Sitta. Tariq is clutching the table leg with one hand, wavering on his unsteady feet while he reaches up for a piece of injera. Ahmed and Sitta take their plates and hold them at eye level in both hands, carrying them into the other room to watch television.

"Is something wrong?" Robin asks, suddenly at my side.

"Nothing," I reply.

"You didn't expect me, did you," he says.

"Amina did neglect to tell me."

"I hope it's not an imposition," he says.

"No, look, we've masses of food." I leave him, busy myself in the kitchen.

"Lilies for his Lilly," Amina croons as I stare into the sink, butchering the flower stems with a bread knife.

"He doesn't belong here, Amina."

She pouts. "Oh, why do you say this? It is a celebration, Lilly."

I stab the stems into a pint glass.

It's all a very happy scene unfolding in the sitting room. Mr. Jahangir is asking, "Your people, are they related to the pharmaceutical Guptas in Bombay? And which college at Cambridge? Do you play chess?"

Robin is bouncing Tariq on his knee, and the boy is in ecstasy. "Bow, wow, wow, wee," he sings, throwing his injera to the floor.

"Oh, pah pah," Yusuf says, "don't be seduced by his mild demeanour, Dr. Gupta. Mr. Jahangir is a shark in a sea of minnows when he sits in front of the chessboard," though what he means is that Mr. Jahangir is an utter cheat. I doubt a brass set or an apology could ever persuade Yusuf to sit down to play with him again.

Mr. J beams, thrilled to be likened to a predator.

Amina decides to ignore me and join the party. I decide to ignore the party and join the children.

"You look very beautiful," Robin says, grasping

my arm as I attempt to breeze by, and I hate the fact that he has seen me in my diri, the nightdress Amina also wears after dusk in her less tartan moments.

"Just going to check on the children."

I switch the channel despite Sitta's objections, turn up the volume, not caring if the news is unsuitable. The bed exhales as I sit down between them.

Ahmed burps. "Excuse me," he says.

—

I make my way to the community association office in the morning. The street is deserted, the light strained. Amina is having a lie-in, I imagine. Or a love-in, given the way Yusuf was staring at her legs last night. I managed to avoid the entire party between eating with the children, washing up and putting Tariq to bed. I managed to avoid having to talk to Robin the whole evening and said only the curtest goodbye.

Amina arrives about half ten, when I'm already halfway through opening the week's mail.

"Have you had buna?" she asks, dropping her purse into a chair.

"Not yet."

She picks up the kettle, about to carry it out to the sink in the hall.

"Real buna?" I ask. "I hate that Nescafé you drink now."

"You are such a habasha," she scoffs. An Ethiopian.

"I'll make it," I mutter, shoving back my chair.

I spill green beans out of a paper bag into my palm. Turn on the Bunsen burner, heat up the tin plate and throw on the beans. I shake the plate with my left hand and rest it over the flame, staring at the marks we have made on the Michelin map on the wall.

"I'm sorry you missed the party, Lilly," she says, flipping through the rest of the unopened mail.

"I'm sorry, I just wasn't up to it."

"But it was such a nice party."

"For you, maybe," I say, still staring at the map.

"You resent me because I have Yusuf, isn't that right?" she says, more statement than question.

She's half right. I do resent her, but more for trying to put Robin in Aziz's place than for the fact that she has Yusuf. For taking such liberties: failing to respect or recognize the space Aziz occupies. Now that she has Yusuf, she can no longer remember how it feels.

"Do you not think it breaks my heart every day to wonder if my sister is still alive, or whether my brothers are being tortured to death in prison?" she demands. "Do you think it has been easy trying to raise three children and deal with a husband who has been traumatized and is afraid of the dark and afraid of other men and sometimes he is even afraid of his own children because he has this nightmare constantly swirling in his head? You know, ever since he has been in England he has not wanted me to touch him because when he was in prison they put matches to his skin. Imagine someone you love looking at you like they fear you will hurt them."

"At least you have a family."

She inhales angrily. "You know, Lilly? You have to stop behaving like an orphaned child."

"Oh shit!" I shriek. Smouldering, blackened beans spill from the tin plate onto the carpet and within seconds they are melting the acrylic at my feet. "Shit, shit, shit!" I stomp up and down.

Amina wordlessly tips the watering can over.

—

I avoid the cafeteria, standing outside during my breaks, watching stray sheets of newspaper take flight, clustered beside other addicts wheeling their drips and exposing their backsides to the wind. "Give us a fag," says one, "I'll catch my death," a minute later.

One of my patients complains that I reek of smoke—this from a woman constantly soaked in her own urine. I have no patience any more. I've even noticed it with the children. Their squabbling has been getting on my nerves.

"Where are you picking up this kind of language?" I shouted at Ahmed the other day when he called his sister a bloody bastard.

His bottom lip began to quiver.

"Tell me! At school?" I persisted.

He shook his head. "From you," he mumbled.

"What?"

"From when you yelled at the cab driver."

Because he'd said he had no change. Because I needed the change to buy milk. Because the only thing I was looking forward to was a cup of tea.

—

It's only a matter of days before I run into Robin. I can't avoid him forever. He looks up when I enter the cafeteria and waves. He offers me Tabasco sauce before peppering his beef stroganoff. He's hating his job today. It's all "shitty bureaucracy" and "shitty petty tyranny" and "shitty miserly shortsightedness" on days when Robin hates his job.

"Look, I honestly didn't realize Amina hadn't told you I was coming," he says, grinding down the gears into awkwardness. "But it was a lovely party. I wish you hadn't disappeared."

"I just didn't think it was appropriate that you were there."

"I was invited," he says, stunned.

"It's not that simple."

"Could you at least *try* and tell me what's the matter?" he pleads. "I'm confused. You said you liked me too."

I'm overcome with a green wave. I hold up my palm. "I can't."

"Can't what?"

"Just can't," I say, fleeing to the loo.

I stare into the warped tin mirror. The whites of my eyes are yellow, my hair is yellow, my teeth are yellow from smoking. Everything about me is sickly and dull. I look as though I've just emerged from a compost heap.

I take off my shoes and socks, run the tap, wash my hands, face and neck, rinse my nostrils and mouth, bathe my forearms, the top of my head, my feet and ankles. I lay down my gown as a prayer rug. I don't usually pray at the hospital; my colleagues complain about the mess, all the water on the floor, and they say that they feel too self-conscious, too respectful to use the toilet when I'm bent over on the floor, there are only two cubicles after all. It makes no difference if I tell them that when I pray I am not of this time and place, I would not notice it even if they were throwing up in the toilet, snorting cocaine off the stainless steel shelf above the sink.

Perhaps they won't notice me here, huddled in one of the cubicles, feet up on the seat, snivelling pathetically, using my gown as a handkerchief.

# Learning Chess.

—

Believing that all has been ordained by God can lead to fatalism, but fatalism is not the same thing as belief. It's a cheat: an abdication of responsibility. Believers take action, while I lie inert. I can't be bothered to get up off the sofa and answer the knock at my door. I'm not in the mood for interruptions, though I'm not doing anything but lying here wearing a flannel nightshirt and slouchy socks, clinging to a lukewarm hot water bottle and contemplating the cracks in the ceiling. I've tried to read, but I can't make it through more than a paragraph at a time. The floor is littered with abandoned newspapers and empty yogurt pots.

Three days ago Robin accompanied me home after my meltdown in the loo. I finally let him into my flat. I put the key in the door, pushed it open and stood in the doorway while he entered my sitting room.

He laughed, looking rather baffled. "Aren't you even going to come in?"

We drank tea at the kitchen table by the window with a view of another identical tower standing lonely in the navy blue dusk. We sat across from each other, our knees near the radiator, the fluorescent light droning above and the thin pane of glass rattling beside our cheeks.

"How long have you lived here?" he asked.

"Why?"

"It's just, well, you don't have any pictures on the walls, or any photographs, or anything."

"I prefer it this way," I said.

"I'm sorry if I've been pushing too hard," he said for the second time. "Perhaps I'm just rather clumsy when it comes to courtship. I thought most women liked to be pursued."

"It's not that."

"Well, I obviously stepped over some kind of line."

He's trying to find a way into a life that has no door. There is an inner courtyard, concealed from the street, but this is a place where sentinels stand guard, the space Aziz inhabits, walking around in his white galabaya, memorizing passages from a book. It is as if I have to protect it all the more fiercely now that Amina does not share it with me.

I reached out to take Robin's hand. "I'm sorry," I said. "I really appreciate all your effort."

He laughed again. "You make it sound like I'm trying to do you some kind of favour! Like fix your plumbing! I may have made a mistake, but I don't think I've entirely misread things. You don't have to shut me out altogether."

I shook my head.

"What is it?"

I looked down at my shoes.

"Is there someone else?"

Finally the right question. The simplest question of all. No matter what I might feel for Robin, there's an organ without a name that only registers the invisible. It's why I sense Aziz in windows, in puddles, in glass; an image thin and distorted, persistent and deadly silent. He does not say: forget me, move on, I have forgotten you, or I am dead, Lilly, long dead, so engage with this man Rabindranath, give him room. He does not say: whatever happened to me is not your fault.

I looked up.

Robin sighed and hung his head. "Lilly, why couldn't you have just told me? Now I feel like an idiot. It's not really fair, you know."

Aziz's silence overwhelms everything else. It blanketed the sound of Robin's footsteps as he retreated to the door, made his way down the concrete corridor, exited the building and walked away. Aziz's silence has blanketed the last three days.

—

Yusuf lets himself in with a key. "It's just that we haven't seen you," he says apologetically.

"Just tired," I reply.

"Sick?" he asks, sitting down by my feet.

"Maybe."

"Can I bring you something? Tea? Soup? I made one yesterday that Amina says she would like to taste every day."

"Not that kind of sick. But I'll be fine."

"Shall I teach you chess?" Yusuf asks. He's had a bit of a set-to with his Oromo friends after discovering one of them served, albeit briefly and coerced, in the Dergue's army. Perhaps the game will distract me too, but it's hard to imagine caring about a board game even though Yusuf insists chess is more like life than most people realize.

He returns with the board and names the pieces in Arabic as he sets them down one by one.

"Aren't you going to answer it?" he asks when I don't move to pick up the phone.

I shake my head.

"Shall I?"

I shrug listlessly and stare at the squares—the burnt orange of an Ethiopian sunset, the dark brown of good earth. Men poised, ready and willing, for battle.

"It was Robin," Yusuf says, sitting back down crossed-legged on the floor. "He was wondering if you were okay."

"What did you tell him?"

"That you are learning chess, of course," Yusuf says, smiling.

"I'm running away from him, Yusuf," I say quietly.

He considers this, scratching his beard. "Perhaps you are not running away from him but from your feelings."

Yusuf says little, but that little is always precise. That is exactly why things with Robin have to end. My feelings for him only threaten to grow, while those for Aziz remain fixed, like the one photograph I have of him—twenty-six years old, staring straight ahead, deadly still in black and white. Staring at me as if I am still nineteen years old.

I pick up a piece from the chessboard. "What did you say this one was called?"

—

I pray for a sign that I have done the right thing, pray throughout the month of Safar, the dangerous month of the Muslim calendar, the one where we must not propose or marry or travel, because calamities will befall us. In Harar, Sheikh Jami used to take care to visit the shrines of every one of the more than three hundred saints of the city during Safar to maximize our protection from evil and illness. He'd visit the forgotten shrines, ones hidden in people's kitchens, in holes in compound walls, in the bend of the river, in the hollow of a tree, ensuring he paid his respects to each saint in the pantheon at least once a year.

Here we have only our flowerpot. And only me to make prayers. Amina won't accompany me to the back because the local imam asserts that these beliefs about Safar are superstitions carried forth from the Jahiliyya. I burn incense every day for thirty days, asking Bilal to reach out to all the other saints. I hope that some descendant of

Sheikh Jami's is doing the same in Harar.

Amina and Yusuf and the children do their best to surround me with the ordinariness of family life. Well-meaning neighbours stop by with curries and stewed cabbage, passing pots into Amina's arms. "Tuck in," I tell Amina and Yusuf. The smells are enticing, but the mouth, the stomach, remain unwilling.

Tariq teeters around looking for trouble and snacking on the inedible, and Ahmed and Sitta squabble in the kitchen. Sitta emerges in tears and Yusuf, who is sitting beside me, spreads his arms and pulls her onto his lap. Ahmed's been teasing her about her mole, saying it looks like an ink stain. It's not the worst of what kids say. I've heard other Ethiopian kids call her nig nog, Galla, Shankilla. They have twice as many cruel words as their parents: the insults of both the old world and the new.

Sitta buries her face in her father's neck, and Yusuf strokes her cheek.

"He telephoned again today," he says to me.

"He shouldn't bother," I reply. "He should just get on with his life."

Amina raised the idea of counselling, which I adamantly rejected, but when I think about how unfair I've been to Robin, I wonder whether counselling might be an act of public service.

My punishment for having missed a second week of work without explanation in the last two years is this mandatory leave of absence. There was no meeting with a board this time, for which I am grateful. It would be too humiliating to have had to see Robin. The head of nursing simply gave me a slip of paper with the phone number of the resident psychiatrist. That went straight in the bin along with my uniform.

When I reached for the tea canister that night, I found a bottle of green and white pills inside my cupboard. Yusuf's prescription for depression. Physician none other than Dr. Gupta.

Part Eight.

—

# Harar, Ethiopia

August–September 1974

Static.

—

Gishta arrived out of breath, out of sorts, interrupting my class. "Send the children home!" she
commanded.

"What's wrong?"

"Send them home now!" she cried.

"Did you have to upset the children like that?"
I asked, after packing them off with their borrowed booklets and the assurance that everything
would be all right.

She was wild with anger, shrieking something
about children and coddling and how she had been
forced to work when she was eight years old. But as
I looked in her eyes I realized it wasn't anger but
fear that had her ranting and waving and smacking the tin fence.

She'd been greeted with a gun in the face that
morning, she confessed once Nouria returned from
the market. The Oromo tenants who farmed
Sheikh Jami's fields were apparently complaining
that they were fed up with having to break their
backs so that the sheikh's wives could wear silk.

They'd turned them away with guns.

Gishta was not the least bit sympathetic, though her own father must have likewise laboured to keep Harari women expensively dressed. But the converted are often more self-righteous than those born to their station. I had only to look at myself to know the truth of this. When I first met Aziz, my religious beliefs had been much more dogmatic than his. But then he held my hand, and in so doing, loosened my grip. And now? Without his hand? I was devastated. I longed for an easier time, when being Muslim was rigid and rule-bound and the past belonged clearly to a pre-Islamic era. I wished there were something absolute in which to believe. It was a time, after all, when one didn't know what to believe, where to turn. You could smell the suspicion in the air—it was being sprayed in all directions, whispers of allegiances, minor peasant revolts, disloyalty, feuding, betrayal. Fear was limiting the movements of women. Silence seemed to dominate the relationships between brothers and best friends. And fewer and fewer students were coming to my class.

In the past, if any child was ever absent for more than one day, I'd always made enquiries. This time was no exception. To my face parents said, "Times are uncertain, we would rather keep them home," but then, as I shortly discovered, my students had been turning up at the Bilal al Habash Madrasa instead, their teacher none other than Idris—Sheikh Jami's other apprentice, a man who, in our couple of encounters, had not hidden the fact that he despised me.

"When times are uncertain, people prefer the authority of a man," Idris said smugly when I dared to confront him outside the madrasa.

The following Sunday, when Sheikh Jami was scheduled to visit his mother in Dire Dawa, I went to Hussein to confirm my suspicions. Hussein, sitting on his own at the shrine, said that Idris had waived the fee as compensation.

"Compensation for what?" I demanded.

There had never been secrets between Hussein and me, but he was reluctant to get involved. I was angry enough to twist his arm without touching him.

For what Idris was apparently calling "their inferior education up to this point."

"And why does it suddenly suit him now?" I shouted. "And why don't you defend me?"

Hussein hung his head.

"You're a coward, Hussein," I said. Even I was stunned by my harshness.

One by one, the channels of communication were turning to static.

And then no students turned up at all.

"Where is Rahile? And where are the boys?" I asked Nouria the next day.

"I sent Rahile to collect laundry. The boys are in the market. If they have no school then they have to work."

"But I can still teach them," I said. "It will be like it was in the beginning."

"Soon, insha'Allah," Nouria said. "But for now, we need an income."

I sat down and stuck my fingers into a hole Bortucan had dug in the dirt.

### Feast and Famine.

—

Despite all the uncertainty, Sadia was still talking about little other than her forthcoming wedding. I didn't understand how she could carry on pretending life was perfectly normal. She hadn't even seen much of Munir over the last few weeks, busy as he was, like Aziz, with these mysterious meetings.

She was insisting we go to Dire Dawa on the weekend to shop. "There are so many things I have to choose," she gushed. "Oh, it will be so much fun! We just walk from shop to shop saying, 'I'll have this and this and this,' and then Munir must come with his mother and they will buy everything. And then when we move into our new home, there it will all be—everything a new wife needs to make her husband comfortable."

I indulged her: her enthusiasm was a refreshing break from the apocalyptic mood that had infected everyone else. Her flippancy shouldn't have surprised me, this was the girl, after all, who, when she talked about Mecca, didn't even mention the Ka'bah. To her, Mecca was a great place for buying perfume and cosmetics. Fashinn gidir, indeed.

We left for Dire Dawa just after dawn on a Saturday. Sadia insisted we take a private taxi now that we had a choice again, not one of the crowded minibuses. In the back seat she chattered on as if there were no politics in the world. We were lucky the driver didn't speak our language.

"You know why we haven't seen Warda in weeks?" she whispered.

"Don't tell me she gets invited to these meetings," I replied.

"No!" Sadia whispered, pulling her skirt outward and inflating her cheeks.

"What?" I shrieked.

"Uss!" Sadia chastised, laughing. Warda's mother was keeping her hidden. Once the baby was born her mother would claim it as her own. "This is normal," Sadia said.

"Sadia?" I ventured hesitantly.

"Yes, farenji?" she cooed.

"Have you and Munir . . . ?"

"Oh my God!" She covered her mouth with both hands and laughed.

"Well, have you?"

She nodded and held up two fingers.

"Did it hurt?"

She winced and mouthed pain.

"Did you have absuma?"

"Of course," she says. "But only the small one. Not like Warda, she has the big one."

"That must really hurt."

"Sure there is pain. But there is much, much bigger pleasure in here," she said, tapping her temple. "And you and Aziz?"

I shook my head.

"It is funny," she said. "They say it is farenji girls who are sharmutas."

The taxi deposited us in Dire Dawa's central market, and Sadia took my hand, pulling me down familiar streets. She stopped outside the unmistakable blue gate of Grandfather Ibrahim's house.

I grabbed her by the wrist. "Why are we here?"

She shrugged. "The old man is my family."

"But I thought he was Munir's grandfather."

"Well, he's my grandfather too. Munir is my cousin. It would be very rude of me not to visit when I am in town, wouldn't it?"

The old man was happy to see me, though he berated me for not having come to visit him again. He teased Sadia about Munir, saying she was like rrata, a piece of meat stuck between the poor boy's teeth.

Sadia giggled at the compliment, and then the old man leaned over to me and said: "He's waiting for you upstairs."

I looked at Sadia, but she only grinned. "Go on," she said coyly.

—

He greeted me with his own apprehension, his smile strained, his gestures tentative. I wanted to press my forehead into his rib cage. I wanted to cry. I wanted to rewind the last few months and sit in the innocent silence of our dark room.

His words took their time, a couple of false starts, beginnings phrased as: "What I mean to say . . . ," "What I thought . . ." and then finally, "Lilly, I didn't mean to be unkind. I've been trying to protect us both. I've never asked you how you knew the emperor, the extent of your involvement with him, but it doesn't matter at this stage because any association puts you in grave danger."

"And I suppose that means your association with me puts *you* in grave danger," I said.

"It does," he admitted. "And if it weren't for the fact that I am committed to a movement that condemns the monarchy, it would be a little less difficult for me to reconcile."

"You're afraid that your new friends will reject you because of your association with me."

"There is something you need to see," he said gently.

"More guns?"

"You'll understand in a few hours," he said and fell silent.

He dared to bridge the distance between us by reaching for my hand. It wasn't fair. His thumb traced the lifeline on my palm. He was trying to pull me back.

"Lilly, please," he implored.

—

In the blue dark we watched as a parade of skeletons wobbled across the screen. Everything—bodies, earth, road and sky—was the colour of sand. The thin membranes stretched over the chest cavities of these creatures fluttered with the profound effort of movement. They fell forward onto their bulbous knees and their rib cages splintered with the impact. Women carried dead babies with crusty mouths and giant eyes framed by fly-covered lashes. There was absolute silence. The parade thinned, leaving a trail of bodies lying on the road that continued into the northern city, where the market was overflowing with sacks of sorghum and teff and wheat and mountains of split peas and lentils.

Members of His Majesty's army were standing guard throughout the market, keeping the beggars at bay with their rifles.

Hundreds of miles south, Haile Selassie was standing on his balcony greeting his royal subjects on the occasion of his eightieth birthday two years before. We watched the emperor tossing copper coins down to the poor and feasting at the palace with white dignitaries, feeding them champagne and caviar flown by the planeload from Paris.

Haile Selassie's officials in the north ordered the army to rid the streets of the embarrassment of these tens of thousands of diseased, walking cadavers. This was a celebration, after all.

We saw footage of the army gunning down starving civilians in honour of the emperor's birth-day, while the emperor roamed the lush palace grounds feeding his pet leopards and dogs choice cuts of meat from silver platters held high by his servants.

We had heard the words *famine* and *starvation*, but we had never seen images before. Haile Selassie had only begun using the words the previous month. Until then, he had denied such things existed in Ethiopia. Now we had the images to accompany the words, thanks to a British journalist.

Sadia hurried from the room partway through with her hand over her mouth.

Grandfather Ibrahim was the first to speak into the dark. "It's over," he said, wonder in his voice.

He was old enough to remember a time before Haile Selassie. He was old enough to remember a time before Ethiopia was even a country.

"It has to be over," replied Aziz, who had known only this country, and known it only to be this way.

—

I saw a pool of blood on the steps of the palace. I saw the imperial lions, starving in their cages, too hungry to discriminate between enemies and friends. I saw cadavers clinging like barnacles to the palace steps and kicked off the sheet over me. It was a stifling night.

The moon cast a silver pool of light over the balcony. To my left, the floorboards creaked. Aziz was beside me. We stood arm against arm.

"They've already shown this film in Britain," he finally said. "The military council thought it was time our own people knew the truth. The emperor has been accused of taking a hundred million dollars of state money and hiding it in a Swiss bank account. The commission sent in its officers and they found thousands of dollars stuck to the floors under the carpets. They seized documents and read lists of figures over the radio—money held in other accounts, foreign properties and investments all in the names of his ministers—assets purchased with money drawn from the state treasury while these hundreds of thousands of people in the north were dying of starvation. Nobody will be able to deny those images."

"But what will happen?"

"The council is talking about an entirely new basis of power—in the hands of the peasants and the workers—the majority. And to do that? The land has to be taken from the wealthy who own it and given back to the poor who actually farm it. From the royal family, the Church, the mosques, the landlords. No more forced labour, no more rights to collect tribute from the peasants, no more payment for military service and allegiance in the form of land grants, no more private ownership."

"That would mean taking land away from the Hararis," I realized aloud. The Hararis thrived under feudalism, it was the basis of their economy, though for them to admit this would be to indict themselves as beneficiaries of the emperor's corrupt system.

"They are one of the wealthiest communities in the country," Aziz said.

"But I don't imagine they will just give over their land."

"That's why it's so important that some of us from Harar, Hararis included, at least some of the young and educated ones, have joined the revolutionary party. We know there's going to be resistance. Hararis have enjoyed centuries of privilege—their wealth comes from the exploitation of peasants. Harar was one of the biggest slave markets in East Africa. The Hararis would trade black people like me for goods from the Orient. A black man for a bolt of silk from China. My father was bought for a vat of gunpowder."

"So even in his lifetime . . ."

"Even in his lifetime. I carry this name—Abdulnasser—slave of his Harari owner."

"But Bilal al Habash was a slave," I offered.

Aziz sighed. "Well, in principle, Islam is about equality. We have tried to believe, but I think . . . Many of us feel socialism, Marxism, might be the only possibility for equality. Not religion. Do you know about Marx?"

I shook my head.

"I could lend you a book," said Aziz. "A small red book."

—

I woke with the call to prayer to find Aziz lying beside me. I stared at his feathery eyelashes, which trembled as if he were watching a film in his sleep, Charlie Chaplin, perhaps, from the way his mouth turned up at the corners. I could feel his whole body swelling, but just as he was about to levitate, I lay across him, my weight barely enough to hold him down.

Aziz opened his eyes, took me by the shoulders and rolled me onto my back. He stared at the middle of me, and began to stroke my stomach through the thin fabric of my diri. He drew hesitant circles, his fingers winding ever closer, my skin melting with his touch, my body begging. He kissed my stomach through the cotton, inching upwards to kiss my nipples. I held his earlobes between my fingers and pinched while he bit me hard and warmth rushed through me.

He tugged up my diri and stroked the insides of my thighs with the backs of his fingers, watching his own hand against my skin. He propped himself up on one hand then and untied his sarong with the other before lowering himself gently on top of me: hard against my stomach and thighs. Life was too short in Africa for this not to happen. I spread my legs and he took his penis in his hand and moved it against me, stroking me with slow rhythm that grew faster until I lunged into his open mouth, my back arched, the clash of teeth, the twist of tongues, the good God, the please, the pleasure.

I dug my nails into his chest as the waves rolled over me. Then a slow burn—a cautious push inward on his part—and my mouth falling open. Tears streaming from the corners of my eyes with wonder and unbelievable pain.

He licked the tears that had fallen into my left

ear, filled my mouth with the salt on his tongue and slowly pushed deeper. I reached out and grabbed him from behind to pull him in as close, as deep, as could be, me the shell, he the snail, home.

"Aziz!" the old man hollered from below. "Why aren't you awake yet?"

Aziz sighed and collapsed on top of me. "Shit," he said harshly, burying his face in my hair. "Shit."

We lay in this defeated heap for a minute, hearts knocking against each other's ribs.

Finally he spoke. "Whatever happens, Lilly, please know that I love you." He pushed himself up onto his arms and looked down as he slowly pulled out of me.

I lay hollow, flat, still, jaw slack. *Whatever happens?* It was as if my stomach was made of glass and a bird had just flown into me, causing a hairline fracture with its beak.

"I love you too, Aziz," I said weakly, holding my stomach, afraid it was about to shatter.

He took the corner of his sarong and gently wiped the blood from between my thighs. No matter how chaste we are, we are guilty until this moment of being proved innocent. If this had been our wedding night, he would have taken that piece of cloth and draped it over a large bowl of sweets that he would present to my mother that morning. Nouria, I suppose. Nouria and Gishta would have run out into the streets waving the sarong and ululating loudly so that everyone could celebrate the proof of my virginity. If this had been our wedding night.

September 12, 1974.

—

It was New Year's Day according to the Ethiopian Orthodox Christian calendar. Aziz and I and the old man sat listening to the radio as we shared a bowl of sorghum porridge. Sadia had left for the shops early, determined to proceed according to plan. The old man was having difficulty, his teeth didn't seem to be sitting quite straight in his mouth that morning. Each time Aziz reached out to spoon another mouthful I felt the hairs on his arm sting my own.

The music came to an end, and the New Year began with a proclamation over the radio in Amharic. Aziz translated.

"Even though the people treated the throne in good faith as a symbol of unity, Haile Selassie I took advantage of its authority, dignity and honour for his own personal ends. As a result, the country found itself in a state of poverty and disintegration. Moreover, an eighty-two-year-old monarch, because of his age, is incapable of meeting his responsibilities. Therefore His Imperial Majesty

Haile Selassie I is being deposed as of September 12, 1974, and power assumed by the Provisional Military Committee. Ethiopia above all."

With that, Parliament was dissolved, the Constitution suspended, and the Supreme Court abolished. The emperor, who was ultimate authority over all three, did not resist arrest. They say that he who had initially denied the famine at all, then denied its extent, then denied any knowledge of military involvement had been forced to sit down with the leaders of the Dergue the previous night at the palace and watch Dimbleby's film as it was broadcast to the nation. He was reputed to have replied, "If revolution is good for the people then I, too, support the revolution," then retired to bed.

—

Sadia managed to select the following items without my help: six sets of Egyptian cotton sheets (even though virtually no Hararis slept in beds), a toaster, a blender, a television (even though very few Hararis had electricity), a telephone (even though there were no telephone lines in Harar), a jug and twelve matching glasses (to serve her guests contaminated, parasite-ridden water?), six ice cube trays (even though there was no refrigeration) and enough clothes, shoes and gold jewellery to keep her looking extraordinarily rich for a lifetime.

She was reciting this list to me when there was a sudden banging on the metal gate of the old man's compound. We all froze, but then the old man came to his senses and sent his servant to open it.

It was Girma from the restaurant.

Aziz jumped up to greet him. They exchanged some whispered words before Aziz turned and said: "Lilly, it's time for you to leave."

"What?"

"To go home," Aziz said simply.

"To Harar," I said cautiously.

"It's not safe for you there."

"But I don't have another home."

"I don't think you have any other choice," said Aziz. "I know *I* don't have any other choice. Girma is here to escort you. You are going to have to leave now."

"A fire is burning," Girma added in a moment too urgent for metaphors.

"The Dergue," Aziz began to explain. "They are taking anyone connected to the emperor in any way." He waved about the room. "We are all at risk."

*Because of your association with me.*

"Djibouti," Aziz and Girma said simultaneously.

Aziz and I stared at each other. This couldn't be happening. Aziz reached into his pocket and pulled out his hospital identification card. He lifted up the plastic and peeled off the small black-and-white photograph.

"I want you to have this," he said, and placed the photo with its curled edges in my hand.

I stared at the tiny photo. "But what can I give you?"

"You have already given it to me," he said, patting his stomach. "It's in here. Whatever happens."

Sweetness in the belly.

Part Nine.

—

# London, England

**1990–91**

A Story of Famine and Refugees.

—

The list of names sent to us each month only grows
longer. It's become impossible to think of individuals
any more; I see a country being turned upside down
and all the people being shaken out and deposited
into the camps that straddle Ethiopia's borders like
a ring of fire. The majority will die there, forty miles
from the borders of home, of starvation and disease,
the newest epidemic of which is AIDS.

"I don't think I can bear it any longer," I say,
throwing the most recent list down on the table
and rubbing my eyes with my palms. "It's all just
a black smear."

"Typical social services burnout," Amina
responds, armed with the language of her new
appointment as interim director of Settlement
Services with the Lambeth Council. She uses this
same language to sugarcoat her own disappointment. She pushes her feelings aside in the pursuit
of order and efficiency.

Amina comes to my flat when she needs peace
and quiet and works at the kitchen table over a

bowl of soup. I leave her to it and go to her flat, where I am of some help with Dickens but none at all with Shakespeare. Yusuf is brilliant with maths and all sciences. At least he's found *some* use for his degree in agricultural economics.

Tariq, at two and a half, is something of a terror. We are generally happy to let him wreak havoc, though, knowing perhaps that in some other time and place he might be selling peanuts to qat addicts in the marketplace rather than banging pots, might soon be learning how to load a gun.

We've found two things that calm him: Marmite, introduced to him by some mumsy-type at nursery, which he licks off toast and sucks off his fingers, and the authoritative voices on the nightly news. He doesn't watch the broadcast but rather sticks his head against the back of the telly, inviting the voices to speak directly into his ear.

I found Yusuf part-time work recently as an orderly at the hospital. He seems to like it well enough, in part, I think, because the relations are so clear. You have doctors, administrators and nurses above orderlies, but below them, you have patients. He does not have to feel intimidated by them because by virtue of being patients they are powerless. Yusuf might feel affectless in the global scheme of things, but at least at the hospital there are people looking up to him, asking him for help. Even white people. He is the one wearing the uniform.

It has clearly gone some way toward restoring his confidence, because lately he's been reading books about farming techniques in modern Britain and asking me questions about soy cultivation and peat moss, things about which I have not a clue. He is slowly nurturing an ember of hope into a flame.

While Tariq continues to stick his head against the back of the television every night, Yusuf has begun to engage with the news. We sit side by side and watch the world uniting and dividing before our eyes. It is impossible to imagine that an empire could have lasted for two thousand years when in one year, the Communists relinquish sole power in the Soviet Union, Yugoslavia explodes and cracks, Nelson Mandela is set free, the Cold War ends, a European Union is agreed upon, Germany is reunited, and Iraq invades a tiny neighbour called Kuwait, sparking a new war more global than the West has ever known.

Yusuf says to me wisely, prophetically: "Muslims will become the new Russians."

"There is never anything about Ethiopia," he laments as we watch the world morphing before our eyes. "It is as if it does not exist."

"Ethiopia doesn't matter to the West," I say, stating the obvious. "We offer them nothing they can exploit."

This has proved both a blessing and a curse. We can feel proud that Ethiopia resisted Europe's colonial overtures, but then we have to accept that the country does not exist in the European imagination as anything but a starving, impoverished nation with just about the highest rates of infant mortality, the lowest average life expectancy and the lowest rates of literacy in the world. As a story of famine and refugees.

"We do offer the West one thing they can exploit," says Yusuf. "A fine example of the evils of communism."

"True. But we were in this position before the Dergue," I argue.

"It could have been different," he says. "Haile Selassie was on the way. Through education, some developments in agriculture . . ."

"For the benefit of a very privileged few, Yusuf. And at the cost of leaving hundreds of thousands to die."

"Well, we are certainly no better off now," he says. "At least during Haile Selassie's time we had some export—coffee—but we lost that market because of communism. Mengistu has alienated the rest of the world by allying himself with the Russians."

"But now the Soviets have given up their monopoly—"

"Which means that very soon, Ethiopia will have *no* friends," Yusuf insists. "Mengistu will be weakened by this change in the Soviet Union, believe me. I predict the end of the Dergue within a year."

—

On Saturday I drift through the lists as I tend to now, more scanning for patterns than reading for details, wondering if Yusuf is right and whether our work here will end as a consequence. There is a whole new generation of refugees coming to live on the estate, mainly Somalis and Kurds. Ethiopians rarely get priority in housing any more even though the numbers have only increased—as if it's simply gone on too long to warrant special attention. A crisis is by definition short lived. An ongoing crisis is at best an oxymoron.

I slide the list across the table to Amina. "Mostly Christian names," I conclude.

Amina glances at the cover sheet. "Huh. They have a new secretary in Rome."

"Do they."

"This Munir Jamal Mahmoud. I guess Nadjmia moved on."

I lean forward. "That name. Say that name again."

She squints through her glasses. "Munir Jamal Mahmoud," she reads. "M.D."

"Munir," I say.

"Who is Munir?" she asks.

"Aziz's best friend."

Amina pulls a fresh sheet of paper from the drawer.

## Some Measure of Happiness.

—

There was a chill between Robin and me for about six months after we stopped dating—if you could ever have called it dating. Whatever it was or wasn't, things have settled now at a polite remove. I assume he just stopped feeling fed up at some point, decided to put his energy somewhere else, perhaps direct it at someone more suitable. A woman who invites him into her well-furnished flat and has inspired hobbies like martial arts, or oil painting; a woman who offers a way in and has a life beyond work. As he should have, as I hope he has, but I wouldn't know because we don't exchange personal information, we exchange brief pleasantries in the corridor and carry on.

I run straight past him the day the letter arrives, charging down to the casualty ward where Yusuf is mopping the floor.

I need a filter. And I need the voice of an Ethiopian man. "Read it to me once," I ask Yusuf, breathless, "but leave out the bad parts. Then read it to me again, this time with the bad parts."

"Here?" Yusuf asks, looking round at the commotion.

I take the mop from his hands and he fumbles in his pocket for his reading glasses. He reads quietly, in the voice of a poet, and the noises of the hospital fade into the background.

October 1990

Dear Lilly,

I hope this letter finds you in good health and with some measure of happiness in your life in London. I cannot tell you how high my heart was lifted to receive this letter from you. I am fine, alhamdullilah. I wish I could offer you the good news that you ask for that would also lift your heart. I have not seen Aziz for several years, but the last time I saw him he was fine except angry like me about this brutal regime. Insha'Allah this Mengistu will die and all truths will be revealed but still it is very dangerous. One must not oppose.

As you know, Aziz and I very much supported this change in our country. We were part of this movement to put an end to imperialism and develop the country according to socialist principles. Our movement was of one mind until this dictator Mengistu started using guns and killing. We have a strong ideology but we believe in peace. Our student group fractured into two parties and then really, all hope for a socialist country is gone. Brothers are fighting brothers and this dictator sends his generals to arrest most of the doctors from the hospital.

They tell us we are counter-revolutionary and send
one of us here and one of us there, to different
prisons all over the country. But in truth, we are
not counter-revolutionary, at least in principle, they
just need doctors for their prisons. The prisons are
overflowing. Everyone in Ethiopia is counter-
revolutionary, it seems.

Aziz and I are lucky in one thing. Since we are a
medical team, we are sent together to Jijiga. Truly,
the conditions are very bad. People sleeping on top
of people and suffocating because there is no room.
Later, of course, they don't even bother with this
pretense of jail. But for now it was jail and first we
were not willing to work for these corrupt captors,
but really they make it so we have no choice. But
we survived this. I walk with a crutch because of my
toes, and Aziz's eye is not so good now, but truly we
were lucky ones, alhamdullilah. They break you in
the beginning and then enough—if they can make
use of you they do.

In 1977 things are very bad with this nightmare
they call Red Terror. They send me to a new prison
in the far southwest where many Ethiopians are
trying to escape to the Sudan. We beg the officers
in Jijiga because we are a medical team, but they
cannot lose two doctors and so they send the one
with the bad foot but not the one with the bad eye.
I feel guilty, oh my God, but this is my chance and
I escape in a truck for Khartoum. And from there
to Egypt and after some years in Cairo, by ship to
Rome because I find my cousin here. For now I am
working part time for the association, but

insha'Allah, I will soon go to Toronto where my
biggest brother is living. If I go to Toronto I will
write to tell you God has granted my wish.

Maybe you can find this man in London. He is
chief of staff from Addis Ababa and was teaching
us at Haile Selassie I University. We hear he went
to London for more training—sent by Mengistu
himself!—but became political asylum seeker. He is
a great man. Maybe he can help you. Mengistu gave
him some Amhara name, but in truth, his name is
Ramadan Sherif.

Insha'Allah there will be some news to lift your
heart. Dear farenji—Aziz was speaking of you every
day.

Assalaamu alaykum,
Munir

There is bad and relative bad. In the course of our
work, I've heard so many stories that I could not
invent a form of torture the Dergue had not already
thought of. Munir has lost his toes and some of his
English (or perhaps it's just that my English has
improved). Poor Aziz has lost an eye. I wonder what
else has been taken from them. Certainly their hope
for a new Ethiopia, in socialism as the way forward.
Revolutions look like this, I have learned. The further left the theory, the greater the speed with which
the pendulum returns to middle, the practice swings
to right. Down falls an iron curtain.

Yusuf reads the letter again. The second version
is identical to the first. These are my thoughts in
order:

I was not the cause of him being sent to prison?

He spoke of me every day?

Sadia. He doesn't even mention her.

Ramadan Sherif.

I was not the cause of him being sent to prison.

He spoke of me every day.

—

A few days later I find myself splayed out on the terrazzo floor, blood in my eyes, spreading in a puddle under my chin.

"Jesus, Lilly, you're bloody lucky you didn't get it in the eye," says Robin, who's supervising the ward that day. "This looks like the culprit," he says, picking a scalpel out of the pool of blood and instruments. The tray has managed to slide halfway down the hall.

He mops up the mess on my face with a handkerchief and helps me up.

"I tripped somehow," I say, looking at my shoes as if they are to blame.

Robin shaves a patch of my hair as I sit on a gurney in the corridor. "What's going on?" he probes, investigating the top of my head.

"I'm useless on a double," I berate myself.

"Do you want me to freeze it first?" he asks.

I shake my head. He is kind. He has never been anything but kind.

"Are you getting enough sleep?" he asks.

"Not the past couple of nights," I admit. There have been late hours and no answers. Amina has not found the name Ramadan Sherif in any of our files. I have not found his name or any variation thereof in any of the staff and faculty registers of the London hospitals and universities.

"Why is that, Lilly?" Robin presses. "Doctor-patient confidentiality."

"I'm trying to find someone," I say as he threads a needle into my skin.

"Uh-uh!" he says. "Keep your head up, I've just started!" He lowers his voice. "You don't have to tell me about it if you don't want to."

I cannot move because there is a needle in my head. The tears tumble down my cheeks.

"Oh, Jesus, I should've frozen you."

"It's not that," I blurt. "I just feel so helpless. Things are such a mess in Ethiopia."

"You've done a lot of work for Ethiopians here. At least that's something, huh?"

"It's not as altruistic as it might seem."

"That doesn't mean it's not good work. I mean, Muslims give alms, right? But that's not exactly altruism. It's about honouring a pillar of faith, being rewarded for being a good Muslim, it's really all about the giver, not the recipient. And Jews make mitzvahs—same thing. And the Catholics say do unto others. Why? Because it's all going to come back and bite them in the behind if they don't. They're still all worthwhile, these acts of goodness or charity, they make the world a better place, but I think it's disingenuous to think of them as altruistic."

I nod.

"Lilly, you've got to keep still! Like most people in the medical profession you're proving to be a terrible patient."

I ask him about Hindus. Acts of goodness.

"Oh, well, it couldn't be more explicitly self-motivated," he says. "Everything is about karma, creating the positive and reducing the negative so that you land somewhere better the next time round."

"I'm so sorry, Robin," I say. "About everything."

"That's okay," he says, stepping back to admire his work. "I'm still standing, right?"

"You were really kind. Really patient. I just couldn't . . ."

He sits down beside me on the gurney in this sterile corridor and in one slow move pulls me into his shoulder. I lean into him, my hands folded in my lap, my mascara making tracks on his white shoulder. Disinfectant. Rubber gloves. And beyond that, the hypnotic dusty warmth of turmeric, the body's honest smell of ground cumin.

## A Final Aria and a Manila Wave.

—

Robin is nodding with vague recognition as we share a cup of tea in the cafeteria. "I'm sure this man was Ethiopian," he says. "It was at that conference I attended last year on AIDS in Africa. You would have loved that conference, Lilly, but we weren't really, you know . . ."

"Friends then."

"In any case," he continues, "it's a shot in the dark but I probably still have the proceedings somewhere. That is, of course, only if you want me to look."

"Can I help you look?" I ask.

"What? At my flat?" He laughs at this uncharacteristic forwardness. "I cannot believe I've finally managed to entice you to my flat. Ah, life is funny. Had I known all it would take was one of my files, I would have waved manila at you years ago."

His flat surprises me. Statues of gods and goddesses with waving arms stand in the bookshelf, on the window ledge, on top of the television. Each is a tangled mass of twisted limbs and I cannot make out which arms belong to which head.

"Smells good," I say.

"I cheated. Marks and Spencer's."

He slides a plate of biriyani in front of me with an oven-mitted hand. I am blinded by polka dots and steam.

When we've finished, I carry the plates into the narrow kitchen. I nearly drop them at the sight of myself in the mirrored glass above the sink. God, what a sight. I touch the stitched line running up my face and finger my bald patch.

Robin stands behind me, his reflection cut off at the neck. He pulls my hair back in his hand. My neck tingles as I stand there with plates in each hand, staring at the reflection of his jumper in the mirror.

"It will indeed make a fantastic scar," he says.

He makes coffee with hot milk and flavours it with cardamom and cloves: not quite Ethiopian, but not at all English. I gulp it down anxiously, scalding my tongue.

"Right." He rises from the table, taking his cue from me.

I follow him into the bedroom. He has a framed poster of elephants above his bed and a bright orange bedspread punctuated by shiny silver discs. A shelf full of books and a dresser topped with photos of family and friends. It feels like the bedroom of a girl. I am ashamed by how little I know about him.

He kneels down and pulls two dusty cardboard boxes out from under the bed.

I pick up one of the photographs on the dresser. "Your parents?"

He looks up. "My aunt and uncle. They live in Manchester, but they treat me like a son. They've had a hard time. Idi Amin threw them out of Uganda in '72 and they've never been the same. They used to have their own import business."

"Why didn't they go back to India?"

"Oh, you know how it is. Once you are outside a place you can never go back. Not really."

He's right, but one can only know that when there is still the option of going back.

I hover over his shoulder as he rifles through the second box. It's sweet the way his life is on display here. I remember him commenting on how I didn't have any photographs or pictures on my walls. I still don't, but I can appreciate now how they cheer a place up. I absentmindedly scan the spines of Robin's books while he digs under his bed for a third box. A title catches my eye: *Tales of the Sufis of the Sahara*. The name tears at my heart: M. Bruce MacDonald. I pull it off the shelf by its thin spine. I open the cover, turn the first and second pages. There, a dedication printed on the creamy white page: "For Lilly."

"My God."

"Eureka!" Robin exclaims, pulling out a file.

I replace the book and swallow the lump in my throat while Robin rubs dust from his nose and sniffs, flipping through a booklet with the words "HIV/AIDS Prevention in Sub-Saharan Africa" stamped across the front. The white moon of his fingernail scans the index. He turns to page twenty-three.

"There it is."

I look over his shoulder. Dr. B. Wondemariam. "Islamic Perceptions of HIV/AIDS Transmission in the Horn of Africa. Wellcome Unit for the History of Medicine, University of Oxford," the heading of the abstract reads. At the end of the article there is a brief biography. Former chief of staff at Addis Ababa Hospital and chair of the faculty of medicine at Addis Ababa University.

"Oh my God!" I exclaim. "Can I use your phone?"

"Of course."

I reach Amina at home.

"Where are you, Lilly?" she asks. "I thought we were taking Sitta and Ahmed to the Ritzy."

I totally forgot. We were supposed to take them to see a film tonight. "I'm so sorry, Amina, please tell the kids I'm sorry. It's just, I'm at Robin's and—"

"Ooh la la," Amina croons—her new favourite expression, one she uses to comment on anything from a ripe piece of fruit to news of a riot.

"That doctor, years ago. The Amhara. Do you remember his name?"

"What doctor? The one I went to visit in Camden? I don't remember, Lilly. That was five years ago or something."

"Wondemariam?" I try.

She pauses. "Yes, that's very possible."

"Initial B."

"Yes." I hear her nodding. "Berhanu was his name."

—

I didn't question it when he said *we*. *We'll take the bus. We'll make a day of it. We'll leave about eleven on Thursday.* I've willingly let him take charge. I even asked him to make the phone call.

"Who is this?" the man had demanded.

"My name is Dr. Gupta, from the South Western Hospital. I am a friend of a friend."

"But why do you call me Ramadan?"

"A friend of a friend from a long time ago."

Robin covered the receiver with his other hand. *It's him*, he mouthed. I leaned in to listen.

"What do you want?"

"I want to ask you about someone we might have known in common, but I don't want to ask you over the phone," Robin said.

"You are not Ethiopian."

"No, Indian."

This must be why he agrees to let us visit. It must have terrified him to hear his real name, but less so than if it had come from the mouth of an Ethiopian. Your status might be legal in the new country, but that is meaningless in the wars of the old.

Amina has packed us a lunch as if we are children heading off on our first day of school. On the bus I unwrap white bread sandwiches with the crusts cut off, a thermos of tea, and a note scribbled on a piece of paper stamped with paw prints and the words *From the desk of Amina Mergessa.* "I hope the day is enjoyable. If not the destination, at least the journey," she has written provocatively.

I stare out the window at the countryside beyond my reflection. "That book," I say to Robin. "By Muhammed Bruce. You never mentioned it."

"I didn't dare. I realized I had really crossed a line."

"What's it like?"

"I haven't read it."

"Why not?"

"Because I bought it for you."

I kiss him. Once, twice, three times, hard on the mouth.

The lashes of his wonky eye flutter. He is startled. He smiles.

Dr. Ramadan's office is a sparse room with a wisteria-wrapped bay window overlooking the road. He is a tall, distinguished man in his sixties, with a neatly trimmed grey beard. He has a formal air and wears a grey suit with a tie tucked behind a waistcoat missing a button. We sit on torn upholstery but keep our coats on. The brittle air is determined, finding its way into the room through invisible cracks, and although the day is dark, our host does not turn on the overhead light.

"Aziz Abdulnasser," he repeats, rolling the name around in his mouth. He swivels in his chair. "And you say he was probably my student when?"

"Sometime in the late 1960s. It could have been as early as '66."

"Hmm. And then imprisoned in Jijiga?"

"In the mid-1970s. Maybe '76, '77."

"I think I know why your friend has sent you to me," he says sombrely, leaning back and stretching the remaining buttons on his waistcoat. He scratches his temple with the eraser-end of a pencil.

"Do you?" I have to tug each sentence from him.

"I am well acquainted with that prison."

"Were you imprisoned there too?"

"No. Not exactly." He puts his palms on the desk. "I'm afraid, Miss, that the prison was destroyed in 1978," he says, talking to his hands. "As was everybody imprisoned there."

I open my mouth but no words come out. Robin reaches for my hand. I have only a feeling that people must have just when the plug is pulled. A few involuntary spasms rattle my ribs.

"During the Dergue's fight with the Somalis," he says, his eyes rolling up towards the ceiling. I see only the bulbs of his eyes in profile—round, meditative moons. "The Somalis saw Haile Selassie's departure as an opportunity to try and take back the Ogaden. They were quite right, I might add. That little mess was due to a bit of deal making between Haile Selassie and the British in Somalia. So, the Dergue did what the Dergue always does and started rounding up everyone suspected not only of fighting but even of *thinking* of fighting—you see, the Dergue prides itself on being able to read minds. As you might imagine, it was not long before the prison in Jijiga was full of Ethiopian Somalis.

"And then the Somali army invaded the area," he continues lecturing to the ceiling. "They occupied Jijiga. They even got as far west as Harar. The Dergue brought in Russian advisers and Cuban forces to fight the Somalis for them and suddenly the area was full of tanks and riddled with landmines and all this machinery we had not seen before in this part of Ethiopia. The Cubans pushed the Somali army back overland as far as Jijiga. And then they dropped down bombs from their airplanes. They deliberately targeted the prison in order to obliterate the Ethiopian Somali rebels. They killed a great many other people as well," he says matter-of-factly.

I should have known. I should have known there was more that Munir did not want to have to say. It is very Ethiopian to spare the bad news. To keep hope, possibility alive. And very Muslim. *Insha'Allah.* There is always a chance that God will will what you wish. Aziz might have mentioned me every day, but those days ended for him, for us, in 1978.

I register that my nails have drawn blood from Robin's hand. He doesn't let go. He squeezes my hand even tighter.

"How do I know this, you might wonder?" continues the doctor, finally looking at us. "I am ashamed to say it, but I was employed by the Dergue. This is when I was forced to take an

Amhara name. I had no choice. I was chief of staff at the hospital in Addis. I was ordered to become the personal physician to Mengistu and his senior officers when he came to power. And in 1978, Mengistu was in Jijiga. Watching this whole scene take place like he was attending the opera," the doctor says with a dramatic wave. "He even gave a standing ovation."

The Ethiopian in me would wail, make her grief known, she would look to the sky and cry at the top of her lungs, begging Allah for mercy, for forgiveness, for compassion for the souls of those she loves. But the English in me is mute.

I have to flee this room. I shake off Robin's hand and tug at the door handle. The two men watch me through the window as I pound down the steps, as I tear down the street, as I look to the sky and rain floods into my open mouth, threatening to fill my lungs.

I cough and splutter and throw my hands onto the iron fence in front of me, clutch the bars beyond which stands a church, St. Giles, and a graveyard so old the names of the dead have been washed away. If this were a Muslim graveyard there would never have been names. And no gravestone would be bigger than any other. We are all equal in the eyes of God. We are all nameless. We all return to Allah in the end.

A black cloud hovers above my head and the rain suddenly stops. Robin peels my fingers from the iron bar and puts the umbrella in my hand.

He turns his jacket inside out and covers me

with it on the bus ride home. I lean my head upon his shoulder.

He whispers: "Hindus believe that the essence of the person—the soul—lives on, reincarnated over and over with greater maturity each time to the point where it ultimately achieves enlightenment, freedom from the body. It is what we all ultimately wish for."

Like a Sufi, I think, only a Sufi attempts to do it in a single lifetime.

Do souls ever immigrate? I wonder later that night. I'll have to ask Robin in the morning. I won't wake him now. He's sleeping soundly, his long legs crossed at the ankles and hanging over the edge of my sofa.

## East, West and Farther West.

—

Yusuf's prediction was dead on. In May 1991, the EPRDF—a coalition of revolutionary forces led by Tigrayan guerilla fighters from the north—rolls its tanks into Addis Ababa and sends Mengistu and his officers into flight.

The Dergue is charged with having killed, unlawfully arrested, imprisoned and tortured hundreds of thousands of Ethiopian citizens, abetting and using famine to kill hundreds of thousands more, creating an epidemic of displaced persons and a worldwide diaspora of refugees.

Aziz was one of millions. But he was my one.

Over the months since Robin and I visited Dr. Ramadan, I have begun to wonder if Aziz has, in some ways, always and only ever been an apparition. It is his absence that is part of me and has been for years. This is who I am, perhaps who we all are, keepers of the absent and the dead. It is the blessing and burden of being alive. It is Muhammed Bruce's dedication. None of us are orphans even if everyone we've ever loved has died.

It's the end of seventeen years of terror and we live on.

—

Yusuf has been offered a junior position at an agricultural college in a city in Canada's west. They know nothing about Calgary except that it is apparently very, very cold in winter, there are mountains, and Yusuf's cousins own a restaurant that is sandwiched between a grocery and a barbershop also owned by Oromo. But this is enough. This is more than London. They were forced into exile and now, several years on, they are ready to make choices about how and where they live. They are no longer refugees. A new wave of refugees has arrived to take their place.

"Where will *you* go?" Amina asks me.

"I don't know. Do I have to go?"

"Well, you don't want to live *here* for the rest of your life."

"Why not? There's nothing wrong with it. I mean, it's been your home for ten years, hasn't it?"

There is a critical difference between us that I'd never fully realized before. For Amina, arriving in London was random; it could have been anywhere. But for me, England was the only logical place, where the roots of my history, as alien as these might seem, are actually buried. My journey ends here. It ended here years ago, in fact, well before I was ready. It's taken seventeen years for my soul to catch up with my body.

I'm reminded of when Hussein and I set off for Harar. I had begged the Great Abdal to tell me what more he knew of the fate of my parents. Just let one chapter end before another begins. He'd always been vague whenever I'd asked, saying only Allah knows, this sort of thing, but on this occasion, perhaps because he knew there might be no other opportunity for the truth, he told me that they had stolen from the coffers, taking a good portion of the money donated by pilgrims to buy an enormous quantity of opium, which they had been trying to sell in the alleyways of the medina in Tangier.

"But why would they have needed to make so much money?" I'd asked him.

"Because they were trying to earn the passage home," was the answer.

You put roots down, they'll start growing, my father used to say.

—

Amina circles the ad, pushes it across the Formica tabletop and accompanies me north on the tube to Finsbury Park. It's not far from Camden Market, for which I have a particular affection, but much more affordable. The flat is in a house, not a high-rise, on a rundown residential street of two-up two-downs with walled front gardens. Many of them have been converted into upper and lower flats.

It has central heating *and* a fireplace and, unlike the estate, my new flat has an English history:

generations live in the hardwood floors, the tobacco brown of the drapes, the remains of a roll of wallpaper in the closet, the ashes in the fireplace. It has a warmth so unlike the concrete corridors of the estate, where the lonely echoes only exaggerate one's sense of living in exile, only feed the desire to live in the past and feast in secret like a bulimic on a closet full of memories.

London will no longer loom large on the other side of the river. I will live on its northern edge and enter its depths as part of my new job as a nurse with a mobile public health unit that operates, among other things, a needle exchange. My nursing qualifications are necessary, but it was my Saturday work that recommended me for the job. Years of dealing with people who are battered and scarred and frightened and depressed and anxious and angry and suicidal have prepared me well for this tough inner-city work.

Robin suggests I take up a relaxing hobby such as yoga or meditation. It is clear there will simply have to be a separation between my work and my private life. Which is okay. I'm ready to cultivate the latter.

Robin borrows a van, and he and Yusuf help me pack up the contents of my flat, meagre as they are. All the years in this place and I have never invested in anything worth keeping. *That can go to Leila down the hall, and if she doesn't want it, we'll take it to Oxfam. Oh no, that thing? It would be too insulting. You can bung that straight in the bin.*

By early evening on the day of the move, Amina has arrived with the children and a large pot of dorro wat she has carried in her arms all the way on the underground. She sets it down on the cooker and nearly loses her eyebrows with the initial burst of flame.

"Amina." I smile, waving a pack of incense. We have to expel the spirits first.

She laughs and tells me that I am very fashinn qadim, just like an old woman of Harar. I ignore her, lighting half a dozen sticks off the flame, and I wave them about, uttering the prayers to wish any ancestors and spirits who have remained in the space good journeys to heaven. When the death of someone is not properly honoured, their spirit remains caught between the earthly and heavenly worlds.

This is goodbye.

Yusuf inhales deeply, Robin looks on fondly, Tariq follows me from room to room, and Ahmed and Sitta, thinking it a game, compete to see who can laugh the loudest. This might be the only time they ever witness this old Harari tradition, I realize. This is what happens in the West. Muslims from Pakistan pray alongside Muslims from Nigeria and Ethiopia and Malaysia and Iran, and because the only thing they share in common is the holy book, that becomes the sole basis of the new community; not culture, not tradition, not place. The book is the only thing that offers consensus, so traditions are discarded as if they are filthy third-world clothes. "We were ignorant before," people say, as if it is only in the West that they have learned the true way of Islam.

Even our own imam, at the mosque we've been attending for years, reinforces this, calling for the importance of uniformity of practice and dress in the face of a hostile world. The imams decry the erosion of Islamic values in the West, particularly the separation between men and women. "The preservation of the community depends on protecting our women," our imam asserts, and obliges us to dress more conservatively and remember that our value on this earth is as mothers of the next generation.

Perhaps I am very fashinn qadim, but to become as orthodox as this imam demands, I would have to abandon the religion I know. He's asking for nothing less than conversion. Why would I do such a thing? My religion is full of colour and possibility and choice; it's a moderate interpretation, one that Aziz showed me was possible, one that allows you to use whatever means allow you to feel closer to God, be it saints, prayer beads, or qat, one that allows you to have the occasional drink, work alongside men, go without a veil when you choose, sit alone with an unrelated man in a room, even hold his hand, or even, dare I say it, to feel love for a Hindu.

It's an interpretation where jihad is as Hussein taught me, one's personal struggle to be a good Muslim, not a fight against those who are not Muslim, as our imam has started preaching.

I've stopped going to the mosque, and I'm

rather glad Amina is moving for this reason. She's already given up her colourful veils for plain ones in navy. I don't think she needs to hear any more from this imam.

She is stirring the chicken stew with her back to me, but despite calling me old-fashioned, I can hear her saying the prayer along with me as I wave incense above her head.

—

We eat Ethiopian-style, sitting on the floor, dorro wat at the centre of a platter covered in injera, a bit of salad and a spoonful of white cheese at the side. We tear the injera with our right hands. I play mother and separate the meat from the bones and divide the hard-boiled eggs into pieces with my fingers. We dig in, and like all Indians who eat our food, Robin looks as though he has been eating this way his entire life.

"Do you have a daughter?" Sitta asks him between mouthfuls.

"No, I don't, Sitta. Not yet."

"Do you have a wife?" she persists, much to my embarrassment.

"No." He laughs, looking at me, and I realize how much I like his slightly wonky eye, and I wonder if the world looks slightly different to him out of that eye or because of it.

"Not even in Ethiopia?" Sitta asks.

Everyone laughs, though it's not surprising. Every adult she knows is missing someone. In her mind, Ethiopia must be the country where missing people live. And I suppose Robin's colouring is not that unlike a Harari.

"Like Lilly's husband," she says.

The laughter stops and we look into our laps.

"He was never my husband, Sitta," I say after a minute.

Sitta looks confused.

"Why are you not married yet, then, Dr. Robin?" asks Amina without a hint of subtlety.

He groans. "Oh, it's my mother. I know it doesn't sound very modern, but she wants me to marry a nice Bengali girl. She sends me pictures all the time. Last time she called me she couldn't stop giggling and I asked her why she was so amused, and then she says in this high-pitched voice: 'Mukulika? Now go ahead and introduce yourself.'

"She had this girl on the other end of the line! Can you believe it? It was terribly awkward. 'And what kind of medicine do you specialize in, Dr. Gupta? My father was a doctor in Bombay. No, he has passed away I'm afraid.' And my mother interjecting: 'Tell Mukulika about the first-class honours, tell her about saving poor Mr. Parminder's life.'"

Ahmed and Sitta find Robin's imitation of his mother highly amusing. "Poor Mr. Parminder," Sitta chirps in imitation.

I can't believe how I've misjudged him. How I used to dismiss him because of his perfect English and his Cambridge education. Resent the ease with which he picked up the phone and called home. It's amazing how similar many of our experiences have been.

"Do you know how to ski?" Ahmed asks Robin.

"Well, I once—"

"Because Ayo says we're going skiing in the Rocky Mountains," Ahmed interrupts.

"Are you really, Amina?" I laugh. "Masha'Allah!"

"Yes!" she exclaims. "You know"—she gestures, as if she is gripping ski poles—"and these special trousers and woolly hats with balls on top, it's very fashinn gidir!"

The two of us shriek with laughter until we both realize that it's not funny at all. This is just what the world looks like now: a veiled Ethiopian woman skiing down the side of a Canadian mountain. The picture of resilience. The new world.

For all the brutality that is inflicted upon us, we still possess the desire to be polite to strangers. We may have blackened eyes, but we still insist on brushing our hair. We may have had our toes shot off by a nine-year-old, but we still believe in the innocence of children. We may have been raped, repeatedly, by two men in a Kenyan refugee camp, but we still open ourselves to the ones we love. We may have lost everything, but we still insist on being generous and sharing the little that remains. We still have dreams.

—

"I have a house-warming present for you," Robin says once Amina and Yusuf and the children have left.

"Oh, you shouldn't have. You've done so much for me already."

He takes the towel from my soapy hands and replaces it with a pair of boots.

"Wellingtons!" I laugh. I bend over to put them on. "Oh," I hesitate, just about to put my foot into the second one. "But they don't match."

"They will in your garden," he says. "'How very peculiar,' your neighbours will say. 'How very English.'"

And how very sweet that he remembers even the tiniest details of my faraway past, that he pulls them near, cherishes them, treats them as if they are precious objects, worthy of a home on the mantel above the fireplace, lined up to be admired, honoured, shared.

## A Bit of Background, a Lot of Thanks.

—

This is a work of fiction inspired by research, relationships and, above all, imagination. As such, I have taken enormous liberties with the histories and geographies of the places and people depicted in this book—most boldly, perhaps, conferring saintly status onto Islam's first muezzin, Bilal al Habash.[1]

That said, I have attempted to maintain some historical accuracy by roughly following the events that led up to the 1974 revolution and beyond, during the years of the Dergue. For this chronology I have relied upon and am indebted to Ryszard Kapuściński's portrait of Haile Selassie, *The Emperor: Downfall of an Autocrat*; Bahru Zewde's

---

[1] For the record, Aw (Father) Abadir 'Umr al-Rida is the patron saint of Harar, but his importance is felt only locally. Perhaps the most influential saint in the Muslim world, one whose influence is felt throughout the Middle East and reaches across North Africa in a way similar to that which I imply for Bilal al Habash here, is Abdul Qadir Jailan.

*A History of Modern Ethiopia*; the Africa Watch report *Evil Days: 30 Years of War and Famine in Ethiopia* prepared by Alex de Waal; and Jonathan Dimbleby's film *Ethiopia: The Unknown Famine*.

The following works have also been invaluable: Sir Richard Burton's *First Footsteps in East Africa: A Journey to Harar*; *The Shorter Encyclopedia of Islam* compiled by H.A.R. Gibb and J.H. Kramers; and Yusuf Ali's Arabic/English version of the Qur'an.

—

I owe a decade and a half of thanks. For first introducing me to the "idea" of Ethiopia and Oromo issues fifteen years ago I owe thanks to my dear friend Agitu Ruda. For introducing the possibility of research in Ethiopia in 1992, when I was starting graduate studies in social anthropology at Oxford, I owe thanks to Dr. Bahru Zewde, former director of the Institute of Ethiopian Studies at Addis Ababa University. Thanks to Dr. Adhana Haile Adhana for his friendship in England and Ethiopia, and to him, Federawit and their children—Haile, Hayget, Biruke and Salam—for opening their home in Addis to me and sharing everything they had. Thanks to Neil and Tigist Chadder for their friendship and generosity—taking me in so warmly and showing me a very different side of Addis.

Thanks to Ahmed Zekaria for his extraordinary generosity not only in sharing his ethnographic work on the city of Harar, but in introducing me to his relatives, with whom I lived in Harar during 1994 and 1995. Thanks to Haji Mohammed Adem and Abai Nafisa and their children—particularly Maria—and Haji Mohammed Adem and Fatima Sitti and their children—especially dear Ekram— for being family to me in Harar.

I am indebted to Mohammed Jami Guleid for assisting me with my research in Harar, to my closest friends in the city—Ekram, Hashim, Abdulaziz, Alemayehu, Biruke, Nouria and Sara—and the acquaintances far too numerous to mention who taught me everything from how to self-diagnose giardiasis to how to buy a decent goat.

For encouragement and guidance during the academic work that inspired this book I owe thanks most of all to Professor Wendy James, my doctoral supervisor. Thanks also to my post-doctoral supervisor, Professor Janice Boddy at the University of Toronto, to Ted Colman and to Professors Celia Rothenberg, Anne Meneley and Michael Levin for conversations about shared ethnographic interests over the years.

I am indebted to the following bodies who helped fund my research: the Harold Hyam Wingate Foundation, the Royal Anthropological Institute, Magdalen College and the Graduate Studies Office of Oxford University (for doctoral work); the Social Sciences and Humanities Research Council of Canada and the University of Toronto (for post-doctoral research).

I want to thank members of the Harari Community Association in Toronto who welcomed me at their events and into their homes. For some of my recent research on the Oromo I owe thanks to Professor Mohammed Hassen of Georgia State University, Dr. Trevor Trueman of the Oromo Support Group, Lydia Namarra and Taha Ali Abdi of the Oromo Relief Association in London, Tesfaye Deressa Kumsa in Toronto and Bonsa Waltajjii in London.

For answers to questions regarding hospitals in London I owe thanks to Patrick Fennessy and Deirdre Graham. Thanks to Richard Gibbs of the Croydon Council and Steve Roud of the Croydon Library for answering my queries about Ethiopian settlement in the area and to Lydia Namarra for reorienting me toward Lambeth. Thanks to my grandfather, Sir Edward Fennessy, for his concern. Thanks to Tammy Gibb and Fraser Tannock for help with London's geography, and Ruth Petrie for giving me some sense of Brixton in the seventies and eighties. Thanks to Ted Woodhead for insights on Methodism and missionaries. Thanks to Sarah Dearing for discussing literature and revolution. Thanks to Bedri Ahmed for answering my queries about Harari terms. And for reacquainting me with the Middle East in the last couple of years, thanks to Maureen Conway and Ken Campbell.

—

For support in the writing of this novel, I wish to acknowledge: the Toronto Arts Council, the Ontario Arts Council, the Canada Council, the Banff

Centre for the Arts and the MacDowell Colony.

Thanks to Anne McDermid for representing me and my work. Thanks to my incredible editors Martha Kanya-Forstner and Maya Mavjee, who brought out in me the book that was meant to be written and to Shaun Oakey for the astute editorial advice that pushed it to completion. Thanks to Anne McDermid, Annie Sommers, Sheila Fennessy, Heather Conway and Christopher Kelly for comments on various drafts, and Kelly Dignan, Suzanne Brandreth and Ravi Mirchandani for their involvement at an early stage in the book's development. Thanks to Louise Dennys for her generosity and ongoing support and to Scott Sellers, Scott Richardson, and Lara Hinchberger at Random House of Canada and Jane Warren at Anne McDermid and Associates for their involvement.

Finally, to my immediate family and friends— Sheila, Stan, Vibika, Annie, Chris K., James, Charly, Drew, Su, and Heather—I am so grateful for your support. And so blessed to have you in my life. Especially you, Miss Heather.

## About the Author.

—

Camilla Gibb was born in London, England, and grew up in Toronto. She has a Ph.D. in social anthropology from Oxford University for which she conducted fieldwork in Ethiopia. Her two previous novels, *Mouthing the Words*, winner of the City of Toronto Book Award in 2000, and *The Petty Details of So-and-so's Life*, have been published in 18 countries, receiving rave reviews around the world. She is one of 21 writers on the "Orange Futures List"—a list of young writers to watch, compiled by the jury of the prestigious Orange Prize. She is currently Writer in Residence at the University of Toronto. Visit Camilla Gibb's website: www.camillagibb.ca.

A Note about the Type.

—

The body of *Sweetness in the Belly* has been set in a digitized version of Century Schoolbook, one of several variations of Century Roman to appear within a decade of its creation in 1895. That original roman face was cut by Linn Boyd Benton in response to a request by publisher and editor Theodore Low De Vinne for an attractive, easy-to-read typeface to fit the narrow columns of his *Century Magazine.*

Century Schoolbook was designed specifically for textbooks in the primary grades, but its great legibility quickly earned it popularity in a range of applications.